CARIBBEANA

CARIBBEANA

An Anthology of English Literature
of the West Indies

1657–1777

Edited and with an Introduction by

THOMAS W. KRISE

The University of Chicago Press
CHICAGO & LONDON

THOMAS W. KRISE is associate professor of English and executive officer of the Air Force Humanities Institute at the U.S. Air Force Academy in Colorado Springs.

THE UNIVERSITY OF CHICAGO PRESS, CHICAGO 60637
THE UNIVERSITY OF CHICAGO PRESS, LTD., LONDON

© 1999 by The University of Chicago
All rights reserved. Published 1999

08 07 06 05 04 03 02 01 00 99 5 4 3 2 1
ISBN (cloth): 0-226-45390-1
ISBN (paper): 0-226-45392-8

Library of Congress Cataloging-in-Publication Data

Caribbeana : an anthology of English literature of the West Indies,
   1657–1777 / edited and with an introduction by Thomas W. Krise.
      p.   cm.
   Includes bibliographical references
   ISBN 0-226-45390-1. — ISBN 0-226-45392-8 (pbk.)
   1. West Indian literature (English)   2. Caribbean Area Literary
collections.   3. West Indies Literary collections.   4. Caribbean
literature (English)   I. Krise, Thomas W.
PR9215.C39   1999
820.8´09729—dc21   99-20932
                                                                           CIP

For Patricia Love Krise

Contents

Acknowledgments

This anthology is a product of a passion for the history and culture of the West Indies that began during my school days in Saint Thomas, Virgin Islands. The encouragement of many teachers, patrons, and friends has enabled me to cultivate that passion ever since. My greatest debts are to Lieutenant Colonel Donald Anderson, Dr. J. Paul Hunter, Dr. Janice Knight, Dr. Bruce Redford, and Colonel Jack M. Shuttleworth. For assistance of various kinds, I am indebted to the following: Dr. Thomas Bonner Jr., Lieutenant Colonel David A. Boxwell, Dr. J. Douglas Canfield, Ms. Barbara Crawford, Colonel Frederick T. Kiley, Dr. Janel Mueller, Dr. Carla Mulford, Mrs. Tanya Rosburg, Dr. Laurie Shannon, Dr. Stuart Sherman, and Dr. David S. Shields.

Generous grants from the Air Force Institute of Technology, the Faculty Research Committee and the Academic Support Fund of the U.S. Air Force Academy, the Frank J. Seiler Research Laboratory, and the Columbia Broadcasting System Foundation's Bicentennial Narrators' Scholarship have allowed me to study at a rich variety of libraries and archives. I am grateful to the National Endowment for the Humanities for enabling me to participate in Dr. Ronald Paulson's and Dr. Frances Ferguson's 1990 Summer Institute at Johns Hopkins University. I am indebted further to Dr. Terry Belanger and Dr. David Gants of the Rare Book School at the University of Virginia, and to the librarians and staffs of the following libraries: the Joseph L. Regenstein Library of the University of Chicago (especially Dr. Alice Shreyer and her Special Collections staff); the James Ford Bell Library of the University of Minnesota; the Air Force Academy Library; the Newberry Library, Chicago; the Special Collections Library of the University of Illinois at Chicago; the Seabury-Western Episcopal Theological Seminary Library, Evanston, Illinois; the Henry E. Huntington Library, San Marino, California (especially Dr. Roy Ritchie); the William Andrews Clark Memorial Library, Los Angeles; the British Library; the Bodleian, Worcester College, and Rhodes House libraries, Oxford; Dr. Williams's Library, London; the Lambeth Palace Library, London; the Guildhall Library, London; the Library of Congress; the Folger Shakespeare Library, Washington; the Bermuda Archives; the National Library of Jamaica, Institute of Jamaica, Kingston; the West Indies and Special Collections Library, University of the West Indies, Mona, Jamaica; and the John Carter Brown Library, Brown University. I am also indebted to the staffs of the following institutions for their helpful correspondence and photocopying support: the McMaster University Libraries, Hamilton, Ontario; the Sutro Library, San Francisco; and the Nevis Public Library, Nevis, West Indies.

For his advice and careful shepherding of this project, I am grateful to Mr. Alan G. Thomas, Senior Editor, and to his excellent staff at the University of Chicago Press, particularly Mr. Randolph Petilos, Ms. Claudia Rex, Ms. Lynne Nugent, and the Press's anonymous readers.

An anthology, like a flower garden, depends on many outside influences. For their sunny encouragement, nourishing suggestions, and pruning questions, I am indebted to my family, friends, teachers, colleagues, and students. *Et les fruits passeront la promesse des fleurs. —Malherbe.*

Colorado Springs
April 1999

A Note on the Texts

In choosing the works for this anthology, I have sought to include the most representative samples of published writing concerning the British West Indies between the Protectorship of Oliver Cromwell and the beginning of the American Revolution. The editorial method of the present edition can be characterized as "cautious eclecticism." In the interest of presenting texts that were available to the reading public, I have chosen the earliest extant editions of each of the texts, and I have collated them against as many other surviving copies as possible, aiming to ensure as accurate a set of texts as possible. No authors' manuscripts survive for any of the texts included here, but, since the aim of the collection is to illuminate the role of the West Indies in the English-speaking culture of the period, the state in which the texts were read at the time supersedes any concern for what the individual authors may have intended to write. Even if original manuscripts did exist, the theory employed here would dictate that the first editions be used as copy texts in preference to the manuscripts, presenting an anthology of texts that were actually available to the public of the period.

In the present edition, the texture (spelling, punctuation, paragraphing) of the originals has been preserved as much as possible to give the reader a sense of the rhythm and "feel" of the texts. The text of each work is drawn from the earliest extant edition, preserving the exact wording, spelling, punctuation, and verse lineation, with the following exceptions:

(a) Obvious errors in spelling and punctuation are corrected based on readings of identical words in other parts of the same edition, or by comparison with words and punctuation in later editions.

(b) Archaic typographical features, such as the long "s" (ſ) and ligatures, are modernized. Other typographical features—italicization and irrational paragraphing—are preserved; confusing passages are explained in the editor's notes.

(c) Footnotes are authors' notes, except for editorial insertions enclosed in square brackets. Editor's notes are collected at the end of the book.

(d) The placement of footnote references has been altered in cases where modern readers might be confused, generally when the original note marker was placed before, rather than after, the related word or phrase.

(e) Latin quotations in the main texts are preserved, and translations are provided in the editor's notes; longer passages in footnotes are replaced by English translations.

The copy texts for the works included in the anthology are as follows: (1) Ligon, first edition, the British Library (shelf number 455.a.18); (2) Hickeringill, first edition, Dr. Williams's Library, London; (3) Tryon, first edition, the British Library (523.c.6); (4) Ward, third edition, the William Andrews Clark Memorial Library, University of California at Los Angeles; (5) "Black of Guardaloupe," first edition, the British Library (104.h.40); (6) "Moses Bon Sàam," first edition, the British Library (8156.de.2); (7) Robertson, first edition, the British Library (8156.de.2); (8) Seymour, first edition, the British Library (840.m.1[41]); (9) "Ingenious Lady of Barbados," first edition, the British Library (871.k.21); (10) Grainger, first edition, the British Library (1651.405); (11) Singleton, first edition, the British Library (11641.g.56); (12) Williams, first edition Long's *History*, the British Library (146.c.7); (13) "*Jamaica* poet," first edition, the British Library (T.25[6]).

In the editorial notes, "OED" refers to *The Oxford English Dictionary* (second edition, 1991). "Partridge" refers to Eric Partridge, *A Dictionary of Slang and Unconventional English*, (eighth edition, ed. Paul Beale, New York: Macmillan, 1984).

Thomas Jeffrey's map of the West Indies (1759). Photo courtesy Thomas W. Krise.

Introduction

I ought to be judged as a captain sent from Spain to conquer a warlike and
numerous people, of rites and customs very much opposed to our own, as far
away as the Indies, where, by God's will, I have reduced a new world to the
lordship of our lord and lady, King and Queen; thanks to which Spain, which
was once called poor, has become the richest of kingdoms.

Christopher Columbus[1]

I

No clash of cultures before or since 1492 has been so stark as Columbus's
meeting of the native inhabitants of the West Indies. More than any other,
the place dubbed "the West Indies" is an amalgam of confused and conflicted
knowledge and desire. The name itself contains traces of these states of mind:
"Indies" not only represents Columbus's goal to reach and exploit the lands
that Marco Polo made so desirable, but also, in time, came to stand for all territories open and available for Western European conquest and use. The
word "West" hints at much more than mere geographical identification and
correction of Columbus's mistake. "West" suggests possession: the Indies—
the "Others"—that belong to those countries self-identified as "the West" at
least since the division of the Roman Empire in the fourth century. "West Indies" also carries with it echoes of the classical myths of the Hesperides, the
islands beyond Ocean in the West where heroes find repose and where the
grove of Hera's golden apples is guarded by the ferocious dragon Ladon. Because the islands and lands in the western Atlantic were imagined by "the
West," "discovered" by Europeans, and reimagined as simultaneously empty,
rich, and defenseless, they became—more thoroughly than any future con-
quests—the possessions of the European imagination.

In the epigraph to this introduction, Columbus strips away all pretense of
altruism from Europe's imperial project in the West Indies and asserts the

1

martial character of his mission: authorized by divine power, Columbus's achievement is conquest, not religious conversion or peaceful trade. He describes the people as being so completely alien that any claims to human dignity fall away, making their territories and persons free for the taking. Columbus, then, can claim the masculine glory of conquest free of the guilt attendant upon the destruction of people granted the dignity of humanity. The result of this achievement is the shame-free enrichment of Spain as if by divine miracle; and yet, the sentence is written as a defense by a man dragged back from the fledgling New World empire in chains to face charges of abuse of power and maladministration. Taken as a whole, this vignette combines all the elements of the representations of the West Indies in the centuries to come: an air of heroic and manly adventure on the fringes of European justice, the assertion of innocent conquest under divine direction, the exercise and abuse of power, the promotion of the new lands as places to accumulate wealth with ease, and the struggle to free oneself of the bonds of imprisonment, slavery, or civilization.

The quincentennial of Columbus's first voyage inspired several scholarly studies of the exploration narratives of the early discoverers and adventurers of the New World.[2] Naturally, such studies usually focus on the contacts between Europeans and Native Americans. But by the time the English made their debut in the region, the native inhabitants were in large part destroyed, and so the specifically English contributions to this literature of exploration tend to focus on English animosity toward and competition with the Spaniards and their American empire. The accounts of the voyages of Sir Francis Drake, Sir John Hawkins, and Sir Walter Ralegh retain some of the heroic adventurer quality found in the accounts of the earliest explorers but are more distinctly belligerent, as these English Sea Dogs also represent the ingenuity and spunk of the Protestant English underdogs against Catholic Spain, the superpower of the sixteenth century. Like the earlier Spanish accounts, the English literary representations of the West Indies are presented in a promotional mode; but to this tradition of promotion the English add the prospect of accumulating great wealth by plundering England's archenemy. With his *Discoverie of Guiana* (1596), Ralegh infused into England excitement over the possibility of the existence of El Dorado by suggesting that the golden city might be explored and exploited by English rather than Spanish adventurers—thus besting the Spanish at the game of imperial conquest.

The English would, of course, discover tremendous wealth in the West Indies, but not in the form of Ralegh's gold. The extraction of this other kind of wealth required seizure and settlement of once-Spanish territories. To attract investment and population, the projectors of the new English empire needed to promote among English readers knowledge of and interest in the new endeavors. The resulting promotional literature—by John White, Thomas Harriot, John Smith, and others—blends elements of exploration narratives with those of promotional tracts and travel narratives. The writers who came to the West Indies after the explorers—the travelers—created accounts that differ in important ways from the earlier literature: there is more interest in the colonial societies; there are echoes of travel narratives of the Grand Tour of Europe, with their concerns about the connection between travel and education; and there is heightened interest in pleasure per se over such preoccupations of the exploration narratives as wonder, savagery, and daring.

II

Until recently, the English literature of the British West Indies has been left out of anthologies of early American and eighteenth-century British literature. But, thanks to the efforts of Philip Gura, Myra Jehlen, David Shields, William Spengemann, Michael Warner, and others to expand the notion of early American literature to include works from and about all parts of the British Empire in America, anthologists are beginning to notice the literatures produced by English-speaking people in the British colonies outside the future United States. Most of the more recent anthologies include a token handful of texts to suggest the presence of literary work being produced outside the mainland colonies.

Caribbeana aims to promote this widening interest by illuminating the English literary representations of the West Indies between the age of exploration and the age of abolitionism. During this period—between the mid-seventeenth and late-eighteenth centuries—the British West Indian colonies were at least as important as the colonies of North America to the expanding British Empire.[3] Unlike the task of creating a school anthology in a field already filled with anthologies, the task of doing the first one of a type presents special problems. Chief among these is the competition between the desire to make important texts available to students and scholars and the desire to reproduce the more famous and well-edited texts that are readily available. I have decided not to produce a comprehensive survey anthology incorporating snippets of all the key texts, but rather to provide access to hitherto unknown or little-known texts.

To orient the reader to the place of West Indian literature within the larger fields of early American and eighteenth-century British literature, I offer the following list of what I consider to be the well-known key texts relating to the Caribbean region in the early period: Ralegh's *Discoverie of Guiana* (1596); William Shakespeare's *The Tempest* (1611); Aphra Behn's *Oroonoko, or the History of the Royal Slave* (1688); Thomas Southerne's *Oroonoko: A Tragedy* (1696); Daniel Defoe's *Robinson Crusoe* (1719); John Gay's *Polly* (1729); Tobias Smollett's *Roderick Random* (1748); Samuel Foote's *The Patron* (1764); Richard Cumberland's *The West Indian: A Comedy* (1771); Olaudah Equiano's *Interesting Narrative* (1789); Philip Freneau's Santa Cruz and Jamaica poems (1770s—1790s); and John Gabriel Stedman's *Narrative* of the Surinam slave revolt (1796). All of these texts are obtainable in twentieth-century editions, and I exclude them from the anthology for this reason.

This anthology provides coverage of the main colonies of the region (Barbados, Jamaica, and the Leeward Islands), while also touching on various themes important to an understanding of the cultural concerns and milieu of the area: slavery and freedom, African culture, obeah, sugar cultivation, piracy, absentee landlordism, military conquest, the making of money to spend at "home" in England. It also brings to light several important, though overlooked, representations of the black experience in the Americas, including two narratives of slave experience that are fifty-one and twenty-five years older, respectively, than the earliest such narratives included in African-American anthologies so far ("A Speech made by a Black of Guardaloupe," 1709, and "The Speech of Moses Bon Sàam," 1735); and two early attempts to ventriloquize black Africans in the service of one side or the other of the slavery question (Tryon's dialogue in *Friendly Advice*, 1684, and Robertson's *Speech of Campo-bell*, 1736). The anthology also includes pieces by two women: Frances Seymour's poem "The Story of Inkle and Yarico" and a collection of the poems of an anonymous "ingenious Lady" published by Samuel Keimer (Benjamin Franklin's employer in Philadelphia) in his *Barbados Gazette* and reprinted in his miscellany *Caribbeana* (1741). Finally, it provides the full text of James Grainger's *The Sugar Cane* (1764), which is one of the most ambitious and well-received poems to be written in the British colonies in America before the Revolution. In his review of the poem in the *Critical Review* of October 1764, Samuel Johnson remarked, "we have been destitute till now of an American poet, that could bear any degree of competition."[4] Grainger's work inspired two other poets included in the collection: John Singleton and the anonymous *Jamaica* poet.

As with any such anthology, many worthy texts must be excluded, most often because of their length. A sampling of such texts would include: Alexander Exquemelin's *The Buccaniers of America* (English edition, 1684); William Walker's tragedy *Victorious Love* (1698); Sir Hans Sloane's *Voyage to the Islands* (1707, 1725); William Pittis's novella *The Jamaica Lady* (1720, based on Ward's *A Trip to Jamaica,* included here); Edward Moore's *Yarico to Inkle: An Epistle* (1736); Edward Trelawny's *Essay Concerning Slavery* (1746); the anonymous novella *The Fortunate Transport* (c. 1750); Samuel Martin's *Essay upon Plantership* (1750); Nathaniel Weekes's *Barbados: A Poem* (1754); William Belgrove's *Treatise upon Husbandry* (1755); and Janet Schaw's *Journal of a Lady of Quality* (c. 1776).

The vast majority of West Indian literary works were printed in London, despite the arrival of the first printing press in the British West Indies (in Jamaica) in 1717. This preference for printing in the metropole reflects both the small population of readers in the island colonies and the writers' evident desire to appeal to the larger literary world of London. The two exceptions to this general rule in this anthology are Singleton's *A General Description* (published first in Barbados, then in London) and Samuel Keimer's *Caribbeana,* which, although published as a miscellany in London, was drawn from some seven years of his *Barbados Gazette,* which he began after leaving Philadelphia in 1731.

In terms of their place in a larger scheme of literary themes, the texts of the anthology can be divided along a fault line represented by the publication of Daniel Defoe's *Robinson Crusoe* in 1719. Before that date, the age of the exploration narratives gives way to an age of travel writing. The adventurers of the middle to later seventeenth century differ from the Sea Dogs of the earlier generation in that they travel to well-established colonies under a degree of state protection to make their fortunes. In the half-century following 1719, the expanding population of African slaves, combined with changes in the sensibilities of Britons at home, forces the issue of slavery to the forefront of West Indian literary representations. These two central concerns of the writing that arises from the British West Indies—travel and slavery—bound up as they are with mercantile imperialism, are also central concerns of *Robinson Crusoe.* Travel, slavery, trade, and imperialism all play roles in Crusoe's fate; Defoe's novel sums up the travel theme of West Indian literature, while adumbrating the centrality of slavery in the representations to come later in the eighteenth century. For these reasons, it is instructive to keep *Crusoe* in mind when exploring the cultural artifacts of the region presented in this work.

III

My Island was now peopled, and I thought my self very rich in Subjects; and it was a merry Reflection which I frequently made, How like a King I look'd.
—Daniel Defoe, *Robinson Crusoe*[5]

The true symbol of the British conquest is in Robinson Crusoe. . . . The whole Anglo-Saxon spirit is in Crusoe; the manly independence and the unconscious cruelty; the persistence; the slow yet efficient intelligence; the sexual apathy; the practical, well-balanced religiousness; the calculating taciturnity.

—James Joyce, "Daniel Defoe"[6]

The very provenance of Robinson Crusoe is symbolic of the West Indies: like the Caribbean islands, Crusoe's island is a territory imagined as simultaneously empty, rich, and defenseless. Defoe adapts a true story of a man marooned on an island in the South Pacific, moves him to an imagined West Indian island with no permanent native inhabitants, makes him master of the place, and provides him with willing and grateful servants. That James Joyce sees this man as an archetypal Englishman should come as no surprise, given that Crusoe represents, among other things, a modern imperial man freed of any feelings of guilt over his elevation to mastery. His story reinscribes the old justification (as old as Columbus) for the seizure of native territory—that the Indians are but transitory visitors, not "settled" owners of the land. And, in his precastaway life, Crusoe engages not only in the Atlantic trade generally, but quite specifically in the same African slave trade that populates the Caribbean and generates its great wealth. Once marooned, Crusoe sets out to alter the landscape as if to replicate his native England as much as possible—a small-scale version of the surveying, planning, and building of distinctly English towns and plantations throughout the region.

Postcolonial studies, ethnocriticism, and ethnohistory have reinvigorated interest in areas of the world subjected to European imperialism. The British West Indies differ from most other regions of the colonialized world in that by the time the first English settlers arrived in the Lesser Antilles, virtually all the native inhabitants had been extirpated by warfare, forced transportation, and disease.[7] Within half a century, the new settlers had begun to create a colonialized subject people by purchasing and transporting culturally diverse peoples from the African slave traders. After the cultivation of sugar cane spread throughout the islands, the West Indies became the final destination of half the Africans transported into American slavery.[8] Once thrown together, these African peoples created their own lingua francas and composite cultures by drawing from their widely diverse religious, linguistic, and cultural backgrounds commingled with the English language and culture of the charter society.[9] The culture of the British West Indies that resulted from this mixture of peoples and circumstances was further altered by nearly continuous international warfare in the region and by the imposition of a seigneurial slave economy based almost solely on the cultivation and manufacture of a single product—sugar—using the world's first large-scale factory system.

Throughout the period covered by the present work (1657–1777), the West Indies constituted the most valuable colonial possessions of Great Britain and France, the world's leading powers of the day. The sugar islands provided their metropolitan powers with enormous wealth; they offered adventurous Britons and Frenchmen places to change and make fortunes; and, by affording places to which to transport criminals and vagrants, the islands served as relief valves for urban overcrowding and other social pressures. Evidence of cultural awareness of the West Indies abounds in English literature in the seventeenth and eighteenth centuries. Besides the Caribbean characters and settings in the works of well-known authors, such as Jane Austen, Daniel Defoe, John Gay, William Shakespeare, and Tobias Smollett, hundreds of other representations of the Caribbean entered into the English-speaking consciousness through countless travel and exploration narratives, abolitionist and pro-slavery polemics, and novels and dramas featuring Creoles and slaves among the minor characters.

IV

Travel is an important emblem of the early West Indies in that it is a sign of empire. The travel-related representations of the Elizabethan Sea Dogs, the swashbuckling pirates, and the fortune hunters all reveal an underlying expansionist and exploitative motivation—a drive to seize whatever wealth was available for use back home. Unlike most of the continental American colonies, where the typical English traveler went to settle, the West Indies attracted travelers who more often than not aimed to amass wealth and experience to spend and use in England.[10] Also unlike the case of the northern colonies, in the West Indies slaves made up eight- or nine-tenths of the total population, making the African presence and the fact of slavery more difficult to elide; these statistics, moreover, made it impossible to imagine an alternative to the elaborately imperial economic system based upon the largest forced migration in history. The theme of slavery gradually assumes greater importance until it becomes the gauntlet over which British commitments to liberty, property, and fair play conflict dramatically during the first half of the nineteenth century. The themes of travel and slavery run through nearly all of the works in the anthology.

The first text in the collection is an excerpt from Richard Ligon's *A True and Exact History of the Island of Barbados* (1657), which provides one of the most detailed accounts of any seventeenth-century English colony. The selection includes Ligon's estimate of the various classes of people in the colony (indentured servants, slaves, and masters), plus his telling of the story of Inkle and Yarico. The tale of the Englishman Inkle, who is saved by the Indian maiden Yarico only to sell her into slavery upon his rescue, was highly popular throughout the eighteenth century, culminating in George Colman's 1787 opera *Inkle and Yarico*.

Edmund Hickeringill's *Jamaica Viewed* (1661) is a succinct account of the newly conquered island together with an evaluation of the military lessons learned from the poorly managed conquest of the island. Hickeringill peppers his account with proleptically Hudibrastic verse[11] that combines the misogyny omnipresent in colonial and imperial discourse with insubordination to his former overlords in Jamaica. The work was received well enough to merit Hickeringill's appointment by Charles II as secretary to the first royal governor of Jamaica (Thomas, Lord Windsor) with the sizable salary of £1,000 per year.

Famous for his popular tracts on vegetarianism and Behmenist mysticism, Thomas Tryon turned his sojourn in Barbados (selling hats) into his *Friendly Advice to the Gentlemen-Planters of the East and West Indies* (1684). The selection from this work included here is his dialogue between an enslaved African and his English master, which is not only one of the earliest attacks on slavery as an institution, but also one of the earliest attempts to represent an African slave's point of view.

Next comes Edward Ward's *A Trip to Jamaica: With a True Character of the People and the Island* (1698), a satiric travel script relating the young Ned Ward's attempt to recoup his fortune in Jamaica following unsuccessful ventures in London. It is notable primarily for three reasons: first, it launched Ned Ward's journalistic career, which was highlighted by his innovative contribution to periodical literature, the *London Spy* (1698–1709); second, in its ranting condemnation of everything Jamaican, the *Trip* serves as a subversive counterweight to promotional travel literature about the Western Hemisphere (like Hickeringill's); and third, its influence was felt for a number of years, as it formed the basis for the novella *The Jamaica Lady* (1720), written by Ward's friend William Pittis.

Ward's satire is followed by "A Speech made by a Black of Guardaloupe, at the Funeral of a Fellow-Negro" (1709), which was appended to an open letter concerning the slave trade. Although this "speech" is most likely a fabrication by an early anti-slavery writer, it may represent attitudes and even language of slaves with whom the writer came in contact. If it is indeed a representation of an enslaved African's speech, it is a full fifty years earlier than the narratives of Jupiter Hammon and Briton Hammon, both published in 1760, which are commonly accepted as the earliest published pieces by African-Americans.

Another early representation of the African slave's point of view comes in the form of "The Speech of Moses Bon Sàam" (1735), which purports to be by a leader of the Jamaican Maroons to his followers, who are waging the ultimately successful guerrilla campaign known as the First Maroon War (1730–39). The publication of this speech prompted two replies: "The Speech of Caribéus" (1735), a ranting attack by a metropolitan pro-slavery advocate; and *The Speech of Mr. John Talbot Campo-bell, a Free Christian-Negro, to his Countrymen in the Mountains of Jamaica* (1736), a much longer and more richly textured reply. The latter piece is the work of the white planter and Anglican priest Robert Robertson, of Nevis in the Leeward Islands, who was a notable pamphleteer during the agitation in favor of stricter navigation acts that led to the Molasses Act of 1732. In *The Speech of Campo-bell*, Robertson creates the character of John Talbot Campo-bell, a freed black African turned slave-owning planter, who speaks for the pro-slavery side against the runaway slaves in the rebel Maroon communities in Jamaica's mountainous interior. This vivid and unsettling text is an attempt by the author to justify the slave system and to construct a new, separate West Indian subjecthood for both blacks and whites, while maintaining white supremacy in the colonial society.

The tale of Inkle and Yarico resurfaces in two 1738 poems by Frances Seymour, countess of Hertford. In "The Story of Inkle and Yarico" and "An Epistle from Yarico to Inkle, After he had left her in Slavery," Seymour provides an early and poetic critique of slavery. Seymour's poems were among many on this subject that were published in the decades following Richard Steele's retelling of Ligon's story in the *Spectator* (number 11, 13 March 1711). Seymour's skilled versifying, high social station, and wide network of prominent literary friends make these poems an important example of metropolitan engagement with issues of imperialism and slavery.

The next selections leave the issue of slavery in the background and focus instead on an intense relationship between a man and a woman. The thirteen poems written by an anonymous "ingenious Lady" to her friend "Damon" include some of the best examples of poetry to come out of the Caribbean in the eighteenth century. All of these poems were first published by Samuel

Keimer in the *Barbados Gazette* and then again in his miscellany *Caribbeana* in 1741. Of special interest is the poet's defense of her style in "On being charged with Writing incorrectly."

Perhaps the best major work to come out of the West Indies in the period (and indeed out of all of America, if we are to agree with Samuel Johnson) is James Grainger's *The Sugar Cane: A Poem, In Four Books* (1764). This long georgic poem details the entire process of running an eighteenth-century sugar plantation, from choosing the proper fields to the selection and "seasoning" of newly arrived African slaves. A physician and student of history, Grainger peppers his poem with extensive footnotes detailing the dietary and medicinal uses of the various plants and animals in the region, together with historical and geographical comments on the islands of the eastern Caribbean. Of particular interest is Book IV, "The Genius of Africa," which provides a fascinatingly conflicted description of Africans, their cultures, and the problems of enslaving them.

Grainger's success inspired other poets, including the actor John Singleton, whose *A General Description of the West-Indian Islands* (1767) is a blank verse topographical poem relating his tour of the Windward and Leeward Islands. Drawing upon Grainger's material and John Milton's style, Singleton's poem is a rich source of information on the cultures of the islands, including the religion, entertainments, and other ways of life among the both the free and slave populations.

The next selection features a Latin ode by Francis Williams, a free black Jamaican whose education was sponsored by the second duke of Montagu as an experiment to prove the educability of people of African descent. Williams attended school in England, graduated from Cambridge University, and returned to head a school for free blacks in his native Jamaica. His poem comes to us through *The History of Jamaica* (1774) by Edward Long, who aimed to discount Williams's learning and skill by belittling his poem. In the event, however, Long manages to provide a good translation of the Latin poem and enough footnoted commentary to prove Williams's wide reading and command of classical literature. The selection on Williams includes both the original Latin ode and Long's translation, together with all of Long's contextual (and virulently racist) commentary.

The final chapter of the anthology contains the anonymous 408-line *Jamaica, A Poem, in Three Parts* (1777), together with its appended 82-line "Poetical Epistle from the Island of Jamaica, to a Gentleman of the Middle-Temple." This topographical poem in heroic couplets blends echoes of Alexander Pope's "Windsor Forest" (1713) and Grainger's *The Sugar Cane* with early abolitionist sentiment. The poem and its verse appendix are quoted extensively in John Gabriel Stedman's *Narrative of a Five Years Expedition against the Revolted Negroes of Surinam* (manuscript 1790; published 1796), a major resource for the abolitionist cause. In *Jamaica* the poet follows the same order of description of the island as did Hickeringill in *Jamaica Viewed* (1661) and employs several of the same techniques (including the poetic resurrection of the exterminated Indians), while suggesting through the poem's form and sentimentality the changes in both English and West Indian society since the Restoration.

Choosing texts for an anthology is always a contest between inclusivity and selectivity. Representativeness vies with practical considerations of space, readability, and coverage. In making the choices, my aim has been threefold: first, to select a group of texts that reflects the major issues and pre-occupations of the British West Indies in the long eighteenth century (1660–1800); second, to ensure that the resulting texts represent a range of genres; and third, to provide a work of manageable length and sufficient quality to spark and sustain the interests of historians and critics of eighteenth-century culture. The resulting collection includes the genres of history, description, dialogue, essay, travel narrative, satire, funeral oration, prose fiction, georgic poem, ode, topographical poem, and verse epistle, all written by an administrator, a hatter, a journalist, soldiers, slaves, a schoolmaster, a clergyman, a peeress, an actor, a physician, and some unknowns. The variety of both genres and authors is itself an indication of the richness of the life and literary culture of the British West Indies between the suzerainties of Oliver Cromwell and George III.

V

The anthology intersects with a variety of critical and theoretical concerns that have moved to the fore in early-American and eighteenth-century studies, particularly colonial discourse, racism, gender roles and patriarchalism, and ethnographic variations of historical and literary studies. Current discussions of these issues have led a number of historians and critics to take up the case of the West Indies as an important arena for understanding these topics.

Among the more prominent recent studies of the West Indies is Peter Hulme's *Colonial Encounters: Europe and the Native Caribbean, 1492–1797* (1986). Focusing on European representations of relations with the dwindling population of native inhabitants of the West Indies, Hulme explicates the colonial discourses within five prominent stories of encounter: Columbus's *Journal* and letters, Shakespeare's *The Tempest*, Smith's accounts of Pocahontas, Defoe's *Robinson Crusoe,* and the various versions of the tale of Inkle and Yarico. Hulme's concentration on the Caribs continues with the anthology he edited with Neil Whitehead entitled *Wild Majesty: Encounters with Caribs from Columbus to the Present Day* (1992).[12] Hulme's analyses of the operation of colonial discourse, particularly the power of such discourse to degrade and delegitimate the "other," have intensified the scholarly community's interest in the Caribbean region.

Influential studies of the earlier, largely Spanish, era of exploration include two works of Stephen Greenblatt: a collection of essays edited by him entitled *New World Encounters* (1993) and his own monograph *Marvelous Possessions: The Wonder of the New World* (1991). Like Hulme, Greenblatt interprets the discourse of colonialism as not only a part of the enterprise of imperial appropriation, but also the central means of promulgating and maintaining conquest.[13]

Studies of European racism and sexism often involve considerations of the slave colonies of the Americas. A relatively early and seminal study of race issues that focuses on the British West Indies is Wylie Sypher's *Guinea's Captive Kings: British Anti-Slavery Literature of the Eighteenth Century* (1942). Sypher sifts through the large mass of pro- and anti-slavery polemics, poems, and novels published in the eighteenth century, providing a useful rubric for categorizing and interpreting the early phases of the abolitionist movement. Sypher also manages to highlight the intrusion of other motives into the British abolitionist movement, such as the desires for parliamentary reform and for public roles for women. Five decades later, Moira Ferguson elaborates one of these overlapping movements—the drive for new roles for women— in *Subject to Others: British Women Writers and Colonial Slavery, 1670–1834* (1992), which provides considerable coverage of the British West Indies.[14]

Ethnographic ways of reading and interpreting history and literature have helped focus attention on the Caribbean region, from which many of the earliest "ethnographies" were drawn. Although few ethnohistorical or ethnocritical studies have been devoted to West Indian examples, the techniques used in these cross-disciplines can be useful to the interpretation of early West Indian texts—particularly to the project of attempting to reconstruct a sense of the culture of the slaves and Maroons when the entire archive is mediated through European languages and discourses.[15] Such studies critique the imperialism inherent in the ethnographic project and help the student of the cultural contact zone to interpret the non-European culture with a degree of nuance that diminishes the bias implicit in the European archive.

The West Indies figure prominently in more than two dozen works of

English prose fiction in the long eighteenth century, chief among which are Aphra Behn's *Oroonoko* and Daniel Defoe's *Robinson Crusoe*. Two of the prose fictions—William Pittis's *The Jamaica Lady*[16] and the anonymous *Fortunate Transport* offer extensive coverage of Jamaica and are useful companion texts to this anthology. The West Indies also figure prominently in more than a dozen comedies and tragedies in the period. Most of these can be grouped into three categories: Shakespeare's *The Tempest* and its variations; stage interpretations of Behn's *Oroonoko* (including *Victorious Love* by the native Barbadian William Walker); and dramatic and operatic retellings of Richard Ligon's story of Inkle and Yarico. As these three thematic groups of dramas indicate, slavery figures prominently in theatrical representations of the West Indies well before African slavery dominates the region's social structure and becomes the central preoccupation of other genres.

Another important theme in the literary representations of the West Indies is piracy. The cult of the pirate—the ultimate criminal and, for some, the symbol of both liberty and the new moneyed economy—infuses much of the cultural representation of the Caribbean, including the texts of this anthology.[17] The two most influential collections of pirate stories are Alexander Exquemelin's *The Buccaniers of America* (English edition, 1684) and Daniel Defoe's *The General History of the Pyrates* (1724). Together, these two popular works supply the stereotype of the pirate that persists into the present time.

Much of the mercantile traffic upon which the pirates preyed was rooted in sugar cane. Sugar cultivation was, of course, the single most important economic activity and the source of the tremendous wealth of the West Indian islands. While brief attention to the processes and hardships of sugar production is paid in Book II of *Jamaica, a Poem*, the most important—and intriguing—literary representation of this agriculture is James Grainger's *The Sugar Cane*.

A study of early slavery writings in English can begin productively with Tryon's *Friendly Advice* and the speeches in the anthology by the "Black of Guardaloupe," "Moses Bon Sàam," and "John Talbot Campo-bell," which provide unusually early and vivid impressions of the impact of slavery on colonial and metropolitan cultures. These texts form an important background and context for the tradition of the slave narrative, which continues with the accounts of Jupiter and Briton Hammon, Job Ben Solomon, Ukawsaw Gronniosaw, Ignatius Sancho, Ottobah Cugoano, and especially Olaudah Equiano, whose 1789 *Interesting Narrative* is the most sophisticated and extensive example of the slave narrative in the eighteenth century.[18] Most of these early slave narratives are heavily edited by Europeans and mediated through European discourse, but as with much other European writing about contacts with oral and nonliterate cultures, some evidence of the realities of those cultures can often be gleaned by reading carefully "through" the bias of the European reportage.[19] A further investigation of early slavery writing would lead one to a number of West Indians and travelers to the West Indies. Richard Baxter and Morgan Godwyn each published tracts concerning West Indian slavery in 1673 and 1680, respectively.[20] Further, one of the earliest condemnations of slavery in English, by Robert Sanderson in 1638, was a response to (then principally Spanish) slavery in the West Indies. And George Fox's comments on slavery during his West Indian and North American tours in 1671 and 1672 can be found in his *Journal,* published posthumously in 1694, which launched the long and distinguished history of Quaker opposition to slavery.

Despite the abundance of accounts of such human-centered phenomena as piracy, sugar cultivation, and slavery, an investigator of early West Indies literature ought not to overlook the large number of natural histories and descriptions. As the first places in which Europeans discovered the exotic flora and fauna of the New World, the West Indies have a long catalogue of important natural histories. As is often the case with early modern scientific texts, these natural histories contain much of interest to the scholar of culture. For example, Richard Blome's account of the English West Indies (1672) describes Jamaica after twenty-three years of English settlement, providing much more specific detail about towns, plantations, and laws than could Hickeringill in the first few years after the conquest.[21] Blome also describes the North American colonies and the rest of the English West Indies at the time: Barbados and the Leeward Islands of Saint Christopher, Nevis, Antigua, and Montserrat. One of the most famous travelers to the region was Sir Hans Sloane, whose voyage prompted his lifelong interest in natural history and whose collection of curiosities became the original inventory of the British Museum. Sloane's *Voyage to the Islands* (1707, 1725) contains intriguing descriptions of the cultures of enslaved Africans in the West Indies; in addition, despite a certain repetitiveness, it provides a detailed picture of Jamaica during Sloane's sojourn as physician to the governor between 1687 and 1689.[22] And finally, Mark Catesby's natural history of Carolina and the Bahamas (then under joint administration) includes considerable description of the Bahamas, which became the chief lair for English pirates after they were forced to leave Jamaica in the wake of the destruction of Port Royal in the massive earthquake of 1692.[23]

In a time of growing globalization of culture, it is natural for students of literary history to pay new attention to the West Indies, where the effects of imperialism were felt earliest and most harshly. In no other region of the world was the native population so thoroughly exterminated, to be replaced by the forced migration of slaves to cultivate a single introduced crop for the pleasure and immense profit of the imperial centers. Despite all this, people of the seventeenth- and eighteenth-century West Indies have left rich artifacts of an equally rich culture formed under extraordinary conditions. This anthology aims to provide a selection of some of the best and most intriguing English literary artifacts of that culture.

FROM

A True & Exact History of the Island of Barbados

RICHARD LIGON

(1634–1703)

Richard Ligon's *A True and Exact History of the Island of Barbados* (1657; second edition, 1673) provides perhaps the best description of any West Indian colony in the seventeenth century. Having been made destitute by being on the losing side of the English Civil War, Ligon embarked for the West Indies to attempt to rebuild his fortune. He arrived in Barbados in 1647, operated a plantation, and worked as an architect. Returning to England in the 1650s, he was imprisoned for a time, during which he wrote his *History*. The engraved map he included in the first edition is the earliest detailed map of the island.

Ligon's account of the people of the island indicates that by the late 1640s the mold was set for the monoculture plantation system that would dominate the region for two centuries more. His report of the treatment of white indentured servants provides a counterpoint for descriptions of the treatment of African slaves in later accounts of the West Indies. Indeed, apologists for the slave system often argued that white indentured servants, miners, soldiers, and sailors were treated at least as poorly as African slaves.

In relating the tale of Inkle and Yarico, Ligon provides the first example of this allegory of European colonization, which would persist in prose, verse, song, and stage throughout the period of British slavery.

FROM

A TRVE & EXACT HISTORY Of the Island of BARBADOS.

Illustrated with a Mapp of the Island, as also the Principall Trees and Plants there, set forth in their due Proportions and Shapes, drawne out by their severall and respective Scales. Together with the Ingenio[1] that makes the Sugar, with the Plots of the severall Houses, Roomes, and other places, that are used in the whole processe of Sugar-making; *viz.* the Grinding-room, the Boyling-room, the Filling-room, the Curing-house, Still-house, and Furnaces;

All cut in Copper.

By Richard Ligon Gent.

LONDON, Printed for *Humphrey Moseley*, at the *Prince's Armes* in *St. Paul's Church-yard*:

1657.

The number and nature of the inhabitants

It were somewhat difficult, to give you an exact account, of the number of persons upon the Iland; there being such store of shipping that brings passengers dayly to the place, but it has been conjectur'd, by those that are long acquainted, and best seen in the knowledge of the Iland, that there are not lesse then 50 thousand soules, besides *Negroes*; and some of them who began upon small fortunes, are now risen to very great and vast estates.

The Iland is divided into three sorts of men, *viz.* Masters, Servants, and slaves. The slaves and their posterity, being subject to their Masters for ever, are kept and preserv'd with greater care then the servants, who are theirs but for five yeers, according to the law of the Iland. So that for the time, the servants have the worser lives, for they are put to very hard labour, ill lodging, and their dyet very sleight. When we came first on the Iland, some Planters themselves did not eate bone meat, above twice a weeke: the rest of the seven dayes, Potatoes, Loblolly, and Bonavist.[2] But the servants no bone meat at all, unlesse an Oxe dyed: and then they were feasted, as long as that lasted, And till they had planted good store of Plantines,[3] the *Negroes* were fed with this kind of food; but most of it Bonavist, and Loblolly, with some eares of Mayes[4] toasted, which food (especially Loblolly,) gave them much discontent: But when they had Plantines enough to serve them, they were heard no more to complaine; for 'tis a food they take great delight in, and their manner of dressing and eating it, is this: 'tis gathered for them (somewhat before it be ripe, for so they desire to have it,) upon Saturday, by the keeper of the Plantine groves; who is an able *Negro*, and knowes well the number of those that are to be fed with this fruite; and as he gathers, layes them all together, till they fetch them away, which is about five a clock in the after noon, for that day they breake off worke sooner by an houre: partly for this purpose, and partly for that the fire in the furnaces is to be put out, and the Ingenio and the roomes made cleane; besides they are to wash, shave and trim themselves against Sunday. But 'tis a lovely sight to see a hundred handsome *Negroes*, men and women, with every one a grasse-green bunch of these fruits on their heads, every bunch twice as big as their heads, all comming in a train one after another, the black and green so well becomming one another. Having brought this fruit home to their own houses, and pilling[5] off the skin of so much as they will use, they boyl it in water, making it into balls, and so they eat it. One bunch a week is a *Negres* allowance. To this, no bread nor drink, but water. Their lodging at night a board, with nothing under, not any thing a top of them. They are happy people, whom so little contents. Very good servants, if they be not spoyled by the English. But more of them hereafter.

[*Indentured Servants*]

As for the usage of the Servants,[6] it is much as the Master is, mercifull or cruell; Those that are mercifull, treat their Servants well, both in their meat, drink, and lodging, and give them such work, as is not unfit for Christians to do. But if the Masters be cruell, the Servants have very wearisome and miserable lives. Upon the arrival of any ship, that brings servants to the Iland, the Planters go aboard; and having bought such of them as they like, send them with a guid to his Plantation; and being come, commands them instantly to make their Cabins, which they not knowing how to do, are to be advised by other of their servants, that are their seniors; but, if they be churlish, and will not shew them, or if materialls be wanting, to make them Cabins, then they are to lie on the ground that night. These Cabins are to be made of sticks, withs,[7] and Plantine leaves, under some little shade that may keep the rain off; Their suppers being a few Potatoes for meat, and water or Mobbie[8] for drink. The next day they are rung out with a Bell to work, at six a clock in the morning, with a severe Overseer to command them, till the Bell ring again, which is at eleven a clock; and then they return, and are set to dinner, either with a messe of Lob-lollie, Bonavist, or Potatoes. At one a clock, they are rung out again to the field, there to work till six, and then home again, to a supper of the same. And if it chance to rain, and wet them through, they have no shift, but must lie so all night. If they put off their cloths, the cold of the night will strike into them; and if they be not strong men, this ill lodging will put them into a sicknesse: if they complain, they are beaten by the Overseer; if they resist, their time is doubled. I have seen an Overseer beat a Servant with a cane about the head, till the blood has followed, for a fault that is not worth the speaking of; and yet he must have patience, or worse will follow. Truly, I have seen such cruelty there done to Servants, as I did not think one Christian could have done to another. But, as discreeter and better natur'd men have come to rule there, the servants lives have been much bettered; for now, most of the servants lie in Hamocks,[9] and in warm rooms, and when they come in wet, have shift of shirts and drawers, which is all the cloths they were,[10] and are fed with *bone meat* twice or thrice a week. Collonell *Walrond*[11] seeing his servants when they came home, toyled with their labour, and wet through with their sweating, thought that shifting of their linnen not sufficient refreshing, nor warmth for their bodies, their pores being much opened by their sweating; and therefore resolved to send into *England* for rug Gownes, such as poor people wear in Hospitalls, that so when they had shifted themselves, they might put on those Gowns, and lie down and rest them in their Hamocks: For the Hamocks being but thin, and they having nothing on but shirts and drawers, when they awak'd out of their sleeps, they found themselves very cold; and a cold taken there, is harder to be recovered, than in *England*, by how much the body is infeebled by the great toyle, and the Sun's heat, which cannot but very much exhaust the spirits of bodies unaccustomed to it. But this care and charity of Collonell *Walrond*'s, lost him nothing in the conclusion; for, he got such love of his servants, as they thought all too little they could do for him; and the love of the servants there, is of much concernment to the Masters, not only in their diligent and painfull labour, but in fore seeing and preventing mischiefes that often happen, by the carelessnesse and slothfulnesse of retchlesse[12] servants; sometimes by laying fire so negligently, as whole lands of Canes and Houses too, are burnt down and consumed, to the utter ruine and undoing of their Masters. . . .

A little before I came from thence, there was such a combination amongst them, as the like was never seen there before. Their sufferings being grown to a great height, & their daily complainings to one another (of the intolerable burdens they labour'd under) being spread throughout the Iland; at the last, some amongst them, whose spirits were not able to endure such slavery, resolved to break through it, or die in the act; and so conspired with some others of their acquaintance, whose sufferings were equall, if not above theirs; and their spirit is no way inferiour, resolved to draw as many of the discontented party into this plot, as possibly they could; and those of this perswasion, were the greatest numbers of the servants in the Iland. So that a day was appointed to fall upon their Masters, and cut all their throats, and by that means, to make themselves not only freemen, but Masters of the Iland. And so closely was this plot carried, as no discovery was made, till the day before they were to put it in act: And then one of them, either by the failing of his courage, or some new obligation from the love of his Master, revealed this long plotted conspiracy; and so by this timely advertisement, the Masters were saved: Justice *Hethersall* (whose servant this was) sending Letters to all his friends, and they to theirs, and so one to another, till they were all secured; and, by examination, found out the greatest part of them; whereof eighteen of the principall men in the conspiracy, and they the first leaders and contrivers of the plot, were put to death, for example to the rest. And the reason why they made examples of so many, was, they found these so haughty in their resolutions, and so incorrigible, as they were like enough to become actors in a second plot; and so they thought good to secure them; and for the rest, to have a speciall eye over them.

Negres

It has been accounted a strange thing, that the Negres, being more then double the numbers of the Christians that are there, and they accounted a bloody people, where they think they have power or advantages; and the more bloody, by how much they are more fearfull than others: that these should not commit some horrid massacre upon the Christians, thereby to enfranchise themselves, and become Masters of the Iland. But there are three reasons that take away this wonder; the one is, They are not suffered to touch or handle any weapons: The other, That they are held in such awe and slavery, as they are fearfull to appear in any daring act; and seeing the mustering of our men, and hearing their Gun-shot, (than which nothing is more terrible to them) their spirits are subjugated to so low a condition, as they dare not look up to any bold attempt. Besides these, there is a third reason, which stops all designes of that kind, and that is, They are fetch'd from severall parts of *Africa*, who speake severall languages, and by that means, one of them understands not another: For, some of them are fetch'd from *Guinny* and *Binny*, some from *Cutchew*, some from *Angola*, and some from the River of *Gambra*.[13] And in some of these places where petty Kingdomes are, they sell their Subjects, and such as they take in Battle, whom they make slaves; and some mean men sell their Servants, their Children, and sometimes their Wives; and think all good traffick, for such commodities as our Merchants sends them.

When they are brought to us, the Planters buy them out of the Ship, where they find them stark naked, and therefore cannot be deceived in any outward infirmity. They choose them as they do Horses in a Market; the strongest, youthfullest, and most beautifull, yield the greatest prices. Thirty pound sterling is a price for the best man Negre; and twenty five, twenty six, or twenty seven pound for a Woman; the Children are at easier rates. And we buy them so, as the sexes may be equall; for, if they have more men then women, the men who are unmarried will come to their Masters, and complain, that they cannot live without Wives, and desire him, they may have Wives. And he tells them, that the next ship that comes, he will buy them Wives, which satisfies them for the present; and so they expect the good time: which the Master performing with them, the bravest is to choose first, and so in order, as they are in place; and every one of them knowes his better, and gives him the precedence, as Cowes do one another, in passing through a narrow gate; for, the most of them are as neer beasts as may be, setting their souls aside. Religion they know none; yet most of them acknowledge a God, as appears by their motions and gestures: For, if one of them do another wrong, and he cannot revenge himselfe, he looks up to Heaven for vengeance, and holds up both his hands, as if the power must come from thence, that must do him right. Chast[14] they are as any people under the Sun; for, when the men and women are together naked, they never cast their eyes towards the parts that ought to be covered; and those amongst us, that have Breeches or Petticoats, I never saw so much as a kisse, or embrace, or a wanton glance with their eyes between them. Jealous they are of their Wives, and hold it for a great injury and scorn, if another man make the least courtship to his Wife. And if any of their Wives have two Children at a birth, they conclude her false to his Bed, and so no more adoe but hang her. We had an excellent Negre in the Plantation, whose name was *Macow*, and was our chiefe Musitian; a very valiant man, and was keeper of our Plantine-groave. This Negres Wife was brought to bed of two Children, and her Husband, as their manner is, had provided a cord to hange her. But the Overseer finding what he was about to do, enformed the Master of it, who sent for *Macow*, to disswade him from this cruell act, of murdering his Wife, and used all perswasions that possibly he could, to let him see, that such double births are in Nature, and that divers presidents[15] were to be found amongst us of the like; so that we rather praised our Wives, for their fertility, than blamed them for their falsenesse. But this prevailed little with him, upon whom custome had taken so deep an impression; but resolved, the next thing he did, should be to hang her. Which when the Master perceived, and that the ignorance of the man, should take away the life of the woman, who was innocent of the crime her Husband condemned her for, told him plainly, that if he hang'd her, he himselfe should be hang'd by her, upon the same bough; and therefore wish'd him to consider what he did. This threatning wrought more with him, then all the reasons of Philosophy that could be given him; and so let her alone; but he never car'd much for her afterward, but chose another which he lik'd better. For the Planters there deny not a slave, that is a brave fellow, and one that has extraordinary qualities, two or three Wives, and above that number they seldome go: But no woman is allowed above one Husband.

At the time the wife is to be brought a bed, her husband removes his board, (which is his bed) to another room (for many severall divisions they have, in their little houses, and none above sixe foot square) And leaves his wife to God, and her good fortune, in the room, and upon the board alone, and calls a neighbour to come to her, who gives little help to her deliverie, but when the child is borne, (which she calls her Pickaninnie) she helps to make a little fire nere her feet and that serves instead of Possets, Broaths, and Caudles.[16] In a fortnight, this woman is at worke with her Pickaninny at her back, as merry a soule as any is there: If the overseer be discreet, shee is suffer'd to rest her selfe a little more then ordinary; but if not, shee is compelled to doe as others doe. Times they have of suckling their Children in the fields, and refreshing themselves; and good reason, for they carry burdens on their backs; and yet work too. Some women, whose Pickaninnies are three yeers old, will, as they worke at weeding, which is a stooping worke, suffer the hee Pickaninnie, to sit astride upon their backs, like St. *George* a horseback; and there spurre his mother with his heeles, and sings and crowes on her backe, clapping his hands, as if he meant to flye; which the mother is so pleas'd with, as shee continues her painfull stooping posture, longer then she would doe, rather than discompose her Joviall Pickaninnie of his pleasure, so glad she is to see him merry. The worke which the women doe, is most of it weeding, a stooping and painfull worke; at noon and night they are call'd home by the ring of a Bell, where they have two hours time for their repast at noone; and at night, they rest from sixe, till sixe a Clock next morning.

On Sunday they rest, and have the whole day at their pleasure; and the most of them use it as a day of rest and pleasure; but some of them who will make benefit of that dayes liberty, goe where the Mangrave trees grow, and gather the barke of which they make ropes, which they trucke[17] away for other Commoditie, as shirts and drawers.

In the afternoons on Sundayes, they have their musicke, which is of kettle drums, and those of severall sises;[18] upon the smallest the best musitian playes, and the other come in as Chorusses: the drum all men know, has but one tone; and therefore varietie of tunes have little to doe in this musick; and yet so strangely they varie their time, as 'tis a pleasure to the most curious eares, and it was to me one of the strangest noyses that ever I heard made of one tone; and if they had the varietie of tune, which gives the greater scope in musick, as they have of time, they would doe wonders in that Art. And if I had not faln[19] sicke before my comming away, at least seven months in one sickness, I had given them some hints of tunes, which being understood, would have serv'd as a great addition to their harmonie; for time without tune, is not an eighth part of the science of Musick.

I found *Macow* very apt for it of himselfe, and one day comming into the house, (which none of the *Negroes* use to doe, unlesse an Officer, as he was,) he found me playing on a Theorbo,[20] and sinking to it which he hearkened very attentively to; and when I had done took the Theorbo in his hand, and strooke one string, stopping it by degrees upon every fret, and finding the notes to varie, till it came to the body of the instrument; and that the neerer the body of the instrument he stopt, the smaller or higher the sound was, which he found was by the shortning of the string, considered with himselfe, how he might make some triall of this experiment upon such an instrument as he could come by; having no hope ever to have any instrument of this kind to practise on. In a day or two after, walking in the Plantine grove, to refresh me in that cool shade, and to delight my selfe with the sight of those plants, which are so beautifull, as though they left a fresh impression in me when I parted with them, yet upon a review, something is discern'd in their beautie more then I remembred at parting: which caused me to make often repair thither: I found this *Negro* (whose office it was to attend there) being the keeper of that grove, sitting on the ground, and before him a piece of large timber, upon which he had laid crosse, sixe Billets,[21] and having a hand-saw and a hatchet by him, would cut the billets by little and little, till he had brought them to the tunes, he would sit them to; so the shorter they were, the higher the Notes which he tryed by knocking upon the ends of them with a sticke, which he had in his hand. When I found him at it, I took the stick out of his hand, and tried the sound, finding the sixe billets to have six distinct notes, one above another, which put me in a wonder, how he of himselfe, should without teaching doe so much. I then shewed him the difference between flats and sharps, which he presently apprehended, as between *Fa*, and *Mi*: and he would have cut two more billets to those tunes, but I had then no time to see it done, and so left him to his own enquiries. I say this much to let you see that some of these people are capable of learning Arts.

Another of another kinde of speculation I found; but more ingenious then he: and this man with three or foure more, were to attend mee into the woods, to cut Church wayes,[22] for I was imployed sometimes upon publique works; and those men were excellent Axe-men, and because there were many gullies in the way, which were impassable, and by that means I was compell'd to make traverses, up and down in the wood; and was by that in danger to misse of the poynt, to which I was to make my passage to the Church, and therefore was faine to take a Compasse with me, which was a Circumferenter,[23] to make my traverses the more exact, and indeed without which, it could not be done, setting up the Circumferenter, and observing the Needle: This *Negre Sambo* comes to me, and seeing the needle wag, desired to know the reason of its stirring, and whether it were alive: I told him no, but it stood upon a poynt, and for a while it would stir, but by and by stand still, which he observ'd and found it to be true.

The next question was, why it stood one way, & would not remove to any other poynt, I told him that it would stand no way but North and South, and upon that shew'd him the foure Cardinall poynts of the compass, East, West, North, South, which he presently learnt by heart, and promis'd me never to forget it. His last question was, why it would stand North, I gave this reason, because of the huge Rocks of Loadstone that were in the North part of the world, which had a quality to draw Iron to it; and this Needle being of Iron, and toucht with a Loadstone, it would alwaies stand that way.

This point of Philosophy was a little too hard for him, and so he stood in a strange muse; which to put him out of, I bad him reach his ax, and put it neer to the Compasse, and remove it about; and as he did so, the Needle turned with it, which put him in the greatest admiration that ever I saw a man, and so quite gave over his questions, and desired me, that he might be made a Christian; for, he thought to be a Christian, was to be endued with all those knowledges he wanted.

I promised to do my best endeavour; and when I came home, spoke to the Master of the Plantation, and told him, that poor *Sambo* desired much to be a Christian. But his answer was, That the people of that Iland were governed by the Lawes of *England*, and by those Lawes, we could not make a Christian a Slave. I told him, my request was far different from that, for I desired to make a Slave a Christian. His answer was, That it was true, there was a great difference in that: But, being once a Christian, he could no more account him a Slave, and so lose the hold they had of them as Slaves, by making them Christians; and by that means should open such a gap, as all the Planters in the Iland would curse him. So I was struck mute, and poor *Sambo* kept out of the Church; as ingenious, as honest, and as good a natur'd poor soul, as ever wore black, or eat green.

On Sundaies in the afternoon, their Musick plaies, and to dancing they go, the men by themselves, and the women by themselves, no mixt dancing. Their motions are rather what they aim at, than what they do; and by that means, transgresse the lesse upon the Sunday; their hands having more of motion than their feet, & their heads more than their hands. They may dance a whole day, and neer heat themselves; yet, now and then, one of the activest amongst them will leap bolt upright, and fall in his place again, but without cutting a capre.[24] When they have danc'd an houre or two, the men fall to wrastle, (the Musick playing all the while) and their manner of wrastling is, to stand like two Cocks, with heads as low as their hipps; and thrusting their heads one against another, hoping to catch one another by the leg, which sometimes they do: But if both parties be weary, and that they cannot get that advantage, then they raise their heads, by pressing hard against one another, and so having nothing to take hold of but their bare flesh, they close, and grasp one another about the middle, and have one another in a hug, and then a fair fall is given on the back. And thus two or three couples of them are engaged at once, for an houre together, the women looking on: for when the men begin to wrastle, the women leave of their dancing, and come to be spectatours of the sport.

When any of them die, they dig a grave, and at evening they bury him, clapping and wringing their hands, and making a dolefull sound with their voyces. They are a people of a timerous and fearfull disposition, and consequently bloody, when they finde advantages. If any of them commit a fault, give him present punishment, but do not threaten him; for if you do, it is an even lay, he will go and hang himselfe, to avoid the punishment.

What their other opinions are in manner of Religion, I know not; but certainly, they are not altogether of the sect of the *Sadduces*:[25] For, they believe a Resurrection, and that they shall go into their own Country again, and have their youth renewed. And lodging this opinion in their hearts, they make it an ordinary practice, upon any great fright, or threatning of their Masters, to hang themselves.

But Collonell *Walrond* having lost three or foure of his best Negres this way, and in a very little time, caused one of their heads to be cut off, and set upon a pole a dozen foot high; and having done that, caused all his Negres to come forth, and march around this head, and bid them look on it, whether this were not the head of such an one that hang'd himselfe. Which they acknowledging, he then told them, That they were in a main errour, in thinking they went into their own Countries, after they were dead; for, this mans head was here, as they all were witnesses of; and how was it possible, the body could go without a head. Being convinc'd by this sad, yet lively spectacle, they changed their opinions; and after that, no more hanged themselves.

When they are sick, there are two remedies that cure them; the one, an outward, the other, an inward medicine. The outward medicine is a thing they call Negre-oyle, and 'tis made in *Barbary*,[26] yellow it is as Bees wax, but soft as butter. When they feel themselves ill, they call for some of that, and annoint their bodies, as their breasts, bellies, and sides, and in two daies they are perfectly well. But this does the greatest cures upon such, as have bruises or strains in their bodies. The inward medicine is taken, when they find any weakness or decay in their spirits and stomacks, and then a dram or two of *kill-devill*[27] revives and comforts them much.

I have been very strict, in observing the shapes of these people; and for the men, they are very well timber'd, that is, broad between the shoulders, full breasted, well filleted,[28] and clean leg'd, and may hold good with *Albert Durers*[29] rules, who allowes *twice the length of the head*, to the breadth of the shoulders; and twice the *length of the face*, to the breadth of the hipps, and according to this rule these men are shap'd. But the women not; for the same great Master of Proportions, allowes to each woman, twice the length of the face to the breadth of the shoulders, and twice the length of her own head to the breadth of the hipps. And in that, these women are faulty; for I have seen very few of them, whose hipps have been broader then their shoulders, unlesse they have been very fat. The young Maides have ordinarily very large breasts, which stand strutting out so hard and firm, as no leaping, jumping or stirring, will cause them to shake any more, then the brawnes of their armes. But when they come to be old, and have had five or six Children, their breasts hang down below their navells, so that when they stoop at their common work of weeding, they hang almost down to the ground, that at a distance, you would think they had six legs: And the reason of this is, they tie the cloaths about their Children's backs, which comes upon their breasts, which by pressing very hard, causes them to hang down to that length. Their Children, when they are first born, have the palmes of their hands and the soles of their feet, of a whitish colour, and the sight of their eyes of a blewish colour, not unlike the eyes of a young Kitling;[30] but, as they grow older, they become black.

Their way of reckoning their ages, or any other notable accident they would remember, is by the Moon; and so accounting from the time of their Childrens births, the time they were brought out of their own Country, or the time of their being taken Prisoners, by some Prince or Potentate of their own Country, or any other notorious accidents, that they are resolved to remember, they account by the Moon; as, so many Moons since one of these, and so many Moons since another; and this account they keep as long as they can: But if any of them live long, their Arithmetick failes them, and then they are at a dead fault, and so give over the chase, wanting the skill to hunt counter.[31] For what can poor people do, that are without Letters and Numbers, which is the soul of all businesse that is acted by Mortalls, upon the Globe of this World.

Some of them, who have been bred up amongst the Portugalls, have some extraordinary qualities, which the others have not; as singing and fencing. I have seen some of these *Portugall Negres*, at Collonell James Draxes,[32] play at Rapier and Dagger very skilfully, with their Stookados, their Imbrocados, and their Passes:[33] And at a single Rapier too, after the manner of *Charanza*, with such comelinesse; as, if the skill had been wanting, the motions would have pleased you; but they were skilfull too, which I perceived by their binding with their points, and nimble and subtle avoidings with their bodies, and the advantages the strongest man had in the close, which the other avoided by the nimblenesse and skilfulnesse of his motion. For, in this Science, I had bin so well vers'd in my youth, as I was now able to be a competent Judge. Upon their first appearance upon the Stage, they march towards one another, with a slow majestick pace, and a bold commanding look, as if they meant both to conquer; and comming neer together, they shake hands, and embrace one another, with a cheerfull look. But their retreat is much quicker then their advance, and, being at first distance, change their countenance, and put themselves into their posture; and so after a passe or two, retire, and then to't again: And when they have done their play, they embrace, shake hands, and putting on their smoother countenances, give their respects to their Master, and so go off. For their Singing, I cannot much commend that, having heard so good in *Europe*; but for their voices, I have heard many of them very loud and sweet.

Excellent Swimmers and Divers they are, both men and women. Collonell *Drax* (*who was not so strict an observer of Sundaies*, as to deny himselfe lawfull recreations) would sometimes, to shew me sport, upon that day in the afternoon, send for one of the *Muscovia* Ducks, and have her put into his largest Pond, and calling for some of his best swimming Negres, commanded them to swim and take this Duck; but forbad them to dive, for if they were not bar'd that play, they would rise up under the Duck, and take her as she swome, or meet her in her diving, and so the sport would have too quick an end. But that play being forbidden, the duck would make them good sport for they are stronger ducks, and better Divers by farre then ours: and in this chase, there was much of pleasure, to see the various swimmings of the *Negroes*; some the ordinarie wayes, upon their bellies, some on their backs, some by striking out their right legge and left arme, and then turning on the other side, and changing both their legge and arme, which is a stronger and swifter way of swimming, then any of the others: and while we were seeing this sport, and observing the diversities, of their swimmings, a *Negro* maid, who was not there at the beginning of the sport; and therefore heard nothing of the forbidding them to dive, put off her peticoate behind a bush, that was at one end of the Pond, and closely sunk down into the water, and at one diving got to the Duck, pul'd her under water, & went back againe the same way she came to the bush, all at one dive. We all thought the Duck had div'd: and expected her appearance above water, but nothing could be seen, till the subtilty was discovered, by a Christian that saw her go in, and so the duck was taken from her. But the trick being so finely and so closely done, I begg'd that the Duck might be given her againe, which was granted, and the young girle much pleased.

Though there be a marke set upon these people, which will hardly ever be wip'd off, as of their cruelties when they have advantages, and of their fearfulnesse and falsnesse; yet no rule so generall but hath his acception:[34] for I believe, and I have strong motives to cause me to bee of that perswasion, that there are as honest, faithfull, and conscionable people amongst them, as amongst those of *Europe*, or any other part of the world.

A hint of this, I will give you in a lively example; and it was in a time when Victuals were scarce, and Plantins were not then so frequently planted, as to afford them enough. So that some of the high spirited and turbulent amongst them, began to mutinie, and had a plot, secretly to be reveng'd on their Master, and one or two of these were Firemen that made the fires in the furnaces, who were never without store of drie wood by them. These villains, were resolved to make fire to such part of the boyling house, as they were sure would fire the rest, and so burn all, and yet seem ignorant of the fact, as a thing done by accident. But this plot was discovered, by some of the others who hated mischiefe, as much as they lov'd it; and so traduc't them to their Master, and brought in so many witnesses against them, as they were forc't to confesse, what they meant should have been put in act the next night: so giving them condigne[35] punishment, the Master gave order to the overseer that the rest should have a dayes liberty to themselves and their wives, to doe what they would; and withall to allow them a double proportion of victual for three dayes, both which they refus'd: which we all wonder'd at knowing well how much they lov'd their liberties, and their meat, having been lately pincht of the one, and not having overmuch of the other; and therefore being doubtfull what their meaning was in this, suspecting some discontent amongst them, sent for three or foure of the best of them, and desir'd to know why they refus'd this favour that was offer'd them, but receiv'd such an answer: as we little expected; for they told us, it was not sullenness, slighting the gratuitie their Master bestow'd on them, but they would not accept any thing as a recompence for doing that which became them in their duties to due, nor would they have him think, it was hope of reward, that made them to accuse their fellow servants, but an act of Justice, which they thought themselves bound in duty to doe, and they thought themselves sufficiently rewarded in the Act. The substance of this, in such language as they had, they delivered, and poor *Sambo* was the Orator; by whose example the others were led both in the discovery of the Plot, and refusall of the gratuitie. And withall they said, that if it pleas'd their Master, at any time, to bestow a voluntary boone upon them, be it never so sleight, they would willingly and thankfully accept it: & this act might have beseem'd the best Christians, though some of them were denied Christianity; when they earnestly sought it. Let others have what opinion they please, yet I am of this beliefe; that there are to be found amongst them, some who are as morally honest, as Conscionable, as humble, as loving to their friends, and as loyall to their Masters, as any that live under the sunne, & one reason that they have to be so, is, they set no great value upon their lives: And this is all I can remember concerning the *Negroes*, except of their games, which I could never learne, because they wanted language to teach me.

As for the Indians, we have but few, and those fetcht from other Countries; some from the neighbouring Ilands, some from the Maine,[36] which we make slaves: the women who are better verst in ordering the Cassavie[37] and making bread, then the *Negroes*, we imploye for that purpose, as also for making Mobbie: the men we use for footmen and killing of fish which they are good at; with their own bowes and arrows they will go out; and in a dayes time, kill as much fish, as will serve a family of a dozen persons, two or three daies, if you can keep the fish so long. They are very active men, and apt to learne any thing, sooner then the *Negroes*, and as different from them in shape, almost as in colour; the men very broad shoulder'd, deep breasted, with large heads and their faces almost three square,[38] broad about the eyes and temples, and sharpe at the chinne, their skins some of them brown, some a bright Bay, they are much craftier, and subtiler then the *Negroes*; and in their nature falser; but in their bodies more active, their women have very small breasts, and have more of the shape of the *Europeans* then the *Negroes*, their haire black and long, a great part whereof hangs downe upon their backs, as low as their hanches, with a large lock hanging over either breast, which seldome or never curles: cloaths they scorne to weare, especially if they be well shap't; a girdle they use of tape, covered with little smooth shels of fishes, white, and from their flanke of one side, to their flank on the other side, a fringe of blew Bugle;[39] which hangs so low as to cover their privities. We had an Indian woman, a slave in the house, who was of excellent shape and colour, for it was a pure bright bay; small brests, with the nipls of a porphyrie colour,[40] this woman would not be woo'd by any means to weare Cloaths. Shee chanc't to be with Child, by a Christian servant, and lodging in the Indian house, amongst other women of her own Country, where the Christian servants, both men and women came; and being very great, and that her time was come to be delivered, loath to fall in labour before the men, walk'd down to a Wood, in which was a Pond of water, and there by the side of the Pond, brought her selfe a bed; and presently washing her Child in some of the water of the Pond, lap'd it up in such rags, as she had begg'd of the Christians; and in three hours time came home, with her Childe in her armes, a lusty Boy, frolick and lively.

This Indian dwelling neer the Sea-coast, upon the Main, an English ship put in to a Bay, and sent some of her men a shoar, to try what victualls or water they could finde, for in some distresse they were: But the Indians perceiving them to go up so far into the Country, as they were sure they could not make a safe retreat, intercepted them in their return, and fell upon them, chasing them into a Wood, and being dispersed there, some were taken, and some kill'd: but a young man amongst them stragling from the rest, was met by this Indian Maid, who upon the first sight fell in love with him, and hid him close from her Countrymen (the Indians) in a Cave, and there fed him, till they could safely go down to the shoar, where the ship lay at anchor, expecting the return of their friends. But at last, seeing them upon the shoar, sent the long-Boat for them, took them aboard, and brought them away. But the youth, when he came ashoar in the *Barbadoes*, forgot the kindnesse of the poor maid, that had ventured her life for his safety, and sold her for a slave, who was as free born as he: And so poor *Yarico* for her love, lost her liberty.

[Masters]

Now for the Masters, I have yet said but little, nor am able to say halfe of what they deserve. They are men of great abilities and parts, otherwise they could not go through, with such great works as they undertake; the managing of one of their Plantations, being a work of such a latitude, as will require a very good head-peece,[41] to put in order, and continue it so.

FROM

Jamaica Viewed

EDMUND HICKERINGILL

(1631-1708)

Although known chiefly for his acerbic pamphleteering against the "popish follies" of his own Church of England, Edmund Hickeringill had an early life punctuated by far travels and radical changes of opinion. He was a pensioner in Saint John's College, Cambridge, and spent a little more than a year as a junior fellow in Caius and Gonville College, Cambridge. The rest of his youth was marked by rapid shifts between political and religious extremes. In 1652, he was rebaptized as an adult, ordained a Baptist minister, and sent as a missionary to Scotland. Early in 1653, he became chaplain to a regiment of horse in Leith, but he was quickly excommunicated from the Baptist church and turned Quaker. Two months later, he renounced Quakerism and became something of an early deist. He then spent 1653 through 1656 as a lieutenant in the garrison at Perth, Scotland, before setting out on a series of mercenary travels to Sweden, Spain, and Portugal.

On his return to England, he was appointed captain and sent to Jamaica, where he collected the data for *Jamaica Viewed* (1661), his first publication. The second edition (1661) was dedicated to the restored King Charles II, who rewarded Hickeringill with an appointment (with the large salary of £1,000) as secretary to Thomas, Lord Windsor, the first governor of Jamaica under the new government. Upon returning from his second West Indian voyage, Hickeringill was ordained a priest of the Church of England by Robert Sanderson (whom Hickeringill called "the presbyterian bishop," and who, incidentally, wrote one of the earliest condemnations of chattel slavery in English). The remainder of Hickeringill's life was spent as rector of All Saints Church, Colchester, author of a series of attacks on the "popish excesses" of the established church and defendant in various libel suits.

An old, possibly eighteenth-century, manuscript note in the flyleaf of the British Library's copy of *The Works of Mr Edmund Hickeringill* (1716) has this to say about the author:

The humorous and very ludicrous author of the following volumes
aptly and minutely delineated the genuine features of priestcraft in
the most masterly manner, and though himself a clergyman, has by
no means favoured his brethren, regardless of denomination. He appears well qualified for the execution of such a task, as having resided
among the Roman Catholics abroad, and been much habituated to
the manners of the Presbyterians in Scotland, During his [being] in
the Army with Monk[1] in the great rebellion. Nor does he spare the
sectaries of England in their turn. He appears to sit amicably in
Company of his brethren of the established Church, levelling his Artillery against all other priests without the least favour or affection,
and with no inconsiderable success; at length he arises from his seat,
forsakes his brethren, and lashes with a potent arm all the religions of
the world—In a word, Mr. Hickeringhill has succeeded in his exhi-
bition of fraud all that Shaftsbury[2] ever suggested and gone farther
than Woolston,[3] or even Bolingbroke.[4]

Jamaica Viewed appeared at a critical moment in the history of Jamaica
and Britain: Charles II had promised Spain the return of Jamaica in exchange for Spain's support for his restoration to the throne. As it turned
out, Charles did not require Spain's assistance, but he was still inclined to
hold to the bargain. *Jamaica Viewed* and other reports of the value of Jamaica helped change Charles's mind. Jamaica remained a British colony
without interruption for another three hundred years. The preface to the
third edition (1705) is included here. The copy text of the remainder is the
first edition (1661).

JAMAICA VIEWED;

WITH All the *Ports*, *Harbours*, and their several *Soundings*, *Towns*,
and *Settlements* thereunto belonging. Together, *With the nature
of it's* Climate; *fruitfulnesse of the* Soile, *and it's suitablenesse
to* English Complexions: With several other collateral
Observations and Reflexions upon the Island.
By *E.H. London*, Printed by *J.R.*
1661.

PREFACE TO THE THIRD EDITION, 1705
The Stationer to the Reader

This View (or Description) of *Jamaica* was printed, and by Two *Editions* Published in 1661. by Captain *Hickeringill*, at his Return from *Jamaica*, soon after
the Restauration of King Charles II. (*to whom* the Book is Dedicated, *and at
whose Command* it was Compiled, to give His Majesty intelligence of a Territory he knew little of: And *in Gratitude* to the Author, for his Pains, that King
made him *Secretary* to the Earl of *Windsor*,[5] then going Governour to *Jamaica*; whose *Instructions* (none so fit *to draw up*) as he had been there, and
made Observations, and had a *Map* of the Soundings toward the Island of *Jamaica* given to him, (to publish for the Benefit of all Mariners that touch upon
that Coast) by Governor *Doyly*,[6] the Author's dear Friend and intimate Acquaintance, &c. But why the *Reverend Author* left the *Secretaries Place* (so very
Profitable and Honourable) to be a *Divine*, I do not know; This I know, that
the Book is *out of Print*, and scarcely to be had *for Love or Mony*; and I having
the Happiness to publish the Authors Two *Books* of *Priest-craft*, with good
Success, cannot but think that I gratify *the Reader*, as well as *my self*, with re-
newing an old Book, especially at this time, *when we have* a War with *Spain*,
very useful and profitable, as well as pleasant to the Reader; in a Stile so peculiar to the Author, that it is near almost needless to prefix his Name, but that
the Stile of his Youth (45 Years ago) is more *Florid* and *Juvenile* than can be expected now, flagging near the *Autumn* of Fourscore Years, when tis time to expect the Fall of the Leaf. But the Book is reprinted now in 1705. *verbatim*, as at
first in 1660.[7] without any one word either *added*, *alter'd* or *diminish'd*, and
therefore if any Phrase seem too Aiery and Comical for a *Divine*, 'tis suitable
enough to what he then was—a *Jolly Captain*, by Sea and Land. Which may
the better compound for these *seemingly wanton Flights* of Juvenile Fancy in
his *Satyr against Marriage*; and his *athlectical Constitution* and *numerous Issue*
secures him from being accounted a *Woman-hater*; he seems *to like* Wives well

enough, so they be content to be *House-Wives*, and keep in their *Kitchings* and *Nurseries*, and not run *Salt* and *Rank* to *Campaigns*, and *Navy's*, Debauching the Camp; and Young Ladies (like *Venable*'s)[8] to be Leaguer-Ladies.[9]

TO THE READER. *The Partial Censures and Nick-names which prejudice and interest have injuriously impos'd upon the Island of* Jamaica, *(after it became the Refuge of that* English *Colony that of late unhappily invaded* Hispaniola*) mov'd me, in the negligence of better Pens, to Apologize for it, in this ensuing Description; For indeed to describe* Jamaica, *is to praise it, nor can it look better then with it's own face, exempt from the adulterate* Fucus *of artificial Pilliary. And believe me, Reader, 'twas no private nor politick design, (hereby to allure and Duckoy the unwary world) but meer zeal to truth, that engag'd me by my opportune continuance there, to do this right to that injur'd Island.*

Jamaica Viewed.

That the Island of *Iamaica* was rather the Grave then Granary to the first *English* Colony (seated there, after their inauspicious Enterprize upon *Hispaniola*) cannot modestly be denied;

Whether occasioned by the griping Monopoly of some hoarding Officers; or through want of timely Recruits, alwaies found necessary for such Infant-settlements: or, through some fatal Conjunction of the superiour Luminaries, (that frown by course with a squint and malignant Aspects on one Nation or other,) I will not now dispute.

But that such a Mortality should proceed, either from the *Clime*, being scituate in the *Torrid Zone*, (a Heresie unpardonable in the ancients;) or from any accidental *Malignity* in any of the Elements, peculiarly entail'd upon it, whereby it should be lesse habitable then any other most auspicious settlement remains here to be controverted. . . .

2. *General.* Second. *Of the improv'd Productions of the Isle*

In the next place, the fruits of *Iamaica* that are produc'd by the improvement of Art, will most methodically present themselves to be considered; wherein I shall purposely omit to give the Reader any account of those usual Household Provisions, of Cassawder, Corn, Potatoes, *&c.* nor of those Merchantable Comodities of Cotton, Indico, Tobacco, Sugar, *&c.* common to it with the rest of the *English* Plantations; But presuming the Reader's acquaintance with those Fruits and Merchandize so vulgarly known; I shall onely treat of those that are more rare and not to be found in any other of the *English* Colonies in *America*.

I. The first that I shall mention is the *Cacoa*-Walks, which are not few in this Island, some of them containing ten or twelve Acres of Ground, some more, some lesse: The Trees are about the bignesse of our largest Plum-trees in *England*, orderly set, like our Orchards, at the distance of 6, or 7. foot from each other; which *Interstitiums* are carefully weeded, & cleared from the Grasse, that the *Cacoa* Trees may without a Rival engrosse the Sap and substance of the *Soil*, which is chosen the most fertile that can be got, and naturally skreen'd and shaded from the piercing rayes of the Sun; Nor indeed can any ground be better employ'd; the *Spaniard*, (who best understands the value of them) reckoning every one of his *Cacoa*-trees to be worth him a Piece of Eight *per ann.* after it begins to bear, which is usually about seven years after it's first planting; in which time they are once or twice transplanted for the two first years, and especially in their Infancy must be protected from the scortching Sun by the favourable interposition of some shady Trees; and therefore the *Plantane*-Walks are usually made choice of, for such Nurseries.

Of the Fruit or Nuts of these Trees is made the so fam'd *Chocoletta*, whose virtues are hiperboliz'd upon every post in *London*: though we must confesse it of excellent nourishment.

The *Spaniard* victualling for a long and wildernesse Journey, with no other Refreshment, then Cakes made of the Kernals of those *Cacoa* Nuts; which he dissolves in water for his meat and drink.

The Composition of these *Cacoa* Cakes or *Chocoletta* is now so vulgar that I will not disparage my Reader by doubting his acquaintance in so known a Recipe; a very *Crambe*[10] in other Authours. . . . I shall conclude with one rarity more, of which in *Iamaica* is too great a plenty; and that is the *Alligator*, or *Indian Crocodile*, an amphibious Creature, that (like an *Otter*) haunts both the land and water.

I have seen many of them upon *Hispaniola*, but never in any of the *Chariby* Islands, nor in the *Wind-ward* Settlements upon the *Main*.

It would be too long to tell what large feats are storied of this Beast; as, that he will pull the Bulls into the water, (catching them like a keen Mastiffe by the cheek) when they come to drink, *&c.*

This is true, that they have an incomparable strength in the water, in which as their most friendly Element, they do usually encounter the prey, especially, if the mastery, will require their utmost strength in the grapple.

But though he winnes the field in the water, (with a Bull) yet he must share the Spoile on the shore; for he cannot (without the danger of drownding) swallow his Booty, through an impediment in his throat. Some of them (I have seen) six or seven yards long, but their usual stretch, may bate the half;

And indeed, though they are fierce and ravenous, yet at the approach of a man, whilest they lie basking upon the Sands, they betake themselves, (though with no great haste) into the water; yet it is not very safe sleeping near the shore where they haunt, lest they take you napping. Yet can they not prejudice a child that is but aware of them: For their motion is very slow; neither can they turn the head, but the whole body must wheele for companie.

Dat Deus immiti cornua curta[11]—

There is as good Civet in the Cods of an old rammish *Alligator*, as in the *Ginny* Civet Cats.

I shall not mention here the plenty of all sorts of Fish, and wild Fowl, as *Ginny* Hens, Ducks, wild Pigeons, &c. because these Collections shall take notice only of what is singular in this Island, without a Copartner, or any Parallel in any other Settlements of our Countrey-men.

But possibly amongst these Rarities some will expect I should (as the most welcome News) discover some Mines of Silver or Gold; as the most undoubted transcendency of a rich Land.

> *Scilicet uxorem cum dote, fidemque & amicos,*
> *Et Genus & formam, regina pecunia donat.*
> *Ac bene nummatum decorat suadela, venusque.*[12]

This *auri sacra fames*[13] of the *Lyrick*, is usually the Grand Inquest; and without it other things seem to want their taste, or relish but unsavoury, especially to such an *Epicurean* as that was that charm'd his sences with this Lullabie;

> *Forbear your Stoick Rules, go read*
> *To bed-rid Age; for I'le not heed*
> *Your peevish Morralls, till dull sence*
> *Despairs to have concupiscence.*[14]
> *No, (whilest my spirits are young and good,*
> *Revelling in my frolick bloud)*
> *Compar'd to me old* Epicure,
> *Shall be a Puritan demure,*
> *Each sence shall play the Parasite,*
> *To humour my coy Appetite,*
> *Till I (bidding all joyes good night)*
> *Prove the* Nil ultra[15] *of delight.*
> *For virtues only, that attend*

A State not needy I commend;
For on your beggar-virtues I
Dote not (except integrity,)
Such as is Patience per force,
A virtue practis'd by my Horse.
When him to th'Manger I do tie
From meat, long'd for with leering eye.
And let humility be gone,
When I have nought to be proud on.
Rather then such poor vertues have,
Some court rich vices, or a grave.

Such is some mens prophane *Boulimy* & insatiable *Poludipsie*[16] after Gold, through the depravement of their canine and pical[17] Appetites.

—nec
Terret ambustus Phaethon avaras
spes. Hor.[18]

Neither heat nor cold can baracade the entrails and womb of the earth from the *Caesarian Section*, and debauch'd midwifery of the greedy Miners; which (as 'tis thought) would not in *Iamaica*, prove labour in vain; for some *Melottoes*[19] and *Negroes*, (that were lately Slaves to the *Spaniards* in this Isle) tell us, that their Masters did certainly know of two Silver Mines; yet are they not hitherto found by the *English*; whose scrutiny therein is not very prying and exact, the which, though assured, were no policy to divulge, 'till their numbers be encreased, & their foot-hold secured; Arguments, that perswaded the *Spaniard* to reclose and dam up a rich Silver Vein in a Mountain near the Sea, a few Leagues to the Norward of *Cape St. Nicholas*, at the west-end of *Hispaniola*: not daring to present such a temptation to the Princes of *Europe*, till his Mines in *Petozo, Peru*, and New *Spain* be worn out; that his spare hands then may not only extract, but secure the *Oare*; a prize, which if now expos'd to publick notice, would create him many an unwelcome Rival, that would not be to seek of pretences enough, to further his suit: since our mother-Earth doth indifferently prostrate her womb to the common embraces of any Ravisher, that hath *Armes* strong enough to secure him, in the Rape; the only *Patent* that the *Spaniard* can show for his *Indie*-Mines.

Which himself very well knowes, and is therefore very unwilling to dispute his Title, but where he can empannell an Army, instead of a Jury to make good the Claime; the which he can hardly levie upon *Hispaniola*; it being so thinly peopled, that he can scarcely muster five hundred fighting men, (in the whole Island) though he should put forth a general Presse (enforc'd with the strictest Commission of *Aray*)[20] except only in the Town of St. *Domingo*; which is distant above one hundred and fifty miles from the fore-mentioned Mine; and are not able with all their skill and strength to root out a few *Buckaneers* or Hunting *French-men*, that follow their Game, in despight of them, though they cannot number three hundred at a general Rendezvouse: and those dispersed at three hundred miles distance from one another, on the North and West sides of the Island; of whom peradventure I may have hereafter more occasion to discourse.

Therefore it is not much material, whether or no, *Iamaica* own any Silver-Mines, though it be more then probable that time will discover some:

Quicquid sub terra est,
in apricum proferet aetas.[21]

For if there were but strength of hands in *Iamaica*, they might procure money with lesse labour then digging: except the *Spaniard* will quietly suffer them to reap the Fruits of the Common Earth. For the propriety whereof he can shew no Bill of Sale but his Sword.

Thus much in General.

I shall now give you a more particular Description of this Isle, with it's Harbours,
Towns, Ports, Soundings, . . .

Wherein the chiefe Harbour at Point Cagway[22] merits Precedency, lying North-West from the said Point in an Arm of the Sea, that shoots in three or four Leagues within the Land.

Where a thousand tall ships may safely ride at one time, and all sufficiently shelter'd from winds and waves; and if they please, close aboard the shore, for an *English* mile in length, incomparably convenient for careening ships of all Burthens.

Upon this Point or sandy Bay is now built above five hundred houses, by the *English*, chiefly for the accommodation of sea-men, especially the *Privateers*, who are their best Customers; and sometimes, as now it is, the Residence of the General, and some Merchants & Manufactures; whose shares to build upon is measured out to them by the Foot, and that immediately forfeited, if not forthwith improv'd by Buildings, which now almost cover the face of the Bay for a mile in length; the breadth thereof being variable, sometimes borrowing of the two Seas, in whose Armes it lies, and then re-paying with unequal Interest; so that about a mile from the Harbours mouth, it is almost Bankerupt.

The Bank in that place not extending to above half a Cables length in bredth: where, if cut through from Sea to Sea, (which very little labour would effect.) This *Isthumus* would lose it's name in an Island; And the Conversion conduce much to it's security.

For there is no landing upon the South-side of the Bay (which is wash'd and Buts upon the main Seas) by reason of the fury of the waves (not pacified by any Breakers,) even in the most becalmest seasons.

And the entrance into the Harbour is commanded with a Fort,[23] built by the *English*: wherein there are at this day, some as good Canon planted, as the Tower of *London* would afford, yet the *Bay*, (or said Town) consisting on nothing but loose sand (in most places whereof you have water, in sinking but 3. or 4. foot) admits no sufficient defence in Teneable Bulworks, without the tribute of forreign Materials; which are not far to seek.

The worst is, their water, which is infected (by the intrusion of the Neighbour-seas) with a brackish taste; and therefore, they make use of none but what is fetch'd three, or four leagues in Boats and Canoues.[24]

Which inconvenience disswaded the *Spaniards* from gracing it with so much as one house, seating themselves near a pleasant River, and by the side of a most lovely *Savana*, in the famous Town of

St. Jago de la Vega.[25]

Which was as well built, and as large as any Town in *England*; but now has lost much of it's pristine lustre, since the Land-Lords became *English*; for it did contain two thousand Houses, & upwards, with sixteen Churches and Chappells, when it was first seized upon by the Army conducted by Gen. Venables; now there remains only the Skeletons of two Churches and an Abbey; with about five or six hundred Houses; some of which are yet very pleasant and habitable.

This Town was first founded by *Columbus*, to whose happy search, the *West-Indies* first discovered it self; (all former Commerce & Traffick thither being till then adjourn'd beyond the Records of Time and Memory) but now by him reviv'd to Correspondency. He was the first Father, and Godfather to this Town, giving it the name of *St. Jago de la Vega*; which it reciprocally retorted to him in his, and his yet remaining Families Title of Honour, by the good pleasure of the King of *Castile*, created Duke *de la Vega*; famous in *Spain*, even to this day.

Here is plenty of *Cassia Ligrea*, and Oranges of excellent relish in abundance, with some other choice Fruits, the Fruits of the *Spanish* Industry.

The mentioned *Savana* that faces this Town is now pretty well stockt with Sheep, Goats, Cowes, and especially tame Horses. But it did contain many thousands of each whilst the *Spaniard* own'd it.

The back side of the Town is wash'd with a fair, but unnavigable River which buries it self in the Sea, near *Passage-Fort*.

About twenty or thirty years agoe, this Town was wonne by a little Fleet of *Englishmen*, fitted out from the *Chariby* Islands, chiefly from St. *Kits*, under the Command of Gen. *Iackson*,[26] who landed about five hundred men at *Passage-Fort*, and fought his way up to the Town, against two thousand *Spaniards*, who still fled before him; but somewhat retarded his Career, by six or seven several Breast-works, cast up athwart the Road, on purpose to Bulwork this Town, (the Jewel of this Isle) from such Inroades and sudden surprizals: for the prevention whereof they kept continual watch upon a great Hill that overlooks the Sea, the Harbour, and the Town, from whence the Centinells, in the twinkling of an eye, by token agreed upon, signified the imminency of approaching dangers; As at this time when Gen. *Iackson* made the On-set; the strength of the Isle being drawn up on the shore, before he could land his men; whom, though the *Spaniards* somewhat resisted, and at their several Brest-works caus'd them to make an unwilling Halt; yet the fury of *Iackson*'s men, greedy of spoil, overcame all difficulties, neglecting dangers in comparison thereof; Thus with the losse of forty men, forcing to the Town, plunder'd it, to their no small enrichment. The booty likewise being advanced by a large Fine paid him by the *Spaniard*, on condition that the Town might be preserved from burning; which was accordingly sav'd, and their retreat to the Fleet undisturb'd.

But when the swelling *Armado* with Gen. *Venables*, attempted this Town, (after their worse successe against St. *Domingo*) they beat the bush so long, till the Bird was flown. For the subtle *Spaniard*, belaying our men with parleys, and fair words, in the interim dispatches away Bag and Baggage; sometimes sending Beeves[27] to stay the stomacks of the hungry Soldiery; and bearing Gen. *Venables*, in hand with choice Viands; and *Spanish* dainties, presented to his Lady; who had more mind to eat then fight.

Thus staving them off, till their Train and best Movables had got so much Law, that afterwards the swiftest pursuit could not give them a *Turn*, before they had got Covert in their Fastnesse, the Woods.

And certainly, the treasure they carried with them could not but be very considerable if we may guess at the worth of the Jewell by the splendor of the Cabinet, that kept it: or estimate the largeness of the Bird by the nest: the Town being then even to magnificence, adorn'd with spatious Houses.

For the safe-guard whereof the *Spaniards* never durst cope with our men in the plain field; yet would sometimes gawl them, when befriended with the treachery, that night and the Woods do afford; in which *Clandestine* encounters, though at first the *Spanish* success was too fortunate; yet dear bought experience did in a little time train up our men in the same Mysteries: in which now they are grown so perfect, that they never ceast beating both *Spaniard* and *Negro* at their own Play, and with their own weapons, till they had cleared the Island of them; In despair now of Recovery (being so often re-frustrated in their reattempts,) except by some invincible *Armado*, which yet will find work enough, e're they make the Island too hot for the *English*, now naturaliz'd to the Countrey, & can never want shelter nor victuals whilst they have the Woods to befriend; with which now they are so well acquainted, that the *Molottoes* and *Negroes*, (which the *Spaniards* left behind them to keep possession of the Island, therein reckoning without our Host, presuming them unconquerable, and past finding out) are now so overmatch'd in their own Arts, that their Captain & the major part of them have submitted; thereby lessening their masters Title by eleven Points of the Law; and craving *English* protection; into which, they are upon submission received, by the truly Honourable General *Dawley*,[28] and now authorized to prey upon and hunt their fellows, that in scattered Parties yet stand it out, having already sealed their allegiance with the bloud of their old Associates, not without the dextrous contrivement of that Noble General, whose happy policy in the wary preservation of this Forlorne in *Iamaica*, hath already without the suspicion of flattery, authoriz'd the stile. To whom our Nation, in some measures stands indebted for the Reprizal of that honour at *Rio-Novo*, which was so shamefully lost under the debauch'd conduct of Gen. *Venables* in *Hispaniola*: the *Spaniards* till then having so mean and despicable thoughts of *English* courage, that upon the On-set at *Rio-Novo* they upbraided our men with the opprobrious mention of *Sancto Domingo*, till the repented assay of their valour, disciplin'd them into better manners.

For though the numbers of the *Spanish* Forces at *Rio-Novo* doubled the *English* (being sent from *Cuba* to reinforce and resettle the Island) and those strongly entrenched; yet such was the enraged earnestnesse of the Soldiery to redeem their wounded Honours, that (regardlesse of all odds and disadvantages) they storm'd them in their trenches with a resolution as undaunted as the successe was prosperous. Hereby not only retriving the Pristine fame of their Countrey men; but also hitherto frustrating all hopes in the *Spaniards* of further attempts to regain the Island.

(Another Party of *Spaniards* reseating themselves at *Point-Pedro*, being attended with a no lesse inauspicious fate.)

And the truth is, the Island, though it were lesse fruitful, is worth the fighting for, though it should cost the *Spaniard* some of his best bloud; for it lies within his Bowells, and in the heart of his Trade.

For all the treasure that his Plate-Fleet brings home from *Carthagina* stear directly for St. *Domingo* in *Hispaniola*, and from thence must passe by one of the ends of this Island to recover the *Havana*, The common Rendezvouse of this whole *Armado*, before it returns home through the *Gulf* of *Florida*. Nor is there any other way (whereby to misse the Island of *Iamaica*) because he cannot in any reasonable time turn it up to the Wind-ward of *Hispaniola*; the which though he might with difficulty perform, yet he would thereby loose the security of his united forces, which at the *Havana* (from all the Parts of the *Bay* of *Mexico*, *New-Spain*, and the rich Merchandize that comes by *Nombre de Dios*, from the South-Seas,) accompany each other home from the said general Rendezvouse.

So that the *Privateers* from *Iamaica* are often fingering the Plate, and other precious commodities, that was never consign'd to them; by picking up their single & straggling Vessells before they are ensur'd by their embodied Fleet.

In which respects (as in many others) Necessity hath made a better choice of a seat for the *English* Dominions, then their intended surprizal of *Hispaniola*, though it had been atchieved: And their winnings, (if the Game be followed) will unexpectedly outvie the stakes.

And here I cannot but take notice of the many convenient Harbours, adjudg'd by the most experienced Mariners to equal the best that they ever came to Anchor in. For besides that already mentioned at *Point Caggoway*. There is another (nothing inferiour) below it to *Lee-ward* at about 4. or 5. Leagues distance; and may as conveniently serve the Town of St. *Iago*, as that other at *Cagg-way*; they being triangularly scituated: It is usually known by the name of *Old Harbour*, where four hundred tall ships may ride together without danger of falling foul upon one another.

And about fourteen Leagues to *Wind-ward*, is another safe Port called by the *Spaniards Porto Morant*, which yet retains the name. In the Confines whereof a Regiment is seated; who with many other Planters, have now made themselves considerable in the Produce of Sugar, Tobacco, Cotton, &c.

But it is besides my scope to mention every Harbour on this and the North side of the Isle, lest this Volume extend beyond the compendious Dimensions of Journal Notes; calculated only for those that are most remarkable . . . ; and be sufficiently Authentick to confute those Traditional *Heterodoxes*, that some mens rashnesse hath published to the contrary upon bare report.*

---

*Amer. desc. p. ult. 1655. [Hickeringill is citing *America: Or An exact Description of the West-Indies: More especially of those Provinces which are under the Dominion of the King of Spain. Faithfully represented by N N Gent* (London: Ric. Hodgkinsonne, 1655). Text of entire reference to Jamaica follows from the last page, 484 ("pagina ultima"): "Jamaica is somewhat a lesser Island, lying Southward of Cuba, and to the West of Hispaniola, almost at an equall distance, viz.

But I shall adjourn a more plenary discovery to these ensuing *Animadversions.*

REFLECTIONS Upon the present Affairs of JAMAICA; And the Expedition against HISPANIOLA; Under the Conduct of General VENNABLES.

I. That Bulky *Armadoes* are many times sunk with their own weight; which, if parcell'd out into seasonable Recruits, had signified more by each Retail, then the prodigal waste of such Whole-sale Adventures.

The Dimensions of this great Preparation vastly exceeding the difficulties that could encounter them, from all the united Forces in *Hispaniola*: and fitted out with strengths sufficient to make Prize of the whole *Spanish* Plate-Fleet, rather then the sacking of a small Town, or an unpeopled Land, such as is St. *Domingo,* and *Hispaniola;* who at the first brunt left this town to the Ransack of Gen *Iackson's* men; though timely Alarum'd by *Iackson's* Demurre, at the Harbours mouth, for four daies space; and then not able to land above five hundred men.

A thousand *English* Soldiers being now an overmatch to all the Power, that the *Spaniards* in *Hispaniola,* can bring into the field; unable at this day to ferrit out a few *French Buckaneers,* or Hunting *Marownaes,*[29] formerly mentioned; who live by killing the wild Beeves for their Hides; and might grow rich by the Trade, did not their lavish Riottings in expence (at the neighbour-*Tortudoes*)[30] exceed the hardship of their Incomes. Their comfort is, they can never be broke whilest they have a Dog and a Gun; both which, are more industriously tended then themselves.

These *Acteon* straglers[31] (that seldome number above five or six in a company) are often affronted with the *Spanish* Rounds (consisting of about one hundred Fire-locks) that once a year compass the Island, yet dare they never cope with these resolute Champions, and wandring Knights; who, setting

---

twenty leagues from them both. They reckon it to be in length about fifty leagues or more in breadth twenty, and to contain in the whole about one hundred and fifty, of a rich and fertil Soil, and in nothing less provided for the necessities of mans life, than either Hispaniola or Cuba; well stock'd with Cattel, and as plentifully stored with Fruits of all sorts, yeelding abundance of Cottowooll, more than either of the other Islands: only it wanteth the conveniency of some good Havens and Ports, which it hath but few; and the Sea round about it so shelvy, and full of rock and broken Islands, that the coast of it is held to be not a little dangerous: and therefore as little frequented by Merchants or others. There being at present three only small Towns inhabited in the whole Island, viz. 1. Sevilla, or New-Sevill, in the North parts of the Island. 2. Melilla ten leagues distant from Sevill towards the East. And lastly Orsitan, 14. leagues distant from it towards the South. Finis."]

back to back, would make sure to sell their lives at a double rate, and in that posture bid defiance to the enemy.

The Grave Seignior scorning to barter a drop of Poenish bloud[32] in exchange for an Ocean of such Rascal-Gaule.[33]

And I am very confident that the small Remnant left in *Iamaica* (knowing how to victual their Camps with what the Woods afford) will be able to disaray the *Spaniards* in *Hispaniola* or *Cuba*, (even to admiration,) and above what the most favouring presage can expect or autume.[34]

And certainly this Foot-hold (yet secur'd, maugre the *Spanish* craft and power,) foiled twice by them in their reattempts doth open so fair a passage into the *Indies*; that if His Sacred *Majesty*, our most excellent Prince do not in mercy balk the *Spaniard*; a few years will immortalize Him one of the greatest Emperours of the World: being happy, and not only in an invincible Navy, but in the Dominion of Northern Kingdomes, that are therefore so fruitful, that they store him with more men than Room; who are soonest likely to leave justling when they are parted with more elbow-room: The very Devision that united *Abraham* and *Lot*, who by too near correspondence fell together by the ears. Thus too nigh neighbourhood begets contentions, whilest distance and absence usually enhanceth the affections of near friends. . . .

REFLEX. 2.

2. That sudden surprizes from an Ambuscade, usually prevailes more then open force. The whole strength of *Hispaniola*, though embodied and in view, not being able to strike that terrour, and make such havock of our amazed Soldiers, as fourty or fifty *Negroes* and *Molettoes* effected by an unlook'd for onset.

Gaining more by this jugling delusion then their whole Army could by Play above-board. The *Spaniards* (like *Hannibal*) obtaining conquest with their heads rather then their hands.

Nor are they so usually foiled, as when encountred with their own weapons: a wary plodding *Fabius*[35] signifying more then a hot Spur *Marcellus*.[36]

To which squint-ey'd Mode in war *Scanderbeg*[37] stands endebted for most of this Victories against the *Ottomanes*; as also *Ioshua*, though back'd with a Divine reserve, for the defeat of *Aj*.

Thus also do the Native *Indians* encounter their Adverse Nations, rather stealing upon them then assailing them; especially, practis'd by the *Meridional*, and more oriental *Americans*; whose diminitive statures call for the assistance of wily stratagems; neglected by the more Northerly and arme-strong Regions, whose Character, (according to mine own knowledge and experience) especially of those *Guiana* and *Chariby Indians*, that cohabit with the *English* in *Surinam*, I deem not much extravagant here to insert.

Under the Line that equal's night and day
Guiana stands, part of America:
On whose head Phoebus[38] *shoots his fiery steams,*
Twice every year, with down-right darted beams.
In his Twelve Houses, *as he travells forth*
Alongst the Zodiack, *'twixt the South and North.*
Whose Native Indian *hath not, nor needs Art*
To clothe himself, Nature supplies that Part.
They're true Philosophers, not much they have,
Nor do they want much, nor much do they crave.
They care not for to morow; no supply,
But just from hand to mouth, no Granary:
If they want Flesh, they take their bow in hand.
And then for Hare or Deer, hunt o're the Land.
For all Game here most eas'ly taken be,
Since they take Covert in some hollow Tree.
Or some such crazie Refuge, whence they are
Dig'd forth at leisure for the Hunters fare.
Or if the stomach do in Fish delight,
With wily Feats he gluts his appetite.
His Bread & drink both made of one root are,
Cassawder[39] *call'd, cook'd by the womens care;*
Who shew their best of duty to their Home,
When their Mates wearied with their Booties come.
For every man in's house is Lord and King,
Hath pow'r of life and death, and every thing:
His will's his law, from him there's no appeal,
No other Monarchy or Commonweale.
If Wives and Children offenders are,
His will's the Judge; hand, Executioner.
To none but to their Chief, they Homage owe,
That's th'Eldest Son, when marry'd, t'him they bowe,
His Father, Mother, Brethren, Nephews, all;
Must low'r to him, and on the knee must fall:
Till his first Son be married, then he

(Depos'd) must to his own Son bend the knee.
Thus do they live by families, thus then
Their alwaies govern'd by middle-ag'd men.
When any dies, into his Urne is hurl'd
All that he hath; (to use; i'th'other world:)
His Axe, Bill, Knife, his Bow and Hammock too,
And this the best of service they can doe
For their dead Friend. If he a Captain be,
Then if he have a Slave, he then must die;
And the same Roge[40] *burn both; thus is supply'd*
Each one i'th'other world, as 'fore he dy'd.
But usually their Slaves, when captive ta'ne,
Are to the English *sold; and some are slain,*
And their Flesh forthwith Barbacu'd[41] *and eat*
By them, their Wives and Children as choice meat.
Thence are they call'd Caribs, *or* Cannibals;
The very same that we Man-eaters *call.*
And yet herein lies not their chief content
To eat for food, but as a Sacrament ;
To bind them and their Children to be fierce,
And into th'entrails of their foes to pierce.
Though in the world no greater Cowards be,
Managing all their Fights with treachery,
Most of their feats by stealth and night are done,
If once it come to handy-gripes they run.
Thus much I'le say, I would not wish to have
A better friend, or foe, or better slave
Then is an Indian; *where he once affects,*
In love and service shall be no neglects.
Command him as your slave, his life, his All,
If he do once you but Bone-aree[42] *call;*
And who would wish an easier foe, then he,
That (like a Buck) at noise of Guns will flie,
But then your slave if that an Indian *be,*
No other Caterer you need but he.
He plenty shall provide for yours and you,
With his Dogs only, and his Bill and Bow.
And thus much for their Men. Their Women are
Lovely, though brown; modest, hiding their Ware,

With several colour'd Beads together knit,
With Art methodical together set;
And this they use whilest they are young and fair,
But when they're old, they're heedlesse, all is bare.
If of your Wine and Brandee, you'le be free,
The'le not leave till they drunk as beggars be.
They call the Devil Yerkin, *him alone*
They worship, saying, God wills harm to none,
But is intirely good; and therefore they,
The mercy of their Yerkin *only pray.*
When they are sick, Yerkin *doth bear the blame,*
Of him they beg Deliverance from the same,
The Muses and their Flamens they cashiere,
Only Diana's *Troops are 'stablish'd here*
Except some Priests, which they do call Peei,
With mumbling charms Yerkin *to pacifie.*
(In summe to say) They're all simplicity,
Almost like Adam, *in's innocency.*
Whatever Nature or their Appetite
Does dictate, they do follow with delight,
Not once with conscience check embittered,
Being by the law of nature only led.
Not coveting large Barns, with hoards to stuffe,
When once their belly's full, they have enough;
For Avarice, *here never makes them jarre,*
Nor warrants, by religions varnish, warre.
His pride so natural, (if 't be a vice,)
Yet costs him nothing, or but little Price;
It never makes him sell his land, nor shut
Shop-windows up, nor a spare Jewel put
To trouble, in a Pawne for Cloak or Gown.
His only pride's a Feather in his Crown:
The cast-clothes of some gaudy Bird fits him.
For which he needs not venture life nor limb,
Nor Hector *it, nor list under Sir* Hugh,
(When known by the old suit, to fish for new;)
Nor cringe to Velvet Title, with a gape,
Like fawning Curre, or mopping Jack-an-Ape:[43]
Nor need to be light finger'd in a crowd;

Nor light heel'd to procure a Scarfe or Hood
Nor with stretch'd Fancies beg a Ladies smile,
Which she (poor soul) scarce understands the while.
They make no Mintage here of Braines, nor be
The sterling *Pence coyn'd with a Comoedie.*
For pomp and fine clothes only are the cause
Of all our shirking Trades, and endlesse lawes.
Since Nature ne're brought forth a Creature yet,
Unfurnish'd, with what Coverlets were fit.
The Back (if not misus'd) in coldest Lands,
Craving no waste-clothes, more then face or hands.

But this Diversion is somewhat out of our way to *Iamaica.* . . .

REFLEX. 7.

7. That though *Infant-Settlements*, like *Infant-years*, are usually most fatal; yet their *Blossomes* once Set, are not so easily Blasted. Happily experimented in *Iamaica*, whose Blooming hopes now thrive so well, and their Stocks so well Rooted, that they are not easily Routed. The Major part of the Inhabitants being old *West-Indians*,[44] who now Naturalized to the Countrey, grow the better by their Transplantation; and flourish in health equivalently comparable to that of their *Mother-Soil.* For which I need not beg credit, since there is no *Countrey Disease* (as at *Virginia* and *Surinam*) endemically raging throughout the Isle; nor any new and unheard of distempers that want a name.

So that a wise man needs no other Physick there but his Temperance, scarcely craving Hospital assistance so much as we in *England*, nor have any more reason to deify an *Aesculapius.*[45]

And therefore we consult our fears, rather then the dangers, when the very name of *Travell* into Foreign Parts, doth so much affright us, especially into so serene an *Aire* as breathes in *Iamaica*, that owns nothing but it's distance to dismay us from it's visit; The *Indies* being no such Bugbear as they are (usually) pourtray'd. In vindication therefore

For Travell, take this

APOLOGY.

Prithee, perswade me not, my Dear,
You do mistake my Fates, I fear.
My Glass will run no sooner out,
Though I do range the World about,

Could my stay here, bribe a delay,
From the pale Sisters,[46] *I would stay.*
But 'tis too true (though't be a Fable)
The Sisters *are Inexorable;*
And are as nimble with their Knife
To those that lead a Home bred life.
Brave Rawleigh *found (too soon) a Tomb!*
Not in the Indies, *but at home.*
The Destinies did Drake *forbeare*
In the Antipodes, not here;
And do, like Ladies coy, neglect
Those most, that Court them with respect.
But will Embraces beg and pray
Of those that are as nice as they.
Or, if the froward Stars dispence
With their Malignant influence,
Adjourning Plagues they use to bring,
In Peccant Autumns or the Spring:
Yet a Consumption or the Gout
In Chimney-corner finds us out:
Or, (what is worse) old driveling Age
With all it's loathed Aequipage
Arrests us, till we have unsaid
The Pray'rs which we for long life made;
Yet, they're forc'd soonest to recant,
That fruits of youthful Travell want:
For knowledge onely doth commend
Old Age; whilest listening Nephews 'tend
With greedy ears to catch up all
Old stories, Grand-sires does let fall;
(Thus shortening long Winters Night)
This palliates *Age with some delight:*
For when the cold Palsey doth seize
On other members, Tongue's at ease.
And is the old man's Commendamus,[47]
Which without Travell is lesse famous.
Nay damn'd Exile in this was blest,
Of Kings, it has made ours the best:
Thus Joseph's *Brethrens (meant) Abuse*

Rais'd him, The Honour *of his House.*
Aeneas *thus enhanc'd his fame*
From Trojan *to the* Roman *Name.*

REFLEX. 8.

8. That an Army once cow'd, especially in their first forreign attempt, seldome bound their fear till it become altogether Panick: like that Punick amaze that epidemically invaded *Carthage,* after the first defeat of *Hannibal* by the more thriving Genius of *Scipio Africanus.*

This is certain, that after the first check given to our Forces by the *Negroes* and *Molettoes* in *Hispaniola;* The very mention of their coming, (though bruted but for experiment) caus'd some to hasten their march, beyond the pace of gravity and valour.

Though after Tryals approv'd them to be *English* men, rather then *Normans,* daring, to Rally defeated Courage. The truth whereof many an *Aethiope* hath now unwillingly asserted by the lavish expence of his sooty bloud. And here I intended to publish some Essayes touching the future Settlement of *Iamaica,* which now are upon second thoughts condemn'd to privacy.

FINIS

FROM

Friendly Advice to the Gentlemen-Planters of the East and West Indies

THOMAS TRYON

(1634-1703)

Thomas Tryon was a noted and well-published promoter of the Pythagorean philosophy of vegetarianism and moderation. Born near Cirencester, England, the son of a tiler, Tryon was apprenticed to a hatter at the age of eighteen. He joined the Anabaptist movement briefly before joining the Behmenists, a Quaker-like group that followed Jakob Böhme (1575–1624). In the 1660s, Tryon moved to Barbados, setting up a hatter's business. After several years there, he returned to London and continued his trade as an exporter of hats to the West Indies. His first dietary regimen was limited to water, bread, fruit, butter, and cheese. He later expanded the list to include vegetables and published a number of tracts advocating vegetarianism and abstention from tobacco, alcohol, and all luxuries. In his *Autobiography*, Benjamin Franklin tells of his adoption of the Tryonist dietary program for a time. Tryon was a pacifist whose spiritual tracts formed a link between the Behmenists and the Quakers.

Tryon's *Friendly Advice to the Gentlemen-Planters of the East and West Indies* (1684) combines travel narrative with social critique. Divided into three parts, the text first examines the vegetables and fruits of the East and West Indies as part of Tryon's promotion of a vegetarian diet. He then details in the second part the ills of the slave system, which are incorporated into the dialogue in the third part. This dialogue, excerpted here, is one of the earliest attempts to represent the enslaved African's point of view. Earlier critiques of slavery by Richard Baxter (*Chapters from a Christian Directory*, 1673) and Morgan Godwyn (*The Negro's and Indians Advocate*, 1680) had pioneered the condemnation of slavery on Christian grounds, but Tryon is the first to place the critique in the mouth of a slave—a technique employed by all sides of the slavery issue for many years afterward.

Friendly Advice to the Gentlemen-Planters of the East and West Indies.
In Three Parts. I. A brief Treatise of the most principal Fruits and
Herbs that grow in the *East & West Indies*; giving an Account of
their respective Vertues both for *Food* and *Physick*, and what
Planet and Sign they are under. Together with some Directions
for the Preservation of Health and Life in those hot Climates.
II. The Complaints of the Negro-Slaves against the hard
Usages and barbarous Cruelties inflicted upon them.
III. A Discourse in way of Dialogue, between
an *Ethiopean* or *Negro-Slave*, and a *Christian*
that was his Master in *America*.
By Philotheos Physiologus.
Printed by Andrew Sowle, *in the Year*
1684.

A Discourse
In way of a Dialogue, Between an Ethiopean or Negro-Slave
And a Christian, That was his Master in America.
The Third Part.

Master. Come hither, *Sambo*! you look as gravely to day as a *Dog Out-law'd*,
or a *Justice of Peace* set in the Stocks; I doubt you have been doing some
Rogury, I call'd you to make us *some Sport*, let us see one of your *Dances*, such as
are used in your own Country, with all your odd Postures and Tricks, for Diversion; I have heard you are the best at it of all my People.

Slave. *Boon Master*! If you will have me Dance upon mine Head, or Caper
on the top of the House, I must do it, though I break my Neck; for you are become Lord both of my *Feet*, and every part of me, but I fear I shall not be able
at present to answer your Expectation handsomly, I am so much out of humour, and unfit for *Feats of Activity*.

Master. Why? What's the matter Sirrah! I'll warrant, you have been frol-
licking so long amongst your Companions, that now you'l pretend you are
Weary.

Slave. Truly, Sir! this being the *only Day* in the Week you spare us from
hard labour, and allow us for Recreation, we do a *Sundayes* amongst our selves,
endeavour to *forget* our Slavery, and skip about, as if our Heels were *our own*,
so long sometimes, till our Limbs are almost as weary with that, as with work-

ing; But that is not my present case, for I have been walking all alone several hours upon the Shoar, viewing that prodigious heap of Waters, that with roaring Waves continually beat upon this little Island, and sometimes casting up my Eyes to that *glorious Eye of Heaven*, which (they say) at one view beholds half the World, I could not satisfie my self which was the greatest Wonder; so that the Contemplation of them *both* together, has fill'd my Brains with abundance of strange Conceits, and made me very Dull and Melancholly.

Master. And what, I pray, might be the Result of our *wise Worships* speculations?

Slave. I had a thousand different Notions offered themselves to my Mind, and amongst the rest, I was thinking, what if the *Sun* should *forget to Rise* to morrow Morning, whether your Man, (our *Over-seer*) would make him get up, as he does us, by *blowing his Horn*? Or else how we should do to work in the Dark? Or if the *Sea* should swell a little higher, and wash the tops of your *Sugar-Canes*, I might not then lawfully swim Home to my own Country, without being beaten to a Jelly for a *Run-away*?

Master. Out you *Rogue*! Are these your Contemplations? nothing but studying Mischief to your Master? Your *Bones* shall presently pay for the busie Idleness of your Brains, and the *Sauciness* of your Tongue.

Slave. O *boon Master*! I beseech you be not angry, I meant no harm in the World: This is a Day on which you do not *Work*, & therefore I hope you will not *Fight*, which I conceive is ten times worse; for I had rather *work* all the *Sunday*, then be *beaten* once: If you will be pleased to lay by your huge Cudgel, and vouchsafe to answer me a few harmless Questions, I doubt not but I shall divert you as much to your satisfaction, as if I had danc'd two Hours.

Mast. Though you are an *Impudent*, yet since you seem to be an *ingenious Raskal*, I am content (for once) to hear your Prate:[1] What is your wise Question?

Sl. I desire first you would lay that frightful Cudgel a little further off, and then begging Pardon for the Presumption, since this is the Day you observe to *serve God* in, I would crave leave to be a little instructed touching that Service, and wherein it consists.

Mast. Why? It consists in being *Christians*, as we are—But what should I talk to such a dark ignorant *Heathen*, scarce capable of *common Sense*, much less able to understand things of such an high and mysterious Nature.

Sl. I confess we are poor silly dark ignorant Creatures, and for ought I find, so are many of the *Bacchararo's** too, as well as we; but that you may not grudge

*So the *Negro's* in their language call the *Whites*.

your Time or Pains, I will assure you, that I will attend very seriously to what you say, and possibly may prove somewhat more docible[2] than some of our Complexion; For I was the Son of a *Phitisheer*, that is, a kind of *Priest* in our Country and Way; he was also a *Sophy*,[3] and had studied the Nature of things, and was well skill'd in *Physick* and natural *Magick*, I have heard him often discourse of a *great* and *mighty Beeing*, (greater far, and *brighter* too than either Moon or Sun) which framed both *Land* and *Sea*, and all the glittering Glories of the *Skie*; and he was wont to say, *Men were the Children of the* great King, *who if they were good, would take them up* (but I think it was after they were dead here) *into* spangled Regions, *where they should do no Work, nor endure any Pain, nor* Fight *one with another, but remain in Joy and Peace, and Happiness*: 'Tis so long ago, that I was taken from him and sold hither, that I have forgot much of his *Talk*, and yet I remember some of his *Skill*, whereby I have Cured several of my Countrymen since I came hither, of Diseases, that your Doctors could not help, either so surely or so suddainly.

Mast. I have heard something of your success that way, and since thou art the Son of an *Heathen Philosopher*, and pretendest to more *Wit* than the rest of thy *Fellow-Brutes*, what is it thou wouldst be at?

Sl. Sir! I desire to be informed, what a *Christian* is, or ought to be.

Mast. Though I think it will be to as little purpose, as to go about to *wash thy Skin* white, to inform such dark *stupid Heathens* as you are; nevertheless I shall endeavour to gratifie your Curiosity.

1st; He that is *a Christian*, ought to believe that God made the *World*, and all things therein.

Sl. O then, Master! I am *a Christian*, for I believe that as well as you.

Mast. Hold your Tongue, there go many other things to make a *Christian* besides that; for he must also know and believe, that Man being thus made, did by transgressing the *Law* of his Maker, *fall* from that good and perfect State, wherein he was made, into a sinful estate, and thereby was liable to the *Wrath of God*, and so to be *Damn'd* forever, or suffer everlasting Punishment. But God out of the unspeakable Riches of his *Grace* and *Goodness* to his Creatures, thus become miserable, determined in his own secret Counsel, and in fulness of time did actually send down his most beloved and eternal Son, *Jesus Christ*, to take upon him mans Nature, who after a most unspotted exemplary Life, and laborious Preaching the *good Tidings* of *Remission of Sins* to all that should believe in him, and enduring many Persecutions and Affronts here on Earth, was at last *put to Death* without the Gates of *Jerusalem*, by the cruel Hands of the *Jews*, and being buried, *rose again to Life* the third day, and ascended into Heaven; by which Death of his, he satisfied the Wrath of God for the Sins of the whole World, as the Scripture witnesseth.

Sl. If Jesus Christ dyed for the Sins of the whole World, or satisfied God's wrath for the Sins of *All Mankind*, then we that you call *Heathens* may justly challenge equal priviledge with your selves.

Mast. O no, you do not *believe* in his Name, nor observe his Commands and Precepts.

Sl. As how I pray?

Mast. You are not *Baptized* in the Name of the *Holy Trinity*, nor do believe the *Merits of Christ's satisfaction*, or that he hath taken away your Sins.

Sl. This is a brave Religion, that by the Death and Suffering of one, all men that in after Generations believe this, shall have their Sins pardon'd, and be blest with eternal Happiness.

Mast. Still, *Sambo!* you are *too quick*, there is more required then a bare Faith, or verbal Belief that such a thing was done, *Christ* is our *Prophet* to teach us, and our *King* to rule us, as well as our *Saviour* to redeem us; They must yield Obedience, and do a *Christian's* Duty, that shall have an Interest or Benefit by his Death.

Sl. I pray then tell me the duty of a *Christian*.

Mast. The Gospel of Christ, or the Doctrine which he taught, and we profess, instructs and requires us; 1*st*, To *fear the Lord* that created all things. 2*dly*; To *be Merciful*, and do unto all men, as we would be done unto. 3*dly*; To be *Sober* and *Temperate* in Meats, Drinks and Exercises, mortifying the *Lusts of the Flesh*, and avoiding all kind of Superfluity, that so we may not waste or abuse the good Creatures of God. 4*thly*; To avoid *evil Communication*, because it corrupts good Manners, and vain Words, but especially wicked Ones. 5thly; To observe the *Rules of Purity*, and abstain from all *appearance* of *Evil*, both in Words and Works. 6*thly*, To free our selves from *Envy, Strife, Malice, Back-biting* and *Slander*; not to accuse men behind their Backs of what they will not speak to their Faces, or cannot prove. 7*thly*; Not to judge of things we *understand not*, lest we be judged; nor condemn those things of which we have no certain Knowledge or Experience. 8*thly*; To be sensible that the Lord by his *all-seeing-Eye* and *divine Principle*, beholds all our Wayes, and that to him there is nothing hidden. 9*thly*; To believe and know for a certain truth, that the Lord will Retaliate and Reward every one according to his Works. 10. To live according to the Gospel and divine Principle, by denying *all Ungodliness* and *worldly Lusts*, and *Uncleanness*, as *Whoredom, Adultery, filthy Speaking*; yea, even all *unchaste Desires*, for so our Lord teacheth us, *That he that looketh on a Woman, and lusteth after her, commits Adultery*. 11. To regulate our Passions and Affections, and to abandon all *Wrath, Anger, Malice, Envy*, vain or immoderate hopes, as also despair, and all perturbations of Mind; to shun and avoid *Covetousness*, (that Root of Evil) *Pride, Ambition*, and all *Uncharitableness*; And on the contrary, to *walk Humbly*, and *Meekly* towards God, and towards man, and to practise *Patience, mutual Forbearance, Moderation, Kindness*, and *Commiseration* in all our wayes. 12. That we be not too confident, nor conceited of our selves, or our own knowledge, but to have regard to the Lord in all our Thoughts, Imaginations and Conclusions, and in every thing to have an Eye to his Providence. 13. To return God the *Praise and Glory* of all the good things we enjoy, as *Health, Strength, Food, Rayment, Knowledge, Understanding*, and the like, acknowledging them all to be the free Gifts of his Bounty; and when we are in any want, trouble, distress or danger to *relie* upon the same God for help, succour and relief, and with earnest, hearty and faithful *Prayers*, to implore the same of him only. 14. To be merciful to all the inferior Creatures, and to use them gently, and with Moderation, avoiding all kind of *Oppressions, Violence, hard Heartedness* or *Cruelty*, either to Men or Beasts.

These, *Sambo*, are some of the Principles or Rules of the *Christian Religion*, the Doctrine which it teacheth, and the Practices it requires.

Negro. *Master Christian!* I give you a thousand hearty Thanks for this account of your *Religion & Philosophy*, which no doubt is the best and noblest of all others: Therefore if these be your Christian Principles, I am already *a Disciple*; but I beseech you be in good earnest, and tell me the truth.

Mast. I do assure thee, they are the Principles of our Lord, Christ, the Son of the living God, that he preached to the World when he was on the Earth, and which his Apostles recommended, and left them on Record in the *Bible*; and which he still continues to Preach by his Spirit in the Hearts of all that are his.

Negr. Since these things are so, I cannot but at once be *surprized*, and as it were *amazed*, with two different Objects of Wonder.

Mast. What are they, prethee?

Negr. First, I admire the *Excellency of your Doctrine*, and the *wonderful Mystery* contained therein; it undoubtedly surpasseth all other Religions in the World, as much as the Sun's Light doth that of the *Glow-Worm*: It seems to me to be an *open Gate* into *Paradise*, and a *Leaf* of the *Tree of Life*; so agreeable to the Nature and Glory of the *great God*, so suitable to the condition of the *weak Man*; no wise Person can make any scruple of the things you have delivered, they command assent; for they proceed from a *true Root*.

But then I cannot but also much wonder and admire that you *Christians* live and walk so wide from, and *contrary* unto all those undeniable Truths, and holy Rules, so that what you preach with your *Tongues*, you pull down with your *Hands*, and your daily Conversation gives the Lye to your Profession.

Mast. You now grow *Saucy* thus to upbraid us; we have indeed *our Failings*, but I hope we do not walk so *Retrograde* as you talk of: What Instances can you produce to maintain so general a Charge?

Negr. I intended not to *upbraid* you, but to satisfie my self, for perhaps you may have *some Reason* that I do not know of, why you act *contrary* to what you teach; nor do I say that all, and *every Christian* does so, there may be Hundreds and Thousands that *I* am not acquainted with, and there are some that I know, of whom I cannot say, but that in a very great measure they live according to that righteous Doctrine; but for the generality or major part, I must say, That in all, and every of the aforesaid Points by you mentioned, the whole Tenour of their Ways, and the continual Practice of their Lives, is directly contrary to the same: And since you command me to instance Particulars, I shall endeavour it in some of the chief.

1. You say, that Christian Religion teacheth *to Fear the Lord*, that created Heaven and Earth: The truth of this we make no doubt of; but how can we believe, that *very many* who go under the Name of *Christians* do obey this Voice of Wisdom, since they so lightly and vainly use the *Name of God* in their Triffling, and wicked Talk, and boldly Swear by it (and that for the most part *falsly* too) in their ordinary Conversation, contrary to his express Commands; nay, not a few, will commonly challenge the great God to *Damn* or *Confound* them, with divers other Blasphemies; And do you call this *Fearing the Lord*?

2. To *be Merciful*, and *do as you would be done by*, you in the next place assign, as a grand and important point of *Christianity*; but where shall we find it? We cannot perceive any thing of *Mercy* to dwell in your Hearts; for you commit *Oppression* with Violence; and that which you call *Trade* or *Traffick* (as 'tis manag'd amongst you) is little better than an Art of *Circumventing* one another; and you practise all sorts of *Cruelty*, not only on the inferior Creatures, but also on those of your *own Kind*, else what makes us your *Slaves*, and to be thus Lorded and Tyrannized over by you? In a word, not only *We*, but the whole Creation groans under your heavy Burthens; & yet you tell us of your *Mercy* and *good Nature*, and boast of your Christian *Charity*.

3. You acknowledge, this divine Religion requires of you to be *Sober* in Meats and Drinks, *&c.* and not to indulge Nature with things Superfluous: But does it not appear by your Conversation, that you never regard its Counsel, since your Wayes are directly opposite? Do not we see it a common Practice amongst the *Christians*, to drink to *Drunkenness*, and eat to *Superfluity* and *Gluttony*? & even of those that seem most reserved, scarce any, that have wherewithal, but will *indulge themselves* great variety of rich compounded Foods, and Cordial-Drinks, that contain too great Nourishment, beyond not

only the *Necessities*, but even the *Power* of Nature, and the *digestive Faculty* of the Stomach, which produces many evil Effects; for besides the waste of the good Creatures, and a most *Ungrateful* abuse of the Creator's Mercies, it heats the *Blood*, makes it thick, hot and sharp, and causeth all the Members to glow with an unnatural Heat, makes both the Body and Mind uneasie, and disables each of them from performing its Offices as it ought, and also sets open the *Gates of Venus* to many lewd Practices: And thus in defiance to the Laws of your Religion, and to his own Personal hurt, one great *over-grown Christian* shall spend as much in *one Day*, to gratifie his Lusts or Vanity, as an *Hundred or Two* of his poor *Slaves* can get by their sore Labour and Sweat. And as for *Exercises*, there is rarely here in this Island any of the *Christians* that will labour, except pure Necessity constrain them to it, but you *lay heavy Burthens* on us, and as your most illuminated Prophet, saith, *will not touch them your selves with one Finger.* So that you make it a *Genteel* Quality, and honourable, to break and violate that great Command of the Creator in the beginning, which I have heard is recorded by a most famous Prophet of the *Jews*, and whom you also receive, viz. *That Man should get his Bread by the Sweat of his Brows;* which yet amongst the more *Noble Christians*, as you call your selves, is counted a *poor*, *low Base* and *shameful* thing.

What *Heathen People* (as you call them) are there in the whole World, that more *pamper their Carkasses*, and indulge themselves like you, with things that are not needful, nor convenient? Do you not invent an hundred Superfluities and needless *Toys*, to gratifie your own, and your Childrens Pallates and Sensuality? the Wind, forsooth! must not blow upon them; and as if the Earth were not good enough to bear them, nor their Legs made to carry them, you provide *Horses* and *Coaches* for them, or we poor *Slaves*, must lugg them about, who are as well able to go as we. For your Garments, Houses, Furniture, *&c.* who can exceed your *Pride*, and *Vanity*? One of your Women shall wear at once as much in value as would clothe an hundred poor People in modest Rayment, each far better than hers, to defend them from the Injuries of the Elements, which is the chief end of Cloathing: Add to this, your great *Palaces*, and sumptuous chargeable[4] Buildings, and all kind of rich superfluous Ornaments, and *Knick-Knacks* in your Houses, wherein you study to out-try and exceed each other, meerly for *State*, *Pride* and *vain Glory*, and to be honoured of men; which extravagancy is attended with another sore Evil, for that it *cannot be maintained* but chiefly by *great Oppression* of Men and Beasts; for those that spend Talents[5] daily, must lay about them for a continual Supply, so that rather then they will be without those chargeable Vanities, they care not how cruelly they use their Servants, and inferior Creatures; They will scourge their

Slaves for a *Penny*, and kill their Beasts with over-labour, and at the same time spend *Pounds* in base depraved Wantonness, and feasting of the Rich, *&c.*

4. You mention the avoidance of *Evil Communications*, as another duty of your Religion, which we *Heathens* do acknowledge, and therefore we have a Proverb amongst us, when any use lewd Discourse, to bid them, *Wash their Mouthes with Water*; but we have observed, that amongst the *Christians* there is nothing more frequent than *Evil Communications*, whensoever any Number meet together, are not your Discourses *vain, idle* and *frothy*, and oft-times such as no *modest Ear* can hear without tingling forth Horror and Indignation? Most of it tending to Debauchery, or injuring the good Name of Persons absent, *Jesting, Lying, Vapouring,*[6] or speaking of Things and People they understand not, nor have any thing to do withal; Nay, a man cannot pass the Way or Street, but his Ears shall be grated with horrid *Swearing*, and *ungodly Speeches*, so that 'tis evident you walk in the greatest opposition imaginable to his command.

5. You say, *You are required to observe Purity, and the natural Rules of* Cleanness, *and to avoid all appearance of Evil*: Which indeed is no inconsiderable point in Nature and Religion, but as far as we have been able to observe, you practice the quite contrary; for not only your Words are very unclean for the generality, but also in your *Foods* and *Drinks* you make no distinction, but rich provoking Food in excess, and all strong intoxicating Drinks, you desire with greedness, which over-heats the whole Body, and irritates the fierce wrathful beastial Nature, whence all *wanton, vain* and *unclean* Thoughts and Imaginations are generated: Also, you make as little distinction between clean and unclean *Beasts* as we, nay, not so much as some of our Country-men; and you eat *Blood*, though I have been told there is not any one thing more frequently, expresly and plainly forbidden in all your *Bible* than that; besides, you make no distinction of the Times and Seasons of the Year, when Beasts are subjects to Surfeits, and other Uncleannesses; neither are your Preparations and cooking of your Food so clean, proper and natural, as they ought to be; and instead of abstaining from all appearances of Evil, we see you court and improve them on all occasions; For do not you appoint *set Meetings*, and make great Feasts? to which you invite the Rich, that will invite you again, where you drink to Drunkenness, and eat to Gluttony, roaring all the while like *mad Bulls*, and mixing your Food with horrid Oaths, and vain Discourses, the fear of the great Creator being banisht from your Hearts, nor any pity shewn to us your poor Vassals, that endure the Heat of the day, and are ready to fall and faint under those heavy Burthens laid upon us, and would rejoyce to partake of *the Crumbs* that fall from your Tables, which you will not afford, & yet spend *our*

Sweat, and the Labours of our Hands, in all kinds of Wantonness and Superfluity, by which many of you contract such grievous Diseases, both to Body
and Mind, that they become themselves more miserable then us their poor
Slaves.

6. You say that the next great point of *Christian* Doctrine, is to free your
selves from *Envy, Strife, Malice, Back-biting* and *Slander;* which is also con-
tradicted by your general practice; for what is more frequent amongst you
than *Envy* and *Revenge?* And though in your Prayers you formally use those
Words, *Lord forgive us our Trespasses as we forgive them that trespass against us,*
yet at the same time Envy lies lurking in your Hearts, and the very next moment shall erect it self; for do not many of you keep your Neighbours and
Brethren in loathsom Prisons for some very little offence, or in truth for none
at all, but only to shew your Power, and gratifie your devilish Fury: And as for
the Gentleman called Strife, he rides the Fore-horse, and is Quarter-master-
General amongst you; what Fighting, Swearing, Damning, Railing, *&c.* is
there in every House between Fathers and Children, Brothers and Sisters,
Relations and Neighbours, ready to destroy and murder one another, and all
about *Things,* not worth a wise mans Thoughts? What swarms of Lawyers,
Clerks, Pettifoggers[7] and Idle-men, does your Strife, and unjust Contention
maintain? And how many are yearly with their Families utterly ruined
thereby? *I'll not leave him worth a Groat,*[8] cries one: *I'll make Dice of his Bones,*
swears the other: *Let him rot in Goal,*[9] says a third. This is your Christian
Charity, and Remission of Injuries.

And for *Backbiting* and *Slandering,* even Eating and Drinking, is scarce
more universally practised among you; almost every man speaks *Evil* or
slighting of those that are not present, though to their Faces he Complements
and Flatters them. Calumny is the Sawce at your great Feasts, and Re-
proaches & scandalous Stories the Entertainments of your *Clubs* and *Visits,*
so that scarce any honest man is free from the Lashes of your invenom'd
Tongues, or from having large Furrows plowed upon his Back, his good
Name wounded, and his Reputation unjustly blasted or called in question, by
your false Stories and malicious Suggestions, whereby many are daily ruined,
there being nothing more base and unmanly than these *whispering Daemons;*
nor is there any Practice that more opposes *Christianity,* and the pure simple
Law of God in Nature, and therefore is a Sin to be condemned forever, and
banisht the Society of all good men.

7. Not to *judge* and *speak of things they understand not,* is a very excellent
Precept, yet nothing is more common among many *Christians* than to judge,
censure, and condemn Things and Persons, though they understand them no

more then a blind man can distinguish Colours, or the Deaf judge of Musick; but right or wrong without any true sight or comprehension, they will pass their Verdict, and shoot their Bolts,[10] for they count their Tongues their own, and think they may say what they list, and so call *Evil* good, and *Good* evil, and abuse their own Consciences, and their Neighbours, so greatly are many of the *Christians* depraved.

8. The eighth Point you mentioned, was, *That the Lord beholds all mens Wayes and Doings, and that unto him, and his Divine Eye there is not any thing hid*: Which without all doubt, is a most certain truth, which neither *Christian* nor *Heathen* dare to deny; for as your own Prophet saith, *It is he that searcheth the Heart, and tryeth the Reigns*. But how can we perswade our selves, that you do in truth and in earnest believe this, since we daily find that you stand more in awe of *Mens seeing*, or *knowing* your Wickedness, than of *God's beholding*, and revenging of it; and therefore you love to *seem*, and be counted *Honest*, and *Just*, and *Merciful*, but scarce a Soul of you seriously endeavours to *be so*; 'tis the *Name* and the *Credit* you look after, not the *Thing*, which shews that you seek to please, and be well spoken of by Men, but regard not the righteous Judgment of God, who looks through the *Fig-Leaves*, and requires Truth and Purity in the inward parts: This Hypocrisie of yours is notorious, and every one almost taxes his Neighbour for it, and yet all generally practice it, and each huggs himself therein, as one of your own *Poets* complaineth;

> *If my foul Deeds of Darkness may*
> *Be wrapt in Clouds as black as they;*
> *If being ugly I can Paint,*
> *And act the* Devil, *yet seem a* Saint,
> *Cheat and Oppress, Forswear and Lye,*
> *Yet scape the* Law *and* Infamy,
> *I mind no further Honesty.*[11]

9. On the contrary, to *believe* and know (as you say) That the Lord will Retaliate every man according to his Work, is a most true and necessary Principle; but if *Christians* did so, surely they could not, nor would do as they do; For what kinds of *Rewards* and *Returns* do or can you expect for all your Oppressions to us your poor Vassals? For do not you oppress us at your pleasure, *beat*, *whip*, *over-labour*, and *half-starve* us, and many of you scruple not *to Kill us* for a small Offence, and possibly for none at all, but in your Drunkenness to satiate your fierce devilish Passions? Nor do our tender *Children*, and dear *Wives* escape your Violence. Now if Retaliation be one point of your Christian Doctrine, and every man shall be rewarded according to his Works, then what a

sad Reckoning will you have to make, when God shall arise to visit for these things? And you would not certainly adventure upon those things, which you must pay *so dear* for, either in this World, or that which is to come, if you were sufficiently sensible of the Compensation that must be made for the same.

10. 'Tis a noble Truth, that men should walk according to the *divine Principle*, and *forsake all Ungodliness* and *worldly Lusts*: But the generality of *Christians* take contrary measures for the Gospel of Truth, neither inwardly nor outwardly doth teach any to *compel others* by outward Force to believe, and do as they do, be it right or wrong; but advises all to do as they would be done by; and to let their *Moderation be known unto all men*; and to *bear with one another in Love*: Whereas you impose upon one another, and *tye up* other men to your own Conceptions, and without any Compassion or Charity, fall upon such as will not go your way, and do as you do, though you have nothing to object against their Lives and Conversations. And whereas you acknowledge the Doctrine of *Christianity*, where-ever it is entertained in the Love thereof, will bruise the Head of the *Serpentine Nature*, that is, of Lust and Uncleanness, and all Ungodliness, yet we see you daily wallowing in all those *Pollutions*; so that you do not only contradict this *holy Doctrine*, which you boast so much of, but some of you do also severely persecute others for *obeying* the same and submitting to its guidance; And as for *brutish Uncleanness*, *Adulteries*, *Whoredoms*, &c. they are but your *Sports* and *Pastimes*, things that many of you *glory in*; and to be *Chaste* and *Modest*, is to be an object of your Scorn and Derision.

11. How well you regulate your *Passions* (which is another thing you say Christian Doctrine teaches you) all the World sees, and we often *feel*; the Sea when agitated with contrary Winds, it throws up *Dirt* and *Sand* from the bottom of the Deep, and spits its *froth* up towards Heaven, is not more disorderly or dangerous to come near, than you are, when the least thing happens contrary to your Minds, your Souls are in a perpetual Tumult, your Lusts duel one another, Covetousness fights with Luxury, Wantonness jostles Ambition, and Revenge is opposed by Cowardize; *Sence* gets above *Reason*, the *Man* is ridden by the *Beast*, and when in this hurry, *Conscience* gets leave to be heard, then presently there is nothing but *Furies* and *Despair*: Is not all this as contrary to that *Calmness* and *Stillness*, that *Peace* and *Serenity of Mind* (which true Christianity, both *requires* and *gives*, and is delighted in) as Light is to Darkness?

12. 'Tis a great point, and as true that men should not be *too resolute*, confident or conceited of their own Wisdom or Knowledge, but ought to have regard to the Lord in all their Thoughts, Imaginations and Conclusions, and to eye the divine Hand of *Providence* in all things, it being better *to Fear*, than *to*

Boast. But tell us, O Master! who do violate this Rule more than the generality of *Christians?* Do not many of your *learnd Ones* boast of their Lights and Knowledge, and count all others little better than *Brutes* in comparison of themselves? And does not every one fancy his *own Opinion* to be the only Truth, and condemn the Sentiments of others, how well grounded soever they may be? And do not many endeavour to spread their Notions by *Violence, Fighting* and *Oppression,* and by Cruelty, to force all to be of their Complexion in Understanding? Which self-conceited Proceedings are a true *token* and *demonstration,* that they love to contradict the whole course of *God* and *Nature;* for he hath made all things *to differ,* and by that difference the Universe is sustained; and from those *various Notes* proceed the sweetest Harmony? Is it not for want of this Spirit of Humility, that you *wrangle, fight, contend, punish* and *imprison* each other, for not thinking as others do, or because they have not all one *coloured Hair?* For alas! men's Minds and Understandings are as different and various, as their Complexions or Visages; wherefore then are you angry with your Creator, because he hath not made you all alike? If you were not blind and ignorant, and yet very presumptuous and Self-admirers, this could never be amongst People that believe all in *one Prophet,* and *one God:* I perceive therefore it is not about *true Virtue* that you make all this ado in the World; 'tis for your own Conceits, your own Inventions, your own *Dreams,* that you thus contend and disquiet your Neighbours.

13. Your thirteenth Point of *Christianity* was to return *God the Glory* of all your Enjoyments, and relie soley upon him in your Distresses and this you observe no better than the rest; to give God the glory of your Health, Strength, Wealth, *&c,* is to use the same *soberly* and *discreetly,* and imploy them as he hath required for the benefit and advantage of our fellow Creatures, and our own Happiness both here and hereafter; but you only *swagger* and *vapour* and *domineer* with them, as if your own right hand had *made them,* your own Wisdom and Power had procured them, and not as *given,* or rather *lent* you by the Lord, for the good ends before mentioned; whereas you use and bestow them only for *Pride* and *Ostentation,* for *Vanity* or *Luxury,* to accomodate your *Lusts,* or gratifie your *Revenge;* this is sure very far from a true Christian improvement of what you enjoy.

Lastly, Whereas you say, your Christian Doctrine enjoyns you to be *merciful to all the Inferior Creatures,* and to *use them with Compassion,* and *avoid all kind of Oppression and Violence* to those of your own kind: How contrary most *Christians* act hereunto, our own *woful Experience* has too sadly informed us, that there is little or no Mercy or Compassion dwells in your Hearts; for on every small occasion you will not only *beat* and *oppress* us, but some of you count it no more Sin in their drunken fits to *Murther us*, than to kill their *Horse*, or their *Dog*; but let them know, we are humane *rational Souls*, and as much the *Image of God* as themselves, and want[12] none of the noble Faculties, therefore our *innocent Blood* will equally call for *Vengeance*, and as powerfully as if you had killed one of the pretended *Christians*. The Voice of God in Nature is the same; and it is not your custom of *Killing* will make it the more *lawful* or excusable in that day, when Accounts and Retaliation must be made, every Principle then apprehends and comprehends its own Children; those that have immers'd, or precipitated themselves through Violence, into the fierce Anger and wrathful Principle, shall be therein captivated even to Eternity: It is not good Words, long Prayers, and fair Speeches, that will break or untye the wrathful Net, which men all their Lives have been tying; but look what Principle has carried the upper Dominion in the Heart, to that Kingdom you belong.

As for the *inferior Creatures*, they groan under your Cruelties, you *hunt*[13] them for your *Pleasure*, and *over-work* them for your *Covetousness*, and *kill* them for your *Gluttony*, and set them to fight one with another till they dye, and count it a *Sport* and a *Pleasure* to behold them *worry* one another; whereas the same should be matter of *Grief* to you, to see the Gate of Wrath thus opened amongst the Creatures, and that you your selves have been the *original Cause* thereof, by violating the Law of your Maker.

Thus, Master *Christian!* have I briefly shewed, that in all the particulars by you mentioned, the generality of you *Christians* do act the clean contrary; what then do you boast of, and wherein are you better than we? Only that you pretend to understand more, and *do* less, and so deserve the greater Condemnation. Will you make us believe, that those men have *any Religion*, who have *no God*? or have they indeed *a God*, who prefer their *Lusts*, or *Wealth*, or *Honour*, or any thing in the World before him, and his holy Commands; Can we think that you know what it is to *believe* that there is a God, and a Life to come, and to *renounce the Flesh*, the *World*, and the *Devil*, and give up your selves to a *Saviour*, and a *Sanctifier*, when we behold you persuing after Vanity with *out-stretched Arms*, and committing all kind of Wickedness with greediness? Can you your selves think, whilst you are awake and sober, that *Perfideousness* will avail you, and *Rebellion* save you? or that the God of Wisdom, Holiness and Justice, will accept you for a *perjured* Profession to be, and to do *that* which never came into your Hearts? Is *Hypocrisie* a Virtue? Or will *Lying* and *Dissembling* bring a man to *Heaven*? Christianity (by that very Description you have given of it) is such a believing in Christ, to bring us unto God and everlasting Glory, as maketh the *Love of God* become the very Nature of the Soul, and thankful *Obedience* its Imployment, and an *heavenly Mind*, and an *humble, pure, harmless* and *holy Life*, to be its *Constitution*, and *constant Trade*; and the Interests of fleshly Lusts, and the Pomps and Vanities, the Riches and Honours of the World to be truly esteemed but as *dross* and *dung*; Now tell us in good earnest, is *this* the Life which you *live*, or which you *hate*? Why will you *profess* a Religion you *abhor*? Or why will you abhor and despise a Religion which you *profess*? Why will you glory in the part of a *Parrot*, or an *Ape*, to say over a few Words, or move your Bodies into such Forms and Ceremonies, whilst you detest the humane and divine part, to *know*, and *love*, and *live* to God? Do you profess your selves *Christians* only for *Self-Condemnation*, to be Witnesses against your selves in Judgment, that you *wilfully lived* Unchristian Lives? What is there in the World that you are so averse to, as to *be seriously* that which you profess to be? That is, to walk uprightly and sincerely in all those fourteen Particulars by you enumerated. Whom do you hate more than those that are *that in Heart and Life*, which you call your selves in customary Words? or that are *serious* in the Religion which you your selves say, You hope to be saved by. Call us *Heathens* as long as you will, I am confident *Christ* hath not more bitter Enemies in the World, than some of you that wear his *Livery*;[14] We *Blacks* are more gentle to you, than you *Christians* are to one another; and I have been assured, that all the *Heathens* in the World have shed *less* Christian Blood, than what *Hypocrite Christians* themselves have greedily let out, or occasioned to be destroyed: Thus you honour *dead Saints*, and abhor the *Living*, and would gladly make more *Martyrs*, whilst you keep *Days* in Commemoration of those that *others* made. Can any thing be more preposterously absurd, more foolishly wicked, than these *interferring* Contradictions? Were it not better to *be* what you call your selves, or to *call* your selves what you are? If you *approve* of these Christian Doctrines, why do not you square your Conversations accordingly? If you think them *needless Notions*, why do not you disown them? Or why do you so much cry up and magnifie them? Be either *Christians* indeed, or cease to upbraid us for being *Heathens*; for such *shuffling Hypocrisie* is more abominable to God and Man, than the most ignorant *Paganism*.

    Mast. I have given you, *Sambo*, a large liberty of Prating, and you have used it very confidently: How come you so *wonderous Wise*? How dare you upbraid us that have the Light of the Gospel? Or indeed why should we mind any thing such *Heathens* as you can say or talk of?

    Negr. We boast not of *Wisdom*; what I have said, arises from plain *matter of Fact*, which no Person whom our Creator hath endued with a rational Soul, can be ignorant of, if he do not wilfully quench and extinguish in himself that

Light which enlighteneth every man that cometh into the World, and which one of your own Prophets calls, *The Candle of the Lord*.[15] Nor are we altogether such ignorant *dark Heathens*, as you call and suppose us; for many of the *Christians* do not esteem, not look on us any otherwise, or better than *Dogs*; for tell me, I pray *boon Master!* what difference has our Creator made between you and us? Hath he endued you with any particular Quality or Property more then we are furnisht with? The Members of our Bodies, the Faculties of our Minds, our *Senses* and all the Furniture of Nature, are equal, and the same in us as in you: We are not *Beasts*, as you count, and use us, but *rational Souls*, and in us is contained the true Nature and Properties of all Elements, and created things; Nor do we contemn or slight the *Light of the Gospel*, as you call it, but we wonder at you that so much *talk* of it, and so *little practise* the good Rules of Life contained therein. Besides, since you are pleased to grant us the Liberty to plead our own Cause, we might tell you, that we have the *same Gospel* that you so much talk of, written in our Hearts, and doing by Nature the things that are written in the Law, being without the Law, are a Law unto our selves, as one of your illuminated Prophets speaks: And if we do the things that are right in the sight of God, and walk in his innocent Law in Nature, according to *our measure* and *understanding*, we have so far discharged our Duty, and we doubt not but the goodness of our Creator will accept thereof, and pardon our *involuntary Misprisions*, and *Failings*; and if you have a *larger* Manifestation of the eternal Light and Love of God, which we have no reason to doubt, then the more is required of you, and therefore the greater and more sore will your Condemnation be.

Mast. And do you *black Heathenish Negroes* then dare compare your selves with us brave *white Christians*? Does not your very *Hue*, that *sooty Skin* of yours, serve for an Emblem of the darkness of your Minds? You eat all unclean Foods, Carrion and Vermine without scruple; you have no Order nor *decent* Ceremonies at your *Marriages*; you go *naked*, and have not wherewithal to cover your Shame; in a Word, you are in most particulars the very next Door to *Beasts*, and therefore we have hardly so much care and esteem for you, as we have for our *Horses*, or other Cattel; Are you not altogether unlearned, and can neither *spue Latine*, nor *sputter Greek*, nor understand the *Hebrew Rabbins*,[16] and the *Talmud*; your Discourses are not trim'd with Flowers of *Rhetorick*, nor can you *chop Logick*, nor make *Syllogisms*, and run down both Truth and Sense with *Mood* and *Figure*, and the *Magick* of a concluding *Ergo*: What Divines or Clergy-men, what cunning *Lawyers* have you to boast of? Though you pretend to do *Cures*, yet you never read *Galen*[17] nor *Paracelsus*,[18] nor have any *Apothecaries* to make a Trade of the *Materia Medica*, nor *Chymists* to tell you the Medicinal Vertues of *Minerals*; you have very few *Persons of Honour* amongst you (except your Kings) and but a few *Misses*, and no *Theaters* or *Play-houses* for the Education of your Youth; your Women are not so notably arrayed, nor have those *charming Arts*, to invite men to love and dote upon them, as *ours* daily study; neither do you drink Wine in Bowls, nor understand the *genteel* mystery of quaffing of Healths with an *Huzza*! or to *Swear* Modishly with a *boon Courage*! All these things *We* enjoy, and make sumptuous *Feasts*, where we spend as much in a few Hours, as two or three Hundred of such Wretches as you can earn in some dayes: We have all sorts of War like Weapons, and murthering Engines to use at our pleasure: We eat and drink of the fattest Foods, and richest Liquors, and take our ease, and clothe us in costly Attire, and study *new Fashions* for our Garments, to render us more honourable and admired, and many other great Priviledges we have, which you are destitute of.

    Negr. These, Sir! are *brave things* indeed to vapour with! Is it possible that *rational men*, much less such illuminated *Christians*, as you account your selves, should thus be taken with things that are so much *below* the Dignity of humane Nature, to boast of your *Evils*, and glory in your *Shame*? As for our *Complexion*, 'tis the Livery of our Creator, the property of the Climate and Soil, wherein his good Providence disposed of us to be born and bred; we made not our selves *Black*, nor do you make your selves *White*; wherein then have you any thing to brag of above us? If for this cause you despise us, you at the same time despise that *adorable Power*, which is the Maker both of us and you: And though *White* be an Emblem of *Innocence*, yet there are *whited Walls* filled within with Filth and Rottenness; what is only *outward*, will stand you in no stead, it is the *inward Candor* that our Creator is well-pleased with, and not the outward; have a care therefore that you be not found as *black within*, as we are externally.

    You upbraid us with eating *unclean Foods*, Carrion, Vermine, &c. But I pray, is it not your *Cruelty*, in not affording us what is sufficient to support Nature otherwise, that makes us do it? This is first to make us *Cripples*, and then beat us with our *Crutches* for being Lame. As for our poor Coverings, or going Naked, as long as Man remained in the innocent State, he wanted no Garments; and you are forced to *Rob* several sorts of Creatures to cover your *Shame*; nor do you bring into the World any greater *Ward-robe* with you, than we do; nor have you occasion to carry out any more. But how depraved and dishonourable does it look, for that *noble Creature*, [Man][19] not only to be glad to borrow of his inferior Creatures to hide his Shame, but also to grow *Proud* of those Ornaments, which are but the *Spoils*, or the *Labours*, and many times the *Excrements* of Beasts and Flies, or Insects, and the like lower Graduates?

As for Order in *Marriages*, we have as much as you; for though Plurality of *Wives* is contrary to your Custom, it is not to *ours*; and he is no wise man that admires or contemns the various Customs of different Regions, any further than they contradict Nature: Now this Custom of *ours*, as it is be-friended with Examples amongst the antient *Patriarchs*, and the Laws of many Nations so renowned for Civility, as to esteem all others *Barbarians*, so it seems somewhat to agree with the Law of *Nature*, and to prevent Out-rages against Nature, it being not fit, nor *natural* for Men to meddle with their Wives when they are *Breeding*, or great with-child: However, these things are more of *Custom*, than any thing else, and we our selves esteem that man most *happy* that contents himself with *one Wife*. But you, although your Customs and Laws forbid *Poligamy*, and *Adultery*, yet whilst you comply somewhat in the former, do make nothing, many of you, to violate the *latter*, as often as you can meet with an opportunity.

When you say, You hardly esteem of us so well as *Beasts*; we have Reason to believe you, from your cruel Usages, and not allowing us what is necessary for Food and Rest, which yet is to be wondred at, since if we are not worthy (forsooth!) to be your *Brethren*, we are however your *Money*. So that this Cruelty towards us, doth favour more of *Envy*, than of *Christianity* or *Frugality*. It is also true, that we have no *Lip-learned Doctors*, nor are confined to the old musty Rules of *Aristotle* or *Galen*, nor acquainted with the new Fancies of your modern *Fire-working Chymists*, or *Vertuosi*, nor will we compare our selves to you in those things; but we have so much understanding, as not to content our selves to *see with other mens Eyes*, and *put out our own*, as many of your learned *Rabbies* do; nor want we amongst us those that God and Nature have endued with Gifts of knowing the *Vertues of Herbs*, and that can by genuine Skill, administer *good Medicines*, and perform greater Cures, than your famous Doctors with their *hard Words* and *affected Methods*. Neither will the Art of *Chymistry* advantage us; for since God hath hid all sorts of *Mettals* in the deep Bowels of the Earth, and on the contrary adorned its *Surface* with so many noble and salutiferous *Herbs* and *Plants*, we conceive he intended the *latter*, not the *former*, both for the *Food* and *Physick* of man; And also we observe, that most who have hazarded their Healths and Lives, to get them out of these *Subterranean Caverns*, have done much hurt by the use of them in the World. Yet in our own Country we have in divers parts the best Metals near at hand, viz. *Gold*, which too many of the *Christians* make their *God*. Our Women, 'tis true, have no other Ornament than what is Natural, which is more than abundance of yours have, for they want the great Ornament of that Sex, *Modesty*; for though ours go *naked*, yet they are not so *impudent* as your Misses, who make a *Trade* of Lasciviousness and Filthiness.

We drink not Wine in Bowls, nor without; and it would be much better and more becoming *Christianity*, if you *did not* too; for doth it not heat our Blood, irritate the central Heat, set the whole Body into an unnatural Flame, & precipitate the Mind into Fury and Madness, and excite the Senses to Uncleanness and Beastiality? For pray, good Master! tell me, how many Villanies of all sorts do some nominal *Christians* commit against God, and his pure Law in Nature, by reason of their Excesses in that kind? And what grievous *Diseases* do such Debauches occasion both present, and for the future? Nay, to the further shame of *Christians*, have you not by lewd Examples *defiled* and *debauched* us *Ethiopeans*, and the *Indians* whom you converse?[20] So that instead of learning us Virtue, and courting us to your Faith and Religion by *Sobriety* and *Godliness*, you set before us *destructive Presidents*,[21] and make us more the Children of the Devil than we were before; which has forced many of your Religion to make strict Laws, that no *Christians* shall suffer *Indians* to *drink* strong intoxicating Liquors, or sell the same unto them; so that we must needs say in that respect, you have been *kinder to us*, than to your selves; for seeing the great Inconveniences and Hurt the drinking thereof does to us, you endeavour to prevent the same, and yet you continue and encrease the evil Practice thereof your selves, and so long as the *Christians* thus trade in Debauchery and Superfluity; there is no likelihood or hopes that they should draw any considerable Number of us, or the neighbouring *Indians* to embrace their Religion, though undoubtedly it is the most excellent Doctrine that ever was communicated to the World: But the vicious Lives of its Professors, their saying, and not *doing*, cuts off in the Bud, and wholly destroys the growth and encrease of those sublim Truths, and makes the World despise both the *Christians* and their Doctrine; for it is not your good Words, and long Prayers, (and indeed some are short enough) that are pleasing to our Creator, or edifying to us; It must be your *good Works* that shall convince any of the Truth, and beget Love and Amity in all men.

But instead thereof, you spend your time in *Riot, Excess, Vanity*, or *wicked Plays*, whereof evil *Daemons* were the Inventers, whilst we *sigh* and *groan* under your heavy Burthens. But our Cries are slighted by you, and your *Ladies* too, who many of them will *Swagger*, and *Curse*, and *Rant*, and equally oppress, and as much abuse us as your selves, which Fierceness and Cruelty looks more *monstrous* in them, though bad in both Sexes, and where-ever practised, must of a certain truth be retaliated. I have heard some of our Mas-

cruel, white woman as a monstrous figure

ter *Christians* talk of, and cry out against the Tyranny of the *Turks*, and the Slavery they impose on what *Christians* they can get into their Clutches at *Algier*; Is it not strange that you should *Practise* the very same thing your selves, that you so much *Condemn* in others? Nay, you do *ten times worse* than they, both because you profess your selves *Christians*, which is a Religion of Love, Sweetness and Beneficience to all the Creation; and for that you use us *worse* than the *Turks* do their Servants; and especially in this, that you rather *hinder*, than *promote* our embracing the *Christian Faith*, whereas amongst the *Turks* any Christian Slave may turn *Mahumetan*, and is encouraged thereunto, and thereby gains his Liberty.

Mast. The World has come to a fine pass, that such ignorant *Slaves* and *Heathens* as you are, that do neither know nor worship the true God, should presume either to *instruct*, or *condemn* us. Do not you know, that most of the hard usage you so much complain of; is occasioned by *your selves*, for if we should not be severe, and rule you with a *Rod of Iron*, you are so stubborn and disobedient, that there would be no governing of you; therefore we are forced to *beat you* into Obedience and good Manners, you are so *morose, surly* and *inhumane*; so that you are the first cause of those Miseries you endure: Have not you made several Attempts to *Rise*, and cut off the *Christians* Root and Branch, and make your selves Masters of all that we have? And do not such Offences require a strict Hand, and severe Punishments? What greater Crime can there be, than for you to betray your Masters?

Negr. True it is, the World is come to that pass, and mens Wickedness is arrived to that height, that good Advertisements, and wholsom *Counsel*, either of *Christian, Jew* or *Gentile*, will not be entertained, let it come from whom it will, if it tend to Vertue, be sure it shall be withstood with various *Pretences*. Whereas you accuse us of *evil Carriage*, and that the same hath been the Original of all our Griefs and sore Oppressions, there is a certain Truth therein, tho' not as you intend it, for if we and our Fore-fathers *had not violated* the innocent Law of Nature by Violence and Transgression, we had never fallen under *your Yoke*, nor been carried away Captives out of our own Native Country; but now we have by the divine Justice been retaliated, for ours, and our Princes Transgressions; However, though we acknowledge this is but just from God, yet that doth not concern you, nor can you from thence justifie your Oppressions, which could not be occasioned by the Miscarriages you speak of, because they had long been practised upon us, *before* any of us made any of those ill Attempts you mention; 'twas your Cruelties put us upon those extravagant courses: And since Oppression (according to the Doctrine of your most holy wise Prophet) *makes Wise Men mad*,[22] 'twas no wonder if some of our silly Countrymen were thereby so far transported, as to seek by unjustifiable means, to gain their Liberty, or a Melioration of their wretched condition.

Besides, if we had indeed offended you, yet you ought not to retaliate *Evil for Evil*, since on the contrary your Christian Doctrine enjoyns you to return *Good for Evil*, & to *love even your Enemies*; how dare you then in Light of this holy and everlasting Gospel, to talk and act after this manner? Do you indeed dream that your Cruelty, and ruling us with a *martial Rod*, and *barbarous Fierceness*, will make us *Tractable* and *Friendly*, or to love our Masters, and do our Labours with willingness? Alas! we imagined you to be greater *Seers* into the Mysteries of God, and his Law in Nature, than to entertain such vain and impossible Conceits; For how contrary is this not only to your Christian Principles, but also to Reason, and the common Sense and Experience of all mankind? *With the Froward thou shalt learn Frowardness*,[23] saith your own Prophet. And again, *Did ever the Wrath of Man accomplish the Righteousness of God*? Or *Tyranny* beget *Love*? If those who have the government of *generous Horses*, or go about to tame *wild Beasts*, and endeavour by *gentle Usage* to make them tractable, and fit for Service, rather then by Cruelty and Beating; much more those who have the command of *Men*, should bring them to Order and Discipline by the mildest and fairest means, and all the Arts of Sweetness and Perswasion; not treating them worse than *Gardiners* do those *wild Plants*, which by careful looking to, and good Usage, lose the Savageness of their Nature, and in a little time come to bear excellent *Fruit*.

In vain therefore you go about to excuse your Tyranny and Oppression towards us, by making the World believe, that you are as it were constrained, or forced to be cruel to us; Though yet the same be true in one Sense, *viz.* you are irritated thereunto from your own innate awakened *Wrath*, which does predominate in your Hearts and Souls, and then those fierce Arrows of *Mars*, and Poysons of *Saturn*, which you let fly at us, do by simily[24] stir up the original Venoms, and wrathful Qualities *in us*: And this, and this only, is it that hath occasioned some of the *worser sort* of our Country-men to Curse you and your Posterity, and to endeavour to kill and destroy you, which is a *crying Sin*, which we neither justifie, nor can excuse, since 'tis condemned by God, and his Law in Nature; And all that have attempted such savage Mischiefs, ought not to go unpunisht, neither will they; for the just Law of Retaliation will take hold of them; but will you therefore punish the Innocent for, or with the *Guilty*? because some called *Christians* commit *Murders* and *Treasons*, must all of that Profession be cut off by the *Ax*, or the *Gibbet*? If you will deal ingenuously, your own Hearts will tell you, that the occasion of these Evils committed, or endeavoured to have been committed, arise from your *Sins*, and the great *Abuses* wherewith you have from time to time afflicted us, *viz.* your Murdering us at your pleasure, and no Account, or just Compensation rendred for the same: Therefore does our innocent Blood call for Vengeance on you, and (without serious Repentance and Amendment) must be reckoned for. Consider well these things, and then tell us; Do you think, or can you in Reason, but expect, that the great Tyranny, Injustice, and cruel Usages you have practised upon us, will in due time be brought back upon you and your Land or Posterity, if you do not atone for these Evils, and give us Ease and Refreshment? And though we are never so submissive, cannot the kindled Wrath raise up other Enemies to destroy you and yours in a Moment? Therefore be intreated to bethink your selves in time, for undoubtedly the Cup of Wrath is almost full.

Mast. I have considered what you alledge, touching the severe Usage, which we have, and do daily offer to your Country-men; & I must confess, I cannot well see how the same can be reconciled to the Doctrine of our holy and harmly Christian Religion: But alas! What would you have us do? If we should *leave off* these Practices, how should we *live at the Rate* we do? fill our Tables daily with variety of costly Dishes, and swill our selves and numerous Visitants with *rich Wines*, and other strong Liquors: How should we maintain our Grandure, and our Pomp, and raise great *Estates* for our selves and Children, and leave our Posterity great, and rich, and honourable in the World? We consider not your Labour, Weariness, Disorders, Sickness, Hunger, Drought, want of due Rest, or convenient Food, nor any the like Hardships that you suffer: If we can but live in State and Abundance, and make vast Quantities of *Sugar*, or other Commodities yearly, which is our chief delight, and the highest good we desire; and he that does thus do, how hard soever he uses his Slaves, is counted a *brave Husband*, and a *good Christian* too, a very notable man, fit for others to make Examples by, and imitate his prudent Conduct.

Negr. But all this time you look not into the *Radix*,[25] nor consider the lamentable Oppressions and Violences that cleave fast to this your *good Husbandry* (as you call it) that your Houses are cemented with *Blood*, and all your *Dainties* and your *Riches* accompanied with the dolorous Complaints, Sighs and Groans of your poor Vassals, which are continually sent up to Heaven against you.

Mast. No, no; we expel all such Melancholly Thoughts with a plentiful *Glass of Wine*, Jovial Company, or other sensual Diversions.

Negr. Those Arts you use to lay your Reason and Consciences to sleep, will in the end both *hasten* and *aggravate* that Vengeance which must necessarily follow all Injustice and Oppression. As for maintaining *Pride, Superfluity*, and other Evils of that nature, I am of your mind, that they cannot be supplied without Oppression and Violence; for all *Extreams* beget their Likenesses: But sure you *Christians* above all others, ought not to regard such *Vanities*, but relinquish and detest all Superfluity, Pride, Gluttony, and other the like Intemperances, since they are so diametrically opposite to your Profession and Religion. Besides, you abuse your selves and Posterity, by thinking to raise great *Estates*, or derive any lasting Temporal Happiness to you or them, by over-charging us with labour; for does not Reason and Experience let you know, that Houses built with *mouldering Stone* and *rotten Timber*, will not long continue; and that Estates heap'd together by Violence, carry along with them *a Curse* and are blasted from the *Radix*, so that at most they seldom descend to the *third Heir*, and rarely out-live the first or second Generation? What are become of all the Glories of the *Nimrods*, and the *Caesars*, and the *Alexanders*? of all the mighty *Tyrants*, and spreading Monarchies of the *Assyrians, Medes, Persians, Macedonians* and *Romans*? Are they not all long since crusht to pieces by one another, because their Foundations were laid in Violence and Spoil, Injustice and Oppressions? The *Spaniards*, who baptized the *New World* in *Blood*, murdered many *Hundred Thousand Indians*, on pretence of propagating the Christian Religion, when in truth it was only to get *Gold* and *Empire*; Have they not met with Retaliation? Have they not decreased in Power *ever since* those Cruelties, and instead of grasping an *universal Monarchy*, (which their Ambition promised themselves) are now scarce able to defend their own antient Patrimony, or keep off an Enemy from the Frontiers of *Castile*? If all these *mighty Men of War* have *Shipwrackt* by *steering this Course*, how hope you with your petty *Pinnaces*, and tottering *Skiffs*, to avoid the like Tempests? If just Vengeance hath overturned whole Empires and Kings, that called themselves *Invincible*, for their Cruelties and Oppressions, how shall your *private Fortunes* be establisht, that have no other Foundation but the like Violence and Injustice?

On the other side, I pray observe, there are many *honest, compassionate*, and truly *Christian*-spirited Men amongst you, that do not willingly oppress either Man or Beast, and yet you see how they are blest, and prosper, and enjoy more true Content and Happiness in one Week, than you whose Minds are continually distracted with greedy Desires, or anxious Fears, do in all your Lives; Nor are any of your Estates so firmly establisht, as those whose Possessors use Mercy and Gentleness in all their Doings; for Vertue and Well-doing will as naturally attract the Influences, and favour both of God and Man, and of the *Coelestials*, as well as inferior Creatures, as a *Loadstone* does *Iron*: And whosoever endeavours sincerely to live according to the innocent Law of God in Nature, shall be filled with good things, but those that study to grow rich by Wickedness and Oppression, shall be sent *empty away*, and both their Estates and their Hopes be scattered like *Leaves* before the Wind.

Nor is your Practice herein less Impudent than Ungodly, all Wickedness being indeed the height of Folly, and Piety and Vertue evermore the *best Policy*. For why should you oppress us, by whose Labours you are sustained? And our Ill is your Loss, are we not your *Money*? And what a small matter more than you allow us, might plentifully supply us? As suppose such Masters as have Fifty, a Hundred or two Hundred *Negroes*, if they would add to our Allowance, Fifty, or one Hundred, or two Hundred Pounds *per annum*, it might maintain us in lively Strength, and sufficient Vigour to go through with our Labour with cheerful Spirits, and brisk Dispositions; then should our Souls (instead of *Cursing*, and calling for Vengeance upon you) *Bless* you, and serve you cordially and willingly, with all our Power. For those that are wise amongst us, matter not their Freedom so much, provided they might but be admitted such necessary Supports, Priviledges and Accomodations, as our bountiful Creator by his Hand-maid, *Nature*, has plentifully provided for all his Creatures, and especially for the race of Men: And then would you have Peace in your own Houses and Spirits, whereas now you are always filled with Contention, Anger, Strife, Jealousie or Suspitions; nor need you ever then fear our *Rising* up against you, to cut you off, or any other Invasion; for nothing does so much disarm the Rage of the fierce Wrath, as Well-doing and Innocency; these being the surest Bulwarks both against inward and outward Enemies.

Mast. I cannot deny the Truth of what you have said, nor know I how to make any further *Objections*, therefore I think it will more become us to *amend* our Practices, than to study Arguments to *cloak* or *defend* them.

Negr. I am over-joy'd, good Master, to hear these Words from your Mouth; they sound well in our Ears, and make most pleasant Musick; nor will you, I dare promise you, ever have cause to Repent of these merciful Resolutions, for the only way for you to have *good Servants*, is for you first to be *good Masters*; and though some of our Country-men are *untractable, sullen, morose, cruel* and *revengeful* (more especially by reason of the Oppressions beforementioned) so others of them have notwithstanding given you strong Motives to believe their Integrity and faithful Honesty towards their Masters, and *Christians* in general, for many of us at several times, and on sundry occasions, have given most clear and demonstrative Testimonies of our

Faithfulness, in discovering several *horrid Plots* and *Conspiracies*, which some of the worst of us had designed against our Masters; And how little do many of us value our dear *Lives*, to save our *Masters*? And how ready are we to go, run, work, watch and defend our Masters, and to preserve their Rights? So that many of our Christian Masters have been heard to say, *That they would as soon, and willingly trust their Lives with some of their* Negro Slaves, *as with the most trusty* Christian Servants *they had*. And I doubt not, but if our Masters deal justly, and with tenderness preserve us, by allowing us such suitable Food, Drinks and Rest as are needful for the support of our Lives and Health, and suitable to the Climate, we should *all in general* become more tractable, obedient and diligent, and thereby not only perform our Labour much better, but secretly attract the sweet Influences of God and Nature on their Heads, and then twenty of us would dispatch as much Work and Business as thirty do, or can do, that have neither Food that is proper, either in Quantity or Quality, nor *due Rest*, for want of which, the whole frame of the Body, and all the Members grow heavy, dull, weak and heartless, and the Mind indisposed and averse from, as well as unable for Work or Business, which can never go on well, and to satisfaction, where the chief motive is *Whip* and *Spur*, Fear on the one side, and Cruelty on the other.

Besides, if we and our *Wives* were kept in good Heart, we should be able to get not only *more strong* and *healthy* Children, but *more in Number*, which would supply your Business far better, than for you every Year to be at that great Charge of buying such Numbers of *new Negroes*, of whom many fail, and many dye upon the change of Climate; For by reason of the Hardships used to us, and especially the Cruelties towards our Women, during their Pregnancy, they so often *Miscarry*, that we upon the Island cannot keep our Number, but decrease so fast, that you are forced every Year (at vast charge) to fetch about *ten Thousand* (as I have heard) new Ones; whereas there is no doubt to be made, but if we were conveniently supplied with Food and competent Rest, and some due Respect or Commiseration had to our *Wives when they are big*, then every of our Masters Families would so encrease by his *own Bread*, that there would be no more occasion for buying of new Ones, which would wonderfully enrich you; so that if either you regard the Rules of your *Holy Religion*, and will not justly be branded for *Hypocrites* or *Atheists*; If you have any respect to *Humanity*, common *Honesty*, and that universal Principle (but almost universally neglected) *to do as you would be done by*; or lastly, if you would avoid *divine Vengeance*, in Retaliation for your Oppressions, and would justly encrease your Estates by such ways, as they may be a comfort to your selves, and continue to your Posterity: If all or any of these things, I say, have any weight with you, then speedily leave off your Severities, and let your usage of us be such as is fit for *Men* to practise towards *Men*, let us see the excellency of the Christian Religion, by the goodness of your *Lives* that profess it, by your Meekness, and Charity, and Benignity, and Compassion towards your fellow Creatures, especially those of the same Species with your selves, and who have no less rational and *immortal Souls* than the best of you: If these things you do, we and our Posterity shall *willingly serve you*, and not count it any *Slavery*, but our unspeakable Happiness; *Peace* shall be in your Dwellings, and *Safety* shall surround your Island, for Innocency is a better defence than Forts and Citadels, than Armies and Fleets, than *Walls of Brass*, flankt with *Towers of Adamant*: In a word, you shall have Satisfaction *within*, and Security *without*, and enjoy the Blessings both of *Time* and *Eternity*. But if neither the Voice of *Religion*, nor *Nature*, can be heard; If neither *Humanity* nor *Self-interest* can prevail with you, be assured, that although you are willfully *Deaf*, our great Creator will be ready to *hear* our Cries; and you must certainly one day make Retaliation to the uttermost Farthing.

Mast. *Sambo*! I have hearkened attentively, and well considered your Discourse, which carries with it such Evidence and Reason, that I must acknowledge I am convinced that our former Conduct towards you, has not been agreeable to our Religion, or common Equity; therefore for my own part, you shall see by *future Usage*, what *Impression* your Words have made upon me, nor shall I be wanting to acquaint *others* with what you have offered—It grows late, therefore you were best be gone, and betake your self *to Rest*.

Negr. *Boon* Master, I return you a thousand of Thanks for the freedom you have given me of speaking to you: And I am over-joyed to hear, that you have thereby received some *satisfaction*; I shall now return to my fellow Servants; and as I have used some Arguments to you to be kind to them, so I shall on all occasions press them with Arguments to be obedient, humble, just and respective to all their Masters.

Mast. Therein honest *Sambo*! you will do very well, and so good Night to you.

Negr. Good Night, my good dear Master!

FINIS

religion works both ways → as an opiate & as a means of resistance

A Trip to Jamaica

EDWARD WARD

(1667–1731)

Edward Ward was an early example of what would later be called a journalist. During the early decades of the eighteenth century, journalism was only in its infancy, so journalistic writers like Ward were relegated by their contemporaries to the category of subliterary hacks, rather than being recognized as founders of a new field of professional writing. Along with other protojournalists, such as John Dunton, Edmund Curll, Daniel Defoe, and Sir Richard Steele, Ward tested new ideas for periodical writing in an attempt to keep a journal running indefinitely and profitably. Ward is best known for the Hudibrastic sketches of London life that he wrote for his periodical the *London Spy*, which he published from 1698 to 1709. In the *London Spy*, Ward adapted the form of the travelogue he first used in *A Trip to Jamaica* to narrative explorations of urban London; the eleven-year run of the periodical places Ward at the top rank of successful journalists of his day.

In *A Trip to Jamaica* (1698), Ward parodies the kind of promotional travel narrative that characterized reports from the settlements in the Americas. Merchants, adventurers, and investors collaborated to squelch bad news from the new colonies; Ward's bitter critique of conditions in the wealthy colony of Jamaica struck a nerve among readers in London. His tract was popular enough to run through at least seven editions within a few years, and Ward developed the persona of the *Trip* into the characteristic journalist's style he made famous in the *London Spy*. The *Trip* also formed the basis for *The Jamaica Lady* (1720), a prose narrative by Ward's friend William Pittis.

A TRIP TO JAMAICA:
With a True CHARACTER OF THE People
and Island. *By the Author of* Sot's Paradise.
The Third Edition.[1] *LONDON*,
Printed in the Year,
1698.

TO THE READER

The Condition of an Author *is much like that of a* Strumpet, *both exposing our* Reputations *to supply our* Necessities, *till at last we contract such an ill habit, thro' our Practices, that we are equally troubl'd with an* Itch *to be always* Doing; *and if the reason be requir'd, Why we betake our selves to so Scandalous a Profession as* Whoring *or* Pamphleteering, *the same excusive Answer will serve us both,* viz. *That the unhappy circumstances of a Narrow Fortune, hath forc'd us to do that for our Subsistance, which we are much asham'd of.*

The chiefest and most commendable Tallent, admir'd in either, is the knack of Pleasing; and He or She amongst us that happily arives to a Perfection in that sort of Witchcraft, may in a little time (to their great Honour) enjoy the Pleasure of being Celebrated by all the Coxcombs *in the Nation.*

The only difference between us is, in this particular, where in the Jilt *has the Advantage, we do our Business First, and stand to the Courtesie of our Benefactors to Reward us after, whilst the other, for her Security, makes her* Rider *pay for his* Journey, *before he mounts the* Saddle.

It is necessary I should say something in relation to the following Matter: I do not therein present you with a formal Journal *of my Voyage, or* Geographical *Description of the* Island *of* Jamaica, *for that has been already done by Persons better Qualifi'd for such a Task.*[2] *I only Entertain you with what I intend for your* Diversion, *not* Instruction; *Digested into such a Stile as might move your* Laughter, *not merit your* Esteem. *I question not but the* Jamaica *Coffee-House be much affronted at my* Character *of their* Sweating Chaos, *and if I was but as well assur'd of Pleasing every body else, as I am of Displeasing those who have an Interest in that Country, I should not question but the* Printer *would gain his End, which are the wishes of the* Author.

A TRIP TO JAMAICA:

In the times of *Adversity* when *Poverty* was held no *Shame* and *Piety* no *Virtue*; When *Honesty* in a Tradesman's Conscience, and *Money* in his Counting-House were as scarce as *Health* in an Hospital, or *Charity* in a Clergyman. The

Sword being advanc'd, and the *Pen* silenc'd; *Printers* being too Poor to pay down *Copy-Money*, and *Authors* too Poor to Trust 'em: *Fools* getting more by hazarding their *Carcasses*, than *Ingenious Men* by imploying their *Wits*; which was well enough observ'd by a Gentleman, in these following Lines.

> *When* Pens *were valu'd less than* Swords,
> *And Blows got Money more than Words*;
> *When Am'rous* Beaux, *and Campaign* Bully,
> *Thriv'd by their* Fighting *and their* Folly;
> *Whilst Men of Parts, as Poor as* Rats,
> *With* Mourning Swords *and* Flapping Hats,
> *Appear by Night, like* Owles *and* Bats:
> *With Hungry hast pursuing way*,
> *To Sir* John Lend, *or 'Squire* Pay.
> *Till* Wit *in* Rags, *and* Fool *in* Feather,
> *Were join'd, by Providence, together.*
> *The one o'er Bottle breaks his Jest,*
> *Like Country Parson at a Feast*;
> *For which he's Treated and Exalted,*
> *By his dear Friend, Sir* Looby Dolthead.
> *Unhappy Age, which so in Vice surpasses,*
> *That Men of Worth must Worship* Golden Asses.

I being influenc'd by my Stars, with an unhappy propensity to the Conversation of those unlucky kind of *Fortune-Hunters*, till at last, tho' I had no more Wit to boast of than another Man, yet I shar'd the Fate of those that had; and to bear them Company, stragled so far from the Paths of *Profit* and *Preferment*, into a Wilderness of *Pleasure* and *Enjoyment*, that I had like to have been stuck fast in a Thicket of Brambles, before I knew where abouts I was; to clear my self of which, I bustled like a *Fox* in a *Gin*, or a *Hare* in a *Patridge-Net*: But before I could free my self from this Entanglement, I had so wounded my Feet, and stuck so many Thorns in my Side, that I halted homewards like a *Gouty Puritan* to an *Election*, or a *Lame Begger* to a *Misers Funeral*.

These little Afflictions mov'd me to reflect upon my Mis-spent Time; and like a *Thief* in a *Goal*,[3] or a *Whore* in a *Flux*, I resolv'd for the future to Reform my Life, change my Measures, and push my self upon something that might recover those lost Moments, I had hitherto converted to the use of others, and not my self. I now began to peep into the *Business* of the World, and chang'd the Company of those who had nothing to do but *Spend Money*, for the Conversation of such whose practice was to *Get it*.

But I, thro' Inadvertency, neglecting to consult Doctor *Troter*,[4] or some other infallible Predicting Wisaker, began my Reformation in an unfortunate Minute, when *Userers* were unbinding their *Fetter'd Trunks*, and breaking up their *Deified Bags* and *Consecrated Sums*, for the security of *Religion*, and the further establishment of *Liberty of Conscience*, without which [*Liberty*][5] join'd, *Conscience* to them would be of no use. *Tradesmen* grumbling at the *Taxes*, *Merchants* at their *Losses*, most Men complaining for want of *Business*, and all Men in *Business*, for want of *Money*: Every Man upon *Change*[6] looking with as peevish a Countenance, as if he had unluckily stumbled upon his *Wife's Failings*, and unhappily become a witness to his own *Cuckoldome*. These I thought but slender Encouragements to a *New Reformist*, who had forsaken *Liberty* for *Restraint*, *Ease* for *Trouble*, *Laziness* for *Industry*, *Wine* for *Coffee*, and the *Pleasures* of *Witty Conversation*, for the *Plagues* of a *Muddy-Brain'd Society*, who could talk of nothing but *Prime Cost* and *Profit*, the *Good Humour* of their *Wives*, the *Wittiness* of their *Children*, and the *Unluckiness* of their *Prentices*, and knew no more how *Handsomly* to Spend their Money, than *Honestly* to Get it.

The *Complaints* of these *Philodenarians*,[7] the *Declination* of *Trade*, and the *Scarcity* of *Money*, gave me no more hopes of mending my Condition, by pursuing my intended measures, than a *Good Husband* has of mending a *Bad Wife* by winking at her *Vices*. I now found my self in great danger of a Relaps, to prevent which, after two or three Gallons of *Derby-Ale* had one day sent my *Wits* a *Woollgathering*, and generated as many *Maggots* in my *Brains*, as there are *Crotchets* in the *Head* of a *Musician*, or *Fools* in the *Million Lottery*, I e'en took up a Resolution to Travel, and Court the Blinking Gipsy *Fortune* in another Country. I then began to Consider what Climate might best suit with my *Constitution*, and what Part of the World with my *Circumstances*; and upon mature Deliberation, found a *Warm Latitude* would best agree with *Thin Apparel*, and a *Money'd Country* with a *Narrow Fortune*; and having often heard such extravagant Encomiums[8] of that Blessed Paradise *Jamaica*, where *Gold* is more plentiful than *Ice*, *Silver* than *Snow*, *Pearl* than *Hailstones*, I at last determin'd to make a trial of my Stars in that Island, and see whether they had the same Unlucky Influence upon me there, as they had, hitherto, in the Land of my Nativity.

In order to proceed my *Voyage*, I took a Passage in the good Ship the *Andalucia*; and about the latter end of *January*, 1697. upon the dissolution of the hard Frost, I passed, with many others, by the Night Tide, in a *Wherry*, to *Gravesend*, where our *Floating Receptacle* lay ready to take in *Goods* and *Passengers*; but our Lady *Thames* being put into a Passion, by the rude Kisses of an

Easterly Wind, drew her Smooth Face into so many Wrinckles, that her ill-favour'd Aspect and Murmurings, were to me as Terrible as the Noise of *Thieves* to a *Miser,* or *Bailiffs* to a *Bankrupt;* and being pent up with my Limbs, in an awkward Posture, lying Heads and Tails, like *Essex* Calves in a *Rumford* Waggon, I was forc'd to endure the Insolence of every Wave, till I was become as Wet as a New Pump'd *Kidnapper.*[9]

In this Condition I Embark'd about Two a Clock in the Morning, where the Chief Mait, as Master of the Ceremonies, conducted me to a wellcome Collation of *Cheese* and *Bisket,* and presented me with a Magnificent *Can* of Soveraign *Flip,*[10] prepar'd with as much Art as an *Apothecary* can well shew in the mixing of a *Cordial.* After this Refreshment, I betook myself to a *Cabin,* which fitted me so well, it sat as tite as a *Jacket* to a *Dutchman,* where I Slep till Morning, as close as a *Snaile* in a *Shell,* or a *Maggot* in an *Apple-Kernel.* Then Rising, and after I had survey'd our Wooden Teretories, I began to Contemplate upon things worthy of a serious Consideration which stir'd up in me that Malignant Spirit of *Poetry,* with which I am oft times unhappily possess'd: And what my Muse dictated to me, her *Emanuensis,*[11] I here present unto the *Reader.*

A Farewell to ENGLAND

I.

Farewell my Country, *and my* Friends,
My Mistres, *and my* Muse,
In distant Regions, diff'rent Ends
My Genious *now pursues.*
Those Blessings which I held most dear,
Are, by my stubborn Destiny,
(That uncontroul'd Necessity)
Abandon'd from me, and no more appear.

II.

Despair of Fortune makes me bold,
I can in Tempests Sleep,
And fearless of my Fate, behold
The Dangers of the Deep.
No Covetous desire of Life,
Can now my Careless Thoughts imploy,
Banish'd from Friendship, Love, and Joy,
To view the Waves and Winds at equal Strife.

III.

O'er threatening Billows can I fly,
And, unconcern'd, conceive,
'Tis here less difficult to Die,
Than 'twas on Land to Live.
To me 'tis equal, Swim or Sink,
I smiling to my Fate can bow,
Bereft of Joy, I think it now
No more to Drown than 'twas before to Drink.

IV.

Dear Friends with Patience bear the Load
Of Troubles, still to come,
You Pitty us who range Abroad,
We Pitty you at Home.
Let no Oppression, Fears, or Cares
Make us our Loyalty Disband,
Which, like a well built Arch, should stand
The more secure, the greater Weight it bears.

V.

Farewell Applause, *that vain Delight*
The Witty *fondly seek;*
He's Blest who like a Dunce *may* Write,
Or like a Fool *may* Speak:
What ever Praise *we gain to day,*
Whether deservedly or no,
We to the Worlds Opinion owe,
Who does as oft Mistake *the same away.*

VI.

Something there is, which touches near,
I scarce can bid Adieu;
'Tis all my Hope, my Care, my Fear,
And all that I pursue:
'Tis what I Love, yet what I Fly,
But what I dare not, must not Name,
Angels Protect the Sacred Frame,
Till I to England *shall Return, or Die.*

Towards the Evening the Captain came on Board, with the rest of our Fellow-Travellours, who, when we were altogether patch'd up as pritty a Society, as a Man under my Circumstances would desire to tumble into: There was Three of the *Troublesome Sex*, as some call them, (tho' I never thought 'em so) whose Curteous Affabillity, and Complaisancy of Temper, admitted of no other Emulation, but to strive who (within the bounds of Modesty) should be most Obliging. One *Unfortunate Lady* was in pursute of a *Stray'd Husband*, who, in *Jamaica*, had Feloniously taken to Wife (for the sake of a Plantation) a *Lacker-fac'd Creolean*,[12] to the great dissatisfaction of his Original Spouse, who had often declar'd (thro' the sweetness of her Disposition) That if he had Marri'd another Handsomer than her self, it would never have vex'd her; but to be Rival'd by a *Gipsy*, a Tawny Fac'd *Moletto*[13] Strumpet, a Pumpkin colour'd Whore, no, her Honour would not suffer her to bear with patience so coroding an Indignity. The other Two were a pritty *Maid*, and a comly *Widow*; so that in these three, we had every Honourable State of the whole Sex: One in the *State* of *Innocency*, another of Fruition, the third of Deprivation; and if we had but one in the *State* of *Corruption*, a Man might have pleas'd himself as well in our *Little World*, as you *Libertines* can do in the *Great One*.

I shall be too tedious if I at large Particularize the whole Company, I shall therefore *Hustle* them together, as a *Morefields Sweetener* does *Luck in a Bag*,[14] and then you may Wink and Choose, for the Devil a Barrel the better Herring amongst us. We had one (as I told you before) *Cherubimical Lass*, who, I fear, had *Lost her Self*, two more, of the same *Gender*, who had lost their *Husbands*; two *Parsons* who had lost their *Livings*; three *Broken Tradesmen*, who had lost their *Credit*; and several, like me, that had lost their *Wits*; a *Creolean Captain*, a *Superannuated Mariner*, an *Independent Merchant*, an *Irish Kidnapper*, and a *Monmothean Sciths-Man*,[15] all going with one Design, to patch up their *Decay'd Fortunes*.

Every thing being in Order for *Sailing*, the *Pilot* came on *Board*, who put on such a Commanding Countenance, that he look'd as Stern as a *Sarazins Head*;[16] and the *Sins* of his *Youth* having crep't into his *Pedestals*, he Limp'd about the *Quarter-Deck*, like a *Cripple* in *Forma Pauperis*[17] upon a *Mountebanks Stage*, making as great a Noise in his *Tarpaulin Cant*, as a *Young Counsel* in a *Bad Cause*, or a *Butcher* at a *Bear-Garden*. As soon as we had weigh'd *Anchor*, under the doleful Cry and hard Service of *Haul Cat haul*, there was nothing heard till we reach'd the *Downs*, but *About Ship my Lads, bring your Fore Tack on Board, haul Fore-Sail haul, Brace about the Main-Yard*, and the Devil to do, That I was more Amaz'd than a *Mouse* at a *Throsters Mill*,[18] or the *Russian Embassador* at a *Clap* of *Thunder*.

By the help of *Providence*, the *Pilots* Care, and *Seamens* Industry, we pass'd safe to *Deal*, where we Anchor'd three or four Days for a fair Wind. In which interim, the *Prince* of the *Air* had puff'd up an unwelcome Blast in the Night, which forc'd a Vessel upon the *Goodwin*. The next Morning the *Salvages* Man'd out a Fleet of their *Deal Skimming-dishes*, and made such unmerciful work with the poor distressed *Bark*, that a *Gang* of *Bailiffs* with an *Execution*, or a *Kennel* of *Hounds* upon a *Dead Horse*, could not have appear'd more *Ravenous*. From thence, with a prosperous Gale, we made the best of our way into the wide *Ocean*, which *Marriners* say, is of such Profundity, that, like a *Misers Conscience*, or a *Womans Concupiscence* 'tis never to be Fathom'd.

'Twas in the midst of Winter, and very Cold Weather when we set out; but in a Fortnights time we were got into a comfortable Climat, which yielded us so pleasant a warmth, that a Man might pluck off his Shirt upon Deck, and commit *Murther* upon his own *Flesh* and *Blood* till he was weary, without the danger of an Ague.[19]

I happen'd one Morning to hear two *Tar-jackets*[20] in a very high Dispute; I went to them, and ask'd the reason of their Difference. *Why Sir*, says one, *I'll tell you, there was my Master* Whistlebooby, *an old* Boatswain *in one of His* Majesties *Ships, who was* Superhanded, *and past his Labour, and the* Ambaraltie Divorc'd *him from his Ship, and the* King *allow'd him a* Suspension, *and this Lubberly Whelp here says I talk like a Fool; and sure I have not used the Sex this Thirty Years, but I can* Argufie *any thing as proper as he can.*

The chief *Sports* we had on Board, to pass away the tedious Hours, were *Hob, Spie the Market, Shove the Slipper, Dilly Dally* and *Back-Gammon*; the Latter of which prov'd as serviceable to me, as a *Book* of *Heraldry* to a *Gentleman Mumper*,[21] or a *Pass*[22] to a *Penniless Vagabond*: For (like the *Whore* who boasted of her *Industry*) I us'd to make my Days Labour worth *Two Shillings*, or *Half a Crown*, at *Two Pence*, or a *Groat* a *Bout*. The most powerful Adversary I engag'd with, was a *Parson*, who, when the Bell Rung to Prayers, would start up in the middle of a Hit, desire my Patience whilst he step'd into the *Great Cabin*, and gave his Sinful Congregation a *Dram* of Evangellical *Comfort*, and he would wait upon me presently. But that *Recreation* in which we took a more peculiar delight, was the Harmony we made, by the assistance of the two *Heaven-drivers*, in Lyricking over some *Antiquated Sonnets*, and for varieties sake, now and then a *Psalme*, which our Canonical *Vice-Whippers* Sung with as Penitential a grace, as a Sorrowful Offender in his *Last Night-Cap*.

To please my self at a Spare-Hour, I had taken with me a *Flute*, and there being on Board a *Spannel Dog*, who (*Seaman like*) had no great kindness for *Wind Musick*, for when ever he heard me *Tooting*, he'd be *Howling*, which, together, made a Noise so surprising, that it frighted away a *Quotidean Ague*, from a Young Fellow who had been three Weeks under the hands of our Doctor.

One Night, after we had well Moisten'd our Drouthy Carcasses with an Exhilerating Dose of Right Honourable *Punch*, there arose a *Storm*, for which I had often wish'd, that I might not be a stranger to any Surprising Accident the Angry Elements, when at Varience, might afford me. The Heavens all round us (in as little time as a *Girl* might loose her *Maidenhead*) had put on such a Malignant Aspect, as if it threaten'd our Destruction; And *Aeolus* gave us such unmerciful Puffs and Whiffs, that I was fearful to stand upon the *Quarter Deck*, lest, before my time, I should be snatch'd up to Heaven in a Whirle-Wind. From all the Corners of the Skie there darted forth such Beams of *Lightning*, that I Vow and Protest the *Fire-Works* in St. *James's-Square*, were no more to be compar'd to't, than a *Gloworms Arse* to a *Cotten Candle*, which were Instantly succeeded with such Vollys of *Thunder*, from every side, that you would have thought the *Clouds* had been Fortifi'd with *Whole Canon*, and weary of being tost about with every Wind, were Fighting their way into a Calmer Region to enjoy their Rest. Then fell such an excessive *Rain*, that as we had one Sea under us, we feard another had been tumbling upon our Heads; for my part, I fear'd the very *Falling* of the *Skie*, and thought of nothing but *Catching of Larks*. My Spirits being a little deprest, by the apprehensions of the Danger we were under, I went down into the *Gunroom*, to consult my *Brandy-Cask* about taking of a *Dram*; where one of our *Ladies*, thro' want of better Accomodation, was forc'd to be Content with a *Cradle*, in which she was *Praying*, with as much Sincerity, for *Fair Weather*, as a *Farmer* for a *Kind Harvest*, or an *Old Maid* for a *Good Husband*: And I being greatly pleas'd at her most Importunat Solicitations, have given you a Repitition of one part, *viz. And if Thou hast Decreed, that we shall Perish in this* Tempest, *I most humbly beseech Thee to Punish with* Pox, Barrenness, *and* Dry-Belly-Ach, *that* Adultrous Strumpet, *who, by Robbing me of my* Husband, *hath been a means of bringing me to this Untimely End; may her whole Life be a continued course of* Sin *without a moments* Repentance, *that she may* Die *without* Forgiveness, *and be* Damn'd *without* Mercy. In which Interim, A Sea wash'd over our *Fore-Castle*, run *Aft*, and came down the *Whip-scuttle*, she concluding we were going to the Bottom, Shreek'd out, and fell into a *Fit*; whilst I, thro' my *Fear*, together with my *Modesty*, scorn'd to take the Advantage of so fair an Oppertunity.

In a doubtful Condition, between this World and the next, we labour'd till near Morning, about which time the Storm abated; But as soon as Day-light appear'd, and the Serenity of the Weather had turn'd our Frightful Apprehensions into a little Alacrity, some of the Men, from *Aloft*, espi'd a Sail bearing after us with all Expedition; and being no great distance from the Coast of *Sally*,[23] a jealousie arose amongst our Officers, of her being a Man of War belonging to that Country, they having, upon the Conclusion of the late Peace with *France*,[24] Proclaim'd a War with *England*; so that we thought our selves now in as great Danger of being knock'd on the Head, or made Slaves, as we were before of being Drown'd. This Alarum kindled up amongst us new fears of approaching Danger, more Terrible than the former we had so happily surviv'd.

Command was given by our Captain, to prepare for a Fight; down Chests, up Hammocks, bring the small Arms upon the Quarter and every Man directed to his Post, by orders fix'd upon the *Mizzen-mast* in the *Steerage*; the *Bulkhead* and *Cabins* nock'd down, the *Deck* clear'd *Fore* and *Aft*, for every Man to have free access to his Business. When all things were in readiness to receive an Enemy, I took a walk on purpose to look about me, and was so animated with the Seamens Activity and Industry, together with the smell of Sweat, Match, and Gun-powder, that like 'Squire *Witherington* in *Chivie Chase*,[25] I could have Fought upon my Stumps. By this time our suppos'd Enemy was almost come up with us, under *English* Colours, but his keeping close upon our *Quarter*, and not bearing off, gave us still reasons to mistrust him; but seeing him a small Ship, and ours a Vessel of 400 Tuns, 28 Guns, and about 50 Men, we *Furl'd* our *Main-Sail* with all our Hands at once, as a stratagem to seem well Man'd; put our *Top-Sailes* aback, and lay by, to let 'em see we were *no more Afraid than Hurt*. We had on Board an *Irish-man* going over a Servant, who I suppose was *Kidnap'd*; I observ'd this Fellow, being quarter'd at a Gun, look'd as pale as a *Pickpocket* new taken: I ask'd him why he put on such a *Cowardly* look; and told him 'twas a shame for a Man to shew so much Fear in his Countenance. *Indeed Sir* (said he) *I cannot halp et, I love the bate of a Drum, the Pop of a Pistol, or the Bounch of a Mushket wall enough, but, by my Shoul, the Roaring of a Great Gun always makesh me start*. I ask'd him whose Servant he was. *By my Fait*, said he, *I cannot tell; I wash upon Change looking for a good Mashter, and a brave Gentleman came to me and ask'd who I wash; and I told him I wash myn nown shelf, and he gave me some good Wine and good Ale, and brought me on Board, and I have not sheen him sinch.*[26] By this time our Adversary was come within hearing, and upon our Hailing of him, prov'd a little Ship bound to *Guinea*, which put an end to our Fears, and made us fly to the *Punch-Bowl* with as much Joy as the *Mob* to a *Bonfire* upon a States *Holyday*.

After we had chas'd away the remembrance of our past Dangers, with a reviving draught of our Infallable Elixir, we began to be *Merry* as so many

Beggars (and indeed were before as *Poor*) beginning to turn that into Redicule, which so lately had chang'd our Jollitry into Fear and Sadness. When we had thus refresh'd our Bodies, and strengthen'd our Spirits, by passing round a Health to our Noble Selves, &c. 'twas thought high time by our Reverend Pastors, to return Thanks for our great Deliverance from the hands of our Enemies, tho' we had none near us, which was accordingly perform'd with all the Solemnity a parcel of *Merry Juvenal* Wags could compose themselves to observe.

By this time we were got into so warm a Latitude, that (God be thanked) a *Louse* would not live in it. We now began to thin our Dress, and, had not Decency forbid it, could have gladly gone Naked, as our first Parents. Kissing here grew out of Fashion; there's no joyning of Lips, but your Noses would drop Sweat in your Mouths. The Sea, and other Elements, began now to entertain us with Curiossities in Nature worth observing, as *Grampos, Sharks, Porpus, Flying-Fish, Albacores, Bonettas, Dolphin, Bottlenoses, Turtle, Blubber, Stingrays, Sea-Adders,* and the Devil and all of *Monsters* without Names, and some without Shape. As for Birds, *Noddys, Boobies, Shear-waters, Shags, Pitternells, Men of War, Tropick Birds, Pellicans,* &c. I shall not undertake here to describe these Creatures, because some of them are so Frightfully Ugly, that if any Friends Wife with Child should long for the Reading of my Book, it should chance to make her Miscarry. But that which I thought most worthy of Observation, were the *Clouds,* whose various Forms, and beautious Colours, were Inimitable by the Pencil of the greatest Artist in the Univers, *Cities, Palaces, Groves, Fields,* and *Gardens; Monuments, Castles, Armies, Bulls, Bears,* and *Dragons,* &c. as if the Air above us had been Frozen into a *Looking-Glass,* and shew'd us by Reflection, all the Rarities in Nature.

By this time we had gain'd the Tropick, and had come into a Trade-Wind; the greatest of our fears being now a *Calm,* which is fine weather to please fearful Tempers; but it brings us more in danger of being *Starv'd,* than a *Storm* does of being *Drown'd:* Tho' it was our Fortune in a few Days after, to make the *Leward-Islands,* and put us past the dread of so terrible a *Catastrophe,* those we pas'd in sight of were, *Deseado,* a rare place for a Bird-catcher to be Governour of, Birds being the only Creatures by which 'tis Inhabited; *Mountserat, Antego, Mevis,* possess'd by the *English; St. Christophers,* by half *English* half *French; Rodunda,* an uninhabitable high Rock. From amongst these *Caribbe* Islands,[27] in a few days, we got to *Hispaniola,* without any thing remarkable; and from thence, in 24 Hours, with a fresh Gail, within sight of *Jamaica,* which (without Malice or Partiallity) I shall proceed to give you some Account of.

A Character of JAMAICA

The Dunghill of the Universe, the Refuse of the whole Creation, the Clippings of the Elements, a shapeless pile of Rubbish confus'ly jumbl'd into an Emblem of the *Chaos*, neglected by Omnipotence when he form'd the World into its admirable Order. The Nursery of Heavens Judgments, where the Malignant Seeds of all Pestilence were first gather'd and scatter'd thro' the Regions of the Earth, to Punnish Mankind for their Offences. The Place where *Pandora* fill'd her Box, where *Vulcan* Forg'd *Joves* Thunder-bolts, and that *Phaeton*,[28] by his rash misguidance of the Sun, scorch'd into a Cinder. The Receptacle of Vagabonds, the Sanctuary of Bankrupts, and a Close-stool for the Purges of our Prisons. As Sickly as an Hospital, as Dangerous as the Plague, as Hot as Hell, and as Wicked as the Devil. Subject to Turnadoes, Hurricans, and Earthquakes, as if the Island, like the People, were troubled with the *Dry Belly-Ach*.

Of their Provisions

The chiefest of their Provisions is *Sea Turtle*, or *Toad in a shell*, stew'd in its own Gravy; its Lean is as White as a Green-sickness[29] Girl, its Fat of a Calves-turd Colour; and is excellently good to put a stranger into a Flux, and purge out part of those ill Humours it infallibly creates. The Belly is call'd *Caillipee*, the Back *Callipach*; and is serv'd up to the Table in its own Shell, instead of a Platter. They have *Guanas*,[30] *Hickeries*, and *Crabs*; the first being an Amphibeous *Serpent*, shap'd like a *Lizard*, but black and larger, the second a *Land-Tortoise*, the last needs no Description, but are as numerous as *Frogs* in *England*, and Borrough in the Ground like *Rabbets*, so that the whole *Island* may be justly call'd, *A Crab-Warren*. They are Fattest near the *Pallasadoes*, where they will make a Skelliton of a Corps in as little time as a *Tanner* will Flea a *Colt*, or a *Hound* after Hunting devour a *Shoulder of Mutton*. They have *Beef* without Fat, Lean *Mutton* without Gravy, and *Fowles* as dry as the Udder of an Old Woman, and as tough as a Stake from the haunches of a Superannuated *Car-Horse*.

Milk is so plenty you may buy it for Fifteen Pence a Quart; but Cream so very scarce, that a Firkin of Butter, of their own making, would be so costly a Jewel, that the Richest Man in the Island would be unable to purchase it. They value themselves greatly upon the sweetness of their Pork, which is indeed lushious, but as flabby as the Flesh of one just risen from a Flux, and ought to be forbid in all hot Countries (as amongst the *Jews*) for the prevention of *Leprosie*, *Scurvy*, and other Distempers, of which it is a great occasion.

There is very little Veal, and that Lean; for in *England* you may Nurse four

Children much cheaper than you can one *Calf* in *Jamaica*. They have course *Teal*, almost as big as *English Ducks*; and *Moscovy Ducks* as big as *Geese*; But as for their *Geese*, they may be all *Swans*, for I never see one in the Island.

There are sundry sorts of *Fish*, under *Indian* Names, without Scales, and of a *Serpentine Complection*; they Eate as dry as a *Shad*, and much stronger than stale *Herrings* or *Old Ling*; with Oyl'd *Butter* to the Sause as rank as *Goose-grease*, improv'd with the palatable Relish of a stinking *Anchove*.

They make a rare *Soop* they call *Pepper-pot*;[31] its an excellent Breakfast for a *Salamander*, or a good preparative for a *Mountebanks Agent*, who Eats Fire one day, that he may get better Victuals the next. Three Spoonfuls so Inflam'd my Mouth, that had I devour'd a Peck of *Horse-Radish*, and Drank after it a Gallon of *Brandy* and *Gunpowder*, (*Dives*[32] like) I could not have been more importunate for a Drop of Water to coole my Tongue.

They greatly abound in a Beautiful Fruit, call'd, a *Cussue*, not unlike an *Apple*, but longer; its soft and very Juicy, but so great an Acid, and of a Nature so Restringent, that by Eating of one, it drew up my Mouth like a *Hens Fundament*, and made my Palate as Rough, and Tongue as Sore as if I had been Gargling it with *Alum-Water*. From whence I conjecture, they are a much fitter Fruit to recover *Lost Maidenheads*, properly apply'd, than to be Eaten. Of *Water-Mellons* and *Mus-Mellons* they have plenty; the former is of as cold a quality as a *Coucumer*, and will dissolve in your *Mouth* like *Ice* in a hot *Frying-pan*, being as *Pleasant* to the *Eater* (and, I believe, as *Wholsom*) as a *Cup* of *Rock-Water* to a Man in a *Hectick Feavour*: The latter are large and lushious, but much too watery to be good.

Coco-Nuts, and *Physick-Nuts* are in great esteem amongst the Inhabitants; the former they reckon *Meat*, *Drink*, and *Cloth*, but the Eatable part is secur'd within so strong a Magazeen, that it requires a lusty *Carpenter*, well Arm'd with *Ax* and *Hand-saw*, to hew a passage to the *Kernel*, and when he has done, it will not recompence his Labour. The latter is as big as a *Filbert*, but (like the *Beautiful Woman* well Drest, and *Infectious*) if you venture to Tast, is of ill consequence: Their Shell is Black, and *Japan'd* by Nature, exceeding Art; the Kernel White, and extream Pleasant to the Palat, but of so powerful an Operation, that by taking two, my Guts were Swep as clean, as ever *Tom-T—d-man*[33] made a *Vault*, or any of the *Black Fraternity*[34] a *Chimney*.

They have *Oranges*, *Lemons*, *Limes*, and several other Fruits, as *Sharp* and *Crabbed* as themselves, not given them as a *Blessing*, but a *Curse*; for Eating so many sower things, Generates a *Corroding Slime* in the Bowels, and is one great occasion of that Fatal and Intolerable Distemper, *The Dry Belly-Ach*; which in a Fortnight, or Three Weeks, takes away the use of their Limbs, that they are forc'd to be led about by *Negro's*. A Man under this Misery, may be said to be the *Scutchion* of the *Island*, the Complection of the Patient being the *Field*, bearing *Or*, Charg'd with all the Emblems of Destruction, *proper*; supported by *Two Devils, Sable*; and *Death* the *Crest, Argent*.[35] Many other Fruits there are, that are neither worth Eating, Naming, or Describing: Some that are never Tasted but in a *Drouth*, and others in a *Famin*.

Of Port Royal

It is an Island distinct from the Main of *Jamaica*, tho' before the *Earthquake*,[36] it joyn'd by a Neck of Land to the *Palisadoes*, but was seperated by the violence of an Inundation (thro' God's Mercy) to prevent the Wickedness of their Metropolis defusing it self, by Communication, over all the Parts of the Country, and so call that Judgment upon the Whole, which fell more particularly upon the Sinfulest part.

From a Spaceous fine Built Town (according to Report) it is now reduc'd, by the encroachments of the Sea, to a little above a quarter of a Mile in Length, and about half so much the Breadth, having so few remains left of its former splendour, I could think no otherwise, but that every Travellour who had given its Description, made large use of his *License*. The Houses are low, little, and irregular; and if I compare the Best of their Streets in *Port Royal*, to the Fag-End of *Kent-street*, where the *Broom-men*[37] Live, I do them more than Justice.

About Ten a Clock in the Morning, their Nostrils are saluted with a *Land-Breeze*, which Blowing o'er the Island, searches the Bowels of the Mountains (being always crack'd and full of vents, by reason of excessive Heat) bringing along with it such *Sulphorous Vapours*, that I have fear'd the whole Island would have burst out into a Flaming *Aetna*,[38] or have stiffled us with Suffocating Fumes, like that of the melted Minerals and Brimstone.

In the Afternoon, about Four a Clock, they might have the refreshment of a *Sea-Breeze*, but suffering the *Negros* to carry all their *Nastiness* to *Windward* of the Town, that the Nauseous Effluvias which arise from their stinking Dunghills, are blown in upon them; thus what they might enjoy as a Blessing, they ingratefully pervert by their own ill management.

They have a Church 'tis true, but built rather like a *Market-House*; and when the *Flock* are in their *Pens*, and the *Pastor* Exalted to over-look his *Sheep*, I took a Survey around me, and saw more variety of *Scare-Crows* than ever was seen at the Feast of *Ugly-Faces*.

Every thing is very Dear, and an Ingenious or an Honest Man may meet with this Encouragement, To spend a Hundred Pounds before he shall get a Penny. *Medera-Wine* and *Bottle-Beer* are Fifteen Pence the Bottle; nasty *Clarrat*, half a Crown; *Rennish*, Five Shillings; and their best *Canary*, Ten Bits, or Six and Three Pence. They have this Pleasure in Drinking, That what they put into their Bellies, they may soon stroak out of their Fingers Ends; for instead of *Exonerating*[39] they *Fart*, and *Sweat* instead of *Pissing*.

Of the PEOPLE

The generality of the Men look as if they had just nock'd off their Fetters, and by an unexpected Providence, escap'd the danger of a near Misfortune, the dread of which, hath imprinted that in their *Looks*, which they can no more alter than an *Etheopian* can his *Colour*.

They are all *Colonels, Majors, Captains, Lieutenants*, and *Ensigns*,[40] the two last being held in such disdain, that they are look'd upon as a *Bungling Diver*[41] amongst a Gang of *Expert Pick-pockets*; *Pride* being their *Greatness*, and *Impudence* their *Virtue*.

They regard nothing but Money, and value not how they get it, there being no other Felicity to be enjoy'd but purely Riches. They are very Civil to Strangers who bring over considerable Effects; and will try a great many ways to Kill him farely, for the lucre of his Cargo: And many have been made Rich by such Wind-falls.

A Broken *Apothecary* will make there a Topping *Physician*; a *Barbers Prentice*, a good *Surgeon*; a *Bailiffs Follower*, a passable *Lawyer*; and an *English Knave*, a very *Honest Fellow*.

They have so great a veneration for *Religion*, That *Bibles* and *Common Prayer Books* are as good a Commodity amongst them, as *Muffs* and *Warming-pans*.

A little Reputation among the *Women*, goes a great way; and if their Actions be answerable to their Looks, they may vie *Wickedness* with the *Devil*: An *Impudent Air*, being the only *Charms* of their *Countenance*, and a *Lewd Carriage*, the *Studi'd Grace* of their *Deportment*. They are such who have been *Scandalous* in *England* to the utmost degre, either *Transported* by the *State*, or led by their *Vicious Inclinations*, where they may be *Wicked* without *Shame*, and *Whore* on without *Punishment*.

They are Stigmatiz'd with *Nick-Names*, which they bear, not with *Patience* only, but with *Pride*, as *Unconscionable Nan, Salt-Beef Peg, Buttock-de-Clink Jenny*, &c. *Swearing, Drinking*, and *Obscene Talk* are the principal Qualifications that render them acceptable to *Male Conversation*; and she that wants a perfection in these admirable acquirments, shall be as much Redicul'd for her *Modesty*, as a *Plain-dealing Man* amongst a Gang of *Knaves*, for his *Honesty*.

In short, *Virtue* is so *Despis'd*, and all sorts of *Vice Encourag'd*, by both *Sexes*, that the Town of *Port Royal* is the very *Sodom* of the Universe.

FINIS

A Speech Made by a Black of Guardaloupe

ANONYMOUS

(fl. 1709)

This anonymous pamphlet, appended to an anonymous open letter, provides one of the earliest purported representations of slave speech and point of view. Although it is likely to be the work of a white English writer, it may represent an actual experience of hearing a slave's funeral oration. In fact, many slave narratives of the late eighteenth and early nineteenth centuries were mediated through literate white editors and scribes.

In contrast to earlier attacks on slavery by the Quakers Richard Baxter (1673) and Morgan Godwyn (1680) and by the Behmenist Thomas Tryon (1684), the "Speech of the Black at Guardeloupe" (1709) offers one of the earliest examples of an anti-slavery tract not connected closely with dissenting Protestant theology. While its origins are likely to remain shrouded in mystery, the "Speech" still represents one of the earliest texts that purports to be from the point of view of an actual enslaved African, and, as such, it is an important step beyond Tryon's overtly fictional representation of "Sambo" in the dialogue in *Friendly Advice* (1684; included in this anthology). Guadeloupe (corrupted by the English to "Guardaloupe") is a French island in the Lesser Antilles.

FROM

A LETTER FROM A Merchant at Jamaica TO A Member
of Parliament in London, Touching the African Trade.
To which is added, A SPEECH made by a BLACK
of *Guardaloupe*, at the Funeral of a Fellow-Negro.
LONDON, Printed for *A. Baldwin*.
MDCCIX [1709]. Price 2 *d*.

A SPEECH made by a BLACK of *Guardaloupe*, at the Funeral of a Fellow-Negro.

The great and beneficent Creator, the Best of Beings, as Reason tells, and as our Master's Books assure us, when he had form'd this Speck of Earth, was pleased to crown the Work, by making Man, on whom he stamp'd the Image of Himself. All he expected in return, was but a just and grateful sense of the kind Maker's Bounty, and an honest Care to copy after the Divine Original in doing good; that is, in other words, promoting his own and others Happiness. The good and wise Maker had sufficiently furnish'd Man with Facultys necessary to so kind and glorious Design. He gave him the Powers of Perceiving, Deliberating, Judging: He implanted in him a strong Desire of preserving his own Being and Happiness, and gave him unexpressible Tenderness towards others. And as God made of the same common Mold all People, so whilst he subjected the inferior Animals to these little Vice-Roys, he left them all free to use and follow the Conduct of that Divine Ray of Reason, whereby they were shew'd and taught that reasonable Service which he requir'd. He made them, I say, free to follow this bright and faithful Guide, so soon as they should grow up to Man, and their Eyes were strong enough to bear the Light; that so the Creator might have the Glory of a free and chearful Service, and the Creature the Reward of Virtue, and an unconstrain'd Obedience. But, alas! how far has Mankind fallen? How much degenerated from the pure and happy State in which God created them? Sin introduc'd Sloth in some, Wantonness and Luxury in others. These were tempted to affect Command over, and Service from others; while those were again inclin'd to a base Submission and Dependence, rather than be at the Pains of exerting those Powers the wise Author of Nature had given them, which were abundantly sufficient to all the Purposes of Life; and so they, like the profane *Esau*,[1] whom we read of in our Master's Books, sold their Birth-right and Inheritance for a poor Mess of Pottage. Thus fond Mankind forsook the Divine Light plac'd in their Breasts, and by first becoming Servants to their own Lusts and Appetites, became Servants to each other. It had been well, comparatively speaking, had Matters stop'd here; for hitherto there is no Wrong, no Violence: Besides, the Infirmitys of Nature made it a necessary and even prudent Charity to serve their Neighbour in time of want, whose Assistance they again in their Turn might need and expect.

And if any set so little Value on the Gem of Liberty, as quite to part with it for a little Bread, which they might have reap'd and made with their own hands, they were to thank themselves for so foolish a Bargain, and had nothing to complain of but their want of Industry and Wit. But still this extended no farther than their own Consent had carry'd it; and the Agreement being mutual, they were no longer bound by it than their Masters perform'd their part, and treated them fairly. But the Lust of Dominion and the Desire of possessing, seizing Mens Brains, they grew fierce and raging, broke thro the Ties of Nature and Humanity; and upon slender, or only pretended Causes, made War upon their weaker and more innocent Neighbours. Hence in the Source of all our Woes and Miserys; to these we owe our Captivity and Bondage; to these we must lay the innocent Blood of our Brother who lies murder'd, barbarously murder'd, before us. Good God! what have we done? What Right have these cruel Men thus to oppress, insult, and inhumanly butcher their Fellow-Creatures? Let us examine all their Title, and see what it amounts to; and then we shall the better know, whether their Usage of us, or our Complaints, are the more just. They say, they bought us with their Money.—Confess'd; but who had power to sell? We were it may be condemn'd by colour of Law,[2] that is, the Will of some Great Man, to be sold by way of Banishment for some suppos'd Crime.—But how did the Buyer know there ever was a Crime committed, or that the Sentence was just? or if he did, what Right did this confer? 'Tis plain, I think, it gives him only Right to carry us whither he pleas'd, and make us work till we repaid him by our Labor what we cost, with other Charges.

It may be we were taken in War; what Right then had the Conqueror? or what did he transfer? Suppose the War against us was just, and that our Buyers knew 'twas so; yet they like-wise know, that 'tis barbarous and cruel to take a conquer'd Enemy's Life, when the Injur'd can be safe without it; and that 'tis still more barbarous and inhumane for another to take it away, to whom he has sold and deliver'd his Prisoner; since by the Sale and Price receiv'd he seems to have taken the Mony for his Security, and upon that Consideration runs the Hazard of the other's setting him at liberty if he thinks fit. So that 'tis plain, this gives them no such Right over our Lives, as any Man that has the least Tenderness or Humanity (I might, I think, say Justice) would make use of. And as for perpetual Slavery—it must be cruel Justice, that for so small a Sum, so soon repaid, wou'd purchase and exact what makes his Fellow-Creature, from whom he has nought to fear, so miserable for Life. If they contend for this as a Right which they are fond of, let them shew it, and let them take it and the sole Glory of it. But who told our present Lords the War was just? Do Victory and Right go always hand in hand? No, our Masters by Experience know they don't. This then at best can give but a dark doubtful Right, which never can defeat that natural and undoubted one the God of Nature has bestow'd on Men, to have, to own, no other Lord but *him*.

It may have happen'd we were sold to pay our Debts: What will this give them? In Equity they have at most hereby a Right to so much Service as will pay the Debt and Charges of transporting us. The first was all the Creditor could ask. But do they know what this Debt was? No, they never so much as once enquir'd or ask'd to be inform'd. We were perhaps bought of some unkind unnatural Father. Be it so. What have they got by this? Can a Father transfer what he has not? or have they what he neither did or cou'd possibly give them? surely no. A Father has Power indeed, and ought to help and feed his young and tender Off-spring, as all Creatures do, but not to cast them out into the Fields, or sell them wantonly to a base Servitude. God gave him Power to beget and become a Father of Men, not Slaves. A Father, as 'tis fit, has Power too to guide and steer his Childrens Actions while Reason's weak; and if by Age, or otherwise, he's brought to want their help, they are oblig'd by Nature, and by Gratitude, to give their helping hand and best Assistance. But still they are not his Slaves or lasting Property; for when wise Nature has fitted them to propagate and educate their Kind, Reason requires, and Nature loudly tells they are at Liberty, they then are Men. It's true, we seem oblig'd to our Lords, that they were pleas'd to take us off the Hands of cruel Conquerors, or such wanton and unnatural Parents as begot us only for their Pleasure; either of which might likely have destroy'd, if they cou'd not have sold us. But it wou'd be remember'd, no Benefit obliges further than the Intention. Was it then for our sakes, or for their own, our Masters built such mighty Ships in which they plow the Main? Was it for us they laid out so much Wealth? Or was it to save our Lives, they so much ventur'd and expos'd their own? Alas! the Answer is too obvious: Our hard Labour, and harder Fare, but most of all, our cruel Punishments, and perpetual Bondage, but too plainly shew for whose sake all this was done. But besides, 'tis certain many Wars are made, many Children parted with, only because there are so many Buyers. So that all we have to thank them for, is, that they sought to serve themselves; and doing so, they sav'd us from those first of Ills their Avarice had wrought. Further,

Many of us, it may be, are bought neither of the Governour or Conquerour, of Creditor or Parent; but of a treacherous Friend, a perfidious Husband, or an odious Man-stealer. These are far from conferring any Right, unless what can arise from the most unjust and inhuman Acts in the world. What's now become of all their boasted Right of absolute Dominion? It is fled. Where all our Obligations to perpetual Servitude? They are vanish'd. However, we may perhaps owe them something; and it were but just, if so, they should be paid. Let us therefore, if from the account I have already given we can, make an Estimate of the Ballance.—Supposing then one half of us were justly sold at first by those that had a Right to all our Services, if that may be suppos'd: Suppose likewise that our Masters knew it too, and who the very persons were: Then they would have at most a Right to the Labour of such Persons during Life; and of the rest, till they had earn'd and clear'd so much as was given to the Captain who brought 'em hither. But since it is impossible for them to know on whom to place their several Demands; and since they bought us all at random, without regard to Right or Wrong: let us for once suppose favourably for them, who never favour'd us; let us suppose our Masters innocent of all the Wrongs we first sustain'd. Suppose us Men, Women, and Children come to their Shoar from some far-off unknown Land, under the Power of a strange Captain of a Ship, who pretends he has a Right to sell us. He offers to deliver us, Great and Small, into their hands at 20 *l.* a-piece.[3] They pay the Mony. We are deliver'd up. What are we now in debt? 'Tis plain, I think, that since they neither know nor did regard his Title, they can at best have one but till they're reimburs'd the Cost and Charge which they've been at. 'Tis sure we had a plain and natural Right to Life and Liberty; which to take away upon a weak, presumptive, or a may-be Title, were to make us of less value than Beasts and Things Inanimate: a Property in which, by Reason's Law, is never gain'd against a true and just Owner upon slight Presumptions, whatever may be done by Laws of particular Societys, to which each one agrees. But were it otherwise in mere Possessions, yet Life and Liberty are hardly things of so low rate, that they're to pass as lightly from the Owner, to whom God gave the sole and certain Property, as Beasts, or Birds, or Things Inanimate, which bounteous Nature laid in common, and wherein strictly no Man has more Right than what is necessary for him and his Dependants.

Let any Man but make the Case his own, and he'l soon see the Hardship. Would not any one think himself greatly injur'd, if another should make him his perpetual Slave, only because he gave 20 *l.* for him, to one who had him in his power? Methinks the very naming it is enough to shock a Man; and he should need no further Argument to convince him of the Injustice of the thing. But Men are hardly brought to see what makes against their Interest. Taking the matter now to be as last stated—Suppose Twenty of us bought at once; the Mony paid would be 400 *l.* suppose six of the Twenty Children; suppose also one of us to die each year; reckon the Labour of each of those of sufficient Age at 10 *l.* a year, which is really less than it may be well accounted, seeing a great part of our poor Sustenance is owing to our own Hands and Industry, which we are forc'd to employ in planting Herbs and Roots, whilst we should rest from our more toilsome Labour. By this Computation we should have paid all our joint Debt in three years time. Yet would our Lords but use us as Men, we should not stick to a nice Computation, but frankly serve them three or four years more, before we claim'd our Freedom. Many of us here present have serv'd twice, some seven times the space our cruel Lords can justly claim. Of our hard Labour, let our weary'd limbs, their well-planted Fields and full Coffers all bear witness. Of their hard and cruel Usage let our torn Backs testify. Of their bloody Inhumanity, let the Corps[4] of our dear Countryman before us, weltring in its Goar; let it, I say, for ever witness against the cruel Authors of our Woe: who not content to make us Slaves, Slaves for Life, do use us worse than Dogs, and deny us the Compassion they would shew a Horse. 'Tis true, they willingly will teach and make us Christians; while they themselves want to be taught, both They and We are Men. In this however we are somewhat better used than are our wretched Friends in English Isles; where their hard Masters forbear to do good, lest that oblige them to do more. Ridiculous Superstition! that will not allow their servants to be Christians, lest they be forc'd to allow them to be Men. This is to found Dominion upon the Gospel of that Divine Teacher Jesus, who told them plain as Words could make it, his Kingdom was not of this World. And as if none were intitled to the common Privileges of Nature, except they please to allow 'em them by Washing or Baptizing, they carefully forbid our Brethren that. What I pray is this, but to make sport with the Creation, and to monopolize the Blessings of our common Mother Earth? Our hardy Tutors know things better. They teach us what themselves seem hardly to believe; and by giving us hopes of another better World, endeavour to make us content that they alone shou'd enjoy this: teach us to do Good for Evil; and when we have done no fault, to turn our Cheeks to the Smiter, and our Backs to the Scourger; to submit not only to froward and unjust, but even to merciless and cruel Masters; remembring us that their Gospel says, *Thro many Sufferings and Tribulations we must enter into the Heavenly Country*; that Country where our dear, our patient, our murder'd Brother's gone. But why shou'd we complain of Death, whose Life's so miserable to us? To kill us, seems the greatest kindness that our bloody Lords can do. We have lost our native Country, our Friends, our Liberty; we are made Slaves to haughty cruel Men; we are fed and work'd hard; their Will's our Law; which when we do transgress, we suffer all the wanton Cruelty they can devise: No Prayers or Tears can touch their harden'd Hearts relentless as Rocks, they know no pity. What now remains in Life to be desir'd? 'Tis better far to die, than, being Men, be forc'd to live like Beasts: Beasts! and of those the most unhappy too. Still, tho our Hardships are as great as the Injustice of our Oppressors; tho our Sufferings are as many as the hated Days we live; tho all their Pleas of Right are false or short: methinks I cou'd forgive them all, did they not pretend Necessity for their inhuman Acts. They tell, it seems, the *European* World, we're of such base, such brutal Natures, that nought will govern us, but downright Force and Fear; That like the Horse we must be broke and rid with Whip and Spur, but with far closer Reins. Abominable Forgery! Hated Imposture! What, are we not Men? Have we not the common Facultys and Passions with others? Why else has Nature given us human Shape and Speech? Whence is't that some of these wise rational Masters of ours give us sometimes Charge, not only of their Works and Cash, but of their Persons too; and make us judg when they're debauch'd enough in Wine, and when it's time to lug them home upon our servile Backs? Whence is it that some of us, without the Help of Books or Letters, are found able to deliver a Message, or do Business better, even by their own Confession, than they who instrust us with it? But were it a wonder, that while they use us so like Beasts, we shou'd not act as Men? If they give us no Motives to Industry and Obedience, but a base servile Fear, is it at all strange, when that's remov'd, the hated Service straight shou'd cease? It wou'd be strange indeed, shou'd it be otherwise. Cou'd they be brought to deal with us as Men, they soon wou'd see, we may be wrought upon by gentler Methods far than Blows and Scourges. But while they use us thus, how can they e're expect we shou'd not hate them? how can they hope our Services shou'd once proceed from Hearts they never touch'd, unless with Detestation? Let them make tryal of their own Countrymen, and see what will be the difference 'twixt them and us. As much Slaves as they are already, this likely will be all the odds, they'l hate them more, and bear their Usage worse than we. To finish and compleat our Miserys, these Lords of ours, not content that we are Slaves, Slaves basely us'd for Life, they make our innocent Babes their Property, as if they sprung from Brutes. If their Right to us be so uncertain or so small, as I have shew'd it is; with what Pretence, with what Face can they enslave our guiltless Children? who have committed nothing to deserve the loss of Liberty in a base servile tedious Life, a Life beneath the State of Brutes. Supposing we were justly theirs for

Life, which they can never shew; yet still, the most they can demand from In-
nocents is some small time of Labour, for the little Sustenance which they receiv'd by means of these our Lords. But not content with this, they carry on
the wrong, and make them Slaves for Life as they made us; and claim our
Childrens Children, and so on, to all Posterity. Thus, our Lords who call
themselves White-men and Christians, led by their Avarice and Luxury,
commit the blackest Crimes without a Blush, and wickedly subvert the Laws
of Nature, and the Order of Creation. Let us, my dearest Countrymen and
Fellow-sufferers! Let us in this our great Distress and Misery, look up to the
great Author of Nature, whose Works and Image are so basely us'd; and
earnestly implore his mighty Aid: Let us beseech him, for sure he hears the
Crys and Groans of his oppressed Creatures, either to soften those Adaman-
tine Hearts, which cut us in pieces; or to put it into the Minds of some great,
some God-like Men, to come to our Deliverance, that we may sing our
Maker's Praise, and with Assurance say, There is a God who governs the
Earth, and restrains the Pride and Cruelty of wicked Men.

FINIS

internal blackness is what really matters

The Speech of Moses Bon Sàam

ANONYMOUS

(fl. 1735)

An early abolitionist tract, "The Speech of Moses Bon Sàam" appeared first in Aaron Hill's periodical the *Prompter* on 10 January 1735. Versions of this text appeared almost immediately afterward in the January issues of both the *Gentleman's Magazine* and the *London Magazine*. A vitriolic reply entitled "The Speech of Caribéus" appeared in the *Gentleman's Magazine* in the following issue in February 1735. *The Speech of Campo-bell*, published a year after the appearance of Bon Sàam, purports to be a reply spoken by a freed African slave, but it is in fact the work of a white pro-slavery advocate named Robert Robertson. Robertson appended the *London Magazine*'s version of the "Speech of Moses Bon Sàam" to the 1736 printed edition of *Campo-bell*, which is the copy text for the "Speech" included here.

Virtually no clue exists as to the authorship or identity of Moses Bon Sàam. Readers are divided over the question of whether this speech is a fabrication by a British abolitionist or a genuine representation of an actual Maroon leader's arguments. In the *Prompter* (3 January 1735), the editor indicates the upcoming publication of Bon Sàam by saying:

> An Eminent Merchant has communicated to me, in a Letter which he lately received from an Island in that Part of the World I have been speaking of [i.e., the West Indies], the Speech of an Old *Free Negro*, who seems to have put himself in the Front of a Revolted Body of those People, who have fortified themselves in the Mountains, and made Head against the united Power of their Masters,—I shall publish it, in another Paper, for the Sake of some *Warnings* that may be drawn from the dangerous and unexpected Use, they are preparing to make, of *Arts*, and *Lessons*, which were *taught*'em, no Doubt, with a View to the *Profit*, of their *Masters*; and without the least Reflection on the Probability of their being, one Day, turn'd, against their Bosoms. (2)

The length of this chain of communicators (a speaker, a letter writer in Jamaica, the "Eminent Merchant," and the editor) suggests a fabrication.

Further, Robert Robertson, the author of *Campo-bell*, appears to have believed the speech to be a fabrication. In his letter to the editor of the *Gentleman's Magazine* (March 1741), he remarks,

> as nothing on the Subject has appeared since from the Author of Moses Bon Sàam's Speech, tho' he was told by Talbot Campo-bell to speak again if he had any Reply to make, I think there is Ground to conclude, that he rests satisfied with Campo-bell's Answers, tho' at the same Time I think his owning so much to the World cou'd have done him no Dishonour. (145)

On the other hand, Wylie Sypher supports the opposite view that Bon Sàam represents an actual Maroon leader: "the tradition of noble-Negro eloquence surely begins with Moses."[1]

If Bon Sàam is a fiction, his life story and name may have been suggested by the life of Job Ben Solomon (c. 1702–73), a learned West African who arrived in London in April 1733, having been purchased by General James Oglethorpe (the founder of Georgia and head of a House of Commons committee that investigated prison conditions in England). Ben Solomon translated Arabic manuscripts at the Bodleian Library at Oxford University and for Sir Hans Sloane in London, and was much feted by London society throughout the 1733–34 social season. His freedom was bought by subscription at Christmas 1733, and he sailed home to Africa in June 1734. Douglas Grant argues that Ben Solomon arrived in England at the "turning point in the relations between the black and white races."[2] Another antecedent may have been Francis Williams, a free black whose education at Cambridge was sponsored by the second duke of Montagu and whose Latin poetry (included in this anthology) is quoted, translated, and derided by Edward Long in his *History of Jamaica* (1774). Williams's life span is much in doubt, with birth year as early as 1697 and as late as 1712 and death date as early as 1762 and as late as 1774. In any case, enough of the story of Williams's extraordinary career may have been known to the author of "The Speech of Moses Bon Sàam" to suggest the character.

The Speech of *Moses Bon Sàam*, a Free Negro, to the revolted Slaves
in one of the most considerable Colonies of the *West Indies*
At the Head of those Revolted Slaves, who have betaken
themselves to the Mountains, in one of the most
considerable Colonies in the *West-Indies*.[3]
Taken from the London Magazine *for
the Month of* January, 1735, p. 13.

Dear Fellows in Arms, and Brothers in Adversity!
HAD your *Sufferings* been less painful, I might have enjoyed my own *Ease*, in
an Exemption from Danger. But in vain did my Courage once exerted, as you
have heard, in Defence of a *Master*, redeem me from the *Name* of a *Slave!* I
found no Blessing in Freedom; tormented with a livelier Sense of your
Groans, because no longer a *Partaker* of your Misery.

While I was, formerly, one of your Number, and but a Wretch, among
Wretches, I wanted *Sentiments* to reflect, with *Justness*, on the Wrongs we are
accustom'd to suffer. Whether ignorant of the *Bliss* of others, I *discern* not my
own *Misery*: Or, that the Part I was condemn'd to bear, in so general a
Calamity, had deaden'd in my Heart that *Pity*, which has been *awaken'd* by my
Change of Fortune. But, I have *since* been *taught* your Wretchedness, by sixteen Years of Liberty; not spent in *Ease* and *Luxury*, like the Lives of your
Oppressors; but in long, laborious Diligence in Pursuit of their *Arts*, and
Capacity; whereby to know, and make known, that only Education, and Accident, *not* Difference of *Genius*, have been the Cause of this provoking *Superi-
ority*, that bids the Pride of a *white* Man despise and trample on a *black* one.

What Preference, in the Name of that *mysterious God*, whom these Insulters of our *Colour* pretend to worship; what wild imaginary Superiority of Dignity has their pale sickly *Whiteness* to boast of, when compar'd with our
Majestick Glossiness! If there is Merit in *Delicacy*, we have *Skins* as soft as their
Velvets: If in *Manliness*, Consider your *Shape*, your *Strength*, and your *Movement!* Are they not all easier, firmer, and more graceful? Let a *white* Man expose his feeble Face to the *Winds*; let him climb Hills *against Rains*: Let him
go burn his uncover'd Temples in the Heat of High-Noon, as *we* do. Will he
bear it too, as *we* do? No: The Variations of his changeable *Countenance* will
make manifest the *Faintness* he was born to. He will be *sick*, and grow *pale*, and
red, by Turns: He will be *haggard*, *rough*, and *Sun-burnt*. Tho' terrible and
haughty to his Slaves, he will *lose* all Fierceness in his Eye, by the smallest
Struggle with those *Elements*, which *we* are *Proof* against the *Rage* of.

The whole *Advantage*, then, of these proud *Spoilers* of the *Works of God*, who dare make *Beasts* of human Forms, as noble and more manly than their own, in *what* consists it, but superior *Happiness*? They are not wiser by *Nature*, but more exercis'd in *Art*, than *we* are. They are not *braver*, but more *crafty*, and assist their Anger by *Discipline*. They have *Rules* and *Modes* in War; which actuate, as by one *Soul*, the most numerous *Bodies* of arm'd People. While *we*, depriv'd of such *Improvement*, and acting resolutely, but not dependently, *divide* and *lose* our Firmness. You saw the Representation of it, but last Week, in an Example, from this neighbouring *River*: As if the *God*, that animates your Purpose, had *commanded* it to *overflow*, for your Instruction and Warning! Observe, how narrow it looks at present: Yet, because it runs confin'd, *within* its *Banks*, hark! How *roaringly* it rushes down upon the Low-Lands of our Enemy! And with how steady and resistless a Torrent! The other Day, you saw it *broader*. For it rose among the Woods, and almost floated our *Savannah*. But, was it the *louder*, for such *Breadth*? Was it, then, *thus foaming* and *terrible*? Far from it; you can all remember, as I do, that it was then *flat*, *tame*, and *muddy*; and had neither *Violence* nor *Tendency*.

As soon as I became able to *read*, I discover'd, in the *holiest* of all Books, in the *Fountain* of white Men's Religion; I discover'd there, with a Mixture of Amazement and *prophetic* Joy, that the very Man, from whom they had deriv'd the *Name* they had given me, of *Moses*, had been the happy *Deliverer* of a *Nation*! Of a Nation *chosen* and *belov'd* by *God*! the Deliverer of this chosen Nation, from just such a *Slavery as ours*! Just so unfair, oppressive, and unnatural; and, in every Act and Circumstance, resembling that, which you and your Forefathers have *groan'd* under! Innumerable Thousands of his captive Countrymen were as darkly ignorant as *you* are: All unknowing their own Rights; and forc'd, like you, to *labour* for ungrateful, and merciless *Masters*: Till this first *Moses*, this great Giver of *my* Name, was called out by *Heaven*; and thro' a Course of miraculous Events, instructed in the *Arts* and *Learning* of those insolent *Enslavers*: That so he might be worthy, in the Fullness of *God's Time*, to stand out, *his Instrument*, for the Redemption of a *People*.

What now will our Task-masters pretend to object against the *Lawfulness* of our Revolt? If they say our *Forefathers were Slaves*: So were the Ancestors of those Heroes, whom *their Moses*, their almost worship'd *Moses*, deliver'd from Slavery. Will they urge, *that they have paid a Price*; *and, therefore, claim us as their Property*? Grant them the *Life* of a *first* unhappy Captive, to repay this Claim of his proud Purchaser. But did they also *buy* his *Race*? Must the *Children's Children* of this *Wretch's Children* be *begotten*, and *transmitted* to *Slavery*, because that single Wretch himself was unsuccessful in a Battle, and had been put to *Sale* instead of *Slaughter?*

Perish the provoking Image of so *shameless* a Pretension! Let them recollect, how soon the *Profits*, which they too well knew to *make*, from any one of our poor Father's *Toils*, repaid them for his barbarous Purchase. Let them *tell us*, (if they dare see *Truth*, in any Light that shews them not their *Interest*) whether all the *Pomp*, the *Pride*, the *Wantonness*, of that Prosperity we see them live in, is not the *Purchase* of *our* Sweat, *our* Tears, and *our* Distresses? And shall they derive their very *Luxury* from Wretches, to whom they grudge the *Bread* of Nourishment? Shall they *rejoice*, but by *our Affliction*, yet deny their *Pity* to our Agonies?

Indulge me, dear Friends! Your Permission, to *stop here* and *weep*. I know it is a *Weakness*: And it shall possess me but a Moment. I will recover my Voice as soon as I am *able*; and go on to *enumerate* your *Miseries!*

Alas! It is not *possible!* It is *too terrible* a Task! I have neither Patience nor Breath enough to *find Names* for your *Sorrows!* Wou'd to Heaven I cou'd as easily banish them from my Memory, as I can forbear to disgrace you by their Description! But *Fancy* will not suffer me to *forget* them. Imagination, officious to *torment* me, invades my *Sleep* with your *Shriekings*. My very Dreams are made *bloody* by your *Whips*. I am insulted by the *Scoffs*, the *Cruelties*, the grinding, biting, *Insolence*, which we train up our poor Children to the Taste of! Why rejoic'd we at their Birth, unhappy, innocent, *Bleeders?* Or, why do they *smile* in our *Faces*, since we intend them but for *Anguish* and *Agony?* Yet, they *know* we have *no Comfort* to *give* them. *Such* as is *ours*, they *inherit! Happier* Parents bequeath *Money*, and *Vanity*, and *Indolence*, to their Offspring. Alas! *these* are *Legacies*, for *Freemen! We* have nothing but our *Shame* to bestow on our Posterity: Nothing, but the *Shame* of our *Baseness*, who have lengthen'd out our *Slavery* to *out-last* even *Life*, by assigning them our Children, on whom to practice our *Tortures*. But I have *done* with the *Horrors* of *this Subject*: You have awaken'd me, by that lamentable *Howl*, into a *Repentance* that I touch'd you *too sensibly*. Let us think then no more upon what we *have suffer'd*. Let us resolve to *suffer no longer*.

In the *Fastnesses* of these *inaccessible Mountains*, and among Forests, so dark and impenetrable, we shall have *little* to *fear*, if we but continue on the *Defensive*. Here are *Savannahs* for Cattle; and *burnt Woods* for Corn: and as other things, which we *have not*, shall be wanted, there are so many Outlets and Descents, on every Side, for *Excursion*, that we can break down, unexpected, upon the scatter'd Plantations below us; and return with whatever we *wish*, from the *Store-houses* of our *Enemy*. Let us therefore repress *Malice* and *Cruelty*: Let us rather study to support our *new Liberty*, than *revenge* our *past Slavery*. While we *train* and *confirm* our Forces, by the Discipline and Exercise they are beginning to practice, we shall grow stronger, both by our *Skill*, and our *Numbers*: For all of our Colour, whose Hearts have not *whiten'd* themselves, in Terror of their imperious Torturers, will borrow Safety from the *Night*, and escape to us from every Quarter. Or, should such Opportunities be taken from them, by the Vigilance of their Masters, we can encourage, and draw them with us, as often as we make *Incursions*, thereby weakening at once our Enemy, and encreasing our own *Strength*, till our very *Numbers* shall have made us *invincible*.

I know there are some rash Spirits among us, who affirm that much *more* is *possible*: Perhaps it may be so, to our *Courage*; but it ought to be unattempted by our *Prudence*. For, even cou'd we extirpate our Enemies, and drive them out of the Island, it wou'd be found an unsurmountable Difficulty, *without Ships*, and unskill'd in *Navigation*, to maintain our Possession of the cultivated and *open* Coasts, against perpetual fresh Supplies, which wou'd be pour'd in, by their Fleets, for Recovery of *rich* Townships, and Settlements. Whereas, *here*, we shall have only their *Pride* to contend with: Their *Avarice* will not envy us our *Mountains*, where, yet, we have every *Art*, within ourselves, that can be necessary for our Support and Security. They *taught* us these *Arts*, for our *Misery*: But *God*, more just, and more merciful, has *turn'd* them to our *Benefit*.

I have shewn *Sulphur* and *Saltpetre* to your Captains, in several Places, upon our Hills. You have Hand-mills in every Company, for preparing your *Gun-powder*, that most precious of all your Possessions. You might every where find *Iron*; but that it abounds in your *Enemies Warehouses*. Having *Artists* too, who are *capable*, we might *forge* our own *Arms*, if so much trouble were necessary: But there is a *nearer* Way to obtain 'em. It is but to prevent the *Return* of those who shall *dare* to *invade* us, and the *Arms*, which *they bring* for our *Ruin*, will enlarge and perpetuate our *Protection*.

Let us understand then, and accept *God's Bounty*. Let us *divide*, and *appropriate*, the Highlands. Let us *plant*, and *possess*, for Posterity. Cultivating *Law*, too, as well as *Land*, let us, by submitting to *Government*, become too *generous* for *Slavery*. As often as the Enemy, from the *Coasts* of the Island, shall attempt to dislodge us from its *Centre*, let 'em find us too *strong* for their *Anger*: But if they content themselves with *their own*, and leave us in *Possession* of our *Lot*, let them acknowledge us *too kind* for their *Cruelty*. They must always *want* the *Cattle*, which we can never be depriv'd of, but in *Traffick*: And we may receive, in *Exchange*, a thousand Things, for our *Ease*; which it will be more for their Benefit to *sell* us, than provoke us to *conquer*.

Be of *Comfort* therefore, my Friends! and *hope all things from Patience*. Even *Time* that runs on encreasing, till it shall be *lost* in *Eternity*, forms its *Progress* but *slowly*. Tho' *Ages* appear *vast Spaces*, they have all been measur'd by *Moments*. Be not, therefore, *too hasty*. Content yourselves to be thought *weak*, for a *while*, till you have secur'd and deepen'd your *Foundation*. The Building will rise, *stronger*, more *broad*, and more *beautiful*. You have all heard talk of the *Dutch*; those Rivals in Riches and Power, to the most considerable Princes of the Earth! What were *these*, about a hundred Years past, but a Kind of *white Slaves*, to a Monarch, who *now* calls them his *Brothers*? Keep this inspiring *Example* in your *Eye*; and assure yourselves, that the proudest of your Enemies will *embrace* you, in spite of your *Colour*, when they foresee *Destruction* in your *Anger*; but *Ease* and *Security*, in your *Friendship*.

FINIS

FROM

The Speech of Mr. John Talbot Campo-bell

ROBERT ROBERTSON

(fl. 1730–40)

The *Speech of Mr. John Talbot Campo-bell* (1736), published a year after the appearance of "The Speech of Moses Bon Sàam" (included in this anthology), purports to be a reply spoken by a freed African slave but is in fact the work of a white pro-slavery advocate named Robert Robertson. The version of the "Speech of Moses Bon Sàam" printed in the *London Magazine* was appended to the 1736 printed edition of *Campo-bell*.

Although published anonymously, *The Speech of Campo-bell* can be confidently attributed to the Reverend Robert Robertson, of Nevis in the Leeward Islands. In a letter to the editor of the *Gentleman's Magazine*, dated 24 December 1740, an anonymous writer recounts his own writing career, acknowledging authorship of a series of political tracts along with *Campo-bell*. Further, the prominent pro-slavery polemicist James Tobin lists the works of Robertson, including *The Speech of Campo-bell*, in his 1785 counterattack on James Ramsay's abolitionist tracts.[1]

Beyond what can be gleaned from his published works, little is known about Robertson's life. The *English Short Title Catalogue* records his birth year as 1681 or 1682. In his 1740 letter to the *Gentleman's Magazine*, he says of Nevis, "I have lived here many Years" (145). This is the last published item attributed to him. He was for some years rector of Saint John's Church, Fig Tree Hill, Nevis, which in later years was the site of the baptism of Alexander Hamilton (January 1755), and of the marriage of Horatio Nelson to Frances Nesbit (March 1787). Much of his earlier argumentation in favor of the West India interest is distilled and placed in the mouth of Campo-bell.

As in the case of the character of Moses Bon Sàam (see chapter 6), Campo-bell's character may derive from the celebrated lives of Job Ben Solomon (c. 1702–73), the learned West African who spent some time in London in 1733 and 1734, and Francis Williams (c. 1697–c. 1774), the Cambridge University graduate and poet (see chapter 12).

The Speech of Mr. John Talbot Campo-bell is one of the most sophisticated defenses of slavery and of the West Indian plantocracy to come out of the eighteenth century. Along the way, it also argues for a distinct West Indian identity for both blacks and whites, while laying the responsibility for the slave trade on bankers and other monied interests in the imperial capital of London.[2]

THE SPEECH of Mr *John Talbot Campo-bell*,

A FREE CHRISTIAN-NEGRO,

TO HIS COUNTRYMEN in The Mountains of *Jamaica*.

In TWO PARTS. To which is subjoin'd the SPEECH

of *Moses Bon Sàam*, another Free Negro.

LONDON: Printed for J. ROBERTS, near the *Oxford-Arms*

in *Warwick-Lane*,

1736.[3]

PART I.

COUNTRYMEN,

IN a War between the Kings of *Congo* and *Angola*, my Father and all his Family, with above Three Hundred of our Neighbours, were taken Prisoners, in one Morning, by one of the Enemy's Parties. The *Slave*-Traders (sent from *Europe* under the Protection of the Nations to which they belong) lay gaping for us on the Coast, whither we were directly carried, and sold (as you know the Custom is in all our Countries) to those Traders by our Captors, or their Agents. Fifty of us, with about Two Hundred and Fifty more of (at least) ten different Nations in *Africa*, were clapp'd on board an *English* Ship, belonging to three or four eminent Merchants in *London*, one of whom, as I have since heard, was then Lord Mayor of that City. All the Men were immediately handcuff'd and shackled, Two and Two, and lodg'd in one Apartment; and the Women and Children in another. As we lay at Anchor, several Designs were formed to kill the Master and Sailors, and make our Escape; but they kept so good a Guard that nothing could be done. And indeed had we destroyed them all, our Condition would have been the same, or rather worse than it was; for we shou'd soon have been reduced by the other Ships that lay near us, and divided amongst them; or, supposing we cou'd have escap'd safe to Land, the *white* People on the Coast, or the *Negro*-Nation that inhabited there, would have made us Prisoners a second Time, and either restor'd us to the Factors of the former Purchasers on a Salvage, or sold us again to some of the other Ships; or if neither of these, they would have kept us for the next Market. Nothing was attempted till eight or nine Days after we had left the Coast; and then one of our stoutest Men having made a Shift to work off his Irons in the dark, he presently knock'd off the Irons of another, and in a little Time almost all of them got unfetter'd, when sallying forth, all of the sudden, on the Ship's Crew, they made towards the Chest of Arms, but in vain; however, what with the Irons they had knock'd off of themselves, and what with the other Implements they could pick up in the Ship, three or four of the Sailors were kill'd, and two toss'd over-board; and before the Insurrection could be quell'd, many of our Men were slain, and more wounded; and some that had been most active in the Fight, being afraid of Punishment, or perhaps disdaining to live, leapp'd into the Sea, and perish'd. I think we lost near Fifty in all. And happy was it for us that we did not gain the Victory, and kill the *Whites* to a Man, as (I suppose) is always done when our Countrymen get the better at Sea; for then we must have perish'd for want of Skill to navigate the Vessel. 'Tis true these Skirmishes happen but now and then, our Men either growing faint-hearted when out of Sight of Land, or else being so narrowly watched as to have no Opportunities of exerting themselves; but thus it was in the Ship that brought me hither, and thus it is too often in others, as these *Whites* know to their Cost. The Small-pox breaking out soon after, swept away about an Hundred more of us. On our Arrival here, the Supercargo, or the Factors of the *London* Merchants who own'd the Ship (I don't remember which) made Publication, that having imported from *Guinea* One hundred and fifty *Negro-Slaves*, Men, Women, and Children, the same wou'd be sold on such a Day to the best Bidders; and accordingly we were all brought ashore, and sold on that and the two following Days; and our Importers gave the Purchasers the same Title to us that our Conquerors in *Africa* had given to them, i.e. neither of them made any other Articles in our Behalf, than a Man who sells a Horse or a Cow in open Market usually does for those Brutes.

I was scarce seven Years old when I was thus sold, with my Father and Eight more of our Kindred and Acquaintance to a Planter up the Country, who taking a Liking to my Face, put me to School for two Years, and then had me baptiz'd. At first he gave me the Name of *John*, but at my Baptism *Talbot* was added to it, as having been the Sirname of my Mistress, and afterwards when I was confirm'd with my young Master by the Bishop of *London*, a Person of Quality then present (by whose Means I have receiv'd many Favours since) wondring and pleas'd to see one of our Colour at Confirmation, vouchsafed to honour me with the further Addition of *Campo-bell*. My Father soon grew weak and sickly, and did not live above three Years; his last Words were (speaking to me in our own Language, as he always did) *Not to forget my Mother-Tongue, but rather to study to improve in it*; for he seem'd to have a strong Apprehension, that I might, one Time or other, contribute to the bringing over some of our Countrymen to the Ways and Religion of the *English*, which was his Heart's Desire; and so punctual have I been in obeying his dying Command, that I can now speak three of the most current Languages in our Parts of *Africa*. Not many Months after his Death, my Master sent his eldest Son, who was about the same Age with me, to *England* for Education, when he was also pleas'd to pitch on me to wait on him, which I did first at a Grammar School in *Yorkshire*, and next at *Oxford*, where, and at *London*, he continu'd till his 21st Year, and then travell'd through *France*, *Holland*, and some other Places for near three Years. I had never been treated like a *Slave*, and in all our Studies and Travels the young Gentleman used me rather as a Companion than a Servant. In his 25th Year he return'd to this Island, when he was to have procur'd my Manumission in Form, but happen'd to be prevented by my old Master, who dying, alas! some Weeks before our Arrival, had not only left me my Freedom in his Will, but also a Dwelling-house, and two *Slaves* of my own Colour to wait upon me. I ought not to conceal that I was born a *Slave*, as all my Forefathers were time out of mind.

Whether the War in which I was made a Captive, was just or no, I was too young to judge; but I have heard my Father say, that, next to the brutal Fierceness and unbounded Avarice of the Two Kings, 'twas chiefly owing to the underhand Practices of the Emissaries of some of those from *Europe* who have Settlements on the *Guinea* Coast, or who come to Trade with our Countrymen there; which is not improbable, considering the Reason of those Settlements, and the Account on which these Merchants come, *viz.* to carry on the *Slave*-Trade; especially if to this it is added, that these Wars are always lasting, and, notwithstanding the savage Temper of our People, seldom bloody. But passing that, 'tis certain that many of yourselves, or of your Forefathers, were taken, and sold in the manner I was; for it is the Custom in our Countries, as some of you cannot but know, to kill the Captives that are not fit for Sale, *i.e.* such as no body will buy, and to sell the rest; and we must all acknowledge, that if our Side had prevail'd, we should have serv'd our Captives no better than we have been serv'd. Men, Women, and Children, are consider'd with us as the Growth or Manufacture of the Country, and are treated accordingly by their Owners, *i.e.* by their Princes, Masters, or Parents; and if at any time this is thought inconvenient, or not sufficient for the Purposes of Trade, the Prince and People of one Nation are easily persuaded to pick a Quarrel, and to go to Blows, with the Prince and People of another Nation, and then the Victors dispose of the Vanquish'd, just as the *white* People here dispose of their Sugar, Rum, and Molasses, to those that will give most for them. Some of you were *Slaves* in Africa, where Servitude, as you know, is propagated from Father to Son for ever, and where the Masters or Owners sell their *Slaves* to one another, or to Foreigners, on the same Condition on which themselves possess them. Among us, bare Suspicion in the Husband will justify him in selling his Wife for a *Slave*. A small matter of Theft will, in many of our Countries, condemn both the guilty Person and his whole Family to Servitude, or, if Purchasers cannot be found, to present Death: and there are many other Laws with us, the Violation whereof will have the same Effect, as you see some *Whites* are banish'd to this Place from *England*, for breaking the Laws of that Country. And tho' I trust there is nothing of it now, yet it might be prov'd from Letters and Depositions* not to be contested, that some of our Countrymen have been stollen or decoy'd from their Homes by some from *England*, who dealt in the *Slave*-Trade; I mean by those who were call'd *Interlopers*, for I have not heard that any from *England*, in the Service of Companies, have been accused of it. And I can assure you, the *stealing* of *Men* looks so black among all the Nations of *Europe*, that could it be legally prov'd on any of their People, no Punishment would be thought too severe for them: All the Difficulty lies in finding that Proof; which, no doubt, is one Reason why these *European* Nations have, in a manner, constantly carry'd on the *Slave*-Trade by exclusive Companies.

The *Portugueze* first began this Trade with us, in order to work their own and the *Spanish* Gold and Silver Mines in *America*. The *Dutch* next, observing what a precious Commodity *Negro-Slaves* soon became in the *West-Indies*, went heartily into it and pursued the Trade so close as quickly to be able to furnish the *Spaniards* and *Portugueze*, and all other *European* Nations that had got footing in *America*, with such *Slaves*, and at a cheaper Rate than any of them cou'd furnish themselves; and wou'd doubtless have done so much

---

*See a Book, intituled, *Reflections on the Constitution and Management of the Trade to Africa*, in Folio, Part II. *London*, printed by *J. Morphew*, 1709. [This book, by Charles Davenant (London: John Morphew, 1709), argues for the enforcement of the Royal African Company's monopoly of the slave trade to boost British power and share of trade. It includes: a four-page overview of British trade in Africa; a description of the "private war" existing between European companies on the African coast; extracts of reports of abuses by various traders in Africa; a number of charts detailing trade goods as well as numbers of Africans transported; slave ships' names and capacities; and an overview of debates in the House of Commons concerning the Royal African Company's monopoly status. The Navigation Acts were the means by which Britain sought to restrict British colonial trade to British shipping.]

longer than they did, had not the *English* Navigation-Act obstructed them.*
For till then, for One *English* there went Ten *Dutch* Ships to *Barbadoes*, and
the other *Sugar* Islands.

England (the Nation I am principally to speak of) has six *Sugar* Colonies
in the *West-Indies*, viz. *Jamaica, Barbadoes*, and the four *Leward Islands*; for
Anguilla, Tortola, and *Spanish*-Town, are scarce worth naming.⁴ *Barbadoes*
and the *Leward Islands* began to be settled by the *English* some time between
the Years 1620 and 1630, when *England* had no great Trade to the Coast of
Guinea, or not for *Slaves*; so that all the Labour in those Islands was, for near
the first Thirty Years (except that the *Dutch* imported some *Negro*-Slaves
among them) perform'd by *white* Servants from Home, and might have continu'd so to this Day with more Advantage, and less Difficulty, to *England*
than any other *European* Nations cou'd have supported their Colonies here
with Hands of their own. During the Civil Wars in *Great Britain*, many *white*
People of the better Sort went, or were sent, over to *Barbadoes* and the *Leward
Islands*; *Cromwell*'s Usurpation, the sore Defeats at *Dunbar* and *Worcester*, and
the Reduction of *Ireland*, made considerable Additions;⁵ and these, with the
vast Numbers that came, and were stocking over both to those Islands and
This, upon King *Charles*'s Restoration, wou'd soon have prov'd a Number
every Way sufficient to have maintain'd the Trade of all the *English Sugar*
Colonies, or at least have enabled them to outstrip any of their Neighbours or
Rivals in the *Sugar* Manufacture, *&c.* But a Notion happened then to prevail
at the Court of *England*, † (and Petitions and Representations were drawn in
to countenance it) That if the People were suffer'd to go to the *West-Indies* in
such Multitudes, the Nation wou'd lose more Hands than was fit for her to
spare. 'Twas not long before this appear'd to be a Mistake; for all the Hands
that came then, whether to the *Northern* or *Southern* Colonies of *England*,
were none of the best, and‡ such as otherwise must have starved at Home or

---

*See Sir *Josiah Child*'s New Discourse of Trade, p. 185. *London* printed 1693. [In this influential text—first published in 1668 as *A Discourse of Trade* (London: John Everingham,
1693)—Child argues that colonies relieve poverty at home and provide necessary raw materials,
countering the then-prevalent arguments that colonies drain England of necessary population
by suggesting that the English poor would be either hanged or starved if they did not emigrate,
and thus they would be lost to the economy anyway.]

†*Reflections on the Constitution, &c. of the Trade to* Africa, Part I. p. 5.

‡Sir *Josiah Child*'s New Discourse, p. 172. [Child's argument that keeping the poor from
emigrating to the plantations would help preserve the wealth of the kingdom is directed against
the contrary arguments set forth by Charles II's government. The discouragement of emigra-
tion in the 1660s and 1670s is identified by many apologists for slavery as a main cause of the rise
in demand for African slaves.]

fled to foreign *European* Countries for Bread or Shelter, as very many did at that Time to *Holland*, and elsewhere. The Truth is, *England* was then beginning to taste the Sweets of the *Sugar*-Trade, and look'd with a wishful Eye on the Gains that Others were making from the *Slave*-Trade, and therefore resolv'd to come in for a Share of it. This she did to some Purpose, notwithstanding the severe Blow *De Ruyter* gave her on the Coast of *Guinea*[6] in 1665,[*] when he destroy'd most of the *English* Factories, took *Cormantine*-Castle, *Tocorary*-Fort, and other Places on that Coast, and seiz'd, in Ships and Goods of their Company, to the Value of above 200,000 *l.* Sterling. This was soon got over by King *Charles* II; the then Duke of *York*, who understood Trade beyond any Man, condescended to be at the Head of this; and had it not been for the Odium of the Thing, which no single Nation coveted to ingross, *England* might have long enough ago been sole Mistress of the *Slave*-Trade. From that Moment it became impossible for the white Hands in the *English Sugar* Colonies, to carry on the *Sugar* Manufacture; the *white* Servants fail'd in a little Time, and no suitable Recruits coming from Home, the Masters were reduced to the Necessity, either of relinquishing the *Sugar* Manufacture, or of carrying it on with the *Slaves* their Mother Country brought to their Door from *Africa*. And to such a Height is the *English* Share of this Trade now arriv'd, that, beside the *Negro-Slaves* in the *North* Colonies of *Virginia*, *Maryland*, South *Carolina*, &c. and those that are or may be revolted in the *West-Indies*, their Number in the *Sugar* Islands is a good deal above 200,000[†], thus

In *Barbadoes*	—	—	70,000
Antego	—	—	23,000
Montserrat	—	—	7,000
Nevis	—	—	7,000
S. Christopher's		—	17,000
Anguilla, Tortola, and *Spanish*-Town			5,000
Jamaica		—	110,000
			239,000

And the Yearly Importation of *Slaves* from *Africa* into the same Islands (not including those that are re-exported on Account of the *Assiento* Contract,[7] or

[*]*Reflections on the Trade to* Africa, Part I. p. 6.

[†]See, *A Supplement to* the Detection of the State of the present *Sugar* Planters of *Barbadoes*, &c. p. 67. *London* printed 1733. [A continuation of Robertson's *Detection* (London: J. Wilford, 1732). The chart showing the numbers of slaves in each colony is copied exactly from this *Supplement*.]

otherwise) cannot be less than 15,000; to make up which Number there must, considering the many *Negroes* that die in the Passage, be upwards of 20,000 exported from *Africa*; and then as, by the common Computation, about two Fifths of the new-imported *Negroes* die in the *Seasoning*;[8] and as the *Decrease* of the *Negroes* in *Barbadoes*,* for Example (by which one may judge how it is in the other *Sugar* Colonies) requires an annual Supply of about 2800; and as *England* seems to have no Thought of carrying on her *Sugar* Manufacture by *white* Labourers, or by any other than the *Slaves* that are and have been brought from *Africa*; and lastly as *England*, in imitation of other *European* Nations, is bent on improving her *Sugar* Settlements in the *West-Indies*, it may be concluded, that this Importation of our Countrymen will rather increase than be diminish'd.

You have heard who they are that sell these *Slaves* in *Africa*, even our own Countrymen; I will now tell you who take them off their Hands. These are of three Sorts: First, the Traders, among whom I reckon those in *England* who fit out Ships, and send out Cargoes to *Guinea* to purchase these Slaves; all that are concern'd in raising or manufacturing the Goods in *England*, or that designedly import such Goods from *Holland*, or elsewhere, as are necessary to purchase them from our Countrymen on the Coast; together with all that are employ'd in navigating the Vessels necessary to carry on the Trade, or that have the Direction of it in *England*, or on the Coast of *Guinea*, or in the several Factories on the *English Sugar* Islands. The next are the *English Planters* and *Inhabitants* of these Islands, who settled here with no other View than to carry on their lawful Business, *viz.* the producing or manufacturing of *Sugar*, *Rum*, *Molasses*, *Cotton*, *Indigo*, *Aloes*, &c. in the Manner that Lands are cultivated, and Manufactures carried on in *England*, with Hands of their own Colour; and who in Fact did so, and would have gone on in the same Tract still, had they not been diverted from it as has been already said. The third is the *Nation*, to whom the Traders who buy us up in *Africa*, and the *white* Inhabitants of these *Sugar* Colonies who buy us again from them, do belong, *viz. England*. Now, when a Ship has clear'd at the Custom-house, and sets out from the Port of *London*, *Liverpool*, or *Bristol*, for the Coast of *Guinea*, to purchase a Loading of rational Creatures, *Men*, *Women*, and *Children*, who differ in nothing from the Purchasers but some unessential Matters—were a Ship thus qualified to be attack'd or molested in her Voyage thither, or from thence to the *British Sugar*-Islands, or from them in her Return home, by any that are not in a declar'd War with *England*, the Persons so attacking or molesting her

*See *The present State of the* British Sugar Colonies *consider'd*, 4 to. p. 23. *London* printed 1731.

would be deem'd Pyrates, or Enemies of Mankind, and be treated every where as such when taken: And were the Planters, to whom these *Slaves* are sold here, to refuse to pay the Purchase-money agreed on with their Importers or Venders, or not to pay it according to Agreement, the Law of *England* would compel Payment in the same manner that it compels other just Debts to be paid. From whence and much more that might be produced, it seems evident, that *England* admits and approves of this Trade in its several Branches.

What kind of People our Countrymen in *Africa* are, who first sell these *Slaves*, some of you have too much Cause to know, and all of you have heard; but I believe you are altogether ignorant of *England*, which promotes and protects this Traffic. Know then that *England* is, and has been, long divided into two grand Factions, *viz. Royalists* and *Republicans*; for to these all the Subdivisions, which are numerous enough, may be referr'd, as either leaning to, or retaining under, the one or the other. The first is for Kingly Government, which hath been tried in *England* for many Ages; the second for being govern'd by the People, or such a number of them as shall be chosen by the Whole to govern the Whole; and this was also tried in *England* for some Years about the Middle of the last Century. Now the former of these, if ask'd, will own, at first Hearing, that the making *Slaves* of our Fellow-creatures is abominable both before God and Man, and one of the Bishops of that Side, who was esteem'd a wise and honest Man, and well skill'd in Matters of Conscience, declares thus concerning it, "Lands, Houses, Cattle, and other like Possessions made for Man's Use, are the proper Subject-matter of Trade and Commerce, and so are fit to pass from Man to Man by Sales, and other Contracts. But that *Man*, a Creature of such *Excellency*, stamped with the *Image* of God, endow'd with a *reasonable Soul*, made capable of *Grace* and *Glory*, should *prostare in foro*,[9] become merchantable Ware, and be chaffer'd in the Markets and Fairs; I suppose had been a thing never heard of in the World to this Hour, had not the Overflowings of *Pride* and *Cruelty*, and *Covetousness*, wash'd out of the Hearts of Men the very Impressions both of *Religion* and *Humanity*."* 'Tis true he preach'd this before the Servitude of our Countrymen was established in the *British Sugar*-Colonies; and it is also true that since its Establishment here, which was about the Time of the Restoration of

*Bishop *Sanderson*'s 7th Sermon *ad Aulam*, preached *July*, 1638. [Robert Sanderson (1587–1663), *XXXIIII Sermons: XVI Ad Aulam. IIII Ad Clerum. VI Ad Magistratum. VIII Ad Populum* (London: R. Norton, 1657), 139. Sanderson was made Bishop of Lincoln at the Restoration. The quotation is from his seventh Sermon Ad Aulam ("of or against the court, or princely power"), preached at Greenwich, July 1638. The attack on slavery is one of the earliest such arguments made in print in English.]

Kingly Government in *England*, the Bishops seem to have avoided to speak of the Merits of the Case, whether at Court, or any where else. At the Revolution, when the latter Party had got, or conceited they had got, a good Interest in the Government, nothing was to be heard every where but *Liberty*, the *Law* of *Nature*, the *natural Rights of Mankind*, whereof *Liberty* is one, *which* ('tis said) *they might be robbed of, but could never forfeit*, and the like; and *the bringing any of the* Human Race *into* Slavery *was pronounc'd execrable.* Then, if ever, it was thought this Servitude of our Countrymen in these *Sugar* Colonies wou'd be look'd into, especially as the *Slave-*Trade began then to be better understood in *England* than it had been formerly; and indeed the Parliament took it several Times into Consideration (as I believe the Representation of the *Board of Trade*, relating to the Strength and Trade of the *British* Islands in *America*,* hath made it once more fall in their Way this very Year, 1735) that is to say, how it might be carried on most to national Advantage, whether by an exclusive Company with a Joint-Stock, or otherwise; but as to the Justice or Legality of the Trade itself, nothing has been hitherto done or said, or not that I have heard of. Nay one of these *Republicans* (and he no small Man of the Party)† gives it as his Opinion, and has writ a Treatise to prove it,

---

*Dated at *Whitehall, January* 14. 1734 – 5, and on the 18th· of *February*, ordered by the *House* of *Lords* to be printed. *Representation from the Commissioners for Trade and Plantations,* London, 1734. [This report records the populations of the various colonies, separated by color and status as free or enslaved. The report also provides a summary of the British holdings at the time of the publication of the *Speech of Campo-bell*: " . . . our Island Colonies in America, namely, Jamaica, Barbadoes, the Leeward Islands, the Bahama's and the Bermuda or Summer Islands, of which the Three first mentioned are called Sugar Colonies, and are of great Importance to the Trade and Navigation of this Kingdom (5) . . . the Territories which compose His Majesty's Government of the Leeward Islands, are, Antigua, St. Christopher's, Nevis, and Mountserrat, with their Dependencies; Barbouda, and Anguilla, Spanish Town, Tortola, and the rest of the Virgin Islands" (9).]

†See the 2d· Discourse of Mr *Andrew Fletcher*, of *Salton*, on the Affairs of *Scotland, Edinburgh*, printed 1698, and *London*, re-printed 1732, *pag.* 134. In which, among other Things remarkable enough, he blames the Clergy for the Share they had in the *Abolition* of *Slavery*, when *Christianity* was first publickly established under *Constantine* the *Great*. And yet he is not so singular in his Notions as some imagined, when that Discourse was first publish'd; for the Baron *Puffendorf* (from whom I guess Mr Fletcher had his Notion) says, that "Some have thought, and not altogether without Reason, that the *Prohibition* of *Slavery* amongst *Christians,* hath chiefly occasion'd that Flood of thieving Vagrants, and sturdy Beggars, which is usually complain'd of." *De Leg. Nat.* & *Gent. lib. VI. cap. iii. Sect.* 10. of Dr *Kennet's* Translation. And as to Captives in War, *Scipio Gentilis* (in Ep. ad *Philem.* Sect. 43) says, "Perhaps it would not be unprofitable if a complete and just slavery is restored today in the wars which Christians wage among themselves: not so many captive soldiers—especially from the lower ranks—would be slain, the price of ransoming them having been despaired of, and the law of the ancients that

that Slaves *are necessary in a well regulated Government.* But to do his Party Justice, I have not heard that any other of them (unless I should except One) ever avow'd such Doctrine.* So far from it, another of good Credit, whom I take to lean that Way, assures us,[†] *that whatever Notions prevail among* Christians *that encourage* Slavery, *or that are not strictly agreeable to* Liberty, *are not* Christian *Notions, but the Mistakes of* Christians. And I think it hath been argued before the Lord Chief Justice of *England*, without Offence, that *it is against the Law of* Nature *for one Man to be a Slave to another,* and *that* Christianity *and* Slavery *are inconsistent;* with more to the same Purpose.[‡]

You will ask then, If all, both *Royalists* and *Republicans,* are Enemies to *Slavery, how comes* England *to protect and encourage the* Slave-*Trade?* I will explain that by and by; but first I must observe, that there are several other Nations of *Europe*, and some of them the very chief that profess *Christianity*, who have, as Matters are order'd in their *American* Settlements, as pressing Occasion for such *Slaves* as *England*, or rather much more. . . .

One Thing more may be worth observing before I answer your Question, and that is, that there is something in *England*, if consider'd as she loves to stand compar'd to other Nations in *Europe*, whether *Popish* or *Protestant* (unless *Holland* shou'd be excepted[§]) that may make her being concern'd in this

---

allowed chattel slavery having been abolished" [Latin in original; my translation]. ["Fletcher": *The Political Works of Andrew Fletcher, Esq* (London: A. Bettesworth, C. Hitch, and J. Clarke, 1732). Fletcher's complaint about the role of Christianity in the suppression of slavery in the later Roman Empire and the early medieval period begins on page 133. "Puffendorf": Freiherr Samuel von Pufendorf (1632–94), *De jure natur et gentium* (Of the Law of Nature and Nations), 2d ed. (Oxford: L. Lichfield, 1710). Robertson's quotation comes from the section headed "The Inconveniences necessarily attending Servitude." The section actually emphasizes the duties of the master, particularly the obligation of the master to provide "perpetual Certainty of Maintenance" in exchange for "perpetual Obligation" to labor. In practice, many West Indian planters manumitted old or infirm slaves rather than be obligated to care for them, a practice sharply criticized by "ameliorationists" (those antiabolitionists who nevertheless agitated for improved conditions) and exploited by abolitionists. Pufendorf's arguments would tend to work in favor of the ameliorationist argument that abolition would result in heartless abandonment of the black population. "Scipio Gentilis": Scipio Gentili (1563–1616) published many editions and commentaries upon the classics, but this citation remains untraced.]

*The *Author* of the *Fable* of the Bees. [Bernard Mandeville (1670–1733), *The Fable of the Bees: Or, Private Vices Publick Benefits* (London: J. Roberts, 1714).]

[†] *Present State of the* Republic *of* Letters, *for* September, 1729, *Vol. IV. pag.* 186.

[‡] *Modern Reports*, Part V. *pag.* 182 to 191. In the *Savoy*, printed 1711.

[§] *England* and *Holland* are now, almost the only *Assertors* of *Liberty.* Davenant's Discourses on the Publick Revenues, Part II. p. 148. [Charles Davenant, *Discourses on the Publick Revenues, and on the Trade of England* (London: James Knapton, 1698). Part 2 is titled "On the Protection and Care of Trade."]

Slave-Trade more taken Notice of than their being concern'd in it. You must have heard that the *Spirit* of *Liberty* (as it is call'd) runs high in *England*: Among the Populace, *Liberty* is the Cry Morning, Noon, and Night; and nothing is more common, even among some of high Rank there, than to brand the Subjects of *Spain*, *France*, *Denmark*, and other Countries with the opprobrious Name of *Slaves*. Nay, a good Writer of theirs says, *We in* England *shou'd, with the last Drop of Blood, defend this almost only Spot of Ground* [England] *which seems remaining in the World to Publick Liberty.** And another, little inferior to him in Fame, will not so much as except even *Holland*, but says of his own Country, "Besides our other Felicities we have one Thing more to boast of, and that is, of being *Freemen* and not *Slaves*, in this unhappy Age, when an universal Deluge of Tyranny has overspread the Face of the whole Earth; so that this [*England*] is the Ark out of which of the Dove [*Liberty*] be sent forth, she will find no Resting-Place till her Return."† Every Nation, 'tis true, has a dark Side as well as a bright, and this high Opinion of Themselves, and base Opinion of Others, is the Foible of the *English*; and a costly Foible it has been, as having too often made them the Dupes of knavish Craftsmen. But however, since they are certainly one of the freest People in the World, since *Liberty* is so much their *Darling*, and *Slavery* so much their *Dread*, your Question (if one may say so of a Question *which puts a Man in Pain when he goes to answer it*) is doubtless pertinent and just, What makes Men of such a Complexion join with Countries whom they call *Slavish* and *Tyrannical*, in making our Countrymen Slaves? or, admitting them to have done it at first incautiously, What has hinder'd them, for above Seventy Years together, from contriving a Retreat, or so much as once offering at some Project or Expedient of a Cure? To fall into Error is consistent enough with Humanity, but to persist in it after Conviction, or to shun the Means of Conviction, is not so. Possibly you may be tempted to think, that they mean none but *Themselves*, and the other *Whites*, shou'd be free, and that of *all our Colour* are born to be *Slaves*. I assure you, they have no such meaning—But, by what hath been said

---

**Davenant's* Essay *on* Ways *and* Means, p. 4. [Charles Davenant, *An Essay upon Ways and Means Of Supplying the War* (London: Jacob Tonson, 1695). Robertson alters the quotation slightly, but preserves the sense of it (his paraphrase is indicated by his use of italics here rather than quotation marks). "The War" in the title is known variously as King William's War, the War of League of Augsburg, and the Nine Years' War (1688–97).]

†Mr *Walter Moyle*, in his *Argument against a Standing Army*, printed in the Year 1697, near the beginning. [Walter Moyle, *An Argument, Shewing, that a Standing Army Is inconsistent with a Free Government, and absolutely destructive to the Constitution of the English Monarchy* (London, 1697), 2. Robertson paraphrases Moyle, but preserves the sense of the passage.]

of the other Nations of *Europe* that possess *Negro-Slaves*, you see all of them are deep, and some of them deeper in this Trade than *England*: Now, shou'd *England*, or any of those other Nations boggle at it, or fancy something iniquitous or wicked in it, and thereupon let drop their Share in this *Slave*-Trade, their Share of the Profits arising from it wou'd presently be lost,* and (which must wound deeper) some other Nation or Nations of Consciences not so strait-lac'd wou'd presently gain the Whole, which wou'd destroy that general Balance of Trade (and, by Consequence, of Power) which wise Men think ought to be maintain'd in the World. If this be the Truth and the whole Truth, it is idle in our Countryman *Moses Bon Sàam* to ask [the *white* People in the *West-Indies*, or (which might have made the Question less impertinent) the People of *England, France, Spain, Denmark, Portugal,* and *Holland*] *What wild imaginary Superiority of Dignity has the pale, sickly* Whiteness *of these Insulters of our* Colour *to boast of, when compar'd with our* Majestick Glossiness? This, and all the rest of his Rhetoric to the same Purpose, will go for nothing with the *Dealers* in *Slaves*; but cou'd *Moses Bon Sàam*, or any other, instruct them how to get a Penny more by quitting the *Slave*-Trade than they do by continuing it, I dare answer for the *English*, every Man, Woman, and Child of us, might be set at Liberty to-morrow; nay I doubt not but *England*, which sent Ships and Men to buy you, or your Fathers in *Guinea*, that you might labour in her *Sugar* Manufacture here, wou'd with equal Ardour, and a much better Heart, send Ships and Men to carry you from hence, and set you down where you were taken up. A Happiness, which none of you needs to covet! For if our Countrymen who rule there (as all of you, that were of Age at your coming from *Guinea*, know very well) cou'd find none to sell you to again, instant Death would be your Portion!—But I see you have got somewhat to eat; I will stop a while, and take a Bit with you—

PART II.

HAVING explain'd some Things which you seem to have been in the dark about, and which, however, ought to be well consider'd before you determine what is to be done at present; I am next to put you in Mind, that when *England* took this Island from *Spain*, near upon Eighty Years ago, the few *Spanish Negro-Slaves* that their Masters cou'd not carry off with them, and that would not come in to the Conqueror, betook themselves to these Mountains, where they continu'd for many Years little observ'd or regarded. But the *English* who

---

*Whatever Business *England* quits, *other Nations* will take up, and from our *Spoils* not only be *Richer,* but much *Stronger. Davenant* on the Publick Revenues, Part II. p. 66.

sat down here, being quickly furnish'd by their Countrymen in *England* with incredible Numbers of our Countrymen from *Guinea*, to work in the *Sugar* Manufacture; as soon as the *Negro-Slaves* then imported understood that some of their Colour and Country had taken Refuge in the Mountains, and lay pretty safe from the Power of the *Whites*, not a few of them (as has been the Practice ever since) came, either out of Affection, or Curiosity, to spend a Day or Two with their Countrymen here; and as often as any such came up hither, you know they were not suffer'd to go down again. Besides these, all of them that had been forced from their Native Country by the Frauds and Villanies of their own Countrymen there, or that had been spirited from thence by the *white* Christian Traders on the Coast; all that were, or that thought themselves cruelly used, by their Masters below; all that had been guilty of Murders, Rapes, Poisoning, Robberies, Burglaries, or any other Crimes for which the Laws have decreed Corporal Punishment, or Death; all that had absented from, or neglected, their Work, and feared to be corrected for it; all that had lived at Ease in their own Countries, and were either harden'd in Idleness, or too proud and stubborn to stoop to Labour; all these, I say, have been flocking hither, for the last Sixty or Seventy Years; and not content to come themselves, have constantly withdrawn as many of the stupid or more ignorant *Slaves* as they cou'd prevail on to bear them Company. I perceive you may be reckon'd into Two Classes chiefly; first the Descendants of the *Spanish Negroes*, and of those who came or fled hither first from below; and next, the *Salt-Water Negroes*, *i.e.* such as have been lately imported from *Guinea*; but in all my Visits here, I have seen very few *Creole Negroes*, i.e. such as were born among the *Whites* in this Colony; but few as they are, they are Monsters in Wickedness, Devils incarnate, Murderers, Ravishers, Robbers, such as have willfully set Fire to Houses, or to the growing *Sugar* Canes; and these being cunninger than you, and well acquainted in every Creek and Corner of the Island, lead you forth in all your Sallies on the *Whites*, and have assum'd the ruling and ordering of you in all other Matters. I need not say what worse than brutal Rulers they are, how they lie with your Wives, and ravish your Daughters before your Eyes, and how in their Wrath, or their Rum, they will plunge their Knives in your Bosoms or Bellies. Nor shou'd I have mention'd them at all, if you had not assur'd me that they are all gone with some of your own People to lay out a new Settlement on a distant Mountain; for it wou'd not have been in your Power to hinder them from cutting me to Pieces. You see then, my Countrymen, what a woful Situation you are now in: I am well acquainted with the Gentleman who governs this Island, and with most of the *white* Inhabitants of Note, and can assure you from them, that you will all be forgiven on your Submission, and treated in much the same Manner as the *Negroes* are who have continu'd in their Obedience. To be return'd to *Africa* you will not desire, for the Reason I just now gave; and if the good People of *England* shou'd dislike your being replac'd in a State of Servitude here, I can only say, that then the Safety of this Island will not suffer you to remain upon it; and then I shall humbly propose, that you may be all sent forthwith, or as soon as Transports can be provided, to *England*. Hands, well employ'd, are said to be the Riches of a Place; and sure you may be trained up as easily to the Plough, feeding of Cattle, carding and spinning of Wool, beating of Hemp, or the like, as the *Negro-Slaves* here are to the *Sugar* Manufacture; and as I know you would gladly work the first seven or fourteen Years for bare Food and Raiment, your Labour wou'd, without doubt, over-balance both that, and the Charges of transporting you thither. But to be plain, the *English* Laws, here and every where else, are such, that Ravishers, willful Murderers, *&c.* are uncapable of being pardon'd; and I hope you do not think they deserve to live: 'Twill be in vain therefore to speak to the Governor in their behalf: They are but a Handful in respect of you; seize the Monsters, and deliver them up to Justice, which will make your own Submission the more readily accepted. This I have said in the Absence of these consummate Villains; but were they now present I would desire to speak to them and you both, as follows.

Countrymen: You are now enrag'd at the *white* People of this Island, whom *Moses Bon Sàam* calls *your Enemies*, your *Oppressors, ungrateful and merciless Masters, insolent Enslavers, imperious Torturers, Insulters of our Colour, and proud Spoilers of the Work of* God, *who dare make Beasts of Human Forms.* How true this is, none can better judge than yourselves. That some *Whites* in these *Sugar* Colonies have treated some of our Colour basely and barbarously, is as certain, as that some Mothers in *England* destroy their Babes, or that some Children there starve or murder their Parents, or that some *Englishmen* once murder'd their King, or that *Woolston* (a Clergyman!) turn'd Infidel,[10] or that too many of their 'Squires, and Others, turn Profligates, and ruin their Estates. But sure the Laws of the *British Sugar* Colonies are express against such Cruelty,* as express as in any of the other *European*

---

*See, *An* Abridgment *of the Laws of the* Plantations, *London* printed for *J. Nicholson,* &c. 1704. At p. 147, If any *Slave* by Punishment from his Owner from running away, or other Offence, suffer in Life or Limb, none shall be liable to the Law for the same; but whoever shall kill a *Slave* out of Willfulness, Wantonness, or Bloodymindedness, shall suffer three Months Imprisonment, and pay Fifty Pound to the Owner of the *Slave*. If the Party so offending be a Servant, he or she, shall have on the bare Back thirty nine Lashes, and also (after the Expiration of the Term with his or her Master, or Mistress) shall serve the Owner of the deceas'd *Slave* the

Colonies in the *West-Indies*; and if *England*, which makes Laws at *Will* for her Colonies in other Matters, does not think them express and severe enough, they may be made what she pleases. As to Facts, I have not known or heard in the last thirty Years, that any of these *Whites* have willfully or wantonly taken away the Life of any one *Slave*, or that (notwithstanding the many Thousands that are here, and their frequent Offences) above three or four single *Slaves* have in all that Time died under Correction, or soon after it. Most of the Instances handed about in *England*, will be found, upon Examination, to be false, or unfairly represented, or misunderstood; and the Gentlemen there who talk so much, and with such Positiveness, of the Cruelty of the Masters to their *Slaves* here, ought certainly to have descended to Particulars, and nam'd their Vouchers, which since none of them are so candid as to do, the impartial Part of Mankind will judge accordingly. The Truth is, these Masters in general run into the other Extreme, and are rather criminally merciful: If one steals a Cow, a Sheep, or a Hog in *England*, or breaks into a House, or robs on the Highway, he will be hang'd for it; but when a *Slave* commits any the like Offence here, as he can in no Case be condemn'd without due Proof before two Justices of the Peace, and three sufficient Freeholders of the Neighbourhood (which is the Rule in trying *Slaves* in these *Sugar* Colonies)* so the common Way is to compound the Matter with the Party injur'd, and to let the *Slave* escape with a Whipping; and he wou'd be look'd on as an unsufferable Neighbour here, who shou'd have Recourse to a Magistrate in any Case where Compensation is ready to be made to him. A *Negroe-Slave* about twenty Years old, and born in my own House (the Cloaths on whose Back are seldom

---

full Term of four Years. And p. 243. If a Master shall of Wantonness, or Cruelty, willfully kill his own *Slave*, he shall pay to the Publick Treasury 15 *l*. Sterling; if he kill another Man's, he shall pay double the Value to the Owner, and 25 *l*. Sterling to the Publick Treasury, and be bound to good behaviour during the Governor's Pleasure. ["Abridgment": *An Abridgment of the Laws In Force and Use in Her Majesty's Plantations* (London: John Nicholson, 1704). Although Robertson quotes nearly verbatim from this source, he mixes citations from the laws of Jamaica and Barbados without signaling the change other than by noting the page numbers.]

*On complaint of any heinous and grievous Crime committed by any *Slaves*, as [Murders, Rapes] Burglary, Robbery, burning of Houses [or Canes] killing or stealing of Cattel, &c. the Justices shall issue out their Warrants, and upon probable Proof, the Offender shall be committed or bailed as the Case shall require. And two Justices shall issue their Summons to three sufficient Freeholders, appointing a Day and Place, when and where the said Justices, and the three Freeholders, shall hear the Matter, and if upon Evidence the Party appears guilty, they shall give Sentence of Death, or such other Punishment as the Crime by Law deserves, and by their Warrant cause immediate Execution to be done.—If any Crime that deserves Death be committed by more than one *Negroe*, one of the Criminals only shall suffer Death, as exemplary. *See* Ibid. p. 146. [Robertson's brackets. Ed.]

worth less than 30 *s.* who can say the whole Church Catechism, and other Things that way, and who has been so taught in House-Service as to be richly worth 60 *l.* Sterling) being sent by her Mistress, last Week, to ask after the Health of a *white* Woman in the Neighbourhood who lies bed-rid, and almost blind; this wicked *Slave,* finding no Body in the House with the poor Woman, robb'd her of 18 *s.* which was all the Money she had: The News coming soon to my Ears, I sent my Wife with 28 *s.* to the poor old Woman, promis'd to correct the *Slave* severely (as indeed I did) and so the Thing was hush'd. And about a Fortnight ago, three Field-*Slaves* of one of my Neighbours breaking into my House by Night, took from thence two Pieces of Bag Holland, three Pieces of stamp'd Linnen, and some Shoes and Stockings; some whereof were found on them the next Day; but my Neighbour offering to make full Satisfaction, I ask'd nothing more but that the Thieves shou'd be soundly whipp'd, which was done to such Purpose, that if *Moses Bon Sàam* had been present, their *Shrieks* and *Howls,* which were loud and *lamentable* enough, cou'd not but have touch'd him to the Quick. This Conduct must appear odd to Strangers, but the Reason of it is substantial; for were the Rigour of the Law to take Place, a Plantation of 100 *Slaves* wou'd in a few Years be reduc'd to 50, and that 50 in a few more to 25, and then farewell the *British Sugar* Manufacture. You know that when you lived with your Masters you were duly provided with *Apparel* suitable to this warm Climate,* and with *Food* fit to support you in their Service;† or if any of them did not so provide for you, they were (as in other Cases) Exceptions from the General Rule, and became obnoxious to the Law. Is it not undeniably their Interest to use their *Slaves* well? Can the *Sugar Colonies* (as Things are order'd) *possibly subsist without Slaves,* or *Slaves* without necessary Food and Raiment?‡ Hath not *England* render'd them the prime Materials for carrying on her *Sugar* Manufacture, and as necessary to the Planter here, as Horses or Oxen are to the Husbandman there? And as none but a Brute, or Booby of a Husbandman, will use those dumb Creatures ill, or with-hold fit and necessary Provender from them, he wou'd

---

*All *Slaves* shall have Cloaths once every Year, *viz.* Drawers and Caps for Men, and Petticoats and Caps for Women, upon Pain of forfeiting 5 *s.* for every *Slave* not so cloathed, *ib.* 240.

†All Owners of Plantations shall have at all Times one Acre of Ground well planted with Provisions for every five *Negroes,* and so proportionably, under the Penalty of 40 *s.* for every Acre wanting, *ibid. p.* 147. See also, *A* Letter *to the Lord Bishop of* London, *concerning the* Conversion *of the* Negro-Slaves, p. 49, &c. where the Particulars of the *Food* and *Cloathing* of the *Negroes* in the *British Sugar* Colonies are describ'd and accounted for.

‡See *the* Representation *of the* Board of Trade *to the* House *of* Lords, dated *January* 14, 1734–5, pag. 16.

be the same, or worse Brute or Booby of a Planter, who should starve his *Slaves*, or use them otherwise than well.* Not that a *Slave* is to live in super-

*"We may apportion to our slaves (1) work, (2) chastisement, and (3) food. If men are given food, but no chastisement nor any work, they become insolent. If they are made to work, and are chastised, but stinted of their food, such treatment is oppressive, and saps their strength. The remaining alternative, therefore, is to give them work, and a sufficiency of food. Unless we pay men, we cannot control them; and food is a slave's pay." *Aristot. de Oeconom. l. i. c.* 5. [Latin in original; translation from *Aristotle: Oeconomica and Magna Moralia,* trans. G. Cyril Armstrong (Cambridge: Harvard University Press, 1936), 337).]

"We ought to punish slaves justly, and not to make them conceited by merely admonishing them as we would free men. An address to a servant should be mostly a simple command: there should be no jesting with servants, either male or female, for by a course of excessively foolish indulgence in their treatment of their slaves, masters often make life harder both for themselves, as rulers, and for their slaves to rule." *Plato lib.* 6. *de Legibus* [Latin in original; translation from *Plato: Laws,* trans. R. G. Bury (New York: G. P. Putnam's Sons, 1926), 477–78).]

Fodder, a Wand, and Burthens, are for the Ass: *and Bread,* (cibus necessarius) *Correction, and Work, for a* Servant. *Siracid. c.* 33. *v.* 24. [Citation untraced.]

Slaves were wholly in the Power of their Masters, who had Power—over their Bodies for Labour, without giving them any Wages or Reward: To do all that they are commanded is but the due Debt to their Masters, which if they perform they are not praised, but punish'd if they do it not. Dr *Hammond*'s Annot. on i Cor. ix. 19. [Henry Hammond (1605–60), *A Paraphrase and Annotations upon all the Books of the New Testament* (London: J. Flesher, 1653). Robertson's citation is from *Annotations,* vol. 4: "19. [b] servant unto all: Servants or , bondmen or slaves, were wholly in the power of their masters; they had power of life and death over them, much more of their bodies for labour, without giving them any wages or reward. To do all that they are commanded is but the due debt to their masters, which if they perform they are not praised, but punished if they do it not; whereas they that are free, if they do any office for any, they may in reason expect to be paid for it. So here St. Paul being a free man, no slave to the Corinthians, that is, under no obligation to preach without maintenance . . . [he] might in reason expect from them reward for all his service, his preaching, &c.; but he did all this for nothing, and that he calls . . . his serving them as a servant doth, without any wages, or as though he were their servant" (119).]

And Archbishop *Tillotson,* in his Sermon on St *John* viii. 36. (near the Beginning) interprets the Proverbial Expression in the preceeding Verse, *The* Servant *abideth not in the House for ever:* thus; that is (saith he) *A* Servant *hath no* Right *to* any Thing, *but is* perfectly *at the* Disposal *of his* Master, *being a Part of* his Goods, which he may use as he pleaseth. [John Tillotson, *The Works Of the Most Reverend Dr. John Tillotson, Late Lord Archbishop of Canterbury,* 2d ed., vol. 2 (London: For Timothy Goodwin, et al., 1717). The quotation comes from Tillotson's Sermon 193, p. 614, on John 8:34–36.]

And Dr *South* (in his Sermon on St *John* xv. 15.) says, The Servant (or *Slave*) neither loves the Thing commanded, not the Person who commands it, but is wholly and only intent upon his own Emolument. All Kindnesses done him, and all that is given him, over and above what is *strictly just,* and his *Due,* makes him rather worse than better. And this is an Observation that never fails, where any one has so much Bounty, and so little Wit, as to make the Experiment. For a Servant (or *Slave*) rarely or never ascribes what he receives to the mere Liberality and Generosity of the Donor, but to his own Worth and Merit, and to the Need which he supposes there

fluity; for that wou'd destroy the Design on which the Master purchas'd him, and for the carrying on whereof he continually provides him with Cloathing and Food convenient for him. They who know not what *Perfect Slavery* is, must (if they will be talking about it) talk out of the Way, or at Random; but you need not be told, how apt *Slaves* are to wax wanton on the least Encouragement above what is *strictly just* and *their due*, what a Propensity is in them to Laziness, Stealing, Lying, Drunkenness, and the like, which, with Murmuring, Stubbornness, Disaffection *to* and Designs upon the Master, arise (as I apprehend) from the very Nature of such *Slavery*. I will not say that there is indefinitely* a Divine Infliction in the Case, but I would ask any *white* Man in *England*, or any where in *Europe*, How, supposing himself, and some Thousands of his Countrymen, to be sold and bought in the Manner we, or our Forefathers, have been, and that he had no more Religion or Learning than we brought from *Africa*, and that he was sold here on the same Conditions the Merchants of *London*, *Liverpool*, or *Bristol*, or their Agents, have sold us; I would ask him how he thinks he wou'd behave in such a Situation? I shall not answer for him; But since he is suppos'd to be a Man of Sense and Sincerity, I presume he will agree, that if the Situation of such *Slaves* must be bad, the Situation of their Masters cannot be desirable, and that in Reason they wou'd chuse to carry on their Business with other Hands, if they knew where to get them. Add to this, that the Mother-Country (to mend the Matter) frequently discharges on her *Sugar* Colonies whole Ship-loads of her own Filth and Ver-

---

is of him. [Robert South, *Sermons preached upon Several Occasions*, vol. 1 (Oxford: H. Hall, 1679). Robertson's quotation is found on page 378 in "Sermon XIV, 'Of the Love of Christ to His Disciples,' A Sermon Preached before the University, at Christ-Church, Oxon, 1664." The parenthetical additions are Robertson's: South does not mention chattel slaves per se, so Robertson is extrapolating "slave" from South's "servant."]

    *"For half of the manhood of man Zeus Thunderer taketh away/ When his feet are caught in the net of bondage-bringing day." *Hom.* Odyss. *lib.* xvii. lin. 322. [Greek, followed by a Latin translation, in original; translation from *Odyssey*, trans. Arthur S. Way (London: Macmillan, 1904), 226.]

    "All servitude (though it be the most righteous) [is] the cage of the soul and a public prison-house." D. *Longin.* de *Sublin.* Sect. 44. [Greek in original; translation from *Longinus: On the Sublime*, trans. W. Rhys Roberts (Cambridge: Cambridge University Press, 1935), 157.]

    Grotius ad *Gen.* ix. v. 25. [*Hugonis Grotii Annotationes in Vetus & Novum Testamentum Juxta Editionem Amstelaedamensem, MDCLXXIX, In Compendium redactae* (London: For Jos. Hazard et al., 1727). Hugo Grotius (1583–1645), was a Dutch jurist and statesman. His annotation on Gen. 9:25 ("Cursed be Canaan; lowest of slaves shall he be to his brothers") appears on page 8: "By the law of nature slavery is the punishment for graver sins." *The New Oxford Annotated Bible* offers the following note: "The curse implies that Canaan's subjugation to Israel was the result of Canaanite sexual practices."]

min, such as, *white* Pick-pockets, Whores, Rogues, Vagrants, Thieves, &c. whom she judges not bad enough for the Gallows, and yet too bad to live among their virtuous Countrymen in *England*. I grant that this affects not you, *Slaves* find themselves to be *Slaves*, and that is all; how they came to be so, is none of their Enquiry: Somebody (they are sure) had a Hand in it; Somebody (they are persuaded) has injur'd them; Somebody, therefore, ought to feel their Revenge: And they have none to revenge it on but their immediate Possessors. At the same time, such of you as were sold from *Africa*, know, that your own Countrymen sold you, and by Consequence were the first Authors of your *Slavery*; but you have nothing to say to them, because they are out of your Reach. For the same Reason you say not one Word against those who bought you from your Countrymen, and sold you again here. And I guess you never heard till now that *England* promotes and protects this *Slave*-Trade, which otherwise cou'd not possibly be carried on. Perhaps you thought the *white* Inhabitants here sent their Ships to *Guinea* for you, or your Fathers: Alas! they have no Ships to send, no Commodities to purchase you with; or, if any Merchant in these Colonies is at all concern'd in this Trade, 'tis only as a Factor for those in *England*, or as he joins his small Stock with that of the rich Merchants there. But you are not out of Humour with the People of *England*, either because you did not know that they had any Hand in your *Slavery*, or because you cannot come at them. All your Anger therefore must be vented on these *white* People here; and yet all the Concern they have in bringing about this *Slave*-Trade, is, that rather than give over the *Sugar*-Manufacture, which was their Calling, and deem'd a Lawful one, they accepted of *Negroe-Slaves* to carry it on with; which they did sore against their Will, and not till *England* declin'd to furnish them with *white* Hands to labour in it. This they reckon a Misfortune, and a very heavy one; insomuch as I have often heard many of the best and wisest of them wish heartily enough, that there was never a *Negro-Slave* more to be brought from *Africa* to *America*; that all the *Slaves* in the *British Sugar* Colonies were in *Africa* again, or any where but where they are; and that their Mother-Country would either send them Hands from herself to carry on the *Sugar* Manufacture, or put them in some other Way of Living that cou'd be carried on without *Negroe-Slaves*; for you, or your Parents, were brought hither in so provoking and uncouth a Manner, and are so perverse and provoking yourselves, as to tire the Spirits, and break the Hearts of all that have to do with you.

Moses Bon Sàam says, *Let them* [the *white* People here] *recollect how soon the* Profits, *which they too well knew to make, from any one of our poor Fathers* Toils, *repaid them for his barbarous Purchase.* This shews him to be a Stranger both to the *Slave*-Trade, and to the State of Things here: To the first, in confining the *Barbarity* of the Purchase to the Planters, as if (supposing, for the present, a *Barbarity* in such Purchases) the Purchase made on the Coast of *Guinea* by the Merchants of *London*, *Liverpool*, and *Bristol*, or their Factors, was not at least equally *barbarous*: To the State of Things in these *Sugar* Colonies,* where the Loss in *Slaves* (beside those immediately from *Africa*, of which about two Fifths die in the *Seasoning*) may well, one Year with another, be reckon'd at One in Fifteen; in Dry-weather Years, when Provisions of the Country Growth are scarce, I have known it One in Seven in many Plantations, and the like or worse in sickly Seasons; and when the Small-Pox (which is almost as much dreaded in these *Sugar* Islands as the Pestilence is any where in *Europe*) happens to be imported, 'tis incredible what Havock it makes among our *Blacks*. As to the Births; 'tis true, the Masters allow, or connive at, *Polygamy* in their *Slaves*; but whatever that may do in *Africa*, it is found, among other sore Mischiefs, to hinder Breeding here; and if we consider the Numbers of Infants that die, the little Work the Mother can do for three Months before, and nine after the Birth, Midwifry, and some other Incidents, and the Maintenance of the Child for seven or eight Years, I dare say a *Slave* rear'd up here costs the Planter as much as one from *Guinea*. The Profits arising from a *Slave*'s Labour does not, therefore, so soon make good the Purchase-Money as our Countryman *Moses* imagines. And when it is made good, to whom is it made good? Does it not now begin to be known in *England*, that the Planters in her *Sugar* Colonies are least Gainers of all that are concern'd in either the *Slave* or *Sugar* Trade? And are not many or most of themselves *Slaves* (very near as much as the *Negroes* are to them) to their Creditors in *England*, to whom their Lands, and these very *Slaves* too, are mortgag'd? Let any Man but reflect on† the frequent Mortality that is here among the *Slaves*, the frequency of Storms and Hurricanes, accidental Fire among Canes, long-continu'd Droughts, and other Misfortunes and Calamities, to which the Masters of these Slaves are always subject; what vast Gains Merchants in the several Branches of Trade always make of them; the great Expence that is necessary to maintain the *Sugar* Manufacture; the heavy

*See *A* Detection *of the* State *and* Situation *of the present* Sugar *Planters of* Barbadoes *and the* Leward Islands, *London,* printed 1732, pag. 44. [Robert Robertson, *A Detection of the State and Situation Of the Present Sugar Planters, of Barbadoes and the Leward Islands; With an Answer to this Query, Why does not England, or her Sugar Islands, or both, make and settle more Sugar Colonies in the West Indies? Written in the Month of December 1731* (London: J. Wilford, 1732).]

†See *A* Letter *to the Lord Bishop of* London, *concerning the* Conversion *of the* Negroe-Slaves, p. 55.

Taxes they have to pay here, and the high Duties on their Manufacture when imported into *Great-Britain*: Let any Man, I say, but attend to these, and he will quickly perceive, that the Masters of the *Slaves* here neither are nor can be rich. And indeed the strange Remissness or Inadvertence of *England*, in suffering the *French* and *Dutch Sugar* Colonies to be supplied with *Provisions* from *Ireland*, and with *Horses*, *Lumber*, and *Provisions* from her *Northern* Colonies, to raise more *Provisions* than can be vended without exporting them to her Rivals in the *Sugar* Trade, and her not providing a Vent for *Sugar* from her *Sugar* Islands to *Spain*, the *Streights*, &c. without introducing it first into *England*, and not lessening the Duties on *Muscovadoes*[11] consum'd within *Great Britain*, has put herself in a fair Way of losing the *Sugar* Trade, and by Consequence very much of the Trade in *Slaves* too.

When our Countryman *Moses Bon Sàam* condemns the Propogation of *Slavery* from Father to Son as a *Shameless Pretension*, methinks he shou'd have told you what the Learned among these *white* Men (whose Arts, he says, he has been studying for Sixteen Years) alledge in Defence of it; but since he has not, I will try to supply his Omission. They affirm then, with respect to the first unhappy *Captive*, that* "As by the Right of War an Enemy may fairly be kill'd, so the Conqueror, if he pleases, may give him his Life, upon his promise of Perpetual Service. In which Contract or Composition, the Good which the vanquish'd receives, is the Security of his Life, which, by the Right of War, might have been taken away; and the Good which he engages to bring to the Victor is his Service and Obedience, and these, as far as possible, *Absolute*. For he that obligeth himself to perform the Commands of another, before he knows the Particulars, is bound without any Limitation or Exception, to do all that the other Party shall enjoin;" and nothing but the Law of *Humanity* can procure him any Relief from this *rigorous Justice*. With respect to the *Children* of *Slaves*, they say, That it is but just *the* Birth *shou'd go with the* Bearer, or *the* Child *with the* Mother who is always known, rather than with the *Father*, who (among *Slaves* especially) cannot be so surely known;† that since in a

---

*Puffendorf *de Leg. Nat.* & *Gent.* l. 6. c. 3. sect. 6.

†Ibid. sect. 9. "Now slavery is a condition of the body, since a slave is to the master a kind of instrument in working: wherefore children follow the mother in freedom and bondage." T. Aquinas in *Supplem.* ad tertiam Partem *Summae*, Quaest. 52. Artic. 4. St Thomas Aquinas. [Latin in original; translation from *The "Summa Theologica" of St Thomas Aquinas*, Literally Translated by Fathers of the English Dominican Province (New York: Benziger Brothers, 1922), 181.]

"But of the children of Captives, which are born of Slaves in their Lords Family, there is yet a more difficult question: For by the Laws of the Romans, and of other Nations, concerning Captives (as we shall elsewhere shew) as of brute Beasts, so of people of a servile condition it

State of *perfect Slavery*, not only the *Works* but the *Persons* belong to the Master, their *Children* will likewise fall under his Dominion, as every thing else which they produce; that the *Mother* is on Account of her Burthen, render'd for some time unfit to perform her usual Work, and consequently brings a Loss and Prejudice to her Master, which ought to be thus repair'd; and that the Master does no Injury to the *Child* in dooming it to perpetual Subjection: For since the *Mother* hath nothing of her own, 'tis impossible she shou'd maintain the *Child* but with her Master's Goods: And since the Master is oblig'd to furnish such an *Infant* with Food and other Necessaries, long before it is capable of making any Requital; and since when the *Child* begins to work,

---

holds true, that, Partus sequitur matrem . . . wherefore the Right that these Lords have in the Children of their bond-servants, springs from the many years Alimony that is given them by the Lord before they could be serviceable to him, which they are to recompense by their future labour. And for this cause, the Parents cannot dispose of them to any other man, neither may the Servant flee from his Lord, until full satisfaction be given unto that Lord for the charge of their education." *Grotius* de jure B. ac P. ex edit. *Barbeyrac, Amst.* 1720. lib. 2. c. 5. sect. 29. p. 268, 269. [Latin in original; Barbeyrac's edition of this work by Grotius is untraced. Period translation from *The Most Excellent Hugo Grotius His Three Books Treating of the Rights of War and Peace . . . Translated into English by William Evats, B.D.* (London: Margaret White, 1682), 116. It is interesting to note that the next sentence—unquoted by Robertson—is, in English: "But if the Lord be too unmercifully cruel, then that even they who have surrendered themselves as Slaves, may provide for their own safety by flight . . ." (116).]

"Neither are the persons of Men and Women only, thus taken and made slaves, but their posterity for ever; for whosoever is born of a Woman after her Captivity, is a slave born. . . . Now all this unlimited Power is by the Law of Nations granted for no other Cause than that the Conquerour being allured by so many advantages might be willing to forbear that utmost cruelty which they may lawfully use by killing their Captives, either in the heat of fight, or afterwards in cold blood. . . . That they may be the more willing to forbear, I say, for it is no bargain or agreement, whereby they stand obliged to save them, if we respect the Law of Nations; but a perswasive argument drawn from profit, it being far more beneficial to the Conquerour to sell his Prisoner then to kill him. And therefore he hath the same power to transfer his Right in his Captive to another, as he hath to assign over unto others the Right and property he hath in any of his own Goods or Chattels (it is allowed, following Gronovius in *Annotations,* thus to sell or donate or relinquish by a last will, or to otherwise give to another person, a man-servant, when the servant is useful or redundant). This Power is also extended to the Children that are born after Captivity because if the Conquerour had used his power to the utmost, they had not been born . . . Therefore by the Law of Nations, the Children born of such Captives follow the Mothers condition, because their Chastity is not provided for by any Law, nor is there any strait guard kept upon them; and therefore no presumption how great soever is sufficient to prove who is the Father." Ibid. 1. 3. c. 7, sect. 2 & 4, pag. 756, 757. [Latin in original; translation from *The Most Excellent Hugo Grotius,* 482. Johannes Fredericus Gronovius (1611–71), Dutch classical scholar and professor at Deventer, edited many classical texts and published commentaries and literary criticism. The work cited in Grotius's parenthesis as *Annotations* is untraced.]

his Labour is scarce equivalent to his daily Maintenance, he cannot escape Servitude, unless by the Master's particular Dispensation. And this Reason (*say they*) will hold, not only whilst he is suppos'd to continue, as it were, in his Master's Debt, but ever after; because the Condition on which the Master first undertook to keep him, was, that he should perform perpetual Service; and to this Condition he is presum'd to have yielded a tacit Consent; especially if it be consider'd, that his very Birth is owing to his Master's Favour, who by the Right of War might have put his Parents to Death. For* as to that *Natural Freedom* with which all Men are invested, it then only takes Place, when no Act or Agreement, or ourselves or others, hath render'd us obnoxious to a State of Inferiority.

Upon these Pillars, in the main, stood the *Perfect Servitude*[†] which from the Days of *Noah*,[‡] or of *Nimrod*,[§] was in Vogue for many Ages in most Coun-

---

*"There is no man by nature servant to another, that is, no man in his primitive state or condition considered, without any fact done by himself, whereby his natural liberty is impeached . . . in which sense our Lawyers may be understood, when they say, that to be another mans slave is against nature: But that this kind of slavery might at first be introduced by some fact done; namely, by some voluntary agreement, or for some crime committed, is not repugnant to natural justice . . ." *Ibid.* l. 3. c. 7. sect. i. p. 755. [Translation from *The Most Excellent Hugo Grotius,* 481.]

†"Now that we call perfect Bondage, which tyes a man during life to perform all manner of work, for no other reward but food and cloathing; which if it extend it self to whatsoever conduceth to the preservation of Nature (that is, says Gronovius, so that the master grants not too much to the servant thus resulting in justice yielding to nature), is not much to be grieved at: For our continual labour is indifferently well recompensed with a constant supply of things necessary for life, which they that hire out themselves by the day only, do often want." *Ibid.* l. 2. c. 5. sect. 27. p. 266, 267. [Ibid., 115–16.]

‡*Laur. Pignorius* de Servis, *Amst.* 1674. p. 1 & 2. [Lorenzo Pignoria (1571–1631), *Laurentii Pignorii Patavini De Servis, & Eorum apud veteres ministeriis* (Of the ancient ministers) (Amsterdam: A. Frisii, 1674). After quoting Gen. 9:25 from the Vulgate, Pignoria continues, in reference to slavery: "And this continues ever since the time of Noah's death; it is often repeated in a succession of comments on the deeds of slaves, Abram gathered many of his servants in haste and mustered them to rescue his son from captivity; [and in] the rule of circumcision and the implementation of that rule; and in other places such as in those records that still exist of maidservants [who were both] home-born servants and purchased servants" (my translation). For comments on the deeds of slaves, see Gen. 14:14, 17, 10, and 22.]

§"Indeed, captivity was nothing new: one may indeed read in Genesis 10:8: 'Cush became the father of Nimrod; he was the first on earth to become a mighty warrior,' that is to be understood in Augustine's *City of God,* book 16, chapter 4 [in which one may learn] of the oppressed and of captivity" [Latin in original; my translation]. D. *Augustin.* de *Civ. Dei,* l. 16. c. 4. de oppressione & captivitate intelligi. *Joannes Saresberiensis* [makes plain] (*Policrat.* l. i. c. 4.): "It has been handed down that (Nimrod) was in such a state of exalted madness, that he was not afraid to violate the laws of nature, when he promised slavery to his partners, partners by contract and

tries of the World. Whether they will also serve to support the present *Slave-Trade* in its *Rise, Progress,* and *Duration,* I cannot say; but you shall hear how this last came about. *C. Columbus,* the first Discoverer of *America,* having taken Possession of some Parts of it for the King of *Spain,* the *Spaniards* and *Portugueze* soon discern'd that there was more profitable Work for them here than cou'd be carried on by their own Hands. About the same Time the *Portugueze* discover'd that the Swarms of Men in *Africa* were more than we cou'd employ, or knew what to do with; that many of our People were *Slaves* to their Princes or other Masters; that by the Law, Custom, Constitution, or whatever one may call it, of our Native Countries, this *Slavery* did descend from Father to Son to latest Posterity; and that these Princes or Masters wou'd sell their *Slaves* (as well as the *Captives* taken in War) on the same Terms themselves held them, to any Body that wou'd buy them. They, therefore, made what haste they could to the Market, which they found to be inexhaustible; and as soon as the *Dutch* saw what a gainful Market it was, away they crowded after them; and the *English, French,* &c. in process of time, getting Possessions in the *West-Indies,* did the same. Now had it not been for the never-ending Tenure of this *Slavery,* none of these *European* Nations (considering the great Expence and Risque of a Voyage from *Europe* to the Coast of *Guinea,* and from thence to the *West-Indies;* the Difficulties and Dangers of trading with our Countrymen; the first Cost of these *Slaves* in *Africa;* the Multitudes of them that die in *Transportation,* and afterwards in the *Seasoning;* the Charges their Owners must be at in the *American* Colonies in maintaining the *Mother* during her Pregnancy, and the *Child* till it grows fit for Labour; the ill Qualities that naturally, as it were, accompany *Perfect Slaves;* the endless plagues their Masters must have to keep them in necessary Subjection, *&c.*) cou'd have judg'd it worth while to buy any of them at all; and let our Countrymen in *Africa* once refuse to sell them on the same Tenure, and from that Moment these *Europeans* will bid *Adieu* to the *Trade*: But since our Countrymen there are in no such Disposition, and the Nations of *Europe* (who have some of their People at work for them here in the *West-Indies*) seem resolv'd rather to continue than to give it over, what wou'd you have the *white* Inhabitants in these Parts to do? Wou'd you have them fly in the Face of all *our* Countries in *Africa* who sell these *Slaves* first, and of *their* Mother Countries in

---

by birth—those whom he had fathered" [Latin in original; my translation]. *Ibid.* p. 3. ["Augustin": Saint Augustine of Hippo, *De civitate Dei* (Of the City of God), book 16, chap. 4. "Joannes Saresberiensis": John of Salisbury (fl. 1120–80), bishop of Chartres, in *Ioanns Saresberiensis Policratus: Sive De nugis Curialium, & vestigiis Philosophorum, libri octo.* Lugduni Batauorum, Ex officina Plantiniana, apud Franciscum Raphelengium, 1595 (orig. 1159), 13.]

Europe who buy them from ours, and after they have paid a very great Price for them, in Consideration that their Servitude is to be perpetual, and have been at no small Cost and Pains besides to train them up in the *Sugar* Manufacture, or otherwise; Wou'd you, I say, have these few *white* Men take upon them to break thro' all, and set their *Slaves* thus transferr'd to them, or their Offspring, at Liberty? And if this is no such reasonable Expectation, can you think it fair in *Moses Bon Sàam* to head you, or for you to march out under his Command against the *white* Men of this Island, and in *your Anger* to bring them to *Destruction*? Cou'd he lead you forth, even against the prime Authors and Instruments of your *Slavery*, those who sold and transported you, or your Forefathers, in the Manner that has been related, he might, for any thing I can see (since the Illegality of this Traffick is plainly a Supposition still) be very much to blame; but if these *white* Men here are not altogether innocent (which they cannot be; if they have given way to a thing in itself evil for the sake of Gain, or to prevent loss) surely they are the least guilty, the most unfortunate, and the poorest Gainers of all that are concern'd in this Trade, and therefore (even admitting it to be prov'd illegal) the least deserving, or the most improper Objects, of your Wrath and Vengeance.

I have again and again told you, how you, or your Forefathers, came to be *Slaves* here, because in your present Situation it is fit you shou'd understand it thoroughly. *Moses Bon Sàam*, to endear himself, and secure (as it wou'd seem) his Command over you, says, that *as soon as he became able to* read, *he discover'd (with a Mixture of Amazement and* prophetick *Joy) in the* holiest *of all Books, how the great Giver of his Name* had deliver'd *a certain Nation from just such a* Slavery *as* this of our Countrymen here; *just so unfair, oppressive, and unnatural; and, in every Act and Circumstance, resembling that which you and your Forefathers have* groaned *under*. Perfect Slavery, 'tis true, is much the same in any Part or Age of the World, otherwise it wou'd not be *Perfect* Slavery, which chiefly consists in one's being oblig'd, by Virtue of some Contract or some Crime, to labour all his Life long for bare Food, and the other common Necessaries of Life.* But I assure you, *Moses Bon Sàam* wrongs that Book; for, not to say that the *Slaves* here are never put to the Task of *making Brick without Straw*,† or any thing that can be deem'd to resemble it, or that their Infants are all tenderly nurs'd up, and the Midwives never *commanded to kill their Male-Children* in the Birth,‡ or any one else to *cast them out into the* Water *to the In-*

---

*Vid. *Grotium* de Jure B. ac P. l. 2. c. 5. Sect. 27. p. 266, 267.
†*Exod.* v.
‡*Ibid.* i. 16.

tent they shou'd not live;[*] To pass over these, I say, the Founders or Patriarchs of the Nation he speaks of were not *sold* as you have been, but were *invited* (by the then King) into that Country, where, in plain Violation of the Publick Faith, they were afterwards *enslav'd;*[†] neither did they go thither *naked,* as our Countrymen in *Africa* sent you, or your Fathers, here, in the most literal Sense of the Word, but *carried with them their Flocks, and their Herds, and the Goods which they had got* in their Native Country.[‡]

But let it be suppos'd that under the Conduct of *Moses Bon Sàam* you cou'd atchieve all the glorious Things he talks of; that far from *continuing on the* defensive, which is what he first advises, you shou'd change your Mind as quick as he contradicts himself in his *Speech, and break down, unexpected, upon the scatter'd Plantations below, and return with whatever you* wish *from the* Storehouses *of these your Enemies,* as he calls the *white* People here; *that you cou'd* train *and* confirm *your Forces, by the Discipline and Exercise they are beginning to practice; that the* Negroes now with their Masters, shou'd flee to you by Night, or be *drawn along with you when you make* Incursions, *till* you shall think *your very* Numbers *have made you* invincible; nay, let it be suppos'd that you cou'd extirpate these *Whites,* or drive them from the Island; What next? why, *Moses* himself, your Captain-General, tells you, *it wou'd be found an unsurmountable Difficulty,* without Ships, *and unskill'd in* Navigation, *to maintain your Possessions against the perpetual fresh Supplies that wou'd be pour'd in by their Fleets.* It wou'd be so; but I hope he does not mean the *Fleets* of the *white* Inhabitants below; for Fleets they have none; he must therefore mean the Fleets of *England,* or *France,* &c. which doubtless wou'd be the Case, as it was at *St John*'s, the *Danish* Island I mention'd to you before.

But it seems your General is not for a total Extirpation of these *Whites*; he would have you *keep to your Mountains, where* he says *you have every* Art *within yourselves, that can be necessary for your Support and Security—can prepare* Gun-powder, *and find* Iron *every where, but that it abounds in your* Ene-

---

[*]*Ibid.* v. 22. and *Acts* vii. 19.

[†]And the Fame thereof was heard in *Pharaoh*'s House, saying, *Joseph*'s Brethren are come; and it pleased *Pharaoh* well, and his Servants. And *Pharaoh* said unto *Joseph,* say unto thy Brethren, this do ye; Lade your Beasts, and go, get you into the Land of Canaan, and take your Father, and your Households, and come unto me, and I will give you the Good of the Land of *Egypt,* and ye shall eat the Fat of the Land. Now thou art commanded, this do ye; Take your Waggons out of the Land of *Egypt* for your little Ones, and for your Wives, and bring your Father, and come. Also regard not your Stuff; for the Good of all the Land of *Egypt* is yours. And the Children of *Israel* did so: And *Joseph* gave them Waggons, according to the Commandment of *Pharaoh,* and Provisions for the Way, *Gen.* xlv. 16, &c. See *Chap.* xlvii. 5, 6, and 11.

[‡]See *Gen.* xlv. 10. xlvi. 6. xlvii. 1.

mies (these *white* Men's) Warehouses—*and are capable of* forging *your own* Arms, *if so much Trouble were necessary*; *but* (says he) *there is a nearer Way to get* Arms; *'tis but to prevent the* Return *of those who shall* dare *to* invade *you, and the* Arms, *which they bring for your* Ruin, *will inlarge and perpetuate your Protection*—Then he concludes thus, "You have all heard talk of the *Dutch*; those Rivals in Riches and Power, to the most considerable Princes of the Earth! What were *these*, about a hundred Years past, but a kind of *white Slaves*, to a Monarch, who now calls them his *Brothers*? Keep this inspiring *Example* in your *Eye*; and assure yourselves that the proudest of your Enemies [still meaning the *white* People here, but not a Word of the prime Authors or Instruments of your *Slavery*, those who began, carried on, and are still improving and extending this *Slave*-Trade from *Africa* to the *West-Indies*] will *embrace* you, in Spite of your *Colour*, when they foresee *Destruction* in your *Anger*, but *Ease* and *Security* in your *Friendship*."

Friendship! Alas! that anything that is called Rational shou'd so prostitute thy sacred Name! You know, none of the Seeds of *Friendship* are to be found in any of you that are come to Years, nor can you shew me one quiet towardly Negro in all your Company, one that has any thing of Good-Nature or Humanity in him. Are not the *Negro-Slaves* among the *white* People in these Colonies, even those of the same Nation and Blood, eternally quarrelling with, and biting and devouring one another? How do the Parents insult and domineer over their Children, whilst young? And the Children, when grown up, over their Parents? Can so much as a Dog be in Subjection to them, which they do not misuse or starve? And is it not a thousand Times worse in these Mountains, where you have got the thing which such as *Moses Bon Sàam* call *Liberty*? Do you not, on the sorriest Provocation, and often without pretending to have had any at all, sheath your Knives or Daggers in one another's Bowels? What Beasts do the best of you shew yourselves, after you have pillag'd a Planter's Still-house of Rum? How do you lie with the Wives of the weaker and more ignorant Sort, in their Sight, and force their Daughters, even before they are ripe? And all this, and more than I can say, without ever shewing the least Sign of Remorse or Repentance? Is not your hatred to these *Whites* implacable? Wou'd you not cut all their Throats with one Knife, and in one Moment, if you knew how? And what Security, then, can you give, when once you have fortified the Highlands, and got a sufficient Provision of Arms and Ammunition in the Manner *Moses Bon Sàam* has pointed out, that you will rest content, and leave them in quiet Possession of the Lowlands? Can you propose Treaties of Friendship, who know not what Treaties or Friendship mean? No! Wild and wicked as you are, you will not pretend to put so manifest a Trick on your old Masters; and tho' *Moses* talks of I know not what Ease and Security in your Friendship, I am sure you are honest and open-hearted enough to own, that as soon as you have Power you will destroy them to a Man. And admit you had Power and Opportunity to destroy them, and shou'd effect their Destruction; since this is a Matter that ought to be well consider'd, give me leave to ask you once more, what must be the Conse-quence? why the same I just now told you: The Fleets and Armies of *England* wou'd destroy you? Or if they shou'd prove tardy, or do the Work *by Halves*, which is not to be imagin'd; I assure you, from the full Knowledge I have of the Men, the *French* from *Hispaniola*, &c. wou'd pursue you with Fire and Sword, and never quit this Island, were your Fortifications ten times larger and stronger than ever you can make them, while there was one Man, Woman, or Child of you, left alive upon it!

Be wise then, my Countrymen, and listen no longer to the Suggestions of *Moses Bon Sàam*: Submit rather forthwith to the *white* People here. They are *Englishmen*, and Cruelty is no Part of their Character; I dare promise, your Lives under them will be safer, easier, and happier than ever they can be in these Mountains.

Had I not been sold from *Africa* myself, I should have been undone! whereas now the Reverse is happily my Lot! But you will say, What is that, or a few such Instances, to the Case of so many hundred Thousands, or rather Millions, or our Countrymen, that are sold from thence? It must not there-fore be dissembled, that there are those among the *Whites* themselves who dislike this *Slave*-Trade from its Commencement in *Africa*, to its Consum-mation (if that may be said to be consummated which is propagating to latest Posterity) in *America*; nay some of them venture farther, and [upon seriously considering the Nature and Circumstances of this Trade throughout, the Maxims of Interest on which the whole of it is founded, how the principal Nations professing *Christianity* are one way or other embarked in it, the many Lives it destroys, and the little Care that is or can be taken of their Souls] doubt not to say, that, in their Opinion, very few such Pieces of Wickedness have ever been acted on the Face of the Earth: At the same time they confess, that all the Parties concerned in it do not appear to them to be equally guilty, or, that the *Whites* in the *West-Indies*, who are the last Receivers of these *Slaves*, are no deeper Sharers in the Guilt than they are in the Gain; which hath been already prov'd (with respect to the *British Sugar* Planters) to be the least of any that are concern'd in it. But whatever may be in these Men's No-tions, whether with regard to this *Slave*-Trade in general, or to the Part the *British* Planters in the *West-Indies* bear in it, 'tis certain that the Part these

Planters bear in it has brought, and daily brings them under the severest Censures in *England*; where the Way of thinking or speaking on this Subject tallies exactly with yours in these Mountains: No Body there, any more than you do here, blames, or is heard to blame, our Countrymen in *Africa* who sells these *Slaves* first, or the *English* Merchants who buy them, and by this Craft have their Wealth, or *England*, the grand Gainer, for protecting and encouraging a Trade, which consists in selling and buying Men and Women in one Quarter of the World, and selling and buying them in another; but the whole Load of Blame and Guilt, if there is any Blame or Guilt in such Traffick, is cast on the *white* People in these Parts, and on them alone. I could tell those in *England* who do so, were they in my Way, or I in theirs, that their Censures have disconcerted not a few of the *Sugar* Planters, and put them at length on casting about for other Employment, which may not be so profitable to their Mother Country as Sugar-making; nor can their great Stock in *Slaves, Sugar*, Utensils, *&c.* hinder them from so doing, there being plenty of Chapmen in the other *European* Colonies here, who wou'd gladly take them off their Hands at any Price: Among the rest, I must own, that their Censures have put me not a little out of Tune; for I have a Family, and from the Date of my Freedom have been set on a Level with the *Whites*, who are pleas'd to reckon me as one of themselves; and what by the Bounty of my old and young Master, what by my own Application to Business, I have for some Time been Owner of a small Freehold Estate in Land; and my Family-Hands not being sufficient to manure the same, and no free Hands being to be got here to manure it, I was therefore (as any Man in *Europe*, who shou'd live on this Island in Circumstances like mine, wou'd also be) forced as it were of Necessity to buy some of our Countrymen from *Guinea*, in the very same fashion I was brought here myself: Now tho', you may believe, I have used them as well as the Nature and Genius of such Servitude will bear; yet it gives me many sad and anxious Thoughts, not that their Colour and mine is the same, or that we are of the same Kindred and Country, but that I, or any other Freeman, shou'd at all contribute to the Support and Propagation of *Slavery*. I often make the Case of the *Negroe-Slaves* my own, and sometimes suppose myself to be accounting for it (as all concern'd must one Day do) at the last *Tribunal*; and being very lately pretty deep in one of these Contemplations, methought the Great Judge ask'd, how I came to be concern'd in the *Slavery* of my Fellow-Creatures; *Why* (said he) *did you not rather quit the Way of Life you was engag'd in, and betake yourself to some other? Or, if you cou'd find no other, why did you not trust to my* Care *and* Providence? *Cou'd you imagine that I descended from* Heaven *to* Earth, *and suffer'd as I did there, to purchase a* Licence *for any* Man, *or* Species *of*

Men, *to violate the* Laws *of* Nature? At these Words (Blessed *Jesu!* have Mercy upon us?) *aghast, upstared my Hair, I speechless stood!* and as soon as my Terror abated, I sent to some that are said to be the ablest Casuists among both *Royalists* and *Republicans*, as well as to some of their several *Retainers*, in *England*, humbly imploring them to clear up the Case; and in Six or Seven Months from this Time I expect an Answer from some one or more of either Party: In particular, had I known where to direct him, I wou'd have ask'd the same Favour of an Illustrious and Learned *Prelate*[50] there (whose Name, tho' consecrated above twenty Years, I don't remember to have seen in any of the *Lists* of the *Society for the Propagation of the Gospel in foreign Parts)* which I'm sure his great Humanity, and concern for Truth and Right above all By-considerations that can be nam'd, and for the Quiet of so many Consciences, and the honest thriving of the Community, wou'd readily have induced him to grant; and I am much out in my Conjectures, if his Lordship has not often wish'd for a fair Opportunity of declaring his Mind on this very Subject.

Well! Let their Determination be what it will, I wou'd have you, my Countrymen, to refrain from all further Violences to the *Whites* below. None of you that considers, will deny that there is such a Being above as these *Englishmen* call GOD, and that He is powerful, good, and just, and sees and over-rules whatever is done upon Earth: And such of you as were come to Years of Discretion before you left *Africa*, are all persuaded, that immediately after Death you will return again to your Native Countries. Now 'tis plain your Bodies cannot return thither; for do but open the Graves of any of our Countrymen that have died here, and you will still find their Bodies, or their Bones and Dust, in the Graves where you buried them. What returns then must be something else, even the Thing that is in every one of us, by which we think, and consider, and can judge of what is right and what is wrong. This these *English* call *the* Soul, which is the same in you as it is in them, and me, and in all Mankind. And wherever these your *Souls* go, whether to your Native Countries, or elsewhere, you may be sure they go there for some End and Purpose. I know you will allow, that such of them that behav'd aright in their Bodies, will enjoy Pleasure, and that such as did not, will suffer Pain. You had need therefore, my Brethren, to take good heed what you do now while you live. Hearken not to this *Moses Bon Sàam*, he will lead you on, *for certain*, to the Death of your Bodies, and, *for ought I see*, to the worse Damage of your *Souls*, which you believe will go from hence to another Place after the Death of your Bodies.

In setting forth the Case of this *Slave*-Trade, nothing has been conceal'd that seemed to me to make *for* or *against* either the *Enslavers* or the *enslaved*;

if *Moses Bon Sàam* thinks otherwise, or that his *Speech* has been unfairly dealt with, he may *speak* again: Nor am I sensible that any thing of Moment, relating to your Case in particular, has been omitted, unless something shou'd have been said of the *Spanish Negroes* who retreated hither when the *English* took this Island; and of them, I can only say, that as their Number was but small, so their Children have all along so intermix'd with the *Slaves* that came up from their Masters below, that there is no distinguishing them now, nor can yourselves tell with any certainty which of you are the Descendants of those *Negroes*. If, after considering what has been, or may be offer'd, you shall still think yourselves injur'd, it remains (and I wou'd say the same to all our *enslav'd* Countrymen every where) that the Resolution of the Matter be left to that GOD I was telling you of, *who made the World and all Things that are in it, and rules over all*. I assure you *He is no Respecter of Persons*, but regards the *Negroes* as much as he does these *English*, or any *white* Men whatever; for we with our black Skins are the Work of his Hands as well as the best of them, and he careth for us all alike; the only thing that weighs with him is the Right and Merits of the Case, and the Behaviour of People, be they *White*, be they *Black*; and He will make such as behave well more happy, and such as behave ill more miserable, than I, or any other Mortal can express. And for your Consolation, I can assure you too, that as the GOD I speak of is a Lover of Truth, Righteousness, and Mercy, so He is an irreconcileable Enemy to all Violence and Injustice, Cruelty and Oppression, and has often interpos'd *specially* to cut them off.

As to the *Slave*-Trade in general, if there is Iniquity in it, if it is an unjust Invasion of the Law of Nature; Who knows but this most mighty, good, and righteous GOD may, sooner than is apprehended, put it into the Hearts of those who bear sway in our Countries, and into the Hearts of such *European* Nations as conspire with them in it, to conspire in breaking it off? Who knows but He may inspire a certain People in *Europe* (whose Strength at Sea is great, and may be made almost what they please) to take the whole upon themselves, and put a Stop to it with their Shipping at the Fountain-head? What then? our Governors in *Africa* must devise some other Way to employ their Hands than by selling them abroad for *Slaves*; the *Slave*-Merchants of *Europe* will lose a very gainful Trade, and be forced to look out for some other, or to rest content with that of *Gold Dust, Elephants Teeth*, &c. which those I now mean might then easily ingross; *Spain* and *Portugal* (notwithstanding all their Seisures, Indultos, *Piezas de India*, and other Rants at present) cou'd not, or not for Ages, and perhaps never to purpose, work their Gold and Silver Mines; *France* and *Holland* must soon decline in the *Sugar* Manufacture;

England cou'd support it better (as might be prov'd) than any Nation what-soever; the Value of some Things at Market wou'd return to what it was when *Columbus* made his first Discoveries; that *European* Country which cou'd best maintain Manufactures, Fishing, and Agriculture, would be the most consid-erable; and the People, thus pursuing the Path to Glory, would become Arbiters of the Affairs (not of one Quarter only, but) of the greater Part of our habitable Globe. But supposing GOD to do neither, and that all probable Means should be laid aside, or come to nought, He has many Ways of setting Things that are wrong to rights, which the wisest of his Creatures are igno-rant of, and must not presume to dive into. Your Part is exceeding plain, even to make yourselves, and all you are concern'd with, as easy as possible; and how that is to be done, you have heard. These *black Creole* Tyrants are but a Hand-ful; Let them be tied Hand and Foot, and I will come up again when you shall think fit, and doubt not but to bring with me such Articles in your behalf, from the *white* People below, as will be to your liking. Till then, farewel.

8

The Story of Inkle and Yarico AND An Epistle from Yarico to Inkle, After he had left her in Slavery

FRANCES SEYMOUR

(1699–1754)

Frances Seymour's poems included here represent two of the best and earliest engagements with issues of imperialism and slavery in the West Indies by a socially and literarily prominent figure in London. The first poem, "The Story of Inkle and Yarico," circulated in manuscript for several years before it was published in *The New Miscellany* (London: J. Cooper, n.d.) about 1726. "The Story of Inkle and Yarico" and "An Epistle from Yarico to Inkle, After he had left her in Slavery" were published under their own titles together in 1738. The poems reflect the continuing interest of English letters with the tale (first told by Richard Ligon; see chapter 1) of the shipwrecked Englishman Inkle who sells his Indian savior-lover Yarico into slavery upon his arrival in Barbados.

Born Frances Thynne in 1699, the poet grew up at Longleat House in Wiltshire, England. In 1713, she married Algernon Seymour (1684–1750), Earl of Hertford, who succeeded as seventh duke of Somerset in 1748. An army officer, her husband served under Marlborough at the battle of Oudenarde in 1708, was promoted to general in 1737, and was governor of Minorca from 1737 to 1742. Frances Seymour served George II's Queen Caroline as lady of the bedchamber and maintained a wide correspondence with literary men and women of her time, including her great aunt, the poet Anne Finch; Henrietta Louisa Fermor, countess of Pomfret; Mrs. Elizabeth Rowe; James Thomson (who dedicated "Spring" from his "The Seasons" to her); William Shenstone; and Richard Savage (whom she helped to secure a pardon for homicide).

The STORY of INKLE and YARICO.

A most moving TALE from the *Spectator.* Attempted in VERSE
by The Right Hon. the Countess of **** *LONDON:*
Printed for J. COOPER, in *Fleetstreet,*

1738.

A Youth there was possess'd of every charm,
Which might the coldest heart with passion warm;
His blooming cheeks with ruddy beauty glow'd,
His hair in waving ringlets graceful flow'd;
Thro' all his person an attractive mien,   5
Just symmetry, and elegance were seen:
But niggard Fortune had her aid withheld,
And poverty th' unhappy Boy compell'd
To distant climes to sail, in search of gain,
Which might in ease his latter days maintain.   10
By chance, or rather the decree of Heaven,
The vessel on a barbarous coast was driven;
He, with a few unhappy Striplings more,
Ventur'd too far upon the fatal shore:
The cruel natives thirsted for their blood,   15
And issued furious from a neighb'ring wood.
His friends all fell by brutal Rage o'erpowr'd,
Their flesh the horrid *Canibals* devour'd;
Whilst he alone escap'd by speedy flight,
And in a thicket lay conceal'd from sight!   20
Now he reflects on his companions fate,
His threat'ning danger, and abandon'd state.
Whilst thus in fruitless grief he spent the day,
A *Negro*[1] Virgin chanc'd to pass that way;
He view'd her naked beauties with surprise,   25
Her well proportion'd limbs and sprightly eyes!
With his complexion and gay dress amaz'd,
The artless Nymph upon the Stranger gaz'd;
Charm'd with his features and alluring grace,
His flowing locks and his enliven'd face.   30
His safety now became her tend'rest care,
A vaulted rock she knew and hid him there;
The choicest fruits the isle produc'd she sought,

And kindly to allay his hunger brought;
And when his thirst requir'd, in search of drink,   35
She led him to a chrystal fountain's brink.
Mutually charm'd by various arts they strove,
To inform each other of their mutual love;
A language soon they form'd, which might express
Their pleasing care and growing tenderness.   40
With tygers speckled skins she deck'd his bed,
O'er which the gayest plumes of birds were spread;
And every morning, with the nicest care,
Adorn'd her well turn'd neck and shining hair,
With all the glittering shells and painted flowers,   45
That serve to deck the Indian Virgins bowers.
And when the sun descended in the sky,
And length'ning shades foretold the ev'ning nigh,
Beneath some spreading palm's delightful shade,
Together sat the Youth and lovely Maid;   50
Or, where some bubbling river gently crept,
She in her arms secur'd him while he slept.
When the bright moon in midnight pomp was seen,
And star-light glitter'd o'er the dewy green,
In some close arbor, or some fragrant grove,   55
He whisper'd vows of everlasting love.
Then, as upon the verdant turf he lay,
He oft would to th' attentive Virgin say,
"Oh could I but, my Yarico, *with thee*
"Once more my dear, my native country see!   60
"In softest silks thy limbs should be array'd,
"Like that of which the cloaths I wear are made;
"What different ways my grateful Soul would find,
"To indulge thy person and divert thy mind?
While she on the enticing accents hung,   65
That smoothly fell from his persuasive tongue;
One evening, from a rock's impending side,
An *European* vessel she descry'd,
And made them signs to touch upon the shore,
Then to her Lover she glad tidings bore;   70
Who with his Mistress to the ship descends,
And found the crew were country-men and friends.
Reflecting now upon the time he past,

Deep melancholy all his thoughts o'ercast,
"Was it for this, said he, *I cross'd the Main*   75
"Only a doating Virgin's heart to gain?
"I needed not for such a prize to roam,
"There are a thousand doating maids at home.
While thus his disappointed mind was toss'd,
The Ship arriv'd on the *Barbarian*[2] coast;   80
Immediately the Planters from the town,
Who trade for goods and *Negro* Slaves, came down;
And now his mind, by sordid int'rest sway'd,
Resolv'd to sell his faithful *Indian* Maid.
Soon at his feet for mercy she implor'd,   85
And thus in moving strains her fate deplor'd:
"O whither can I turn to seek redress,
"When thou'rt the cruel cause of my distress!
"If the remembrance of our former love,
"And all thy plighted vows want force to move;   90
"Yet, for the helpless Infant's sake I bear,
"Listen with pity to my just despair,
"Oh let me not in slavery remain,
"Doom'd all my life to drag a servile chain!
"It cannot surely be! thy generous breast   95
"An act so vile, so sordid must detest:
"But, if thou hate me, rather let me meet
"A gentler fate, and stab me at thy feet;
"Then will I bless thee with my dying breath,
"And sink contented in the shades of death.   100
Not all she said could his compassion move,
Forgetful of his vows and promis'd love;
The weeping Damsel from his knees he spurn'd,
And with her price pleas'd to the ship return'd.

AN EPISTLE FROM *YARICO* to *INKLE,*
After he had left her in SLAVERY. *LONDON:*
Printed for J. Cooper, in *Fleetstreet,*
1738.

If yet thou any memory retain
Of her thou doom'dst in slavery to remain,

Oh hear my Sorrow! 'twill be some relief
To the dear Author to unfold my grief.
'Tis thy injustice, thy destructive scorn,   5
And not the chain I drag, for which I mourn:
That to my limbs alone doth pain impart,
But thy ingratitude torments my heart.
Close in the deep recesses of my breast,
Thy lovely image still remains imprest;   10
And, spite of thy barbarity to me,
My faithful Soul for ever doats on thee.
I well remember that unhappy day,
In which I gaz'd my liberty away;
Charm'd with thy face like polish'd iv'ry fair,   15
Thy beauteous features and enticing hair.
How did I tremble, lest thy bloom of life
Shou'd fall a prey to some *Barbarian's* knife!
By love instructed first thy life to save,
I hid thee from them in a mossy cave;   20
And scarce durst venture out in search of food,
Lest they the while shou'd revel in thy blood.
Yet, by a sordid thirst of gain subdu'd,
You destin'd me to endless servitude;
And, when in vain thy stubborn heart to move   25
By the remembrance of our love I strove,
I begg'd thee, for thy unborn Infant's sake,
Compassion on my mis'ry to take:
But you, o'erpower'd by cruel avarice,
For my condition only rais'd my price.   30
When I beheld thee leave the fatal coast,
And every hope to move thy Soul was lost,
How did I my neglected bosom tear,
With all the fury of a wild despair!
Then on the sands a stupid corpse I lay,   35
Till by my Master's order dragg'd away;
My suff'rings were thy wretched Infant's death,
Who in one hour receiv'd and lost his Breath!
Yet still I must my hated life sustain,
Still linger on my anxious years in pain;   40
For once I knew a hoary Christian Priest

His every act strict piety confest,
Who told me, that *Beyond the azure skies*
And silver moon another region lies;
Where after death those Souls would surely go   45
Who here unjustly were depress'd with woe,
If they petition'd the all-powerful God,
To smooth their passage and direct their road:
And there in chrystal palaces or bowers,
Deck'd with eternal greens and fragrant flowers,   50
In songs and praises they their lives should spend,
Entranc'd in pleasures which will never end.
But those, who tir'd of life themselves destroy,
He said, *must never taste celestial joy;*
But underneath the earth to pits retire,   55
Where they will burn in everlasting fire.
And, spite of all the ills which I endure
I dare not venture such a dang'rous cure.
He told me too, but oh avert it Love,
And thou great over-ruling Power above!   60
That *Perjur'd men would to those pits be driven*
And ne'er must enter through the gates of heaven.
Think, if this sad conjecture should be true,
Dear faithless Youth, oh think, what wilt thou do!

FINIS

POEMS FROM
Caribbeana
THE "INGENIOUS LADY" OF BARBADOS
(fl. 1731–41)

The poems collected here all appeared in Samuel Keimer's *Barbados Gazette* between 1732 and 1735 and were reprinted in his two-volume miscellany *Caribbeana* in 1741. The identity of the poet remains obscure; the only hints are offered by Keimer's introductory remarks to each selection of poetry, which are reprinted here, along with his preface to volume 1. She was apparently born in England, spent some years in Barbados, and returned to England. Although the poems included here were first published in Barbados, a number of them were reprinted in various magazines in London. The object of her love poems seems to spend some time in Barbados, which is the cause for some of her laments. *Caribbeana* contains scores of examples of verse by both men and women, but the poems of this "ingenious Lady" are notable for their passion and skill.

Through his correspondence with other newspaper editors and by his publication of her poems in *Caribbeana*, Samuel Keimer is responsible for making the Ingenious Lady's works known. Keimer is best known as Benjamin Franklin's employer in Philadelphia, where he attempted to publish the newspaper *Universal Instructor in all the arts and sciences and Pennsylvania Gazette*. When it failed, Keimer moved to Barbados and established the first newspaper in the West Indies, the biweekly *Barbados Gazette*. Keimer returned to his native London about 1739 and published the *Caribbeana*, imitating the style of Richard Steele's periodical *Tatler* (1709–11) and using works drawn from some seven years of the *Barbados Gazette*. He died soon after.

Poems of the "Ingenious Lady" of Barbados

FROM

CARIBBEANA.

CONTAINING LETTERS and DISSERTATIONS,

Together with Poetical Essays, On various SUBJECTS and OCCASIONS;
Chiefly wrote by several Hands in the *WEST-INDIES,* And some of
them to Gentlemen residing there. Now collected together in
Two VOLUMES. Wherein are also comprised, divers Papers
relating to TRADE, GOVERNMENT, and LAWS in general;
but more especially, to those of the *British* Sugar-Colonies,
and of *Barbados* in particular: As likewise the Characters
of the most eminent Men that have died, of late Years,
in that Island. To which are added in
an APPENDIX, Some Pieces
never before Published.

LONDON: Printed for T. OSBORNE and W. SMITH, in *Gray's-Inn;*
J. CLARKE, at the *Royal Exchange;* S. AUSTIN, in *St. Paul's Church-Yard;*
G. HAWKINS, at *Temple-Bar;* R. DODSLEY, in *Pall-Mall,*
and W. LEWIS, in *Covent Garden.* M.DCC.XLI
[1741].

[From Samuel Keimer's Preface to Volume 1]

But we cannot drop the Poetry *of this Collection without distinguishing a considerable Number which were wrote to a Gentleman of* Barbados, *by a Lady then
living here (since deceased) and whom to name, would be an additional Credit to
the Work. Such of her Productions as have already appeared in any other Shape,
have been much called for, and greatly admired by the best Judges. These which were
in no other Hands till they first came abroad in the* West-Indies, *are certainly not
inferior to any of them; and if we may take her own Opinion for it, which we have
seen in a Letter to a Friend of her's, they are some of the best she ever wrote. But as
they would probably have soon been utterly lost, were it not for this our Care, so it
may perhaps be a Pleasure to her Acquaintance (which was very extensive) to trace
her Pen where they could little expect to find it; and which, 'tis apprehended, several
will be able to do. However, she is not the only Author of the fair Sex, to be found in
this Miscellany, which is all we think convenient to say, at present, on that Head.
Several other Copies of Verses there are, of a different Sort, which though composed*

here, were also first made publick from the Original Manuscripts by the only Press
that ever was known in any of the Caribbee Islands; *and which we shall now
leave to speak for themselves.* (ix)

Saturday, June 17, 1732.

The following Copy of Verses was never before in Print, tho' wrote many
Years ago. There are Instances enough of the Havock which *Love* makes
among the Men, and we hardly know a Dabler in Poetry, or indeed a good
Poet, who does not complain of the Cruelty of his Mistress. What I now present the Publick, is the tender Lamentation of a fair Lady, on being disappointed of suitable Returns to her Passion; and whether her's was sincere, or
not, is submitted to the experienced Readers of either Sex. For my own Part,
I do not doubt it; nor can I help wishing, therefore, as old as I am, that 'twas in
my Power to administer Relief to so much Anguish in a Female Breast.

Written at Midnight.

How tedious the long wintry Night appears,	
To unclos'd Eyes, which pass it all in Tears!	
Or if they close, how dreadful is the Dream!	
Some raging Lion, or some rapid Stream!	
My Spirits sunk, all pale and out of Breath,	5
Toiling with this imaginary Death;	
The melancholy Shadows of the Day,	
Does on my Soul in mournful Slumbers stay;	
For oh! my Griefs are of so sad a Kind,	
They pierce my Sense, and even kill my Mind;	10
My Dreams are with a thousand Dangers fraught,	
The mournful Pictures of my waking Thought;	
My Passions stagger underneath the Blow,	
And my Heart-breaking Strings refuse to go:	
Shou'd Fate grow kind, and my lost Love restore,	15
It cou'd leap up to meet his Eyes no more.	
Why nam'st thou Love, the Tyrant of thy Breast,	
That blights thy Bays, and murders all thy Rest?	
The fatal Sound is Poison to my Frame,	
Wakes all my Wounds, and fewels every Flame.	20
Oh, how I did burn, for a cold Icy Breast,	
Which, like a God, is by my Love addrest,	
With Sighs and Tears, and Groans, and broken Rest!	

Oh! witness for me, ev'ry doubled Hour,
To my Soul's Anguish, and my Passion's Pow'r.   25
A thousand Times, and more, I change my Side;
Restless I lie, and my poor Pillow chide;
Like a pale Ghost, I pass the heavy Night,
Traverse the Room out, watch the dying Light.
Alas! behold, the weary Taper fades,   30
And gives my Sorrow up to gloomy Shades;
To Thoughts, to mournful Thoughts, that darker are,
Than the veil'd Midnight Skies, without a Star.
Be still, ye Winds, my louder Sighs attend,
And you, fair Stream, to which my Tears descend,   35
The Sun will not this many an Hour arise,
The happy Sun in *Thetis'*[1] Bosom lies;
He needs ye not; alas! my Griefs alone
Are waking now, or Souls that Grief have known.
This is the Hour that troubled Spirits rove,   40
Sacred to melancholy hopeless Love.
All Things but Death, and Deathless Sorrow, rest,
Such as alarm my ever waking Breast.
Oh, could this Hand some friendly Weapon find,
To let out Life, and free my Captive Mind!   45
What holds it back? alas! Is there a Fear
I cou'd be more undone than I am here?
In some new World I long my Fate to try;
Vouchsafe, then, Heav'ns! to let your Mortal die.
Prometheus, fasten'd to the Rock, complains,   50
Whilst the rag'd Vulture drinks his bleeding Veins;
Thus Love and Sorrow every Joy devours,
Feeds on my Soul, and all my tender Hours.

Wednesday, November 28, 1733. From my CHAPEL.

Having lately obliged the Learned, I now hope to please the lovely Part of my
Readers, by inserting the following *Pieces,* which were wrote above Twelve
Years ago, by one of their own Sex, who made a considerable Figure in the
Beau Monde at Home. The Poems, which have never been in Print before,
were addressed, on different Occasions, to the Object of the Author's tender-
est Affections, who, 'tis said, is, and has been some Time, in this Island; and, if
I guess right at the Gentleman, the Lady is no more to be wondered at for her

Passion than she can be discommended for her Taste. But this, it seems, must be a Secret, which, if discovered, would at once deprive me of the Expectations I have of being often favoured with some of the politest Compositions that can possibly adorn my Paper.

To ********

Believe me; but my Actions speak
Thy Merit and my Truth;
Here all Expressions are too weak,
My dear engaging Youth.

Words faintly would my Love define,   5
If Words thou did'st approve;
My Eyes, my Arms, my Soul are thine,
And all reveal my Love.

There is no Atom in this Frame
That does not talk to thee,   10
And sigh and tremble at thy Name,
And plead for Love, and me.

Oh! listen to my beating Heart,
When thy dear Head reclines;
But, if it fail to speak its Part,   15
Attend my melting Lines.

With tender Passion they are fraught,
Nor dread the Critick's Ear,
While gentle *Cupid* tunes my Thought,
And is the Poet here.   20

To the SAME.

Lost to my longing Arms and Eyes,
My Heart to this soft Method flies;
The only One that has a Pow'r
From me to give thee one soft Hour:
Not all the Artful of thy Kind   5
Can, like this Paper, sooth my Mind;
Such Pow'r thy much lov'd Name can give
To this, that, while I write, *I live*.
Oh! so extravagant's my Flame,
I kiss each Letter of thy Name: 10

My Lips do oft too rudely press
The Lines with cruel Tenderness.
Love to my Soul ungentle grows;
Nor Bounds, nor Moderation knows:
A Thousand foolish Things I do;   15
Myself forgetting, while I think on you;
My Life, my Soul, my Pleasure and Employ;
The Business of my Thought, my lovely Boy;
My tender Master who has taught me more,
In one short Year, than Ages did before.   20

To the SAME. A PASTORAL.

With what unwearied Fondness I admire,
Tell to my gentle Love, my gentle Lyre:
The Words of *Antony* how I approve;
"One Day past by, and nothing saw but Love;
"Another Day, till Months and Years were tir'd,   5
"With looking on, our Passions unexpir'd."
Near thee for ever I could pass the Hours,
But Friends or Business half the Time devours;
A very few are left to Love and me;
Oh! wer't thou all my own, from Business free,   10
Enough Employment wou'd my Fondness find,
A thousand Methods to amuse thy Mind.
To some sweet Grotto I'd my Dearest guide,
Where the Sun shou'd not see me by thy Side;
My Head shou'd on thy dear lov'd Bosom lean,   15
And Love be by, to bless the tender Scene.
When tir'd with hearing my unweary'd Flame,
I then would woo thee in some other Name.
Waller [2] himself my Advocate should be,
Reading his Passion, gazing oft on thee.   20
Oh! with what Pride I should thy Bosom dress,
Kissing the Flowers with jealous Tenderness;
The tuneful Linnets to thy Hand I'll bring,
And teach them on thy very Breast to sing;
My Favourite Dog shall at thy Feet attend,   25
If e'er I go, my Charmer to defend;
Safe may'st thou slumber, if the grateful Brute,

Who loves thee well, but watches at thy Foot.
What shall I say to shew I love indeed?
Accept my Darling Crook, my tuneful Reed;   30
My Books, and all the Sonnets you approve;
Oh! read them well; for they express my Love;
Nor Tongue, nor Eyes, nor Numbers can explain
My Deathless Passion, for my lovely Swain.

Wednesday, February 7, 1733.[3]

As several of my future Papers will probably be filled with Matters of a more
serious and publick Nature, I intend to dedicate this to the Service of the
Ladies, by presenting them with some other Pieces of the amorous Fair one
mentioned formerly, who has long since distinguished herself amongst the
finest Writers in Poetry. They are all addressed to the same Gentleman, and
there is no Reason therefore to question but her Passion was as steady as it appears to be ardent. How well she has painted it, they are the best Judges who
have ever been in the like Circumstances; but I must declare I think there is a
peculiar Softness in the Verse, and a Tenderness in the Sentiments, which are
hardly to be met with in any of the best Performances of those of our own Sex,
on the same Subject. These Manuscripts were, I understand, put into the
Hands of a Friend of mine, to dispose of, as he should think proper, with these
Restrictions only from the Owner (who is now, it seems, a Man of Business)
that *Names* be concealed, and that he did not by publishing them at any Time
postpone what might be of more immediate Service to the Island. For my
Part, I have Reason to rejoice that having often been obliged to my Fellow-
Labourers in *Europe,* by borrowing from their Weekly Papers, I am like to be
able to return the Favour; since they will, no doubt, readily enough transcribe
from me what cannot but be acceptable to the politest Readers of the Age.

Occasioned by his Illness.

While for thy precious Life I fear,
From every Pore descends a Tear;
My Soul and Body feels, for thee,
An Universal Agony:
No Wonder if my Fears are more,   5
Who loves as none e'er lov'd before;
The little Floods will not suffice,
That Nature gives the weeping Eyes;
O'er all my Limbs a deathly Dew;

Others may mourn, but I shall die with you.   10
With thine, behold my Face grow pale,
My Speech all broken, and my Spirits fail.
My Eyes are on thy Features fix'd;
My Looks with Death and Sorrow mixt.
Something beyond ev'n Death, I find,   15
That hurts not the impassive Mind:
But here my very Soul is press'd,
And languishes within my Breast:
My trembling Hands the Pen refuse,
And Sorrow has undone my Muse.   20
Oh! Can I ever live to see
That Bosom press'd so oft by me,
Panting and lost for Want of Breath,
And those dear Eyes shut up in Death?
Distracting Thought! for thee I'll drain ⎤   25
My own Heart's Blood, and every Vein, ⎬
To make thy Channels flow again. ⎦
But if thy Soul will force its Way;
If Tears nor Groans will bribe its Stay,
Our Lips in the last Gasp shall join,   30
I'll catch thy Soul and give thee mine:
Till then, I'll near thy Bed attend,
My Eyes shall watch, my Knees shall bend;
The Stars my Midnight Hours shall see,
The Stars shall learn to watch of me: 35
Thy Cordials I will give with Care,
But, if a Tear shou'd mingle there,
Forgive my Fondness,—know that she,
Who weeps, as soon wou'd die for thee.
If thy Pulse move too slow a Pace,   40
My Sighs shall wing them in their Race;
Or, if too fast, my Tears shall chide
Thy beating Veins, and check the Tide.

To DAMON.[4]

Go, faithful Paper, to my Love impart
All the soft Things his Eyes have taught my Heart;

Learn from my Cheeks a paler Look to wear,
And copy every Tear that's streaming there;
Catch of my Sighs the melancholy Tone;   5
And imitate the Midnight dying Groan.
To his dear Soul my Agonies impart,
The everlasting Beatings of my Heart:
Oh! let my Sorrow an Adviser be;
For Grief itself might learn to look of me: 10
Tremble, as I do now, when you complain,
And say, *Thus shook her Soul at every Strain.*
Thus sunk her Voice, all faint her Accents grew;
But her last parting Breath was blessing you.
Then will he fold thee to his lovely Breast,   15
Where *Venus'* Doves, or Venus' self might rest.
The Spring's united Sweetness you will find,
The Damask Rose, and new-born Vi'let join'd;
The *Tuby-Rose, Carnation,* and *John-quill;*
Fraught with new Sweets, from every Pore distil.   20
But why do I his fragrant Bosom Wrong,
With Similes that only grace my Song?
For, oh! its matchless Sweetness is above
All Things on Earth, form'd by the God of Love,
Who has adorn'd him with his Mother's Charms;   25
And to her killing Eyes has join'd his Arms.
    Oh! who can say which Sense he pleases most?
      He has peculiar Art to touch them all;
    Not Virtue's self its Icy Pow'r can boast;
      The Soul and Body hastens to his Call.   30
Superior Magick to his Arms convey'd,
Than *His** who warm'd to Life the jolly Maid;
He has a Godlike Power to create;
He made me love, ah, cou'd he make me hate!
I then no soft Ambassador shou'd need;   35
Nor would I trouble thee, soft Friend, to plead.
I tremble, lest the Paper, I've convey'd,

Pygmalion. [The legendary king of Cyprus who sculpted a figure of Aphrodite with which he fell in love. The goddess gave the statue life, and Pygmalion married her.]

Itself be warm'd into some happy Maid;
Cou'd the cold Statue kindle into Fire?
What wilt thou do, who burns with my Desire!   40

To the SAME.

Let the God of Passion hear me,
It is Heaven to be near thee,
By thy lovely Eyes I swear,
And the Train of *Cupids* there;
I wou'd not thy Arms resign,   5
If a Monarch sigh'd for mine.
Thou wer't for my Wishes made,
To inchant me, to perswade;
While I fondly gaze upon thee,
While my Soul is doating on thee,   10
To my Lips it eager flies,
Or to my desiring Eyes.
On my Breast it will not stay,
By its Master charm'd away;
If thou lik'st, my Soul, then prithee   15
Keep the Fondling ever with thee;
For I have no Use for one,
When my dearer Soul is gone;
Then a kind of Corps[5] I seem,
And not *live,* but only *dream.*   20
In thy Absence I am dead,
Folded Arms and drooping Head:
If a Lover talks to me;
Still I answer him with thee;
Hear, he cries, *my raging Flame,*   25
Unawares, I sigh *thy Name;*
Oh! what Hope for any other,
Wheresoe'er thou art a Lover?
By thy Tenderness ingross'd,
None can land upon that Coast.   30
To some other Island bear
Common Sighs of empty Air;
Damon's Empire in my Heart
Interest will not shock, nor Art.

Saturday, April 20, 1734.

Sir,

Most of your Readers, I presume, who have seen the Performances of the *amorous* Lady already published in your Paper, will observe a Freedom in them which seems to despise the Rules of Criticks, and which must expose her therefore sometimes to their Censure. For my own Part, however, I think I see more Beauties in those Faults than in the most exact Compositions, without her Fire and Ease. But I am now to acquaint you that the lovely young *Minx* (who was not then above Nineteen) being once told the Opinion of others concerning her Writings, immediately took up a Pen in a Hand fairer than Alabaster, and, with the same Readiness that others dictate in Prose, wrote the following Verses, which probably may not be unentertaining to the Curious, as it is a true Specimen of the Genius and Spirit of the Author.

On being charged with Writing incorrectly.

I'm incorrect, the Learned say,
That *I write well, but not their Way.*
For this to every Star I bend;
From their dull Method Heaven defend;
Who labour up the Hill of Fame,   5
And pant and struggle for a Name;
My freeborn Thoughts I'll not confine,
Tho' all *Parnassus* could be mine.
No, let my Genius have its Way,
My Genius I will still obey;   10
Nor, with their stupid Rules, controul
The sacred Pulse that beats within my Soul.
I, from my very Heart, despise
These mighty dull, these mighty wise,
Who were the Slaves of *Busby's*[6] Nod,   15
And learn'd their Methods from his Rod.
Shall bright *Apollo* drudge at School,
And whimper till he grows a Fool?
Apollo, to the Learned coy,
In Nouns and Verbs finds little Joy;   20
The tuneful Sisters still he leads
To Silver Streams and flow'ry Meads;
He glories in an artless Breast,
And loves the Goddess Nature best.

Let *Dennis*[7] hunt me with his Spite,   25
Let me read *Dennis* every Night,
Or any Punishment sustain,
To 'scape the Labour of the Brain.
Let the Dull think, or let 'em mend
The trifling Errors they pretend;   30
Writing's my Pleasure, which my Muse
Wou'd not for all their Glory lose:
With Transport I the Pen employ,
And every Line reveals my Joy:
No Pangs of Thought I undergo,   35
My Words descend, my Numbers flow;
Tho' disallow'd, my Friend, I'd swear,
I wou'd not think, I wou'd not care,
If I a Pleasure can impart,
Or to my own, or thy dear Heart;   40
If I thy gentle Passions move;
'Tis all I ask of Fame, or Love.
This to the very Learned say;
If they are angry,—why they may;
I, from my very Soul, despise   45
These mighty dull, these mighty wise.

Saturday, June 1, 1734. From my CHAPEL.

Lest the above[8] should be thought to smell too much of the Counting-House by some of our Readers, we have subjoin'd another Piece from the *Fair-Fountain* which has so often entertain'd them. There have been great Inquiries concerning the *happy Man,* on whom so much Female Incense is bestow'd, but to no Purpose. However, as this Performance will help us to one Circumstance, *viz.* his being himself no Stranger to the Muses, so I am now able to add another, which is, that he has been in the Island at least seven Years.

To my gentle Damon *haste;* ⎫
Pour my Soul into his Breast, ⎬
Where I wish myself to rest. ⎭

To my Breast thy Verse applying,
Jealousy is heard no more;
Were I on the Point of dying,

It would every Pulse restore.
Now I am with Transport crying,   5
As I did with Pain before.

While thy Soul itself expressing
In so dear, so sweet a Key;
Mine, an equal Flame confessing,
Sounds in every Line to thee;   10
Oh my everlasting Blessing,
Form'd by Love himself for me!

While I to thy Arms am pressing,
All the World is lost to me:
If *Apollo* were addressing,   15
I would turn into a *Tree*,⁹
And be cold to his Caressing,
Fondly thus to gaze on thee.

If he with his Stars descended,
And would give them all to me;   20
Wer't thou poor and unbefriended,
I would yield them all for thee;
With such Truths the Love's attended,
Which now fills my Breast for thee.

I, no Tenderness disguising,   25
Pour out every Thought to thee;
Every little Art despising,
Which with meaner Hearts agree;
Take my Soul, as it is rising,
Flowing in my Verse to Thee,   30

If with Truth I can retain thee,
Oh how happy I shall be!
Let these Arms for ever chain thee;
Never wishing to be free;
If their eager Pressings pain thee,   35
Pay back all the Wrongs on me.

Be with Tenderness surveying,
Think how great my Love must be;
My Heart, for Numbers never staying,

Flies almost in Prose to thee;   40
And the God of Love, obeying,
Thinks not of my Fame, nor me.

The following Poetical Epistle, from the ingenious Lady so often mentioned
in this Paper, I have before me, in her own Hand-Writing. It is directed exactly as I have printed it; which my curious Readers, I presume, will not be
displeas'd to see.

A Letter to my Love.—All alone, past 12, in the Dumps.
        Absent from all that cou'd inspire
        My Numbers, or my Soul, with Fire.[10]

Oh! weep with me, the changing Scene,
Torn from my Arms; devour'd with Spleen;
Instead of those dear Eyes, I look
Upon the Fire, or else a Book:
But Oh how dull must either be   5
To Eyes that have been studying thee!
Unless the Poet does express
Something that strikes my Tenderness,
I throw the Leaves neglected by,
And in my Chair supinely lie;   10
Or to the Pen and Ink I haste,
And there a World of Paper waste.
All I can write, tho' Love is here,
Does much unlike my Soul appear.
Angry, the scrawling Side I turn,   15
I write and blot, and write and burn;
Then to the Bottle I repair,
The Poets tell us Ease is there:
But I thy absent Hand repine,
Whose Sweetness us'd to *zest* the Wine;   20
Wine in this sullen Moment fails;
I burn my Pen, I bite my Nails,
Rail at my Stars, nay, I accuse
Even my Lover, and my Muse.
Why did he let me go, I cry,   25
—And, now I think on't, tell me why?

You might have kind Excuses made
To one so willing to ha' staid:
The Night was rainy, and the Wind
To all thy softest Wishes kind.   30
For thee and Love methought it blew,
As if my parting Pains it knew,
As if I was a Lover too.
I'm safely shaded from its Pow'r;
But I regard its Rage no more: 35
Now let it tempest as it please,
Or move the Groves, or fright the Seas;
It cannot now alarm my Rest,
Unless it reach thy dearer Breast.
Oh! hasten to me; let my Arms   40
Protect thee from the wintry Storms.
I tremble lest the Cold should dare
To pierce thee—let my Image, there,
Defend it, if it has a Charm,
From these and every other Harm.   45
I want thy Bosom to repose
My beating Heart, oppress'd with Woes;
I want thy Voice my Soul to chear,
Thy Voice is Musick to my Ear;
I want thy dear lov'd Hand to press   50
My Neck, with silent Tenderness;
I want thy Eyes to make me bright,
And charm this sullen Hour of Night.
This Hour, when Pallid Ghosts appear,
Oh! cou'd it bring thy Shadow here;   55
I every Substance wou'd resign,
To clasp thy Aerial Breast to mine;
Or if, my Love, that could not be,
I would turn Air to mix with thee.

Occasion'd by some Lines of his.
1.

While you so sweetly sing your Flame,
My list'ning Soul admires;
But Jealous of its dying Fame,

While thine so high aspires.
Where has thy Genius slept so long?   5
Oh! thou hast done my Fondness wrong!

2.

Coud'st thou a softer Subject chose,
Than Passion so refin'd;
It wou'd have tun'd ungentle Prose,
And every Letter join'd.   10
The Words would, like our Bosoms, meet,
And, as our Arms, the downy Feet.

3.

Behold, great God of soft Desire,
My Love's harmonious Strain;
I bless thy Power that aids his Lyre,   15
So gently to complain;
In all the Arts of Verse unknown,
He trusted to thy Dart alone.

4.

Let others stupid Methods seek,
And to *Parnassus* toil,   20
By *Latin* and loud sounding *Greek,*
And plough the rugged Soil;
Love, in one Hour, informs them more
Than *Busby*[11] cou'd in Years before.

5.

Oh! with thy gentle Master stay,   25
Who has such Wonders wrought;
Nor from these Arms depart away,
Where first thy Soul was taught;
My Lips shall pay thee every Line,
And all *Parnassus* shall be thine.   30

6.

The labouring Poets, distanc'd now
By thy superior Race,
Shall rave and pant, and wonder how
You reach'd, so soon, the Place.
They for thy Master will enquire,   35
Say, *'Twas a Mistress tun'd thy Lyre.*

7.

Bid 'em unlearn the odious Rules,
That keep them back so long;
The heavy Luggage of the Schools,
Which does their Fancy wrong.   40
Oh! bid them read thy artless Lines,
Where Love, and lovely Nature, shines.

8.

Trust me, my most belov'd and dear,
Thy Heart will Credit find;
The Musick of it enters here,   45
And softens all my Mind:
Now every Passion, to thy Lays,
A new and sweet Obedience pays.

9.

So lavish Nature was before
To thy engaging Face,   50
She had but this one Beauty more,
This one resistless Grace;
With this the Victory is whole,
And I deliver up my Soul.
—*Sign'd and Seal'd in the Presence of the* God of Love *and the* Muses.

To DAMON.[12]

In vain, oh! much in vain, for Rest I seek;
My Lips miss thine, my Cheek thy softer Cheek:
From Side to Side, the live-long Night I move,
No longer press'd by the dear Arms I love:
No longer I thy trembling Accents hear,   5
Soft as an Angel's, melting in my Ear,
My Life, my Angel, my enchanting Dear.
Oh what a Harmony thy Voice affords,
When tun'd by Love to those endearing Words!
Softer than Reeds that do the Herdlings call,   10
Or Summer-Winds, or Waters when they fall.
Oh my Delight! when thy dear Form was made,
The Gods of Love and Musick lent their Aid;
The gentle Atoms in such Order fell,
That Nature smiling said, *The Piece is well.*   15

A Thousand *Cupids,* with peculiar Grace,
Command the muscles of thy pleasing Face.
How oft my Heart has bless'd their little Toil,
And leap'd within my Breast at ev'ry Smile;
Various Attractions call my Muse to praise,   20
My Verse, my Wishes charm'd a Thousand Ways:
Shall I the Beauties of thy Soul commend,
Which warms the Form I love, and is my Friend?
'Tis that, my lovely Youth, inspires thy Charms,
Sits on thy Lips, and strains me to thy Arms: 25
A Thousand Blessings all its Wishes wait,
Sweeten its Hours, and Death be wondrous late:
E're that arrives, Oh! may I right divine!
May I be dead, if I'm no longer thine;
If thou, my Soul, art parted from my Breast,   30
By Time, new Friends, or cruel Interest;
The killing Thought my ready Tears demands,
Stabs my poor Heart, and sinks my trembling Hands.
Oh! come, my dearest Life, and give me Rest,
My Arms are tir'd with folding on my Breast: 35
My weeping Eyes do for thy Features long;
My Hearing, for the Musick of thy Tongue.
Oh! ev'ry Sense will die without thee soon,
And Soul and Body both be out of Tune.

To my LOVE. Wrote in Tears.

Dearest Creature of thy Kind,
All that can transport my Mind;
While I hold thee to my Breast,
Ev'ry Wish but *one* is blest;
That some sad Hour (O Heav'n remove   5
It far!) must take me from my Love.
Seas must our longing Arms divide,
The Winds oppose, and raging Tide;
Then shall I wish *Leander's*[13] Arms,
To force the Waves, and meet thy Charms,   10
Then shall I curse my feeble Kind,
And wish my Body all o'er Mind.
Oh! wilt thou then, far from my Sight,

Forget to love, forbear to write?
Or wilt thou sigh, when thou art told   15
——, thy once belov'd, is cold.
Thy Absence gave the mortal Blow;
She ceas'd to live, she lov'd thee so.
When Fate or Chance directs thy Way
To *England,* visit my sad Clay.   20
Oh! as you kneel before my Shrine,
Wonder not if thy Sighs I join;
My Bosom, us'd to mourn for thee,
Will to thy Voice an Eccho be.

The Sugar Cane: A Poem, In Four Books

JAMES GRAINGER

(c. 1721–1766)

James Grainger was born in Berwickshire in southeast Scotland, the son of a tax collector. He studied medicine at the University of Edinburgh, spent three years as an army surgeon in Scotland and Holland, and made a grand tour of Europe before receiving the degree of M.D. in 1753. Moving on to London, Grainger became a member of the Royal College of Physicians but met with difficulty in making a living as a physician. He supplemented his income by writing for various magazines on medical and literary topics and by publishing poetry of his own. A self-taught Latinist, Grainger published translations of classical Latin poems, the most notable being the *Elegies of Tibullus,* which was scathingly reviewed by his fellow Scot and onetime friend Tobias Smollett, prompting a bitter exchange of insults in print between the two. His later works include what became the standard reference work on West Indian diseases and a ballad included in Thomas Percy's *Reliques of Ancient English Poetry.* His literary interests led to friendships with the crème de la crème of London's cultural world at mid-century: Robert Dodsley, Oliver Goldsmith, Samuel Johnson, Thomas Percy, Sir Joshua Reynolds, William Shenstone. In his *Life of Johnson,* James Boswell records Bishop Percy's opinion of Grainger: "He was not only a man of genius and learning, but had many excellent virtues; being one of the most generous, friendly, and benevolent men I ever knew."[1]

In hopes of improving his fortune, Grainger set out in 1759 to the West Indies as a paid companion to John Bourryau, a wealthy friend who owned plantations in the island of Saint Christopher (now Saint Kitts). Shortly after arriving, Grainger met and married a local heiress, whose family made him manager of their estates. Grainger continued his medical practice on the side, hoping one day to be able to buy his own sugar plantation. His authorship of *The Sugar Cane* (1764) represents his education in the cultivation and manufacture of sugar, combined with his continuing interest in medicine and his growing interest in the history, geography, and natural history of the islands. After four years in the Caribbean, Grainger traveled back to London, where he presented his long georgic poem to his circle of literary friends for their opinions. According to Boswell, the manuscript of the poem was read at Sir Joshua Reynolds's house, where the company was amused by Grainger's account of the ravages caused in the sugar cane fields by rats. The amusement caused among this literary group by the explicit descriptions of the conditions of sugar cane plantations demonstrates how unusual was Grainger's innovation of including specific technical and medical terminology in the neoclassical form of the georgic poem. One of the ways Grainger manages to maintain the high tone of the blank verse while also providing accurate and useful information is to use extensive footnotes detailing the various names and uses of local flora and fauna. The effect of reading the full poem with the full footnotes is to enjoy a tour de force of the West Indies at the height of the sugar-and-slavery system, when these small island colonies produced more wealth for Great Britain than all the North American colonies combined.

🐛

THE SUGAR-CANE:

A POEM. IN FOUR BOOKS. WITH NOTES. Agredior primusque

novis Helicona movere Cantibus, et viridi nutantes vertice sylvas;

Hospita sacra ferens, nulli memorata priorum. MANIL.[2]

By JAMES GRAINGER, M.D. &c. LONDON: Printed

for R. and J. Dodsley, in Pall-mall. MDCCLXIV

[1764].

PREFACE.

Soon after my arrival in the West-Indies, I conceived the design of writing a poem on the cultivation of the Sugar-Cane. My inducements to this arduous undertaking were, not only the importance and novelty of the subject, but more especially this consideration; that, as the face of this country was wholly differ-ent from that of Europe, so whatever hand copied its appearances, however rude, could not fail to enrich poetry with many new and picturesque images.

I cannot, indeed, say I have satisfied my own ideas in this particular: yet I must be permitted to recommend the precepts contained in this Poem. They are the children of Truth, not of Genius; the result of Experience, not the pro-ductions of Fancy. Thus, though I may not be able to please, I shall stand some chance of instructing the Reader; which, as it is the nobler end of all poetry, so should it be the principal aim of every writer who wishes to be thought a good man.

It must, however, be observed, that, though the general precepts are suited to every climate, where the Cane will grow; yet, the more minute rules are chiefly drawn from the practice of St. Christopher. Some selection was necessary; and I could adopt no modes of planting, with such propriety, as those I had seen practiced in that island, where it has been my good fortune chiefly to reside since I came to the West-Indies.

I have often been astonished, that so little has been published on the cultivation of the Sugar-Cane, while the press has groaned under folios on every other branch of rural oeconomy. It were unjust to suppose planters were not solicitous for the improvement of their art, and injurious to assert they were incapable of obliging mankind with their improvements.

And yet, except some scattered hints in Pere Labat,[3] and other French travellers in America; an Essay, by Colonel Martyn of Antigua,[4] is the only piece on plantership I have seen deserving a perusal. That gentleman's pamphlet is, indeed, an excellent performance; and to it I own myself indebted.

It must be confessed, that terms of art look awkward in poetry; yet didactic compositions cannot wholly dispense with them. Accordingly we find that Hesiod[5] and Virgil,[6] among the ancients, with Philips[7] and Dyer,[8] (not to mention some other poets now living in our own country); have been obliged to insert them in their poems. Their example is a sufficient apology for me, for in their steps I shall always be proud to tread.

> *vos sequor, ô Graiæ gentis decus, inque vestris nunc*
> *Fixa pedum pono pressis vestigia signis;*
> *Non ita certandi cupidus, quam propter amorem,*
> *Quod vos imitari aveo.*—[9]

Yet, like them too, I have generally preferred the way of description, wherever that could be done without hurting the subject.

Such words as are not common in Europe, I have briefly explained: because an obscure poem affords both less pleasure and profit to the reader.— For the same reason, some notes have been added, which, it is presumed, will not be disagreeable to those who have never been in the West-Indies.

In a West-India georgic, the mention of many indigenous remedies, as well as diseases, was unavoidable. The truth is, I have rather courted opportunities of this nature, than avoided them. Medicines of such amazing efficacy, as I have had occasion to make trials of in these islands, deserve to be universally known. And wherever, in the following poem, I recommend any such, I beg leave to be understood as a physician, and not as a poet.

Basseterre, Jan. 1763.

BOOK I.
ARGUMENT

Subject proposed. Invocation and address. What soils the Cane grows best in. The grey light earth. Praise of St. Christopher. The red brick mould. Praise of Jamaica, and of Christopher Columbus. The black soil mixed with clay and gravel. Praise of Barbadoes, Nevis, and Mountserrat. Composts may improve other soils. Advantages and disadvantages of a level plantation. Of a mountain-estate. Of a midland one. Advantages of proper cultivation. Of fallowing. Of compost. Of leaving the Woura, and penning cattle on the distant Cane-pieces. Whether yams improve the soil. Whether dung should be buried in each hole, or scattered over the piece. Cane-lands may be holed at any time. The ridges should be open to the trade-wind. The beauty of holing regularly by a line. Alternate holing, and the wheel-plough recommended to trial. When to plant. Wet weather the best. Rain often falls in the West-Indies, almost without any previous signs. The signs of rainy weather. Of fogs round the high mountains. Planting described. Begin to plant mountain-land in July: the low ground in November, and the subsequent months, till May. The advantage of changing tops in planting. Whether the Moon has any influence over the Cane-plant. What quantity of mountain and of low Cane-land may be annually planted. The last Cane-piece should be cut off before the end of July. Of hedges. Of stone inclosures. Myrtle hedges recommended. Whether trees breed the blast. The character of a good planter. Of weeding. Of moulding. Of stripping.

BOOK I.

What soil the Cane affects; what care demands;
Beneath what signs to plant; what ills await;
How the hot nectar best to christallize;
And Afric's sable progeny to treat:
A Muse, that long hath wander'd in the groves   5
Of myrtle-indolence, attempts to sing.

    Spirit of Inspiration, that did'st lead
Th' Ascrean Poet[10] to the sacred Mount,
And taught'st him all the precepts of the swain;
Descend from Heaven, and guide my trembling steps   10
To Fame's eternal Dome, where Maro reigns;
Where pastoral Dyer, where Pomona's Bard,[11]
And Smart[12] and Sommerville[13] in varying strains,
Their sylvan lore convey: O may I join
This choral band, and from their precepts learn   15
To deck my theme, which though to song unknown,
Is most momentous to my Country's weal!

    So shall my numbers win the Public ear;
And not displease Aurelius;[14] him to whom,

Imperial George,[15] the monarch of the main,   20
Hath given to wield the scepter of those isles,
Where first the Muse beheld the spiry Cane,*
Supreme of plants, rich subject of my song.

* The botanical name of the Cane is *Saccharum*. The Greeks and Romans seem to have known very little of this most useful and beautiful plant. Lucan and Pliny are the only Authors among the former [*sic*] who mention it; and, so far as I can find, Arrian is the only Greek. The first of these Writers, in enumerating Pompey's Eastern auxiliaries, describes a nation who made use of the Cane-juice as a drink: *Dulces bibebant ex arundine succos.* The industrious Naturalist says, *Saccharum et Arabia fert, sed laudatius India;* and the Greek Historian, in his περιπλους of the Red-sea, tells us of a neighbouring nation who drank it also; his words are, μελι το καλαμινον το λεγομενον σακχαρι. The Cane, however, as it was a native of the East, so has it been probably cultivated there time immemorial. The raw juice was doubtless first made use of; they afterwards boiled it into a syrup; and, in the process of time, an inebriating spirit was prepared therefrom by fermentation. This conjecture is confirmed by the etymology, for the Arabic word סבד is evidently derived from the Hebrew שבד, which signifies an *intoxicating liquor.* When the Indians began to make the Cane-juice into sugar, I cannot discover; probably, it soon found its way into Europe in that form, first by the Red-sea, and afterwards through Persia, by the Black-sea and Caspian; but the plant itself was not known to Europe, till the Arabians introduced it into the southern parts of Spain, Sicily, and those provinces of France which border on the Pyrenean mountains. It was also successfully cultivated in Egypt, and in many places on the Barbary-coast. From the Mediterranean, the Spaniards and Portuguese transported the Cane to the Azores, the Medeiras, the Canary and the Cape-Verd islands, soon after they had been discovered in the fifteenth century: and, in most of these, particularly Madeira, it throve exceedingly. Whether the Cane is a native of either the Great or Lesser Antilles cannot now be determined, for their discoverers were so wholly employed in searching after imaginary gold-mines, that they took little or no notice of the natural productions. Indeed the wars, wherein they wantonly engaged themselves with the natives, was another hindrance to physical investigation. But whether the Cane was a production of the West-Indies or not, it is probable, the Spaniards and Portuguese did not begin to cultivate it either there or in South-America (where it certainly was found), till some years after their discovery. It is also equally uncertain whether Sugar was first made in the Islands or on the Continent, and whether the Spaniards or Portuguese were the first planters in the new world: it is indeed most likely that the latter erected the first sugar-works in Brazil, as they are more lively and enterprizing than the Spaniards. However they had not long the start of the latter; for, in 1506, Ferdinand the Catholic ordered the Cane to be carried from the Canaries to St. Domingo, in which island one Pedro de Atenca soon after built an *Ingenio de açucar,* for so the Spaniards call a Sugar-work. But, though they began thus early to turn their thoughts to sugar, the Portuguese far outstripped them in that trade; for Lisbon soon supplied most of Europe with that commodity; and, notwithstanding the English then paid the Portuguese at the rate of 4 *l. per* C. wt. for muscovado, yet that price, great as it may now appear, was probably much less than what the Sugar from the East-Indies had commonly been sold for. Indeed, so intent was the Crown of Portugal on extending their Brazil-trade, that that of the East-Indies began to be neglected, and soon after suffered a manifest decay. However, their sugar made them ample amends, in which trade their continued almost without a rival for upwards of a century. At last the Dutch, in 1623, drove the

Where'er the clouds relent in frequent rains,
And the Sun fiercely darts his Tropic beam,   25
The Cane will joint, ungenial tho' the soil.
But would'st thou see huge casks, in order due,
Roll'd numerous on the Bay, all fully fraught
With strong-grain'd muscovado,* silvery-grey,
Joy of the planter; and if happy Fate   30
Permit a choice: avoid the rocky slope,
The clay-cold bottom, and the sandy beach.
But let thy biting ax with ceaseless stroke
The wild red cedar,† the tough locust‡ fell:
Nor let his nectar, nor his silken pods,   35
The sweet-smell'd cassia, or vast ceiba save.§

Portuguese out of all the northern part of Brazil; and, during the one and twenty years they kept that conquest, those industrious republicans learned the art of making sugar. This probably inspired the English with a desire of coming in for a share of the sugar-trade; accordingly they, renouncing their chimerical search after gold mines in Florida and Guiana, settled themselves soon after at the mouth of the river Surinam, where they cultivated the Cane with such success, that when the colony was ceded to the Dutch by the treaty of Breda, it maintained not less than 40,000 Whites, half that number of slaves, and employed one year with another 15,000 ton of shipping. This cession was a severe blow to the English trade, which it did not recover for several years, though many of the Surinam Planters carried their art and Negroes to the Leeward Islands and Jamaica, which then began to be the object of political consideration in England.

Sugar is twice mentioned by Chaucer, who flourished in the fourteenth century; and succeeding poets, down to the middle of the last, use the epithet *Sugar'd,* whenever they would express any thing uncommonly pleasing: since that time, the more elegant writers seldom admit of that adjective in a metaphorical sense; but herein perhaps they are affectedly squeamish.

*The Cane-juice being brought to the consistence of syrup, and, by subsequent coction, granulated, is then called *muscovado* (a Spanish word probably, though not found in Pineda) vulgarly brown Sugar; the French term it *sucre brut.*

†There are two species of Cedar commonly to be met with in the West Indies, the white and red, which differ from the cedars cultivated in the Bermudas: both are lofty, shady, and of quick growth. The white succeeds in any soil, and produces a flower which, infused like tea, is useful against fish poison. The red requires a better mould, and always emits a disagreeable smell before rain. The wood of both are highly useful for many mechanical purposes, and but too little planted.

‡This is also a lofty tree. It is of quick growth and handsome, and produces a not disagreeable fruit in a flat pod or legumen, about three inches long. It is a serviceable wood. In botanical books, I find three different names for the locust tree; that meant here is the *Siliqua edulis.*

§Canoes have been scooped out of this tree, capable of holding upwards of a hundred people; and many hundreds, as authors relate, have been at once sheltered by its shade. Its pods contain a very soft short cotton, like silk: hence the English call the tree the Silk-cotton-tree; and the Spaniards name its cotton *Lana de ceiba.* It has been wrought into stockings; but its com-

Yet spare the guava,* yet the guaiac spare;[†]
A wholesome food the ripened guava yields,
Boast of the housewife; while the guaiac grows
A sovereign antidote, in wood, bark, gum,   40
To cause the lame his useless crutch forego,
And dry the sources of corrupted love.
Nor let thy bright impatient flames destroy
The golden shaddoc,[‡] the forbidden fruit,
The white acajou, and rich sabbaca:[§]   45

---

monest use is to stuff pillows and mattrasses. It might be made an article of commerce, as the
tree grows without trouble, and is yearly covered with pods. An infusion of the leaves is a gentle
diaphoretic, and much recommended in the small-pox. The botanical name of the ceiba is *Bombax;* and the French call it *Fromager.* There are two species; the stem of the one being prickly, and
that of the other smooth.

*The Spaniards call this tree *guayava.* It bears a fruit as large, and of much the same shape
as a golden pippen. This is of three species, the yellow, the amazon, and the white; the last is the
most delicate, but the second sort the largest: All are equally wholesome, when stewed or made
into jelly, or marmalade. When raw, they are supposed to generate worms. Strangers do not always at first like their flavour, which is peculiarly strong. This, however, goes off by use, and they
become exceedingly agreeable. Acosta says the Peruvian guavas surpass those of any other part
of America. The bark of the tree is an astringent, and tanns leather as well as that of oak. The
French call the tree *Goyavier.* ["Acosta": José de Acosta (1539–1600), a Jesuit missionary to Peru,
published *Historia natural y moral de las Indias* (Madrid, 1590); published in English as *Natural
and Moral History of the Indies* (London: Val. Sims, 1604).]

[†]The lignum-vitae, or pockwood-tree. The virtues of every part of this truly medical tree
are too well known to be enumerated here. The hardness and incorruptibility of its timber make
abundant amends for the great slowness of its growth, for of it are formed the best posts for
houses against hurricanes, and it is no less usefully employed in building wind-mills and cattle-
mills.

[‡]This is the largest and finest kind of orange. It is not a native of America, but was brought
to the islands, from the East-Indies, by an Englishman, whose name it bears. It is of three kinds,
the sweet, the sour, and the bitter; the juice of all of them is wholesome, and the rind medical. In
flavour and wholesomeness, the sweet shaddoc excels the other two, and indeed every other
kind of orange, except the *forbidden fruit,* which scarce yields to any known fruit in the four
quarters of the world.

[§]This is the Indian name of the avocato, avocado, avigato, or, as the English corruptly call
it, alligator pear. The Spaniards in South-America name it aguacate, and under that name it is
described by *Ulloa.* However, in Peru and Mexico, it is better known by the appellation of *palta*
or *palto.* It is a sightly tree, of two species; the one bearing a green fruit, which is the most delicate, and the other a red, which is less esteemed, and grows chiefly in Mexico. When ripe, the
skin peels easily off, and discovers a butyraceous, or rather marrowy like substance, with greenish veins interspersed. Being eat with salt and pepper, or sugar and lime-juice, it is not only
agreeable, but highly nourishing; hence *Sir Hans Sloane* used to stile it Vegetable marrow. The

For, where these trees their leafy banners raise
Aloft in air, a grey deep earth abounds,
Fat, light; yet, when it feels the wounding hoe,
Rising in clods, which ripening suns and rain
Resolve to crumbles, yet not pulverize: 50
In this the soul of vegetation wakes,
Pleas'd at the planter's call, the burst on day.

    Thrice happy he, to whom such fields are given!
For him the Cane with little labour grows;
'Spite of the dog-star,[16] shoots long yellow joints;   55
Concocts rich juice, tho' deluges descend.
What if an after-offspring it reject?
This land, for many a crop, will feed his mills;
Disdain supplies, nor ask from compost aid.

    Such, green St. Christopher,* thy happy soil!—   60
Not Grecian Tempé, where Arcadian Pan,

fruit is of the size and shape of the pear named Lady's-thighs, and contains a large stone, from whence the tree is propagated. These trees bear fruit but once a year. Few strangers care for it; but, by use, soon become fond of it. The juice of the kernal marks linen with a violet-colour. Its wood is soft, and consequently of little use. The French call it *Bois d'anise,* and the tree *Avocat:* the botanical name is *Persea.* ["Ulloa": Don Antonio de Ulloa (1716 – 1795), author of *A Voyage to South-America* (London, 1758). "Sloane": author of *Voyage to the Islands* (London, 1707 & 1725).]

    *This beautiful and fertile island, and which, in Shakespear's words, may justly be stiled "A precious stone set in the silver sea," lies in seventeenth degree N[orth] L[atitude]. It was discovered by the great Christopher Columbus, in his second voyage, 1493, who was so pleased with its appearance, that he honoured it with his Christian name. Though others pretend, that appellation was given it from an imaginary resemblance between a high mountain in its centre, now called Mount Misery, to the fabulous legend of the Devil's carrying St. Christopher on his shoulders. But, be this as it will, the Spaniards soon after settled it, and lived in tolerable harmony with the natives for many years; and, as their fleets commonly called in there to and from America for provision and water, the settlers, no doubt, reaped some advantage from their situation. By *Templeman's Survey,* it contains eighty square miles, and is about seventy miles in circumference. It is of an irregular oblong figure, and has a chain of mountains, that run South and North almost from one end of it to the other, formerly covered with wood, but now the Cane plantations reach almost to their summits, and extend all the way, down their easy declining sides, to the sea. From these mountains some rivers take their rise, which never dry up; and there are many others which, after rain, run into the sea, but which, at other times, are lost before they reach it. Hence, as this island consists of mountain-land and valley, it must always make a middling crop; for when the low grounds fail, the uplands supply that deficiency; and, when the mountain canes are lodged (or become watery from too much rain) those in the plains yield surprisingly. Nor are the plantations here only seasonable, their Sugar sells for more than the Sugar of any other of his Majesty's islands; as their produce cannot be refined to the best advantage,

Knit with the Graces, tun'd his sylvan pipe,
While mute Attention hush'd each charmed rill;
Not purple Enna,[17] whose irriguous[18] lap,
Strow'd with each fruit of taste, each flower of smell,   65
Sicilian Proserpine, delighted, sought;
Can vie, blest-Isle, with thee.—Tho' no soft sound
Of pastoral stop thine echoes e'er awak'd;
Nor raptured poet, lost in holy trance,
Thy streams arrested with enchanting song: 70
Yet virgins,* far more beautiful than she

---

without a mixture of *St. Kitts'* muscovado. In the barren part of the island, which runs out toward Nevis, are several ponds, which in dry weather crystallize into good salt; and below Mount Misery is a small Solfaterre and collection of fresh water, where fugitive Negroes often take shelter, and escape their pursuers. Not far below is a large plain which affords good pasture, water, and wood; and, if the approaches thereto were fortified, which might be done at a moderate expence, it would be rendered inaccessible. The English, repulsing the few natives and Spaniards, who opposed them, began to plant tobacco here *A.D.* 1623. Two years after, the French landed in St. Christopher on the same day that the English-settlers received a considerable reinforcement from their mother-country; and, the chiefs of both nations, being men of sound policy, entered into an agreement to divide the island between them: the French retaining both extremities, and the English possessing themselves of the middle parts of the island. Some time after both nations erected sugar-works, but there were more tobacco, indigo, coffee, and cotton-plantations, than Sugar ones, as these require a much greater fund to carry them on, than those other. All the planters, however, lived easy in their circumstances; for, though the Spaniards, who could not bear to be spectators of their thriving condition, did repossess themselves of the island, yet they were soon obliged to retire, and the colony succeeded better than ever. One reason for this was, that it had been agreed between the two nations, that they should here remain neutral whatever wars their mother-countries might wage against each other in Europe. This was a wise regulation for an infant settlement; but, when King James [II] abdicated the British throne [in 1688], the French suddenly rose, and drove out the unprepared English by force of arms. The French colonists of St. Christopher had soon reason, however, to repent their impolitic breach of faith; for the expelled planters, being assisted by their countrymen from the neighbouring isles, and supported by a formidable fleet, soon recovered, not only their lost plantations, but obliged the French totally to abandon the island. After the treaty of *Ryswick* [1697], indeed, some few of those among them, who had not obtained settlements in Martinico and Hispaniola, returned to St. Christopher: but the war of the partition soon after breaking out [1701], they were finally expelled, and the whole island was ceded in Sovereignty to the crown of Great Britain, by the treaty of Utrecht [1713]. Since that time, St. Christopher has gradually improved, and it is now at the height of perfection. The Indian name of St. Christopher is *Liamuiga*, or the Fertile Island. ["Templeman's Survey": Thomas Templeman (d. 1729), *A New Survey of the Globe* (London, c. 1729).]

*The inhabitants of St. Christopher look whiter, are less sallow, and enjoy finer complexions, than any of the dwellers on the other islands. *Sloane.*

Whom Pluto ravish'd,[19] and more chaste, are thine:
Yet probity, from principle, not fear,
Actuates thy sons, bold, hospitable, free:
Yet a fertility, unknown of old,   75
To other climes denied, adorns thy hills;
Thy vales, thy dells adorns.—O might my strain
As far transcend the immortal songs of Greece,
As thou the partial subject of their praise!
Thy fame should float familiar thro' the world;   80
Each plant should own thy Cane her lawful lord;
Nor should old Time, song stops the flight of Time,
Obscure thy lustre with his shadowy wing.

    Scarce less impregnated, with every power
Of vegetation, is the red brick-mould,   85
That lies on marly beds.—The renter, this
Can scarce exhaust; how happy for the heir!

    Such the glad soil, from whence Jamaica's sons
Derive their opulence: thrice fertile land,
"The pride, the glory of the sea-girt isles,   90
Which, like to rich and various gems, inlay
The unadorned bosom of the deep,"[20]
Which first Columbus' daring keel explor'd.

    Daughters of Heaven, with reverential awe,
Pause at that godlike name; for not your flights   95
Of happiest fancy, can outsoar his fame.

    Columbus, boast of science, boast of man!
Yet, by the great, the learned, and the wise,
Long held a visionary; who, like thee,
Could brook their scorn; wait seven long years at court,   100
A selfish, sullen, dilatory court;
Yet never from thy purpos'd plan decline?
No God, no Hero, of poetic times,
In Truth's fair annals, may compare with thee!
Each passion, weakness of mankind, thou knew'st,   105
Thine own concealing; firmest base of power:
Rich in expedients; what most adverse seem'd,
And least expected, most advanc'd thine aim.
What storms, what monsters, what new forms of death,

In a vast ocean, never cut by keel,   110
And where the magnet* first its aid declin'd;
Alone, unterrified, didst thou not view?
Wise Legislator, had the Iberian King[21]
Thy plan adopted, murder had not drench'd
In blood vast kingdoms; nor had hell-born Zeal,   115
And hell-born Avarice, his arms disgrac'd.
Yet, for a world, discover'd and subdu'd,
What meed[22] had'st thou? With toil, disease, worn out,
Thine age was spent solliciting the Prince,
To whom thou gav'st the sceptre of that world.   120
Yet, blessed spirit, where inthron'd thou sit'st,
Chief 'mid the friends of man, repine not thou:
Dear to the Nine, thy glory shall remain
While winged Commerce either ocean ploughs;
While its lov'd pole the magnet coyly shuns;   125
While weeps the guaiac, and while joints the Cane.

    Shall the Muse celebrate the dark deep mould,
With clay or gravel mix'd?—This soil the Cane

---

*The declension of the needle was discovered, *A.D.* 1492, by Columbus, in his first voyage to America; and would have been highly alarming to any, but one of his undaunted and philosophical turn of mind.

    This century [i.e., the fifteenth] will always make a distinguished figure in the history of the human mind; for, during that period, printing was invented, Greek-learning took refuge in Italy, the Reformation began, and America was discovered.

    The island of Jamaica was bestowed on Columbus, as some compensation for his discovery of the new world; accordingly his son James settled, and planted it, early (*A.D.* 1509) the following century. What improvements the Spaniards made therein is no where mentioned; but, had their industry been equal to their opportunities, their improvements should have been considerable; for they continued in the undisturbed possession of it till the year 1596, when Sir Anthony Shirley, with a single man of war, took and plundered St. Jago de la Vega, which then consisted of 2000 houses. In the year 1635, St. Jago de la Vega was a second time plundered by 500 English from the Leeward islands, tho' that capital, and the fort, (which they also took) were defended by four times their number of Spaniards. One and twenty years afterwards [1655, actually.], the whole island was reduced by the forces sent thither by Oliver Cromwell, and has ever since belonged to England. It is by far the largest island possessed by the English in the West Indies. Sir Thomas Modyford, a rich and eminent planter of Barbadoes, removed to Jamaica *A.D.* 1660, to the great advantage of that island, for he instructed the young English settlers to cultivate the Sugar-cane; for which, and other great improvements which he then made them acquainted with, King Charles, three years afterwards, appointed him Governour thereof, in which honourable employment he continued till the year 1669.

With partial fondness loves; and oft surveys
Its progeny with wonder.—Such rich veins   130
Are plenteous scatter'd o'er the Sugar-isles:
But chief that land, to which the bearded fig,*
Prince of the forest, gave Barbadoes name:
Chief Nevis,† justly for its hot baths fam'd:

*This wonderful tree, by the Indians called the Banian-tree; and by the botanists *Ficus Indica,* or *Bengaliensis,* is exactly described by *Q. Curtius,* and beautifully by Milton in the following lines:

> The Fig-tree, not that kind renowned for fruit,
> But such as at this day to Indians known,
> In Malabar and Decan spreads her arms;
> Branching so broad and long, that in the ground,
> The bended twigs take root, and daughters grow
> About the mother-tree, a pillar'd shade,
> High over-arch'd, and echoing walks between.
> There oft the Indian herdsman, shunning heat,
> Shelters in cool, and tends his pasturing herds
> At Loop-holes cut through thickest shade.

What year the Spaniards first discovered Barbadoes is not certainly known; this however is certain, that they never settled there, but only made use of it as a stock-island in their voyages to and from South-America, and the Islands; accordingly we are told, when the English first landed there, which was about the end of the sixteenth or beginning of the seventeenth century, they found in it an excellent breed of wild hogs, but no inhabitants. In the year 1627, Barbadoes, with most of the other Caribbee-islands, were granted by Charles I. to the Earl of Carlisle, that nobleman agreeing to pay the Earl of Marlborough, and his heirs, a perpetual annuity of 300 *l. per annum,* for waving his claim to Barbadoes, which he had obtained, by patent, in the preceding reign. The adventurers to whom that nobleman parcelled out this island, at first cultivated tobacco; but, that not turning out to their advantage, they applied, with better success, to cotton, indigo, and ginger. At last, some cavaliers of good fortune transporting themselves thither, and introducing the Sugar-cane (*A.D.* 1647) probably from Brazil, in ten years time the island was peopled with upwards of 30,000 Whites, and twice that number of Negroes, and sent yearly very considerable quantities of sugar to the mother-country. At the Restoration, King Charles II. bought off the claim of the Carlisle-family; and, in consideration of its then becoming a royal instead of a proprietary government, the planters gave the Crown 4½ *per cent.* on their sugars; which duty still continues, although the island is said to be less able to pay it now than it was a hundred years ago. It is upwards of 20 miles long, and in some places almost 14 broad. ["Q. Curtius": (fl. first century A.D.) Roman historian and biographer of Alexander the Great.]

†This island, which does not contain many fewer square miles than St. Christopher, is more rocky, and almost of a circular figure. It is separated from that island by a channel not above one mile and a half over, and lies to windward. Its warm bath possesses all the medical properties of the hot well at Bristol, and its water, being properly bottled, keeps as well at sea, and is no less agreeable to the palate. It was for many years the capital of the Leeward Island government; and, at that period, contained both more Whites and Blacks than it does at present, often mus-

And breezy Mountserrat,* whose wonderous springs   135
Change, like Medusa's head, whate'er they touch,
To stony hardness; boast this fertile glebe.[23]

    Tho' such the soils the Antillean Cane
Supremely loves; yet other soils abound,
Which art may tutor to obtain its smile.   140
Say, shall the experienc'd Muse that art recite?
How sand will fertilize stiff barren clay?
How sand unites the light, the porous mould,
Sport of each breeze? And how the torpid nymph
Of the rank pool, so noisome to the smell,   145
May be solicited, by wily ways,
To draw her humid train, and, prattling, run
Down the reviving slopes? Or shall she say
What glebes ungrateful to each other art,
Their genial treasures ope to fire alone?   150
Record the different composts; which the cold
To plastic gladness warm? The torrid, which
By soothing coolness win? The sharp saline,
Which best subdue? Which mollify the sour?

    To thee, if Fate low level land assign,   155
Slightly cohering, and of sable hue,
Far from the hill; be parsimony thine.
For tho' this year when constant showers descend;
The speeding gale, thy sturdy numerous stock,

---

tering 3000 men. The English first settled there *A.D.* 1628. Sixty-two years afterwards, the chief town was almost wholly destroyed by an earthquake; and, in 1706, the planters were well-nigh ruined by the French, who carried off their slaves contrary to *capitulation* [i.e., the terms of the treaty]. It must have been discovered in Columbus's second voyage, *A.D.* 1493.

    *This island, which lies about 30 miles to the south-west of Antigua, is not less famous for its solfaterre (or volcano), and hot petrifying spring, than for the goodness of its sugars. Being almost circular in its shape, it cannot contain much less land than either Nevis or St. Christopher. It is naturally strong, so that when the French made descents thereon, in K. William and Q. Anne's time, they were always repulsed with considerable loss. It was settled by that great adventurer Sir Thomas Warner, *A.D.* 1632, who sent thither some of his people from St. Christopher, for that purpose. In the beginning of the reign of Charles II. the French took it, but it was restored, *A.D.* 1667, by the treaty of Breda. In this island, the Roman-catholics, who behaved well when our enemies attempted to conquer it, have many privileges, and of course are more numerous there, than in any other of the English Caribbee-islands. Its capital is called Plymouth. Columbus discovered it in his second voyage.

Scarcely suffice to grind thy mighty Canes: 160
Yet thou with rueful eye, for many a year,
Shalt view thy plants burnt by the torch of day;
Hear their parch'd wan blades rustle in the air;
While their black sugars, doughy to the feel,
Will not ev'n pay the labour of thy swains.   165

    Or, if the mountain be thy happier lot,
Let prudent foresight still thy coffers guard.
For tho' the clouds relent in nightly rain,
Tho' thy rank Canes wave lofty in the gale:
Yet will the arrow,* ornament of woe,   170
(Such monarchs oft-times give) their jointing stint;
Yet will winds lodge them, ravening rats destroy,
Or troops of monkeys thy rich harvest steal.
The earth must also wheel around the sun,
And half perform that circuit; ere the bill   175
Mow down thy sugars: and tho' all thy mills,
Crackling, o'erflow with a redundant juice;
Poor tastes the liquor; coction long demands,
And highest temper,† ere it saccharize;
A meagre produce. Such is Virtue's meed,   180
Alas, too oft in these degenerate days.
Thy cattle likewise, as they drag the wain,[24]
Charg'd from the beach; in spite of whips and shouts,
Will stop, will pant, will sink beneath the load;
A better fate deserving.—   185
Besides, thy land itself is insecure:
For oft the glebe, and all its wavering load,
Will journey, forc'd off by the mining rain;
And, with its faithless burden, disarrange
Thy neighbour's vale. So Markley-hill[25] of old,   190

---

*That part of the Cane which shoots up into the fructification, is called by planters its Arrow, having been probably used for that purpose by the Indians. Till the arrow drops, all additional jointing in the Cane is supposed to be stopped.

†Shell, or rather marble quick-lime, is so called by the planters: Without this, the juice of the Cane cannot be concreted into sugar, at least to advantage. See Book III. With quick-lime the French join ashes as a temper, and this mixture they call *Enyvrage*. It is hoped the Reader will pardon the introduction of the verb *saccharize*, as no other so emphatically expressed the Author's meaning; for some chemists define sugar to be a native salt, and others a soap.

As sung thy bard, Pomona, (in these isles
Yet unador'd;) with all its spreading trees,
Full fraught with apples, chang'd its lofty site.

But, as in life, the golden mean is best;
So happiest he whose green plantation lies   195
Nor from the hill too far, nor from the shore.

Planter, if thou with wonder wouldst survey
Redundant harvests load thy willing soil;
Let sun and rain mature thy deep-hoed land,
And old fat dung co-operate with these.   200
Be this great truth still present to thy mind;
The half well-cultur'd far exceeds the whole,
Which lust of gain, unconscious of its end,
Ungrateful vexes with unceasing toil.

As, not indulg'd, the richest lands grow poor;   205
And Liamuiga* may, in future times,
If too much urg'd, her barrenness bewail:
So cultivation, on the shallowest soil,
O'erspread with rocky cliffs, will bid the Cane,
With spiry pomp, all bountifully rise.   210
Thus Britain's flag, should discipline relent,
'Spite of the native courage of her sons,
Would to the lily strike: ah, very far,
Far be that woful day: the lily then
Will rule wide ocean with resistless sway;   215
And to old Gallia's haughty shore transport
The lessening crops of these delicious isles.

Of composts shall the Muse descend to sing,
Nor soil her heavenly plumes? The sacred Muse
Nought sordid deems, but what is base; nought fair   220
Unless true Virtue stamp it with her seal.
Then, Planter, wouldst thou double thine estate;
Never, ah never, be asham'd to tread
Thy dung-heaps, where the refuse of thy mills,
With all the ashes, all thy coppers yield,   225
With weeds, mould, dung, and stale, a compost form,
Of force to fertilize the poorest soil.

*The Caribbean name of St. Christopher.

But, planter, if thy lands lie far remote
And of access are difficult; on these,
Leave the Cane's sapless foliage; and with pens   230
Wattled, (like those the Muse hath oft-times seen
When frolic fancy led her youthful steps,
In green Dorchestria's[26] plains), the whole inclose:
There well thy stock with provender supply;
The well-fed stock will soon that food repay.   235

    Some of the skilful teach, and some deny,
That yams improve the soil.* In meagre lands,
'Tis known the yam will ne'er to bigness swell;
And from each mould the vegetable tribes,
However frugal, nutriment derive: 240
Yet may their sheltering vines, their dropping leaves,
Their roots dividing the tenacious glebe,
More than refund the sustenance they draw.

    Whether the fattening compost, in each hole,
'Tis best to throw; or, on the surface spread;   245
Is undetermin'd: Trials must decide.
Unless kind rains and fostering dews descend,
To melt the compost's fertilizing salts;
A stinted plant, deceitful of thy hopes,
Will from those beds slow spring where hot dung lies: 250
But, if 'tis scatter'd generously o'er all,
The Cane will better bear the solar blaze;
Less rain demand; and, by repeated crops,
Thy land improv'd, its gratitude will show.

    Enough of composts, Muse; of soils, enough: 255
When best to dig, and when inhume the Cane;
A task how arduous! next demands thy song.

    It not imports beneath what sign thy hoes
The deep trough sink, and ridge alternate raise:

---

*The botanical name of this plant is *Dioscoria*. Its leaves, like those of the water-melon, or gourd, soon mantle over the ground where it is planted. It takes about eight months to come to perfection, and then is a wholesome root, either boiled or roasted. They will sometimes weigh one and an half, or two pounds, but their commonest size is from six ounces to nine. They cannot be kept good above half a year. They are a native of South-America, the West Indies, and of *most parts of Guinea*. [I.e., the coastal regions of West Africa.]

If this from washes guard thy gemmy tops;*   260
And that arrest the moisture these require.

Yet, should the site of thine estate permit,
Let the trade-wind thy ridges ventilate;
So shall a greener, loftier Cane arise,
And richest nectar in thy coppers foam.   265

As art transforms the savage face of things,
And order captivates the harmonious mind;
Let not thy Blacks irregularly hoe:
But, aided by the line, consult the site
Of thy demesnes; and beautify the whole.   270
So when a monarch rushes to the war,
To drive invasion from his frighted realm;
Some delegated chief the frontier views,
And to each squadron, and brigade, assigns
Their order'd station: Soon the tented field   275
Brigade and squadron, whiten on the sight;
And fill spectators with an awful joy.

Planter, improvement is the child of time;
What your sires knew not, ye their offspring know:
But hath your art receiv'd Perfection's stamp?   280
Thou can'st not say.—Unprejudic'd, then learn
Of ancient modes to doubt, and new to try:
And if Philosophy, with Wisdom, deign
Thee to enlighten with their useful lore;
Fair Fame and riches will reward thy toil.   285

Then say, ye swains, whom wealth and fame inspire,
Might not the plough, that rolls on rapid wheels,
Save no small labour to the hoe-arm'd gang?
Might not the culture taught the British hinds,
By Ceres' son,† unfailing crops secure;   290
Tho' neither dung nor fallowing lent their aid?

*The summit of the Cane being smaller-jointed as well as softer, and consequently having
more gems, from whence the young sprouts shoot, is properer for planting than any other part
of it. From one to four junks, each about a foot long, are put in every hole. Where too many junks
are planted in one hole, the Canes may be numerous, but can neither become vigorous, nor yield
such a quantity of rich liquor as they otherwise would. In case the young shoots do not appear
above ground in four or five weeks, the deficiencies must be supplied with new tops.

†Jethro Tull, Esq; the greatest improver in modern husbandry.

The cultur'd land recalls the devious Muse;
Propitious to the planter be the call:
For much, my friend, it thee imports to know
The meetest season to commit thy tops,   295
With best advantage, to the well-dug mould.
The task how difficult, to cull the best
From thwarting sentiments; and best adorn
What Wisdom chuses, in poetic garb!
Yet, Inspiration, come; the theme unsung,   300
Whence never poet cropt one bloomy wreath;
Its vast importance to my native land,
Whose sweet idea rushes on my mind,
And makes me 'mid this paradise repine;
Urge me to pluck, from Fancy's soaring wing,   305
A plume to deck Experience' hoary brow.

Attend.—The son of Time and Truth declares;
Unless the low-hung clouds drop fatness down,
No bunching plants of vivid green will spring,
In goodly ranks, to fill the planter's eye.   310
Let then Sagacity, with curious ken,
Remark the various signs of future rain.
The signs of rain, the Matuan Bard hath sung
In loftiest numbers; friendly to thy swains,
Once fertile Italy: but other marks   315
Portend the approaching shower, in these hot climes.

Short sudden rains, from Ocean's ruffled bed,
Driven by some momentary squalls, will oft
With frequent heavy bubbling drops, down-fall;
While yet the Sun, in cloudless lustre, shines: 320
And draw their humid train o'er half the isle.
Unhappy he! who journeys then from home,
No shade to screen him. His untimely fate
His wife, his babes, his friends, will soon deplore;
Unless hot wines, dry cloaths, and friction's aid,   325
His fleeting spirits stay. Yet not even these,
Nor all Apollo's arts, will always bribe
The insidious tyrant death, thrice tyrant here:
Else good Amyntor,[27] him the graces lov'd,
Wisdom caress'd, and Themis call'd her own,   330

Had liv'd by all admir'd, had now perus'd
"These lines, with all the malice of a friend."[28]

Yet future rains the careful may foretell:
Mosquitos,* sand-flies,[†] seek the shelter'd roof,
And with fell rage the stranger-guest assail,   335
Nor spare the sportive child; from their retreats
Cockroaches[‡] crawl displeasingly abroad:
These, without pity, let thy slaves destroy:
(Like Harpies,[29] they defile whate'er they touch:)
While those, the smother of combustion quells.   340
The speckled lizard[§] to its hole retreats,

---

*This is a Spanish word, signifying a Gnat, or Fly. They are very troublesome, especially to strangers, whom they bite unmercifully, causing a yellow coloured tumour, attended with excessive itching. Ugly ulcers have often been occasioned by scratching those swellings, in persons of bad habit of body. Though natives of the West Indies, they are not less common in the coldest regions; for *Mr. Maupertius* takes notice how troublesome they were to him and his attendants on the snowy summit of certain mountains within the arctic circle. They, however, chiefly love shady, moist, and warm places. Accordingly they are commonest to be met with in the corners of rooms, towards evening, and before rain. They are so light, as not to be felt when they pitch on the skin; and, as soon as they have darted in their proboscis, fly off, so that the first intimation one has of being bit by them, is the itching tumour. Warm lime-juice is the remedy. The Mosquito makes a humming noise, especially in the night-time. ["Mr. Maupertius": (1698–1759), author of *Essai de philosophie morale* (Berlin: Jacques Brakstone, 1750).]

[†]This insect the Spaniards call *Mosquitilla*, being much smaller than the Mosquito. Its bite is like a spark of fire, falling on the skin, which it raises into a small tumour accompanied with itching. But if the sand-fly causes a sharper and more sudden pain than the Mosquito, yet it is a more honourable enemy, for remaining upon the skin after the puncture, it may easily be killed. Its colour is grey and black, striped. Lemon-juice or first runnings cure its bite. ["First runnings": "kill-devil," or newly distilled rum.]

[‡]This is a large species of the chafer, or scaribaeus, and is a most disagreeable as well as destructive insect. There is scarce any thing which it will not devour, and wherever it has remained for any time, it leaves a nauseous smell behind it. Though better than an inch long, their thickness is no ways correspondent, so that they can insinuate themselves almost through any crevice, &c. into cabinets, drawers, &c. The smell of cedar is said to frighten them away, but this is a popular mistake, for I have often killed them in presses of that wood. There is a species of Cockroach, which, on account of a beating noise which it makes, especially in the night, is called the Drummer. Though larger, it is neither of so burnished a colour, nor so quick in its motions as the common sort, than which it is also less frequent, and not so pernicious; yet both will nibble peoples toe-ends, especially if not well-washed, and have sometimes occasioned uneasy sores there. They are natives of a warm climate. The French call them *Ravets*.

[§]This is meant of the ground-lizard, and not of the tree-lizard, which is of a fine green colour. There are many kinds of ground-lizards, which, as they are common in the hot parts of

And black crabs* travel from the mountain down;
Thy ducks their feathers prune; thy doves return,
In faithful flocks, and, on the neighbouring roof,
Perch frequent; where, with pleas'd attention, they   345
Behold the deepening congregated clouds,
With sadness, blot the azure vault of heaven.

    Now, while the shower depends, and rattle loud
Your doors and windows, haste ye housewives, place
Your spouts and pails; ye Negroes, seek the shade,   350
Save those who open with the ready hoe
The enriching water-course: for, see, the drops,
Which fell with slight aspersion, now descend
In streams continuous on the laughing land.
The coyest Naiads[30] quit their rocky caves,   355
And, with delight, run brawling to the main;
While those, who love still visible to glad
The thirsty plains from never-ceasing urns,
Assume more awful majesty, and pour,
With force resistless, down the channel'd rocks.   360
The rocks, or split, or hurried from their base,
With trees, are whirl'd impetuous to the sea:
Fluctuates the forest; the torn mountains roar:
The main itself recoils for many a league,
While its green face is chang'd to sordid brown.   365

Europe, I shall not describe. All of them are perfectly innocent. The Caribbeans used to eat them; they are not inferiour to snakes as a medicated food. Snuff forced into their mouth soon convulses them. They change colour, and become torpid; but, in a few hours, recover. The guana, or rather Iguana, is the largest sort of lizard. This, when irritated, will fly at one. It lives mostly upon fruit. It has a saw-like appearance, which ranges from its head all along its back, to its tail. The flesh of it is esteemed a great delicacy. The first writers on the *Lues Venerea,* forbid its use, to those who labour under that disease. It is a very ugly animal. In some parts of South-America, the alligator is called *Iguana.*

    *Black land-crabs are excellent eating; but as they sometimes will occasion a most violent *cholera morbus,* (owing, say planters, to their feeding on the mahoe-berry) they should never be dressed till they have fed for some weeks in a crab-house, after being caught by the Negroes. When they moult, they are most delicate; and then, it is believed, never poison. This however is certain, that at that time they have no gall, but, in its stead, the petrifaction called a Crabs-eye is found. As I have frequently observed their great claws (with which they severely bite the unwary) of very unequal sizes, it is probable, these regenerate when broke off by accident, or otherwise.

A grateful freshness every sense pervades;
While beats the heart with unaccustom'd joy:
Her stores fugacious Memory now recalls;
And Fancy prunes her wings for loftiest flights.
The mute creation share the enlivening hour;   370
Bounds the brisk kid, and wanton plays the lamb.
The drooping plants revive; ten thousand blooms,
Which, with their fragrant scents, perfume the air,
Burst into being; while the Canes put on
Glad Nature's liveliest robe, the vivid green.   375

    But chief, let fix'd Attention cast his eye
On the capt mountain, whose high rocky verge
The wild fig canopies, (vast woodland king,
Beneath thy branching shade a banner'd host
May lie in ambush!) and whose shaggy sides,   380
Trees shade, of endless green, enormous size,
Wondrous in shape, to botany unknown,
Old as the deluge.—There, in secret haunts,
The watery spirits ope their liquid court;
There, with the wood-nymphs, link'd in festal band,   385
(Soft airs and Phoebus wing them to their arms)
Hold amorous dalliance. Ah, may none profane,
With fire, or steel, their mystic privacy:
For there their fluent offspring first see day,
Coy infants sporting; silver-footed dew   390
To bathe by night thy sprouts in genial balm;
The green-stol'd Naiad of the tinkling rill,
Whose brow the fern-tree* shades; the power of rain
To glad the thirsty soil on which, arrang'd,
The gemmy summits of the Cane await   395
Thy Negroe-train, (in linen lightly wrapt,)
Who now that painted Iris girds the sky,
(Aerial arch, which Fancy loves to stride!)
Disperse, all-jocund, o'er the long-hoed land.

*This only grows in mountainous situations. Its stem shoots up to a considerable height,
but it does not divide into branches, till near the summit, where it shoots out horizontally, like
an umbrella, into leaves, which resemble those of the common fern. I know of no medical uses,
whereto this singularly beautiful tree has been applied, and indeed its wood, being spungy, is seldom used to oeconomical purposes. It, however, serves well enough for building mountain-
huts, and temporary fences for cattle.

The bundles some untie; the withered leaves,   400
Others strip artful off, and careful lay,
Twice one junk, distant in the amplest bed:
O'er these, with hasty hoe, some lightly spread
The mounted interval; and smooth the trench:
Well-pleas'd, the master-swain reviews their toil;   405
And rolls, in fancy, many a full-fraught cask.
So, when the shield was forg'd for Peleus' Son;[31]
The swarthy Cyclops shar'd the important task:
With bellows, some reviv'd the seeds of fire;
Some, gold, and brass, and steel, together fus'd   410
In the vast furnace; while a chosen few,
In equal measures lifting their bare arms,
Inform the mass; and, hissing in the wave,
Temper the glowing orb: their fire beholds,
Amaz'd, the wonders of his futile art.   415

While Procyon[32] reigns yet fervid in the sky;
While yet the fiery Sun in Leo rides;
And the Sun's child, the mail'd anana,* yields
His regal apple to the ravish'd taste;
And thou green avocato, charm of sense,   420
Thy ripened marrow liberally bestow'st;
Begin the distant mountain-land to plant:
So shall thy Canes defy November's cold,
Ungenial to the upland young; so best,
Unstinted by the arrow's deadening power,   425
Long yellow joint shall flow with generous juice.

But, till the lemon, orange, and the lime,
Amid their verdant umbrage, countless glow
With fragrant fruit of vegetable gold;
'Till yellow plantanes bend the unstain'd bough   430
With crooked clusters, prodigally full;
'Till Capricorn command the cloudy sky;
And moist Aquarius melt in daily showers,
Friend to the Cane-isles; trust not thou thy tops,

---

*This is the pine-apple, and needs no description; the *cherimoya,* a South-American fruit, is by all, who have tasted both, allowed to surpass the pine, and is even said to be more wholesome. The botanical name of the pine-apple is *bromelia.* Of the wild pine-apple, or ananas bravo, hedges are made in South-America. It produces an inferior sort of fruit.

Thy future riches, to the low-land plain: 435
And if kind Heaven, in pity to thy prayers,
Shed genial influence; as the earth absolves
Her annual circuit, thy rich ripened Canes
Shall load thy waggons, mules, and Negroe-train.

But chief thee, Planter, it imports to mark   440
(Whether thou breathe the mountain's humid air,
Or pant with heat continual on the plain;)
What months relent, and which from rain are free.

In different islands of the ocean-stream,
Even in the different parts of the same isle,   445
The seasons vary; yet attention soon
Will give thee each variety to know.
This once observ'd; at such a time inhume
Thy plants, that, when they joint, (important age,
Like youth just stepping into life) the clouds   450
May constantly bedew them: so shall they
Avoid those ails, which else their manhood kill.

Six times the changeful moon must blunt her horns,
And fill with borrowed light her silvery urn;
Ere thy tops, trusted to the mountain-land,   455
Commence their jointing: but four moons suffice
To bring to puberty the low-land Cane.

In plants, in beasts, in man's imperial race,
An alien mixture meliorates the breed;
Hence Canes, that sickened dwarfish on the plain,   460
Will shoot with giant-vigour on the hill.
Thus all depends on all; so God ordains.
Then let not man for little selfish ends,
(Britain, remember this important truth;)
Presume the principle to counteract   465
Of universal love; for God is love,
And wide creation shares alike his care.

'Tis said by some, and not unletter'd they,
That chief the Planter, if wealth desire,
Should note the phases of the fickle moon.   470
On thee, sweet empress of the night, depend

The tides; stern Neptune pays his court to thee;
The winds, obedient at thy bidding shift,
And tempests rise or fall; even lordly man,
Thine energy controls.—Not so the Cane;   475
The Cane its independency may boast,
Tho' some less noble plants thine influence own.

    Of mountain-lands oeconomy permits
A third, in Canes of mighty growth to rise:
But, in the low-land plain, the half will yield   480
Tho' not so lofty, yet a richer Cane,
For many a crop; if seasons glad the soil.*

    While rolls the Sun from Aries to the Bull,
And till the Virgin his hot beams inflame;
The Cane, with richest, most redundant juice,   485
Thy spacious coppers fills. Then manage so,
By planting in succession; that thy crops
The wondering daughters of the main may waft
To Britain's shore, ere Libra weigh the year:
So shall thy merchant chearful credit grant,   490
And well-earn'd opulence thy cares repay.

    Thy fields thus planted; to secure the Canes
From the Goat's baneful tooth; the churning boar;
From thieves; from fire or casual or design'd;
Unfailing herbage to thy toiling herds   495
Would'st thou afford; and the spectators charm
With beauteous prospects: let the frequent hedge
Thy green plantation, regular, divide.

    With limes, with lemons, let thy fences glow,
Grateful to sense; now children of this clime:†   500
And here and there let oranges erect
Their shapely beauties, and perfume the sky.
Nor less delightful blooms the logwood-hedge,‡

*Long-continued and violent rains are called *Seasons* in the West-Indies.

†It is supposed that oranges, lemons, and limes were introduced into America by the Spaniards; but I am more inclined to believe they are natural to the climate. The Spaniards themselves probably had the two first from the Saracens, for the Spanish noun *Naranja,* whence the English word *Orange,* is plainly Arabic.

‡Linnaeus's name for this useful tree is *Haemotoxylon,* but it is better known to physicians

Whose wood to coction yields a precious balm,
Specific in the flux: Endemial ail,   505
Much cause have I to weep thy fatal sway.—
But God is just, and man must not repine.
Nor shall the ricinus* unnoted pass;
Yet, if the cholic's deathful pangs thou dread'st,
Taste not its lucious nut. The acassee,†   510
With which the sons of Jewry, stiff-neck'd race,
Conjecture says, our God-Messiah crown'd;
Soon shoots a thick impenetrable fence,
Whose scent perfumes the night and morning sky,
Tho' baneful be its root. The privet‡ too,   515
Whose white flowers rival the first drifts of snow
On Grampia's piny hills;[33] (O might the muse
Tread, flush'd with health, the Grampian hills again!)
Emblem of innocence shall grace my song.
Boast of the shrubby tribe, carnation fair,§   520

---

by that of *Lignum campechense.* Its virtues, as a medicine, and properties as an ingredient in dying, need not to be enumerated in this place. It makes no less strong than beautiful hedge in the West-Indies, where it rises to a considerable height.

    *This shrub is commonly called the physic-nut. It is generally divided into three kinds, the common, the French, and the Spanish, which differ from each other in their leaves and flowers, if not in their fruit or seeds. The plant from which the castor-oil is extracted is also called *Ricinus,* though it has no resemblance to any of the former, in leaves, flowers, or seeds. In one particular they all agree, *viz.* in their yielding to coction or expression a purgative or emetic oil. The Spaniards name these nuts *Avellanas purgativas;* hence *Ray* terms them *Avellanae purgatrices novi orbis.* By roasting they are supposed to lose part of their virulency, which is wholly destroyed, say some people, by taking out a leaf-like substance that is to be found between the lobes. The nut exceeds a walnut, or even an almond, in sweetness, and yet three or four of them will operate briskly both up and down. The French call this useful shrub *Medecinier.* That species of it which bears red coral-like flowers is named *Bellyach* by Barbadians; and its ripe seeds are supposed to be specific against melancholy. ["Ray": John Ray (1627–1705), *A Collection of Curious Travels and Voyages* (Latin ed., 1633; English ed., 1705).]

    †*Acacia.* This is a species of thorn; the juice of the root is supposed to be poisonous. Its seeds are contained in a pod or ligumen. It is of the class of the syngenesia. No astringent juice is extracted from it. Its trivial name is *Cashaw. Tournefort* describes it in his voyage to the Levant. Some call it the Holy Thorn, and others Sweet Brier. The half ripe pod affords a strong cement; and the main stem, being wounded, produces a transparent gum, like the Arabic, to which tree this bears a strong resemblance. ["Tournefort": Joseph Pitton de Tournefort (1656–1708), author of *Materia Medica* (1708) and *The Complete Herbal* (1716).]

    ‡*Ligustrum.* This shrub is sufficiently known. Its leaves and flowers make a good gargle in the aphthae, and ulcered throat.

    §This is indeed a most beautiful flowering shrub. It is a native of the West-Indies, and

Nor thou repine, tho' late the muse record
Thy bloomy honours. Tipt with burnish'd gold,
And with imperial purple crested high,
More gorgeous than the train of Juno's bird,[34]
Thy bloomy honours oft the curious muse   525
Hath seen transported: seen the humming bird,*
Whose burnish'd neck bright glows with verdant gold;
Least of the winged vagrants of the sky,
Yet dauntless as the strong-pounc'd bird of Jove;[35]
With fluttering vehemence attack thy cups,   530
To rob them of their nectar's luscious store.

    But if with stones thy meagre lands are spread;
Be these collected, they will pay thy toil:
And let Vitruvius,[36] aided by the line,
Fence thy plantations with a thick-built wall.   535
On this lay cuttings of the prickly pear;†

---

called, from a French governor, named *Depoinci, Poinciana*. If permitted, it will grow twenty feet high; but, in order to make it a good fence, it should be kept low. It is always in blossom. Tho' not purgative, it is of the senna kind. Its leaves and flowers are stomachic, carminative, and emmenagogue. Some authors name it *Cauda pavonis*, on account of its inimitable beauty; the flowers have a physicky smell. How it came to be called Doodle-doo I know not; the Barbadians more properly term it *Flower Fence*. This plant grows also in Guinea.

    *The humming bird is called *Picaflore* by the Spaniards, on account of its hovering over flowers, and sucking their juices, without lacerating, or even so much as discomposing their petals. Its Indian name, says *Ulloa*, is *Guinde*, though it is also known by the appellation of *Rabilargo* and *Lizongero*. By the Caribbeans it was called *Collobree*. It is common in all the warm parts of America. There are various species of them, all exceeding small, beautiful and bold. The crested one, though not so frequent, is yet more beautiful than the others. It is chiefly to be found in the woody parts of the mountains. *Edwards* has described a very beautiful humming bird, with a long tail, which is a native of Surinam, but which I never saw in these islands. They are easily caught in rainy weather. ["Edwards": Bryan Edwards (1743–1800), author of *Observations … of the Maroon Negroes* (1801)].

    †The botanical name of this plant is *Opuntia;* it will grow in the barrenest soils, and on top of walls, if a small portion of earth be added. There are two sorts of it, one whose fruit is roundish and sweet, the other, which has more the shape of a fig, is sour. The former is sometimes eaten, but the other seldom. The French call them *Pomme de Raquette*. Both fruit and leaves are guarded with sharp prickles, and, even in the interior part of the fruit, there is one which must be removed before it is eaten. The leaves, which are half an inch thick, having a sort of pulp interposed between their surfaces, being deprived of their spines, and softened by the fire, make no bad poultice for inflammations. The juice of the fruit is an innocent fucus, and is often used to tinge guava jellies. The opuntia, upon which the cochineal insect breeds, has no spines, and is cultivated with care in South-America, where it also grows wild. The prickly pear makes a strong fence, and is easily trimmed with a scymitar. It grows naturally in some parts of Spain.

They soon a formidable fence will shoot:
Wild liquorice* here its red beads loves to hang,
Whilst scandent blossoms, yellow, purple, blue,
Unhurt, wind round its shield-like leaf and spears.   540
Nor is its fruit inelegant of taste,
Tho' more its colour charms the ravish'd eye;
Vermeil, as youthful beauty's roseat hue;
As thine, fair Christobelle: ah, when will fate,
That long hath scowl'd relentless on the bard,   545
Give him some small plantation to inclose,
Which he may call his own? Not wealth he craves,
But independence: yet if thou, sweet maid,
In health and virtue bloom; tho' worse betide,
Thy smile will smoothe adversity's rough brow.   550

    In Italy's green bounds, the myrtle shoots
A fragrant fence, and blossoms in the sun.
Here, on the rockiest verge of these blest isles,
With little care, the plant of love would grow.   555
Then to the citron join the plant of love,
And with their scent and shade enrich your isles.

    Yet some pretend, and not unspecious they,
The wood-nymphs foster the contagious blast.†
Foes to the Dryads,37 they remorseless fell   560
Each shrub of shade, each tree of spreading root,
That woo the first glad fannings of the breeze.
Far from the muse be such inhuman thoughts;
Far better recks she of the woodland tribes,
Earth's eldest birth, and earth's best ornament.   565
Ask him, whom rude necessity compels
To dare the noontide fervor, in this clime,
Ah, most intensely hot; how much he longs

---

*This is a scandent plant, from which the Negroes gather what they call *Jumbee Beeds*. These are about the size of pigeon-peas, almost round, of a red colour, with a black speck on one extremity. They act as an emetic, but, being violent in their operation, great caution should be observed in using them. The leaves make a good pectoral drink in disorders of the breast. By the French it is named *Petit Panacoco,* to distinguish it from a large tree, which bears seeds of the same colours, only much bigger. This tree is a species of black ebony.

†So a particular species of blight is called in the West-Indies. See its description in the second book.

For cooling vast impenetrable shade?
The muse, alas, th' experienc'd muse can tell: 570
Oft hath she travell'd, while solstitial beams,
Shot yellow deaths* on the devoted land;
Oft, oft hath she their ill-judg'd avarice blam'd,
Who, to the stranger, to their slaves and herds,
Denied this best of joys, the breezy shade.   575
And are there none, whom generous pity warms,
Friends to the woodland reign; whom shades delight?
Who, round their green domains, plant hedge-row trees;
And with cool cedars, screen the public way?
Yes, good Montano;[38] friend of man was he: 580
Him persecution, virtue's deadliest foe,
Drove, a lorn exile, from his native shore;
From his green hills, where many a fleecy flock,
Where many a heifer cropt their wholesome food;
And many a swain, obedient to his rule,   585
Him their lov'd master, their protector, own'd.
Yet, from that paradise, to Indian wilds,
To tropic suns, to fell barbaric hinds,
A poor outcast, an alien, did he roam;
His wife, the partner of his better hours,   590
And one sweet infant, chear'd his dismal way.
Unus'd to labour; yet the orient sun,
Yet western Phoebus, saw him wield the hoe.
At first a garden all his wants supplied,
(For Temperance sat chearful at his board,)   595
With yams, cassada,† and the food of strength,

---

*The yellow fever, to which Europeans of a sanguine habit of body, and who exceed in drinking or exercise, are liable on their arrival in the West Indies. The French call it *Maladie de Siame*, or more properly, *La Fievre des Matelots*. Those who have lived any time in the islands are no more subject to this disease than the Creoles, whence, however, some physicians have too hastily concluded, that it was of foreign extraction.

†Cassavi, cassava, is called Jatropha by botanists. Its meal makes a wholesome and well-tasted bread, although its juice be poisonous. There is a species of cassada which may be eat with safety, without expressing the juice; this the French call *Camagnoc*. The colour of its root is white, like a parsnip; that of the common kind is of a brownish red, before it is scraped. By coction the cassada-juice becomes an excellent sauce for fish; and the Indians prepare many wholesome dishes from it. I have given it internally mixed with flour without any bad consequences; it did not however produce any of the salutary effects I expected. A good starch is made

Thrice-wholesome tanies:* while a neighbouring dell,
(Which nature to the soursop† had resign'd,)
With ginger, and with Raleigh's pungent plant,[39]
Gave wealth; and gold bought better land and slaves.   600
Heaven bless'd his labour: now the cotton-shrub,‡
Grac'd with broad yellow flowers, unhurt by worms,
O'er many an acre shed its whitest down:
The power of rain, in genial moisture bath'd
His cacao-walk,§ which teem'd with marrowy pods;   605

from it. The stem is knotty, and, being cut into small junks and planted, young sprouts shoot up
from each knob. Horses have been poisoned by eating its leaves. The French name it *Manihot,*
Magnoc, and *Manioc,* and the Spaniards *Mandiocha.* It is pretended that all creatures but man
eat the raw root of the cassada with impunity; and, when dried, that it is a sovereign antidote
against venomous bites. A wholesome drink is prepared from this root by the Indians,
Spaniards, and Portuguese, according to *Pineda.* There is one species of this plant which the
Indians only use, and is by them called *Baccacoua.*

*This wholesome root, in some of the islands, is called *Edda:* Its botanical name is *Arum*
maximum Aegyptiacum. There are three species of tanies, the blue, the scratching, and that
which is commonly roasted. The blossoms of all three are very fragrant, in a morning or evening.
The young leaves, as well as the spiral stalks which support the flower, are eaten by Negroes as a
salad. The root makes a good broth in dysenteric complaints. They are seldom so large as the
yam, but most people think them preferable in point of taste.

†The true Indian name of this tree is *Suirsaak.* It grows in the barrenest places to a considerable height. Its fruit will often weigh two pounds. Its skin is green, and somewhat prickly. The
pulp is not disagreeable to the palate, being cool, and having its sweetness tempered with some
degree of an acid. It is one of the *Anonas,* as are also the custard, star, and sugar-apples. The
leaves of the soursop are very shining and green. The fruit is wholesome, but seldom admitted
to the tables of the elegant. The seeds are dispersed through the pulp like the guava. It has a
peculiar flavour. It grows in the East as well as the West-Indies. The botanical name is *Guana-*
banus. The French call it *Petit Corosol,* or *Coeur de Boeuf,* to which the fruit bears a resemblance.
The root, being reduced to a powder, and snuffed up the nose, produces the same effect as
tobacco. Taken by the mouth, the Indians pretend it is a specific in the epilepsy.

‡The fine down, which this shrub produces to invelope its seeds, is sufficiently known. The
English, Italian, and French names, evidently are derived from the Arabic *Algodon,* as the
Spaniards at this day call it. It was first brought by the Arabians into the Levant, where it is now
cultivated with great success. Authors mention four species of cotton, but they confound the
silk-cotton tree, or *Ceiba,* among them. The flower of the West-India cotton shrub is yellow,
and campanulated. It produces twice every year. That of Cayenne is the best of any that comes
from America. This plant is very apt to be destroyed by a grub within a short time; bating that,
it is a profitable production. Pliny mentions *Gossipium,* which is the common botanical name of
cotton. It is likewise called *Zylon. Martinus,* in his Philological Lexicon, derives cotton from the
Hebrew word קטון *Katon,* (or, as pronounced by the German-Jews, Kotoun).

§It is also called *Cocao* and *Cocô.* It is a native of some of the provinces of South-America,
and a drink made from it was the common food of the Indians before the Spaniards came among

His coffee* bath'd, that glow'd with berries, red
As Danae's[40] lip, or, Theodosia, thine,
Yet countless as the pebbles on the shore;
Oft, while drought kill'd his impious neighbour's grove.
In time, a numerous gang of sturdy slaves,   610
Well-fed, well-cloath'd, all emulous to gain
Their master's smile, who treated them like men;
Blacken'd his Cane-lands: which with vast increase,
Beyond the wish of avarice, paid his toil.
No cramps, with sudden death, surpriz'd his mules;   615

---

them, who were some time in those countries ere they could be prevailed upon to taste it; and it must be confessed, that the Indian chocolate had not a tempting aspect; yet I much doubt whether the Europeans have greatly improved its wholesomeness, by the addition of vanellas and other hot ingredients. The tree often grows fifteen or twenty feet high, and is streight and handsome. The pods, which seldom contain less than thirty nuts of the size of a flatted olive, grow upon the stem and principal branches. The tree loves a moist, rich, and shaded soil: Hence those who plant cacao-walks, sometimes screen them by a hardier tree, which the Spaniards aptly term *Madre de Cacao*. They may be planted fifteen or twenty feet distant, though some advise to plant them much nearer, and perhaps wisely; for it is an easy matter to thin them, when they are past the danger of being destroyed by dry weather, &c. Some recommend planting cassada, or bananas, in the intervals, when the cacao-trees are young, to destroy weeds, from which the walk cannot be kept too free. It is generally three years before they produce good pods; but, in six years, they are in highest perfection. The pods are commonly of the size and shape of a large cucumber. There are three or four sorts of cacao, which differ from one another in the colour and goodness of their nuts. That from the Caraccas is certainly the best. None of the species grow in Peru. Its alimentary, as well as physical properties, are sufficiently known. The word is Indian.

*This is certainly of Arabic derivation; and has been used in the East, as a drink, time immemorial. The inhabitants about the mouth of the Red-Sea were taught the use of it by the Persians, say authors, in the fifteenth century; and the coffee-shrub was gradually introduced into Arabia Felix, whence it passed into Egypt, Syria, and lastly Constantinople. The Turks, though so excessively fond of coffee, have not known it much above one hundred and fifty years; whereas the English have been acquainted therewith for upwards of an hundred, on *Pasqua,* a Greek, having opened a coffee-house in London about the middle of the last century. The famous traveller, Thevenot, introduced coffee into France. This plant is cultivated in the West-Indies, particularly by the French, with great success; but the berry from thence is not equal to that from Mocha. It is a species of Arabian jasmine; the flower is particularly redolent, and from it a pleasant cordial water is distilled. It produces fruit twice every year; but the shrub must be three years old before any can be gathered. It should not be allowed to grow above six foot high. It is very apt to be destroyed by a large fly, which the French call *Mouche a caffe;* as well as by the white grub, which they name *Puceron.* Its medical and alimentary qualities are as generally known as those of tea. ["Thevenot": Jean de Thevenot (1633–1667), author of *The Travels of Monsieur de Thevenot* (London: H. Clark, 1687).]

No glander-pest his airy stables thinn'd:
And, if disorder seiz'd his Negroe-train,
Celsus[41] was call'd, and pining Illness flew.
His gate stood wide to all; but chief the poor,
The unfriended stranger, and the sickly, shar'd   620
His prompt munificence: No surly dog,
Nor surlier Ethiop, their approach debarr'd.
The Muse, that pays this tribute to his fame,
Oft hath escap'd the sun's meridian blaze,
Beneath yon tamarind-vista,* which his hands   625
Planted; and which, impervious to the sun,
His latter days beheld.—One noon he sat
Beneath its breezy shade, what time the sun
His sultry vengeance from the Lion pour'd;
And calmly thus his eldest hope addrest.   630

      "Be pious, be industrious, be humane;
From proud oppression guard the labouring hind.
Whate'er their creed, God is the Sire of man,
His image they; then dare not thou, my son,
To bar the gates of mercy on mankind.   635
Your foes forgive, for merit must make foes;
And in each virtue far surpass your sire.
Your means are ample, Heaven a heart bestow!
So health and peace shall be your portion here;
And yon bright sky, to which my soul aspires,   640
Shall bless you with eternity of joy."

      He spoke, and ere the swift-wing'd zumbadore†
The mountain-desert startl'd with his hum;

*This large, shady, and beautiful tree grows fast even in the driest soils, and lasts long; and
yet its wood is hard, and very fit for mechanical uses. The leaves are smaller than those of senna,
and pennated: they taste sourish, as does the pulp, which is contained in pods four or five inches
long. They bear once a year. An excellent vinegar may be made from the fruit; but the Creoles
chiefly preserve it with sugar, as the Spaniards with salt. A pleasant syrup may be made from it.
The name is, in Arabic, *Tamara*. The Antients were not acquainted therewith; for the Arabians
first introduced tamarinds into physic; it is a native of the East as well as of the West-Indies and
South-America, where different provinces call it by different names. Its cathartic qualities are
well known. It is good in sea-sickness. The botanical name is *Tamarindus*.
      †This bird, which is one of the largest and swiftest known, is only seen at night, or rather
heard; for it makes a hideous humming noise (whence its name) on the desert tops of the An-

Ere fire-flies* trimm'd their vital lamps; and ere
Dun Evening trod on rapid Twilight's heel:†   645
His knell was rung;—
And all the Cane-lands wept their father lost.

    Muse, yet awhile indulge my rapid course;
And I'll unharness, soon, the foaming steeds.

    If Jove descend, propitious to thy vows,   650
In frequent floods of rain; successive crops
Of weeds will spring. Nor venture to repine,
Tho' oft their toil thy little gang renew;
Their toil tenfold the melting heavens repay:
For soon thy plants will magnitude acquire,   655
To crush all undergrowth; before the sun,
The planets thus withdraw their puny fires.
And tho' untutor'd, then, thy Canes will shoot:
Care meliorates their growth. The trenches fill
With their collateral mold; as in a town   660
Which foes have long beleaguer'd, unawares
A strong detachment sallies from each gate,
And levels all the labours of the plain.

    And now thy Cane's first blades their verdure lose,
And hang their idle heads. Be these stript off;   665
So shall fresh sportive airs their joints embrace,
And by their dalliance give the sap to rise.
But, O beware, let no unskilful hand
The vivid foliage tear: Their channel'd spouts,
Well-pleas'd, the watery nutriment convey,   670
With filial duty, to the thirsty stem;
And, spreading wide their reverential arms,
Defend their parent from solstitial skies.
                    The End of Book I.

---

des. See Ulloa's Voyage to South-America. It is also called *Condor.* Its wings, when expanded, have been known to exceed sixteen feet from tip to tip. See *Philosophical Transactions.* No 208.

    *This surprising insect is frequent in Guadaloupe, &c. and all the warmer parts of America. There are none in the English Caribbee, or Virgin-Islands.

    †There is little or no twilight in the West-Indies. All the year round it is dark before eight at night. The dawn is equally short.

Book II.
Advertisement to Book II.

The following Book having been originally addressed to William Shenstone, Esq;[42] and by him approved of; the Author should deem it a kind of poetical sacrilege, now, to address it to any other. To his memory, therefore, be it sacred; as a small but sincere testimony of the high opinion the Author entertained of that Gentleman's genius and manners; and as the only return now, alas! in his power to make, for the friendship wherewith Mr. Shenstone had condescended to honour him.

ARGUMENT

Subject proposed. Address to William Shenstone, Esq. Of monkeys. Of rats and other vermin. Of weeds. Of the yellow fly. Of the greasy fly. Of the blast. A hurricane described. Of calms and earthquakes. A tale.

Book II.

Enough of culture.—A less pleasing theme,
What ills await the ripening Cane, demands
My serious numbers: these, the thoughtful Muse
Hath oft beheld, deep-pierc'd with generous woe.
For she, poor exile! boasts no waving crops;　　　　　　　5
For her no circling mules press dulcet streams;
No Negro-band huge foaming coppers skim;
Nor fermentation (wine's dread fire) for her,
With Vulcan's[43] aid, from Cane a spirit draws,
Potent to quell the madness of despair.　　　　　　　　10
Yet, oft, the range she walks, at shut of eve;
Oft sees red lightning at the midnight-hour,
When nod the watches, stream along the sky;
Not innocent, as what the learned call
The Boreal morn,[44] which, through the azure air,　　　15
Flashes its tremulous rays, in painted streaks,
While o'er night's veil her lucid tresses flow:
Nor quits the Muse her walk, immers'd in thought,
How she the planter, haply, may advise;
Till tardy morn unbar the gates of light,　　　　　　　20
And, opening on the main with sultry beam,
To burnish'd silver turns the blue-green wave.

Say, will my Shenstone lend a patient ear,
And weep at woes unknown to Britain's isle?
Yes, thou wilt weep; for pity chose thy breast,   25
With taste and science, for their soft abode:
Yes, thou wilt weep: thine own distress thou bear'st
Undaunted; but another's melts thy soul.

     "O were my pipe as soft, my dittied song"
As smooth as thine, my too too distant friend,   30
Shenstone; my soft pipe, and my dittied song
Should hush the hurricanes tremendous roar,
And from each evil guard the ripening Cane!

     Destructive, on the upland sugar-groves
The monkey-nation preys: from rocky heights,   35
In silent parties, they descend by night,
And posting watchful sentinels, to warn
When hostile steps approach; with gambols, they
Pour o'er the Cane-grove. Luckless he to whom
That land pertains! in evil hour, perhaps,   40
And thoughtless of to-morrow, on a die
He hazards millions; or, perhaps, reclines
On Luxury's soft lap, the pest of wealth;
And, inconsiderate, deems his Indian crops
Will amply her insatiate wants supply.   45

     From these insidious droles (peculiar pest*
Of Liamuiga's hills) would'st thou defend
Thy waving wealth; in traps put not thy trust,
However baited: Treble every watch,
And well with arms provide them; faithful dogs,   50
Of nose sagacious, on their footsteps wait.
With these attack the predatory bands;
Quickly the unequal conflict they decline,
And, chattering, fling their ill-got spoils away.

*The monkeys which are now so numerous in the mountainous parts of St. Christopher, were brought thither by the French when they possessed half that island. This circumstance we learn from *Pere Labat,* who farther tells us that they are a most delicate food. The English-Negroes are very fond of them, but the White-inhabitants do not eat them. They do a great deal of mischief in St. Kitts, destroying many thousand pounds *Sterling's* worth of Canes every year.

So when, of late, innumerous Gallic hosts   55
Fierce, wanton, cruel, did by stealth invade
The peaceable American's domains,
While desolation mark'd their faithless rout;
No sooner Albion's martial sons advanc'd,
Than the gay dastards to their forests fled,   60
And left their spoils and tomahawks behind.

    Nor with less waste the whisker'd vermine-race,
A countless clan, despoil the low-land Cane.

    These to destroy,* while commerce hoists the sail,
Loose rocks abound, or tangling bushes bloom,   65
What Planter knows?—Yet prudence may reduce.
Encourage then the breed of savage cats,
Nor kill the winding snake, thy foes they eat.
Thus, on the mangrove-banks† of Guayaquil,[45]
Child of the rocky desert, sea-like stream,   70
With studious care, the American preserves
The gallinazo,[46] else that sea-like stream
(Whence traffic pours her bounties on mankind)
Dread alligators would alone possess.
Thy foes, the teeth-fil'd Ibbos‡ also love;   75
Nor thou their wayward appetite restrain.§

*Rats, &c. are not natives of America, but came by shipping from Europe. They breed in the ground, under loose rocks and bushes. *Durante*, a Roman, who was physician to Pope Sixtus Quintus, and who wrote a Latin poem on the preservation of health, enumerates domestic rats among animals that may be eaten with safety. But if these are wholesome, cane-rats must be much more delicate, as well as more nourishing. Accordingly we find most field Negroes fond of them, and I have heard that straps of cane-rats are publicly sold in the markets of Jamaica.

†This tree, which botanists call *Rizophora*, grows in marshy soils, and on the sides of rivers; and, as the branches take root, they frequently render narrow streams impassable to boats. Oysters often adhere to their roots, &c. The French name of this strange water-shrub is *Paltuvier*. The species meant here is the red mangrove.

‡Or *Ebbos*, as they are more commonly called, are a numerous nation. Many of them have their teeth filed, and blackened in an extraordinary manner. They make good slaves when bought young; but are, in general, foul feeders, many of them greedily devouring the raw guts of fowls: They also feed on dead mules and horses; whose carcasses, therefore, should be buried deep, that the Negroes may not come at them. But the surest way is to burn them; otherwise they will be apt, privily, to kill those useful animals, in order to feast on them.

§Pere Labat says that Cane-rats give those Negroes who eat them pulmonic disorders, but the good Jesuit was no physician. I have been told by those who have eat them, that they are very delicate food.

Some place decoys, nor will they not avail,
Replete with roasted crabs, in every grove
These fell marauders gnaw; and pay their slaves
Some small reward for every captive foe.   80
So practice Gallia's sons; but Britons trust
In other wiles; and surer their success.

With Misnian[47] arsenic, deleterious bane,
Pound up the ripe cassada's well-rasp'd root,
And form in pellets; these profusely spread   85
Round the Cane-groves, where sculk the vermin-breed:
They, greedy, and unweeting of the bait,
Crowd to the inviting cates,[48] and swift devour
Their palatable Death; for soon they seek
The neighbouring spring; and drink, and swell, and die.   90
But dare not thou, if life deserve thy care,
The infected rivulet taste; nor let thy herds
Graze its polluted brinks, till rolling time
Have fin'd the water, and destroyed the bane.
'Tis safer then to mingle nightshade's juice*   95
With flour, and throw it liberal 'mong thy Canes:
They tough not this; its deadly scent they fly,
And sudden colonize some distant vale.

Shall the muse deign to sing of humble weeds,
That check the progress of the imperial cane?   100

In every soil, unnumber'd weeds will spring;
Nor fewest in the best: (thus oft we find
Enormous vices taint the noblest souls!)
These let thy little gang, with skilful hand,
Oft as they spread abroad, and oft they spread;   105
Careful pluck up, to swell thy growing heap
Of rich manure. And yet some weeds arise,
Of aspect mean, with wondrous virtues fraught:
(And doth not oft uncommon merit dwell
In men of vulgar looks, and trivial air?)   110

*See the article *Solanum in Newman's Chemistry published by Dr. Lewis*. There is a species of East-Indian animal, called a Mungoes [i.e., mongoose], which bears a natural antipathy to rats. Its introduction into the Sugar-Islands would, probably, effectuate the extirpation of this destructive vermin.

Such, planter, be not thou asham'd to save
From foul pollution, and unseemly rot;
Much will they benefit thy house and thee.
But chief the yellow thistle* thou select,
Whose seed the stomach frees from nauseous loads;   115
And, if the music of the mountain-dove
Delight thy pensive ear, sweet friend to thought!
This prompts their cooing, and enflames their love.
Nor let rude hands the knotted grass profane,†
Whose juice worms fly: Ah, dire endemial ill!   120
How many fathers, fathers now no more;
How many orphans, now lament thy rage?
The cow-itch‡ also save; but let thick gloves
Thine hands defend, or thou wilt sadly rue
Thy rash imprudence, when ten thousand darts   125
Sharp as the bee-sting, fasten in thy flesh,
And give thee up to torture. But, unhurt,
Planter, thou may'st the humble chickweed§ cull;
And that, which coyly flies the astonish'd grasp.
Not the confection‖ nam'd from Pontus' King;   130

*The seeds of this plant are an excellent emetic; and almost as useful in dysenteric complaints as ipecacuan. It grows every where.

†This is a truly powerful vermifuge; but, uncautiously administered, has often proved mortal. The juice of it clarified, is sometimes given; but a decoction of it is greatly preferable. Its botanical name is *Spigelia.*

‡This extraordinary vine should not be permitted to grow in a Cane-piece; for Negroes have been known to fire the Canes, to save themselves from the torture which attends working in grounds where it has abounded. Mixed with melasses, it is a safe and excellent vermifuge. Its seeds, which resemble blackish small beans, are purgative. Its flower is purple; and its pods, on which the stinging brown *Setae* are found, are as large as a full-grown English field-pea.

§There are two kinds of chickweed, which grow spontaneously in the Caribbees, and both possess very considerable virtues, particularly that which botanists call *Cajacia,* and which the Spaniards emphatically name *Erudos Cobres,* or Snakeweed, on account of its remarkable qualities against poisonous bites. It is really of use against fish-poison; as is also the sensitive plant, which the Spaniards prettily call the *Vergonzoza,* the Bashful, and *La Donzella,* or the Maiden. There are many kinds of this extraordinary plant, which grow every where in the Islands and South-America. The botanical name of the former is *Alsine,* and that of the latter *Mimosa.*

‖This medicine is called *Mithridatium,* in honour of Mithridates king of Pontus; who, by using it constantly, had secured himself from the effects of poison, in such a manner, that, when he actually attempted to put an end to his life, by that means, he failed in his purpose. So, at least, Pliny informs us. But we happily are not obliged to believe, implicitly, whatever that elaborate compiler has told us. When poisons immediately operate on the nervous system, and their

Not the bless'd apple* Median climes produce,
Tho' lofty Maro (whose immortal muse
Distant I follow, and, submiss, adore)
Hath sung its properties, to counteract
Dire spells, slow-mutter'd o'er the baneful bowl,   135
Where cruel stepdames poisonous drugs have brewed;
Can vie with these low tenants of the vale,
In driving poisons from the infected frame:
For here, alas! (ye sons of luxury mark!)
The sea, tho' on its bosom Halcyons sleep,   140
Abounds with poison'd fish; whose crimson fins,
Whose eyes, whose scales, bedropt with azure, gold,
Purple, and green, in all gay Summer's pride,
Amuse the sight; whose taste the palate charms;
Yet death, in ambush, on the banquet waits,   145
Unless these antidotes be timely given.
But, say what strains, what numbers can recite,
Thy praises, vervain; or wild liquorice, thine?
For not the costly root,† the gift of God,
Gather'd by those, who drink the Volga's wave,   150
(Prince of Europa's streams, itself a sea)
Equals your potency! Did planters know
But half your virtues; not the Cane itself,
Would they with greater, fonder pains preserve!

    Still other maladies infest the Cane,   155
And worse to be subdu'd. The insect-tribe
That, fluttering, spread their pinions to the sun,
Recal the muse: nor shall their many eyes,

---

effects are to be expelled by the skin, this electuary is no contemptible antidote. But how many poisons do we know at present, which produce their effects in a different manner? and, from the accounts of authors, we have reason to be persuaded, that the antients were not much behind us in their variety of poisons. If, therefore, the King of Pontus had really intended to have destroyed himself, he could have been at no loss for the means, notwithstanding the daily use of this antidote.

    *Authors are not agreed what the apple is, to which Virgil attributes such remarkable virtues, nor is it indeed possible they ever should. However, we have this comfort on our side, that our not knowing it is of no detriment to us; for as spells cannot affect us, we are at no loss for antidotes to guard against them.

    †Some medical writers have bestowed the high appellation of *Donum Dei* on rhubarb.

Tho' edg'd with gold, their many-colour'd down,
From Death preserve them. In what distant clime,   160
In what recesses are the plunderers hatch'd?
Say, are they wafted in the living gale,
From distant islands? Thus, the locust-breed,
In winged caravans, that blot the sky,
Descend from far, and, ere bright morning dawn,   165
Astonish'd Afric sees her crop devour'd.
Or, doth the Cane a proper nest afford,
And food adapted to the yellow fly?—
The skill'd in Nature's mystic lore observe,
Each tree, each plant, that drinks the golden day,   170
Some reptile life sustains: Thus cochinille*
Feeds on the Indian fig; and, should it harm
The foster plant, its worth that harm repays:
But Ye, base insects! no bright scarlet yield,
To deck the British Wolf;[49] who now, perhaps,   175
(So Heaven and George ordain) in triumph mounts
Some strong-built fortress, won from haughty Gaul!
And tho' no plant such luscious nectar yields,
As yields the Cane-plant; yet, vile paricides!
Ungrateful ye! the Parent-cane destroy.   180

    Muse! say, what remedy hath skill devis'd
To quell this noxious foe? Thy Blacks send forth,
A strong detachment! ere the encreasing pest
Have made too firm a lodgment; and, with care,
Wipe every tainted blade, and liberal lave   185
With sacred Neptune's purifying stream.
But this Augaean[50] toil long time demands,
Which thou to more advantage may'st employ:
If vows for rain thou ever did'st prefer,
Planter, prefer them now: the rattling shower,   190
Pour'd down in constant streams, for days and nights,
Not only swells, with nectar sweet, thy Canes;
But, in the deluge, drowns thy plundering foe.

*This is a Spanish word. For the manner of propagating this useful insect, see *Sir Hans Sloane's Natural History of Jamaica.* It was long believed in Europe to be a seed, or vegetable production. The botanical name of the plant on which the cochinille feeds, is *Opuntia maxima, folio oblongo, majore, spinulis obtusis, mollibus et innocentibus obsito, flore, striis rubris variegato.* Sloane.

    When may the planter idly fold his arms,
And say, "My soul take rest?" Superior ills,   195
Ills which no care nor wisdom can avert,
In black succession rise. Ye men of Kent,
When nipping Eurus,[51] with the brutal force
Of Boreas,[52] join'd in ruffian league, assail
Your ripen'd hop-grounds; tell me what you feel,   200
And pity the poor planter; when the blast,
Fell plague of Heaven! perdition of the isles!
Attacks his waving gold. Tho' well-manur'd;
A richness tho' thy fields from nature boast;
Though seasons* pour; this pestilence† invades: 205
Too oft it seizes the glad infant-throng,
Nor pities their green nonage:[53] Their broad blades
Of which the graceful wood-nymphs erst compos'd
The greenest garlands to adorn their brows,
First pallid, sickly, dry, and withered show;   210
Unseemly stains succeed; which, nearer viewed
By microscopic arts, small eggs appear,
Dire fraught with reptile life; alas, too soon
They burst their filmy jail, and crawl abroad,
Bugs of uncommon shape; thrice hideous show!   215
Innumerous as the painted shells, that load
The wave-worn margin of the Virgin-isles!
Innumerous as the leaves the plumb-tree sheds,‡
When, proud of her faecundity, she shows,
Naked, her gold fruit to the God of noon.   220
Remorseless to its youth; what pity, say,
Can the Cane's age expect? In vain, its pith
With juice nectarious flows; to pungent sour,

*Without a rainy season, the Sugar-cane could not be cultivated to any advantage: For what Pliny the Elder writes of another plant may be applied to this, *Gaudet irriguis, et toto anno bibere amat.* [*Naturalis Historia*, book 13, section 28, line 3, actually reads (referring to palms): "gaudet riguis totoque anno bibere cum amet sitientia"; "It likes running water, and to drink all the year round, though it loves dry places." Translation from *Natural History*, trans. H. Rackham (London: Heineman, 1915), 115).]

†It must, however, be confessed, that the blast is less frequent in lands naturally rich, or such as are made so by well-rotted manure.

‡This is the Jamaica plumb tree. When covered with fruit, it has no leaves upon it. The fruit is wholesome. In like manner, the panspan is destitute of foliage when covered with flowers. The latter is a species of jessamine, and grows as large as an apple-tree.

Foe to the bowels, soon its nectar turns:
Vain every joint a gemmy embryo bears,   225
Alternate rang'd; from these no filial young
Shall grateful spring, to bless the planter's eye.—
With bugs confederate, in destructive league,
The ants' republic joins; a villain crew,
As the waves, countless, that plough up the deep,   230
(Where Eurus reigns* vicegerent of the sky,
Whom Rhea bore to the bright God of day)
When furious Auster[54] dire commotions stirs:
These wind, by subtle sap, their secret way,
Pernicious pioneers! while those invest,   235
More firmly daring, in the face of Heaven,
And win, by regular approach, the Cane.

    'Gainst such ferocious, such unnumber'd bands,
What arts, what arms shall sage experience use?

    Some bid the planter load the favouring gale,   240
With pitch, and sulphur's suffocating steam:—
Useless the vapour o'er the Cane-grove flies,
In curling volumes lost; such feeble arms,
To man tho' fatal, not the blast subdue.
Others again, and better their success,   245
Command their slaves each tainted blade to pick
With care, and burn them in vindictive flames.
Labour immense! and yet, if small the pest;
If numerous, if industrious be thy gang;
At length, thou may'st the victory obtain.   250
But, if the living taint be far diffus'd,
Bootless this toil; nor will it then avail
(Tho' ashes lend their suffocating aid)
To bare the broad roots, and the mining swarms
Expose, remorseless, to the burning noon.   255
Ah! must then ruin desolate the plain?
Must the lost planter other climes explore?
Howe'er reluctant, let the hoe uproot

*The East is the centre of the trade-wind in the West-Indies, which veers a few points to the North or South. What Homer says of the West-wind, in his islands of the blessed, may more aptly be applied to the trade-winds.

The infected Cane-piece; and, with eager flames,
The hostile myriads thou to embers turn: 260
Far better, thus, a mighty loss sustain,
Which happier years and prudence may retrieve;
Than risque thine all. As when an adverse storm,
Impetuous, thunders on some luckless ship,
From green St. Christopher, or Cathäy* bound: 265
Each nautic art the reeling seamen try:
The storm redoubles: death rides every wave:
Down by the board the cracking masts they hew;
And heave their precious cargo in the main.

    Say, can the Muse, the pencil in her hand,   270
The all-wasting hurricane observant ride?
Can she, undazzled, view the lightning's glare,
That fires the welkin?[55] Can she, unappall'd,
When all the flood-gates of the sky are ope,
The shoreless deluge stem? The Muse hath seen   275
The pillar'd flame, whose top hath reach'd the stars;
Seen rocky, molten fragments, flung in the air
From Aetna's vext abyss; seen burning streams
Pour down its channel'd sides; tremendous scenes!—
Yet not vext Aetna's pillar'd flames, that strike   280
The stars; nor molten mountains hurl'd on high;
Nor ponderous rapid deluges, that burn
Its deeply channel'd sides: cause such dismay,
Such desolation, Hurricane! as thou;
When the Almighty gives thy rage to blow,   285
And all the battles of thy winds engage.

    Soon as the Virgin's charms ingross the Sun;
And till his weaker flame the Scorpion feels;
But, chief, while Libra weighs the unsteddy year:
Planter, with mighty props thy dome support;   290
Each flaw repair; and well, with massy bars,
Thy doors and windows guard; securely lodge
Thy stocks and mill-points.† —Then, or calms obtain;

*An old name for China.
   †The sails are fastened to the mill-points, as those are to the stocks. They should always be
taken down before the hurricane-season.

Breathless the royal palm-tree's airiest van;
While, o'er the panting isle, the daemon Heat   295
High hurls his flaming brand; vast, distant waves
The main drives furious in, and heaps the shore
With strange productions: Or, the blue serene
Assumes a louring aspect, as the clouds
Fly, wild-careering, thro' the vault of heaven;   300
Then transient birds, of various kinds, frequent
Each stagnant pool; some hover o'er thy roof;
Then Eurus reigns no more; but each bold wind,
By turns, usurps the empire of the air
With quick inconstancy;   305
Thy herds, as sapient of the coming storm,
(For beasts partake some portion of the sky,)
In troops associate; and, in cold sweats bath'd,
Wild-bellowing, eye the pole. Ye seamen, now,
Ply to the southward, if the changeful moon,   310
Or, in her interlunar palace hid,
Shuns night; or, full-orb'd, in Night's forehead glows:
For, see! the mists, that late involv'd the hill,
Disperse; the midday sun looks red; strange burs*
Surround the stars, which vaster fill the eye.   315
A horrid stench the pools, the main emits;
Fearful the genius of the forest sighs;
The mountains moan; deep groans the cavern'd cliff.
A night of vapour, closing fast around,
Snatches the golden noon.—Each wind appeas'd,   320
The North flies forth, and hurls the frighted air:
Not all the brazen engineries[56] of man,
At once exploded, the wild burst surpass.
Yet thunder, yok'd with lightning and with rain,
Water with fire, increase the infernal din: 325
Canes, shrubs, trees, huts, are whirl'd aloft in air.—
The wind is spent; and "all the isle below
Is hush as death."[57]
Soon issues forth the West, with sudden burst;

*These are astral halos. Columbus soon made himself master of the signs that precede a hurricane in the West-Indies, by which means he saved his own squadron; while another large fleet, whose commander despised his prognostics, put to sea, and was wrecked.

And blasts more rapid, more resistless drives: 330
Rushes the headlong sky; the city rocks;
The good man throws him on the trembling ground;
And dies the murderer in his inmost soul.—
Sullen the West withdraws his eager storms.—
Will not the tempest now his furies chain?   335
Ah, no! as when in Indian forests, wild,
Barbaric armies suddenly retire
After some furious onset, and, behind
Vast rocks and trees, their horrid forms conceal,
Brooding on slaughter, not repuls'd; for soon   340
Their growing yell the affrighted welkin rends,
And bloodier carnage mows th' ensanguin'd plain:
So the South, sallying from his iron caves
With mightier force, renews the aerial war;
Sleep, frighted, flies; and, see! yon lofty palm,   345
Fair nature's triumph, pride of Indian groves,
Cleft by the sulphurous bolt! See yonder dome,[58]
Where grandeur with propriety combin'd,
And Theodorus[59] with devotion dwelt;
Involv'd in smouldering flames.—From every rock,   350
Dashes the turbid torrent; thro' each street
A river foams, which sweeps, with untam'd might,
Men, oxen, Cane-lands to the billowy main.—
Pauses the wind.—Anon the savage East
Bids his wing'd tempests more relentless rave;   355
Now brighter, vaster corruscations[60] flash;
Deepens the deluge; nearer thunders roll;
Earth trembles; ocean reels; and, in her fangs,
Grim Desolation tears the shrieking isle,
Ere rosy Morn possess the ethereal plain,   360
To pour on darkness the full flood of day.—

 Nor does the hurricane's all-wasting wrath
Alone bring ruin on its sounding wing:
Even calms are dreadful, and the fiery South
Oft reigns a tyrant in these fervid isles: 365
For, from its burning furnace, when it breathes,
Europe and Asia's vegetable sons,
Touch'd by its tainting vapour, shrivel'd, die.

The hardiest children of the rocks repine:
And all the upland Tropic-plants hang down   370
Their drooping heads; shew arid, coil'd, adust.[61] —
The main itself seems parted into streams,
Clear as a mirror; and, with deadly scents,
Annoys the rower; who, heart-fainting, eyes
The sails hang idly, noiseless, from the mast.   375
Thrice hapless he, whom thus the hand of fate
Compels to risque the insufferable beam!
A fiend, the worst the angry skies ordain
To punish sinful man, shall fatal seize
His wretched life, and to the tomb consign.   380

    When such the ravage of the burning calm,
On the stout, sunny children of the hill;
What must thy Cane-lands feel? Thy late green sprouts
Nor bunch, nor joint; but, sapless, arid, pine:
Those, who have manhood reach'd, of yellow hue,   385
(Symptom of health and strength) soon ruddy show;
While the rich juice that circled in their veins,
Acescent,[62] watery, poor, unwholesome tastes.

    Nor only, planter, are thy Cane-groves burnt;
Thy life is threatened. Muse, the manner sing.   390

    Then earthquakes, nature's agonizing pangs,
Oft shake the astonied[63] isles: The solfaterre*
Or sends forth thick, blue, suffocating steams;
Or shoots to temporary flame. A din,
Wild, thro' the mountain's quivering rocky caves,   395
Like the dread crash of tumbling planets, roars.
When tremble thus the pillars of the globe,
Like the tall coco by the fierce North blown;
Can the poor, brittle, tenements of man
Withstand the dread convulsion? Their dear homes,   400
(Which shaking, tottering, crashing, bursting, fall,)
The boldest fly; and, on the open plain

---

*Volcanos are called *sulphurs*, or *solfaterres*, in the West-Indies. There are few mountainous islands in that part of the globe without them, and those probably will destroy them in time. I saw much sulphur and alum in the solfaterre at Mountserrat. The stream that runs through it, is almost as hot as boiling water, and its steams soon blacken silver, &c.

Appal'd, in agony the moment wait,
When, with disrupture vast, the waving earth
Shall whelm them in her sea-disgorging womb.   405

    Nor less affrighted are the bestial kind.
The bold steed quivers in each panting vein,
And staggers, bath'd in deluges of sweat:
Thy lowing herds forsake their grassy food,
And send forth frighted, woful, hollow sounds: 410
The dog, thy trusty centinel of night,
Deserts his post assign'd; and, piteous, howls.—
Wide ocean feels:—
The mountain-waves, passing their custom'd bounds,
Make direful, loud incursions on the land,   415
All-overwhelming: Sudden they retreat,
With their whole troubled waters; but, anon,
Sudden return, with louder, mightier force;
(The black rocks whiten, the vext shores resound;)
And yet, more rapid, distant they retire.   420
Vast coruscations lighten all the sky,
With volum'd flames; while thunder's awful voice,
From forth his shrine, by night and horror girt,
Astounds the guilty, and appals the good:
For oft the best, smote by the bolt of heaven,   425
Wrapt in ethereal flame, forget to live:
Else, fair Theana.[64] —Muse, her fate deplore.

    Soon as young reason dawn'd in Junio's breast,
His father sent him from these genial isles,
To where old Thames with conscious pride surveys   430
Green Eton,[65] soft abode of every Muse.
Each classic beauty soon he made his own;
And soon fam'd Isis[66] saw him woo the Nine,[67]
On her inspiring banks: Love tun'd his song;
For fair Theana was his only theme,   435
Acasto's daughter,[68] whom, in early youth,
He oft distinguished; and for whom he oft
Had climb'd the bending coco's* airy height,

---

*The coco-nut tree is of the palm genus; there are several species of them, which grow nat-
urally in the Torrid Zone. The coco-nut tree is, by no means, so useful as travellers have repre-

To rob it of its nectar; which the maid,
When he presented, more nectarious deem'd.—   440
The sweetest sappadillas* oft he brought;
From him more sweet ripe sappadillas seem'd.—
Nor had long absence yet effac'd her form;
Her charms still triumph'd o'er Britannia's fair.
One morn he met her in Sheen's royal walks;   445
Nor knew, till then, sweet Sheen contain'd his all.
His taste mature approv'd his infant choice.
In colour, form, expression, and in grace,
She shone all perfect; while each pleasing art,
And each soft virtue that the sex adorns,   450
Adorn'd the woman. My imperfect strain,

---

sented it. The wood is of little or no service, being spungy, and the brown covering of the nuts is of too rough a texture to serve as apparel. The shell of the nut receives a good polish; and, having a handle put to it, is commonly used to drink water out of. The milk, or water of the nut, is cooling and pleasant; but, if drunk too freely, will frequently occasion a pain in the stomach. A salutary oil may be extracted from the kernal; which, if old, and eaten too plentifully, is apt to produce a shortness of breathing. A species of arrack is made from this tree, in the East-Indies. The largest coco-nut trees grow on the banks of the river Oronoko. They thrive best near the sea, and look beautiful at a distance. They afford no great shade. Ripe nuts have been produced from them in three years after planting. The nuts should be macerated in water, before they are put in the ground. Coco is an Indian name; the Spaniards call it also *palma de las Indias;* as the smallest kind, whose nuts are less than walnuts, is termed by them *Coquillo.* This grows in Chili, and the nuts are esteemed more delicate than those of a larger size. In the Maldivy Islands, it is pretended, they not only build houses of the coco-nut tree, but also vessels, with all their rigging; nay, and load them too with wine, oil, vinegar, black sugar, fruit, and strong water, from the same tree. If this be true, the Maldivian coco-nut trees must differ widely from those that grow in the West Indies. The coco [i.e., coca] must not be confounded with the coco-nut tree. That shrub grows in the hottest and moistest vales of the Andes. Its leaf, which is gathered two or three times a year, is much coveted by the natives of South-America, who will travel great journeys upon a single handful of the leaves, which they do not swallow, but only chew. It is of an unpleasant taste, but, by use, soon grows agreeable. Some authors have also confounded the coconut palm, with the coco, or chocolate tree. The French call the coco-nut tree, *Cocotier.* Its stem, which is very lofty, is always bent; for which reason it looks better in an orchard than in a regular garden. As one limb fades, another shoots up in the center, like a pike. The botanical name is *Palma indica, coccifera, angulosa.*

*This is a pleasant-tasted fruit, somewhat resembling a bergamot-pear, in shape and colour. The tree which produces it, is large and shady. Its leaves are of a shining green; but the flowers, which are monopetalous, are of a palish white. The fruit is coronated when ripe, and contains, in its pulp, several longish black seeds. It is wholesome. Antigua produces the best sappadillas I ever tasted. The trivial name is Spanish. Botanists call it *Cainito.*

Which Percy's[69] happier pencil would demand,
Can ill describe the transports Junio felt
At this discovery: He declar'd his love;
She own'd his merit, nor refus'd his hand.   455

    And shall not Hymen light his brightest torch,
For this delighted pair? Ah, Junio knew,
His sire detested his Theana's House!—
Thus duty, reverence, gratitude, conspir'd
To check their happy union. He resolv'd   460
(And many a sigh that resolution cost)
To pass the time, till death his sire remov'd,
In visiting old Europe's letter'd climes:
While she (and many a tear that parting drew)
Embark'd, reluctant, for her native isle.   465

    Tho' learned, curious, and tho' nobly bent,
With each rare talent to adorn his mind,
His native land to serve; no joys he found.—
Yet sprightly Gaul, yet Belgium, Saturn's reign;
Yet Greece, of old the seat of every Muse,   470
Of freedom, courage; yet Ausonia's[70] clime,
His steps explor'd; where painting, music's strains,
Where arts, where laws, (philosophy's best child),
With rival beauties, his attention claim'd.
To his just-judging, his instructed eye,   475
The all-perfect Medicean Venus seem'd
A perfect semblance of his Indian fair:
But, when she spoke of love, her voice surpass'd
The harmonious warblings of Italian song.

    Twice one long year elaps'd. when letters came,   480
Which briefly told him of his father's death.
Afflicted, filial, yet to Heaven resign'd,
Soon he reach'd Albion, and as soon embark'd,
Eager to clasp the object of his love.

    Blow, prosperous breezes; swiftly sail, thou Po: 485
Swift sail'd the Po, and happy breezes blew.

    In Biscay's stormy seas an armed ship,
Of force superiour, from loud Charente's[71] wave

Clapt them on board. The frighted flying crew
Their colours strike; when dauntless Junio, fir'd   490
With noble indignation, kill'd the chief,
Who on the bloody deck dealt slaughter round.
The Gauls retreat; the Britons loud huzza;
And touch'd with shame, with emulation stung,
So plied their cannon, plied their missil fires,   495
That soon in air the hapless Thunderer blew.

    Blow prosperous breezes, swiftly sail thou Po,
May no more dangerous fights retard thy way!

    Soon Porto Santo's* rocky heights they spy,
Like clouds dim rising in the distant air.   500
Glad Eurus whistles; laugh the sportive crew,
Each sail is set to catch the favouring gale,
While on the yard-arm the harpooner sits,
Strikes the boneta,† or the shark‡ insnares.
The fring'd urtica§ spreads her purple form   505
To catch the gale, and dances o'er the waves:
Small winged fishes‖ on the shrouds alight;
And beauteous dolphins# gently played around.

---

*This is one of the Madeira islands, and of course subject to the King of Portugal. It lies in 32.33 degrees of N. latitude. It is neither so fruitful nor so large as Madeira Proper, and is chiefly peopled by convicts, &c.

†This fish, which is equal in size to the largest salmon, is only to be found in the warm latitudes. It is not a delicate food, but those who have lived for any length of time on salt meats at sea, do not dislike it. Sir Hans Sloane, in his voyage to Jamaica, describes the method of striking them.

‡This voracious fish needs no description; I have seen them from 15 to 20 foot long. Some naturalists call it Canis Carharias. They have been known to follow a slave-ship from Guinea to the West Indies. They swim with incredible celerity, and are found in some of the warmer seas of Europe, as well as between the tropics.

§This fish the seamen call the Portuguese man of war. It makes a most beautiful appearance on the water.

‖This extraordinary species of fish is only found in the warm latitudes. Being pursued in the water by a fish of prey called Albacores, they betake themselves in shoals to flight, and in the air are often snapt up by the Garayio, a sea fowl. They sometimes fall on the shrouds or decks of ships. They are well tasted, and commonly sold at Barbadoes.

#This is a most beautiful fish, when first taken out of the sea; but its beauty vanishes, almost as soon as it is dead. [Now known commonly by its Hawaiian name, Mahi Mahi.]

Tho' faster than the Tropic-bird* they flew,
Oft Junio cried, ah! when shall we see land?   510
Soon land they made: and now in thought he claspt
His Indian bride, and deem'd his toils o'erpaid.

 She, no less amorous, every evening walk'd
On the cool margin of the purple main,
Intent her Junio's vessel to descry.   515

 One eve, (faint calms for many a day had rag'd,)
The winged daemons of the tempest rose;
Thunder, and rain, and lightning's awful power.
She fled: could innocence, could beauty claim
Exemption from the grave; the aethereal Bolt,   520
That stretch'd her speechless, o'er her lovely head
Had innocently roll'd.

 Mean while, impatient Junio lept ashore,
Regardless of the Daemons of the storm.
Ah youth! what woes, too great for man to bear,   525
Are ready to burst on thee? Urge not so
Thy flying courser. Soon Theana's porch
Receiv'd him: at his sight, the antient slaves
Affrighted shriek, and to the chamber point:—
Confounded, yet unknowing what they meant,   530
He entered hasty—

 Ah! what a sight for one who lov'd so well!
All pale and cold, in every feature death,
Theana lay; and yet a glimpse of joy
Played on her face, while with faint, faultering voice,   535
She thus addrest the youth, whom yet she knew.

 "Welcome, my Junio, to thy native shore!
Thy sight repays this summons of my fate:
Live, and live happy; sometimes think of me:
By night, by day, you still engag'd my care;   540
And next to God, you now my thoughts employ:
Accept of this—My little all I give;

---

*The French call this bird Fregate, on account of its swift flying. It is only to be met with in the warm latitudes.

Would it were larger"—Nature could no more;
She look'd, embrac'd him, with a groan expir'd.

But say, what strains, what language can express   545
The thousand pangs, which tore the lover's breast?
Upon her breathless corse himself he threw,
And to her clay-cold lips, with trembling haste,
Ten thousand kisses gave. He strove to speak;
Nor words he found: he claspt her in his arms;   550
He sigh'd, he swoon'd, look'd up, and died away.

One grave contains this hapless, faithful pair;
And still the Cane-isles tell their matchless love!
The End of Book II.

BOOK III.
ARGUMENT

Hymn to the month of January, when crop begins. Address. Planters have employment all year round. Planters should be pious. A ripe Cane piece on fire at midnight. Crop begun. Cane cutting described. Effects of music. Great care requisite in feeding the mill. Humanity towards the maimed recommended. The tainted Canes should not be ground. Their use. How to preserve the laths and mill-points from sudden squalls. Address to the Sun, and praise of Antigua. A cattle-mill described. Care of mules, &c. Diseases to which they are subject. A water-mill the least liable to interruption. Common in Guadaloupe and Martinico. Praise of Lord Romney.[72] The necessity of a strong, clear fire, in boiling. Planters should always have a spare set of vessels, because the iron furnaces are apt to crack, and copper vessels to melt. The danger of throwing cold water in a thorough-heated furnace. Cleanliness, and skimming well, recommended. A boiling house should be lofty, and open at the top, to the leeward. Constituent parts of vegetables. Sugar an essential salt. What retards its granulation. How to forward it. Dumb Cane. Effects of it. Bristol-lime the best temper. Various uses of Bristol lime. Good muscovado described. Bermudas-lime recommended. The Negroes should not be hindered from drinking the hot liquor. The chearfulness and healthiness of the Negroes in crop-time. Boilers to be encouraged. They should neither boil the Sugar too little, nor too much. When the Sugar is of too loose a grain, and about to boil over the teache, or last copper, a little grease settles it, and makes it boil closer. The French often mix sand with their Sugars. This practice not followed by the English. A character. Of the skimmings. Their various uses. Of rum. Its praise. A West-India prospect, when crop is finished. An address to the Creoles, to live more upon their estates than they do. The reasons.

BOOK III.

From scenes of deep distress, the heavenly Muse,
Emerging joyous, claps her dewy wings.

As when a pilgrim, in the howling waste,
Hath long time wandered, fearful at each step,
Of tumbling cliffs, fell serpents, whelming bogs;   5
At last, from some long eminence, descries
Fair haunts of social life; wide-cultur'd plains,
O'er which glad reapers pour; he chearly sings:
So she to sprightlier notes her pipe attunes,
Than e'er these mountains heard; to gratulate,   10
With duteous carols, the beginning year.

    Hail, eldest birth of Time! in other climes,
In the old world, with tempests usher'd in;
While rifled nature thine appearance wails,
And savage winter wields his iron mace: 15
But not the rockiest verge of these green isles,
Tho' mountains heapt on mountains* brave the sky,
Dares winter, by his residence, prophane.
At times the ruffian, wrapt in murky state,
Inroads will, fly, attempt; but soon the sun,   20
Benign protector of the Cane-land isles,
Repells the invader, and his rude mace breaks.
Here, every mountain, every winding dell,
(Haunt of the Dryads; where, beneath the shade
Of broad-leaf'd china,† idly they repose,   25
Charm'd with the murmur of the tinkling rill;
Charm'd with the hummings of the neighbouring hive;)
Welcome thy glad approach: but chief the Cane,

*This more particularly alludes to St. Kitts; where one of the highest ridges of that chain of mountains, which run through its center, from one end of it to the other, bears upon it another mountain, which, somewhat resembling the legendary prints of the devil's carrying on his shoulders St. Christopher; or, as others write, of a giant, of that appellation, carrying our Saviour, in the form of a child, in the same manner, through a deep sea; gave name, to this island.

†The leaves of this medicinal tree are so large, that the Negroes commonly use them to cover the water, which they bring in pails from the mountain, where it chiefly grows. The roots of this tree were introduced into European practice, soon after the venereal disease; but, unless they are fresh, it must be confessed they possess fewer virtues than either sarsaparilla or lignum vitae. It also grows in China, and many parts of the East-Indies, where it is greatly recommended in the gout, palsy, sciatica, obstructions, and obstinate headachs: but it can surely not effect the removal of these terrible disorders; since, in China, the people eat the fresh root, boiled with their meat, as we do turnips; and the better sort, there, use a water distilled from it. The Spaniards call it *Palo de China.* The botanical name is *Smilax.*

Whose juice now longs to murmur down the spout,
Hails thy lov'd coming; January, hail!   30

　　OM***![73] thou, whose polish'd mind contains
Each science useful to thy native isle!
Philosopher, without the hermit's spleen!
Polite, yet learned; and, tho' solid, gay!
Critic, whose head each beauty, fond, admires;   35
Whose heart each error flings in friendly shade!
Planter, whose youth sage cultivation taught
Each secret lesson of her sylvan school:
To thee the Muse a grateful tribute pays;
She owes to thee the precepts of her song: 40
Nor wilt thou, sour, refuse; tho' other cares,
The public welfare, claim thy busy hour;
With her to roam (thrice pleasing devious walk)
The ripened cane-piece; and, with her, to taste
(Delicious draught!) the nectar of the mill!   45

　　The planter's labour in a round revolves;
Ends with the year, and with the year begins.

　　Ye swains, to Heaven bend low in grateful prayer,
Worship the Almighty; whose kind-fostering hand
Hath blest your labour, and hath given the cane   50
To rise superior to each menac'd ill.

　　Nor less, ye planters, in devotion, sue,
That nor the heavenly bolt, nor casual spark,
Nor hand of malice may the crop destroy.

　　Ah me! what numerous, deafning bells, resound?   55
What cries of horror startle the dull sleep?
What gleaming brightness makes, at midnight, day?
By its portentuous glare, too well I see
Palaemon's[74] fate; the virtuous, and the wise!
Where were ye, watches, when the flame burst forth?   60
A little care had then the hydra quell'd:
But, now, what clouds of white smoke load the sky!
How strong, how rapid the combustion pours!
Aid not, ye winds! with your destroying breath,
The spreading vengeance.—They contemn my prayer.   65

Rous'd by the deafning bells, the cries, the blaze;
From every quarter, in tumultuous bands,
The Negroes rush; and, 'mid the crackling flames,
Plunge, daemon-like! All, all, urge every nerve:
This way, tear up those Canes; dash the fire out,   70
Which sweeps, with serpent-error, o'er the ground.
There, hew these down; their topmost branches burn:
And here bid all thy watery engines play;
For here the wind the burning deluge drives.

In vain.—More wide the blazing torrent rolls;   75
More loud it roars, more bright it fires the pole!
And toward thy mansion, see, it bends its way.
Haste, far, O far, your infant-throng remove:
Quick from your stables drag your steeds and mules:
With well-wet blankets guard your cypress-roofs;   80
And where thy dried Canes* in large stacks are pil'd.—

Efforts but serve to irritate the flames:
Naught but thy ruin can their wrath appease.
Ah, my Palaemon! what avail'd thy care,
Oft to prevent the earliest dawn of day,   85
And walk thy ranges, at the noon of night?
What tho' no ills assail'd thy bunching sprouts,
And seasons pour'd obedient to thy will:
All, all must perish; nor shalt thou preserve
Wherewith to feed thy little orphan-throng.   90

Oh, may the Cane-isles know few nights, like this!
For now the sail-clad points, impatient, wait
The hour of sweet release, to court the gale.
The late-hung coppers wish to feel the warmth,
Which well-dried fewel from the Cane imparts: 95
The Negroe-train, with placid looks, survey
Thy fields, which full perfection have attain'd,
And pant to wield the bill: (no surly watch
Dare now deprive them of the luscious Cane:)
Nor thou, my friend, their willing ardour check;   100

*The Cane-stalks which have been ground, are called *Magoss;* probably a corruption of the
French word *Bagasse,* which signifies the same thing. They make an excellent fewel.

Encourage rather; cheerful toil is light.
So from no field, shall slow-pac'd oxen draw
More frequent loaded wanes; which many a day,
And many a night shall feed thy crackling mills
With richest offerings: while thy far seen flames,   105
Bursting thro' many a chimney, bright emblaze
The Aethiop-brow of night. And see, they pour
(Ere Phosphor his pale circlet yet withdraws,
What time grey dawn stands tip-toe on the hill,)
O'er the rich Cane-grove: Muse, their labour sing.   110

  Some bending, of their sapless burden ease
The yellow jointed canes, (whose height exceeds
A mounted trooper, and whose clammy round
Measures two inches full;) and near the root
Lop the stem off, which quivers in their hand   115
With fond impatience: soon its branchy spires,
(Food to thy cattle) it resigns; and soon
It's tender prickly tops, with eyes thick set,
To load with future crops thy long-hoed land.
These with their green, their pliant branches bound,   120
(For not a part of this amazing plant,
But serves some useful purpose) charge the young:
Not laziness declines this easy toil;
Even lameness from it's leafy pallet crawls,
To join the favoured gang. What of the Cane   125
Remains, and much the largest part remains,
Cut into junks a yard in length, and tied
In small light bundles; load the broad-wheel'd wane,
The mules crook-harnest, and the sturdier crew,
With sweet abundance. As on Lincoln-plains,   130
(Ye plains of Lincoln sound your Dyer's praise!)
When the lav'd snow-white flocks are numerous penn'd;
The senior swains, with sharpen'd shears, cut off
The fleecy vestment; others stir the tar;
And some impress, upon their captives sides,   135
Their master's cypher; while the infant throng
Strive by the horns to hold the struggling ram,
Proud of their prowess. Nor meanwhile the jest

Light-bandied round, but innocent of ill;
Nor choral song are wanting: eccho rings.   140

 Nor need the driver, Aethiop authoriz'd,[75]
Thence more inhuman, crack his horrid whip;
From such dire sounds the indignant muse averts
Her virgin-ear, where musick loves to dwell:
'Tis malice now, 'tis wantonness of power   145
To lash the laughing, labouring, singing throng.

 What cannot song? all nature feels its power:
The hind's blithe whistle, as thro' stubborn soils
He drives the shining share;[76] more than the goad,
His tardy steers impells.—The muse hath seen,   150
When health danc'd frolic in her youthful veins,
And vacant gambols wing'd the laughing hours;
The muse hath seen on Annan's[77] pastoral hills,
Of theft and slaughter erst the fell retreat,
But now the shepherd's best-beloved walk: 155
Hath seen the shepherd, with his sylvan pipe,
Lead on his flock o'er crags, thro' bogs, and streams,
A tedious journey; yet not weary they,
Drawn by the enchantment of his artless song.
What cannot musick?—When brown Ceres asks   160
The reapers sickle; what like magic sound,
Puff'd from sonorous bellows by the squeeze
Of tuneful artist, can the rage disarm
Of the swart dog-star, and make harvest light?

 And now thy mills dance eager in the gale;   165
Feed well their eagerness: but O beware;
Nor trust, between the steel-cas'd cylinders,
The hand incautious: off the member snapt*
Thou'lt ever rue; sad spectacle of woe!

*This accident will sometimes happen, especially in the night: and the unfortunate wretch must fall a victim to his imprudence or sleepiness, if a hatchet do not immediately strike off the entangled member; or the mill be not instantly put out of the wind.

 Pere Labat says, he was informed the English were wont, as a punishment, thus to grind their negroes to death. But one may venture to affirm this punishment never had the sanction of law; and if any Englishman ever did grind his negroes to death, I will take upon me to aver, he was universally detested by his countrymen.

Are there, the muse can scarce believe the tale;   170
Are there, who lost to every feeling sense,
To reason, interest lost; their slaves desert,
And manumit them, generous boon! to starve
Maim'd by imprudence, or the hand of Heaven?
The good man feeds his blind, his aged steed,   175
That in his service spent his vigorous prime:
And dares a mortal to his fellow man,
(For spite of vanity, thy slaves are men)
Deny protection? Muse suppress the tale.

Ye! who in bundles bind the lopt-off Canes;   180
But chiefly ye! who feed the tight-brac'd mill;
In separate parcels, far, the infected fling:
Of bad Cane-juice the least admixture spoils
The richest, soundest; thus, in pastoral walks,
One tainted sheep contaminates the fold.   185

Nor yet to dung-heaps thou resign the canes,
Which or the sun hath burnt, or rats have gnaw'd.
These, to small junks reduc'd, and in huge casks
Steept, where no cool winds blow; do thou ferment:—
Then, when from his entanglements inlarg'd   190
Th' evasive spirit mounts; by Vulcan's aid,
(Nor Amphitryte* will her help deny,)
Do thou through all his winding ways pursue
The runaway; till in thy sparkling bowl
Confin'd, he dances; more a friend to life,   195
And joy, than that Nepenthe[78] fam'd of yore,
Which Polydamna, Thone's imperial queen,
Taught Jove-born Helen on the banks of Nile.

Indeed the bare suspicion of such a piece of barbarity leaves a stain: and therefore authors cannot be too cautious of admitting into their writings, any insinuation that bears hard on the humanity of a people.

Daily observation affords but too many proofs, where domestic slavery does not obtain, of the fatal consequences of indulged passion and revenge; but where one man is the absolute property of another, those passions may perhaps receive additional activity: planters, therefore, cannot be too much on their guard against the first sallies of passion; as by indulgence, passion, like a favourite, will at last grow independently powerful.

*A mixture of sea water, is a real improvement in the distillation of rum.

As on old ocean, then the wind blows high,
The cautious mariner contracts his sail;   200
So here, when squaly bursts the speeding gale,
If thou from ruin would'st thy points preserve,
Less-bellying canvas to the storm oppose.

    Yet the faint breeze oft flags on listless wings,
Nor tremulates the coco's airiest arch,   205
While the red sun darts deluges of fire;
And soon (if on the gale thy crop depend,)
Will all thy hopes of opulence defeat.

    "Informer of the planetary train!"[79]
Source undiminished of all-cheering light,   210
Of roseat beauty, and heart-gladning joy!
Fountain of being, on whose water broods
The organic spirit, principle of life!
Lord of the seasons! who in courtly pomp
Lacquay[80] thy presence, and with glad dispatch,   215
Pour at thy bidding, o'er the land and sea!
Parent of Vegetation, whose fond grasp
The Sugar-Cane displays; and whose green car
Soft-stealing dews, with liquid pearls adorn'd,
Fat-fostering rains, and buxom genial airs   220
Attend triumphant! Why, ah why so oft,
Why hath Antigua,* sweetly social isle,
Nurse of each art; where science yet finds friends
Amid this waste of waters; wept thy rage?

    Then trust not, planter, to the unsteddy gale;   225
But in Tobago's endless forests fell
The tall tough hiccory,† or calaba.‡

---

*This beautiful island lies in 16 degrees and 14 min. N. lat. It was long uninhabited on ac-
count of its wanting fresh-water rivers; but is now more fully peopled, and as well cultivated as
any of the leeward islands. In a seasonable year, it has made 30,000 hogsheads of sugar. It has no
very high mountains. The soil is, in general, clayey. The water of the body-ponds may be used
for every purpose of life. Antigua is well fortified, and has a good militia.

†This is a lofty spreading tree, of very hard wood, excellently adapted to the purposes of the
mill-wright. The nut, whose shell is thick, hard, and roughish, contains an agreeable
and wholesome kernal. It grows in great abundance in St. Croix, Crab island [Culebra], and
Tobago.

‡This lofty tree is commonly called Mastic: it is a hard wood, and is found in the places

Of this, be forc'd two pillars in the ground,
Four paces distant, and two cubits high:
Other two pillars raise; the wood the same,   230
Of equal size and height. The Calaba
Than steel more durable, contemns the rain,
And sun's intensest beam; the worm, that pest
Of mariners, which winds its fatal way
Through heart of British oak, reluctant leaves   235
The closer calaba.—By transverse beams
Secure the whole; and in the pillar'd frame,
Sink, artist, the vast bridge-tree's mortis'd[81] form
Of ponderous hiccory; hiccory time defies:
To this be nail'd three polish'd iron plates;   240
Whereon, three steel Capouces, turn with ease,
Of three long rollers, twice-nine inches round,
With iron cas'd, and jagg'd with many a cogg.
The central Cylinder exceeds the rest
In portly size, thence aptly Captain nam'd.   245
To this be rivetted th' extended sweeps;
And harness to each sweep two seasoned mules:
They pacing round, give motion to the whole.
The close brac'd cylinders with ease revolve
On their greas'd axle; and with ease reduce   250
To trash, the Canes thy negroes throw between.
Fast flows the liquor through the lead-lin'd spouts;
And depurated[82] by opposing wires,
In the receiver floats a limpid stream.
So twice five casks, with muscovado fill'd,   255
Shall from thy staunchions drip, ere Day's bright god
Hath in the Atlantic six times cool'd his wheels.

Wouldst thou against calamity provide?
Let a well shingled roof, from Raleigh's land,*

---

where the Hiccory grows. The flowers are yellow, and are succeeded by a fruit, which bears a distant resemblance to a shrub.

*Sir Walter Raleigh gave the name of Virginia, in honour of Q. Elizabeth, to the whole of the north-east of North America, which Sebastian Cabot, a native of Bristol, (though others call him a Venetian,) first discovered, *A.D.* 1497, in the time of King Henry VII. by whom he was employed; but no advantages could be reaped from this discovery, on account of the various disturbances that ensued in England during the succeeding reigns, till about the year 1584, Q. Eliz-

Defend thy stock from noon's inclement blaze,   260
And from night-dews; for night no respite knows.

    Nor, when their destin'd labour is perform'd,
Be thou asham'd to lead the panting mules
(The muse, soft parent of each social grace,
With eyes of love God's whole creation views)   265
To the warm pen; where copious forage strowed,
And strenuous rubbing, renovate their strength.
So, fewer ails, (alas, how prone to ails!)
Their days shall shorten; ah, too short at best!

    For not, even then, my friend, art thou secure   270
From fortune: spite of all thy steady care,
What ills, that laugh to scorn Machaon's[83] art,
Await thy cattle! farcy's tabid form,[84]
Joint-racking spasms, and cholic's pungent pang,
Need the muse tell? which, in one luckless moon,   275
Thy sheds dispeople; when perhaps thy groves,
To full perfection shot, by day, by night,
Indesinent[85] demand their vigorous toil.

    Then happiest he, for whom the Naiads pour,
From rocky urns, the never-ceasing stream,   280
To turn his rollers with unbought dispatch.

    In Karukera's* rich well-water'd isle!
In Matanina!† boast of Albion's arms,
The brawling Naiads for the planters toil,
Howe'er unworthy; and, through solemn scenes,   285
Romantic, cool, with rocks and woods between,

---

abeth gave Sir Walter Raleigh a patent for all such land, from 33. to 40. N. lat. as he should chuse
to settle with English, reserving only to the crown a fifth part of all the gold and silver which
should therein be discovered, in lieu of all services. Accordingly several imbarkations were fitted out from England, but all to no purpose. Some farther attempts, however, were made to settle this part of the country in the succeeding reign; but it was not till the year 1620 [actually, 1619],
that a regular form of government took place. Then was tobacco planted, and negroes imported
into Virginia. Since that time it has gradually improved, and does not now contain fewer than
100,000 white people of better condition, besides twice as many servants and slaves. The best
shingles come from *Egg-Harbour.*

    *The Indian name of Guadaloupe.

    †The Caribbean name of *Martinico.* The *Havannah* had not then been taken.

Enchant the senses! but, among thy swains,
Sweet Liamuiga! who such bliss can boast?
Yes, Romney, thou may'st boast; of British heart,
Of courtly manners, join'd to antient worth: 290
Friend to thy Britain's every blood-earn'd right,
From tyrants wrung, the many or the few.
By wealth, by titles, by ambition's lure,
Not to be tempted from fair honour's path:
While others, falsely flattering their Prince,   295
Bold disapprov'd, or by oblique surmise
Their terror hinted, of the people arm'd;
Indignant, in the senate, he uprose,
And, with the well-urg'd energy of zeal,
Their specious, subtle sophistry disprov'd;   300
The importance, the necessity display'd,
Of civil armies, freedom's surest guard!
Nor in the senate didst thou only win
The palm of eloquence, securely bold;
But rear'd'st thy banners, fluttering in the wind: 305
Kent, from each hamlet, pour'd her marshal'd swains,
To hurl defiance on the threatening Gaul.

　　　Thy foaming coppers well with fewel feed;
For a clear, strong, continued fire improves
Thy muscovado's colour, and its grain.—   310
Yet vehement heat, protracted, will consume
Thy vessels,* whether from the martial mine,
Or from thine ore, bright Venus, they are drawn;
Or hammer, or hot fusion, give them form.
If prudence guides thee then, thy stores shall hold   315
Of well-siz'd vessels a complete supply:
For every hour, thy boilers cease to skim,
(Now Cancer reddens with the solar ray,)
Defeats thy honest purposes of gain.

---

*The vessels, wherein the Cane-juice is reduced to Sugar by coction, are either made of iron or of copper. Each sort hath its advantages and disadvantages. The teache, or smallest vessel from whence the Sugar is laved into the cooler, is generally copper. When it melts, it can be patched; but, when the large sort of vessels, called iron-furnaces, crack, which they are too apt to do, no further use can be made of them.

Nor small the risque, (when piety, or chance,   320
Force thee from boiling to desist) to lave
Thy heated furnace, with the gelid[86] stream.
The chemist knows, when all-dissolving fire
Bids the metalline ore abruptly flow;
What dread explosions, and what dire effects,   325
A few cold drops of water will produce,
Uncautious, on the novel fluid thrown.

For grain and colour, wouldst thou win, my friend,
At every curious mart, the constant palm?
O'er all thy works let cleanliness preside,   330
Child of frugality; and, as the skum
Thick mantles o'er the boiling wave, do thou
The skum that mantles carefully remove.

From bloating dropsy, from pulmonic ails,
Would'st thou defend thy boilers, (prime of slaves,)   335
For days, for nights, for weeks, for months, involv'd
In the warm vapour's all-relaxing steam;
Thy boiling house be lofty: all atop
Open, and pervious* to the tropic breeze;
Whose cool perflation,[87] wooed through many a grate,   340
Dispells the steam, and gives the lungs to play.

The skill'd in chemia, boast of modern arts,
Know from experiment, the fire of truth,
In many a plant that oil, and acid juice,
And ropy mucilage,[88] by nature live: 345
These envious, stop the much desir'd embrace
Of the essential salts, tho' coction bid
The aqueous particles to mount in air.

'Mong salts essential, sugar wins the palm,
For taste, for colour, and for various use:†   350

*This also assists the christallization of the Sugar.
†It were impossible, in the short limits of a note, to ennumerate the various uses of Sugar;
and indeed, as these are in general so well known, it is needless. A few properties of it, however,
wherewith the learned are not commonly acquainted, I shall mention. In some places of the
East-Indies, an excellent *arrack* [i.e., distilled liquor] is made from the Sugar-Cane: And, in
South-America, Sugar is used as an antidote against one of the most sudden, as well as fatal poisons in the world. Taken by mouth, *pocula morte carent,* this poison is quite innocent; but the

And, in the nectar of the yellowest Cane,
Much acor,[89] oil, and mucilage abound:
But in the less mature, from mountain-land,
These harsh intruders so redundant float;
Muster so strong, as scarce to be subdued.   355

    Muse, sing the ways to quell them. Some use Cane,
That Cane* whose juices to the tongue apply'd,
In silence lock it, sudden, and constrain'd,
(Death to Xantippe,)[90] with distorting pain.

    Nor is it not effectual: But wouldst thou   360
Have rival brokers for thy cades[91] contend;
Superior arts remain.—Small casks provide,
Replete with lime-stone thoroughly calcin'd,
And from the air secur'd: This Bristol sends,
Bristol, Britannia's second mart and eye!   365

    Nor "to thy waters only trust for fame,"[92]
Bristol; nor to thy beamy diamonds trust:
Tho' these oft deck Britannia's lovely fair;
And those oft save the guardians of her realm.
Thy marble-quarries claim the voice of praise,   370
Which rich incrusts thy Avon's banks, sweet banks!
Tho' not to you young Shakespear, Fancy's child,
All-rudely warbled his first woodland notes;
Tho' not your caves, while terror stalk'd around,
Saw him essay to clutch the ideal sword,   375
With drops of blood distain'd: yet, lovely banks,

---

slightest wound made by an arrow, whose point is tinged therewith, proves immediate death; for, by driving all the blood of the body immediately to the heart, it forthwith bursts it. The fish and birds killed by these poisoned arrows (in the use of which the Indians are astonishingly expert) are perfectly wholesome to feed on. See *Ulloa* and *De la Condamine's* account of the great river of Amazon. It is a vegetable preparation.

    *This, by the natives, is emphatically called the *Dumb Cane;* for a small quantity of its juice being rubbed on the brim of a drinking vessel, whoever drinks out of it, soon after will have his lips and tongue enormously swelled. A physician, however, who wrote a short account of the diseases of Jamaica, in Charles II.'s time, recommends it both by the mouth and externally, in *dropsical* and other cases: But I cannot say, I have had any experience of its efficacy in these disorders. It grows wild in the mountains; and, by its use in Sugar-making, should seem to be somewhat of an *alcalescent* nature. It grows to four feet high, having, at the top, two green shining leaves, about nine inches long; and, between these, a small spire emerges.

On you reclin'd, another tun'd his pipe;
Whom all the Muses emulously love,
And in whose strains your praises shall endure,
While to Sabrina[93] speeds your healing stream.   380

    Bristol, without thy marble, by the flame
Calcin'd to whiteness, vain the stately reed
Would swell with juice mellifluent; heat would soon
The strongest, best-hung furnaces, consume.
Without its aid the cool-imprison'd stream,   385
Seldom allow'd to view the face of day,
Tho' late it roam'd a denizen of air;
Would steal from its involuntary bounds,
And, by sly windings, set itself at large.
But chief thy lime the experienc'd boiler loves,   390
Nor loves ill-founded; when no other art
Can bribe to union the coy floating salts,
A proper portion of this precious dust,
Cast in the wave, (so showers alone of gold
Could win fair Danae[94] to the God's embrace;)   395
With nectar'd muscovado soon will charge
Thy shelving coolers, which, severely press'd
Between the fingers, not resolves; and which
Rings in the cask; and or a light-brown hue,
Or thine, more precious silvery-grey, assumes.   400

    The fam'd Bermuda's ever-healthy isles,
More fam'd by gentle Waller's deathless strains,[95]
Than for their cedars, which, insulting, fly
O'er the wide ocean; 'mid their rocks contain
A stone, which, when calcin'd, (experience says;)   405
Is only second to Sabrina's lime.

    While flows the juice mellifluent from the Cane,
Grudge not, my friend, to let thy slaves, each morn,
But chief the sick and young, at setting day,
Themselves regale with oft-repeated draughts   410
Of tepid Nectar; so shall health and strength
Confirm thy Negroes, and make labour light.

    While flame the chimneys, while thy coppers foam,
How blithe, how jocund, the plantation smiles!

By day, by night, resounds the choral song   415
Of glad barbarity; serene, the sun
Shines not intensely hot; the trade-wind blows:
How sweet, how silken, is its noontide breath?
While to far climes the fell destroyer, Death,
Wings his dark flight. Then seldom pray for rain: 420
Rather for cloudless days thy prayers prefer;
For, if the skies too frequently relent,
Crude flows the Cane-juice, and will long elude
The boiler's wariest skill: thy Canes will spring
To an unthrifty loftiness; or, weigh'd   425
Down by their load, (Ambition's curse,) decay.

    Encourage thou thy boilers; much depends
On their skill'd efforts. If too soon they strike,*
E'er all the watery particles have fled;
Or lime sufficient granulate the juice: 430
In vain the thickning liquor is effus'd;
An heterogeneous, and uncertain mass,
And never in thy coolers to condense.

    Or, planter, if the coction they prolong
Beyond its stated time; the viscous wave   435
Will in huge flinty masses chrystalize,
Which forceful fingers scarce can crumble down;
And which with its melasses ne'er will part.
Yet this, fast-dripping in nectarious drops,
Not only betters what remains, but when   440
With art fermented, yields a noble wine,
Than which nor Gallia, nor the Indian clime,
Where rolls the Ganges, can a nobler show.
So misers in their coffers lock that gold;

---

*When the Cane-juice is granulated sufficiently, which is known by the Sugar's sticking to the ladle, and roping like a syrup, but breaking off from its edges; it is poured into a cooler, where, its surface being smoothed, the christallization is soon completed. This is called *striking*. The general precept is to temper high, and strike low. When the Muscovado is of a proper consistence, it is dug out of the cooler, and put into hogsheads; this is called *potting*. The casks being placed upon staunchions, the melasses drips from them into a cistern, made on purpose, below them, to receive it. The Sugar is sufficiently cured, when the hogshead rings upon being struck with a stick; and when the two canes, which are put into every cask, shew no melasses upon them, when drawn out of it.

Which, if allowed at liberty to roam,   445
Would better them, and benefit mankind.

    In the last coppers, when the embrowning wave
With sudden fury swells; some grease immix'd,
The foaming tumult sudden will compose,
And force to union the divided grain.   450
So when two swarms in airy battles join,
The winged heroes heap the bloody field;
Until some dust, thrown upward in the sky,
Quell the wild conflict, and sweet peace restore.

    False Gallia's sons, that hoe the ocean-isles,   455
Mix with their Sugar, loads of worthless sand,
Fraudful, their weight of sugar to increase,
Far be such guile from Britain's honest swains.
Such arts, awhile, the unwary may surprise,
And benefit the Impostor; but, ere long,   460
The skilful buyer will the fraud detect,
And, with abhorrence, reprobate the name.

    Fortune had crown'd Avaro's[96] younger years,
With a vast tract of land, on which the cane
Delighted grew, nor ask'd the toil of art.   465
The Sugar-bakers deem'd themselves secure,
Of mighty profit, could they buy his cades;
For, whiteness, hardness, to the leeward-crop,
His muscovado gave. But, not content
With this pre-eminence of honest gain,   470
He baser sugars started in his casks;
His own, by mixing sordid things, debas'd.
One year the fraud succeeded; wealth immense
Flowed in upon him, and he blest his wiles:
The next, the brokers spurn'd the adulterate mass,   475
Both on the Avon and the banks of Thame.

    Be thrifty, planter, even thy skimmings save:
For, planter, know, the refuse of the Cane
Serves needful purposes. Are barbecues
The cates thou lov'st? What like rich skimmings feed   480
The grunting, bristly kind? Your labouring mules
They soon invigorate: Give old Baynard these,

Untir'd he trudges in the destin'd round;
Nor need the driver crack his horrid lash.

Yet, with small quantities indulge the steed,   485
Whom skimmings ne'er have fatten'd: else, too fond,
So gluttons use, he'll eat intemperate meals;
And, staggering, fall the prey of ravening sharks.

But say, ye boon companions, in what strains,
What grateful strains, shall I record the praise   490
Of their best produce, heart-recruiting rum?
Thrice wholesome spirit! well-matur'd with age,
Thrice grateful to the palate! when, with thirst,
With heat, with labour, and wan care opprest,
I quaff thy bowl, where fruit my hands have cull'd,   495
Round, golden fruit; where water from the spring,
Which dripping coolness spreads her umbrage round;
With hardest, whitest sugar, thrice refin'd;
Dilates my soul with genuine joy; low care
I spurn indignant; toil a pleasure seems.   500
For not Marne's flowery banks, nor Tille's* green bounds,
Where Ceres with the God of vintage reigns,
In happiest union; not Vigornian hills,[97]
Pomona's lov'd abode, afford to man
Goblets more priz'd, or laudable of taste,   505
To slake parch'd thirst, and mitigate the clime.

Yet, 'mid this blest ebriety,[98] some tears,
For friends I left in Albion's distant isle,
For Johnson, Percy, White,[99] escape mine eyes:
For her, fair Auth'ress!† whom first Calpe's rocks   510
A sportive infant saw; and whose green years
True genius blest with her benignest gifts
Of happiest fancy. O, were ye all here,
O, were ye here; with him, my Paeon's[100] son!
Long-known, of worth approv'd, thrice candid soul!   515
How would your converse charm the lonely hour?
Your converse, where mild wisdom tempers mirth;

*Two rivers in France, along whose banks the best Burgundy and Champagne-grapes grow.
†Mrs. Lennox. [Charlotte Lennox (1720–1804), New York–born English novelist.]

And charity, the petulance of wit;
How would your converse polish my rude lays,
With what new, noble images adorn?   520
Then should I scarce regret the banks of Thames,
All as we sat beneath that sand-box* shade;
Whence the delighted eye expatiates wide
O'er the fair landscape; where in loveliest forms,
Green cultivation hath array'd the land.   525

   See! there, what mills, like giants raise their arms,
To quell the speeding gale! what smoke ascends
From every boiling house! What structures rise,
Neat tho' not lofty, pervious to the breeze;
With galleries, porches, or piazzas grac'd!   530
Nor not delightful are those reed-built huts,
On yonder hill, that front the rising sun;
With plantanes, with banana's bosom'd-deep,
That flutter in the wind: where frolick goats,
Butt the young negroes, while their swarthy fires,   535
With ardent gladness wield the bill; and hark,
The crop is finish'd, how they rend the sky!—

   Nor, beauteous only shows the cultured soil,
From this cool station. No less charms the eye
That wild interminable waste of waves: 540
While on the horizon's farthest verge are seen
Islands of different shape, and different size;
While sail-clad ships, with their sweet produce fraught,
Swell on the straining sight; while near yon rock,
On which ten thousand wings with ceaseless clang   545
Their airies build, a water spout descends,
And shakes mid ocean; and while there below,
That town, embower'd in the different shade

*So called, from the *pericarpium*'s being often made use of for containing sand; when the
seeds, which are a violent emetic, are taken out. This is a fine shady tree, especially when young;
and its leaves are efficaciously applied in headachs to the temples, which they sweat. It grows
fast; but loses much of its beauty with age. Its wood is brittle, and when cut emits a milky juice,
which is not caustic. The sand-box thrives best in warm shady places. The sun often splits the
pericarpium, which then cracks like a pistol. It is round, flatted both above and below, and divided into a great number of regular compartments, each of which contains one seed flatted
ovularly. The botanical name is *Hura*.

Of tamarinds, panspans,* and papaws,† o'er which
A double Iris throws her painted arch,   550
Shows commerce toiling in each crowded street,
And each throng'd street with limpid currents lav'd.

    What tho' no bird of song, here charms the sense
With her wild minstrelsy; far, far beyond,
The unnatural quavers of Hesperian[101] throats!   555
Tho' the chaste poet of the vernal woods,
That shuns rude folly's din, delight not here
The listening eve; and tho' no herald-lark
Here leave his couch, high-towering to descry
The approach of dawn, and hail her with his song: 560
Yet not unmusical the tinkling lapse
Of yon cool argent rill, which Phoebus gilds
With his first orient rays; yet musical,
Those buxom airs that through the plantanes play,
And tear with wantonness their leafy scrolls;   565
Yet not unmusical the waves hoarse sound,
That dashes, sullen, on the distant shore;
Yet musical those little insects hum,
That hover round us, and to reason's ear,
Deep, moral truths convey; while every beam   570
Flings on them transient tints, which vary when
They wave their purple plumes; yet musical
The love-lorn cooing of the mountain-dove,
That woos to pleasing thoughtfulness the soul;
But chief the breeze, that murmurs through yon canes,   575
Enchants the ear with tunable delight.

---

*See the notes on Book II.

†This singular tree, whose fruits surround its summit immediately under the branches and leaves, like a necklace; grows quicker than almost any other in the West Indies. The wood is of no use, being spungy, hollow, and herbacious; however, the blossoms and fruit make excellent sweet-meats; but above all, the juice of the fruit being rubbed upon a spit, will *intenerate* [i.e., soften] new killed fowls, &c. a circumstance of great consequence in a climate, where the warmth soon renders whatever meats are attempted to be made tender by keeping, unfit for culinary purposes. Nor, will it only intenerate fresh meat; but, being boiled with salted beef, will render it easily digestible. Its milky juice is sometimes used to cure ringworms. It is said, that the guts of hogs would in time be lacerated, were they to feed on the ripe, unpeeled fruit. Its seed is said to be *anthelmintic.* The botanical name is *Papaya.*

While such fair scenes adorn these blissful isles;
Why will their sons, ungrateful, roam abroad?
Why spend their opulence in other climes?

Say, is pre-eminence your partial aim?—   580
Distinction courts you here; the senate calls.
Here, crouching slaves, attendant wait your nod:
While there, unnoted, but for folly's garb,
For folly's jargon; your dull hours ye pass,
Eclips'd by titles, and superior wealth.   585

Does martial ardour fire your generous veins?
Fly to your native isles: Bellona,[102] there,
Hath long time rear'd her bloody flag; these isles
Your strenuous arms demand; for ye are brave!
Nor longer to the lute and taber's sound   590
Weave antic[103] measures. O, could my weak song,
O could my song, like his, heaven-favoured bard,
Who led desponding Sparta's oft-beat hosts,
To victory, to glory; fire your souls
With English ardor! for now England's swains,   595
(The Man of Norfolk,* swains of England, thank;)
All emulous, to Freedom's standard fly,
And drive invasion from their native shore:
How would my soul exult with conscious pride;
Nor grudge those wreaths Tyrtaeus[104] gain'd of yore.   600

Or are ye fond of rich luxurious cates?[105] —
Can aught in Europe emulate the pine,
Or fruit forbidden, native of your isles?
Sons of Apicius,[106] say, can Europe's seas,
Can aught the edible creation yields,   605
Compare with turtle, boast of land and wave?
Can Europe's seas, in all their finny realms,
Aught so delicious as the Jew-fish† show?
Tell me what viands, land or streams produce,

*The Honourable General George Townshend. [1724–1807; later fourth viscount and first marquess Townshend; commander at the conquest of Quebec after Wolfe's death.]

†This, tho' a very large, is one of the most delicate fishes that swim; being preferable to caramaw, king-fish, or camaree; some even chuse it before turtle. The Jew-fish is often met with at Antigua, which enjoys the happiness of having on its coast few, if any, poisoned fishes.

The large, black, female, moulting crab excel?   610
A richer flavour not wild Cambria's hills,[107]
Nor Scotia's rocks with heath and thyme o'erspread,
Give to their flocks; than, lone Barbuda,* you,
Than you, Anguilla,† to your sheep impart.
Even Britain's vintage, here, improv'd, we quaff;   615
Even Lusitanian,[108] even Hesperian wines.[109]
Those from the Rhine's imperial banks (poor Rhine!
How have thy banks been died with brother-blood?
Unnatural warfare!) strength and flavour gain
In this delicious clime. Besides, the Cane   620
Wafted to every quarter of the globe,
Makes the vast produce of the world your own.

    Or rather, doth the love of nature charm;
Its mighty love your chief attention claim?
Leave Europe; there, through all her coyest ways,   625
Her secret mazes, nature is pursued:
But here, with savage loneliness, she reigns
On yonder peak, whence giddy fancy looks,
Affrighted, on the labouring main below.
Heavens! what stupendous, what unnumbered trees,   630
"Stage above stage, in various verdure drest,"[110]
Unprofitable shag its airy cliffs!
Heavens! what new shrubs, what herbs with useless bloom,
Adorn its channel'd sides; and, in its caves
What sulphurs, ores, what earths and stones abound!   635

---

*This is a low, and not large stock-island, belonging to the *Codrington family*. Part of this island, as also two plantations in Barbadoes, were left by Colonel Christopher Codrington, for building a college in Barbadoes, and converting Negroes to the Christian religion. ["Codring-ton": Christopher Codrington (1668–1710), born in Barbados to Christopher Codring-ton the elder, captain-general of the Leeward Islands; after seven years as a fellow of All Souls College, Oxford, he succeeded his father as governor of the Leeward Islands; on his death, he endowed both Codrington Library at All Souls and Codrington College in Barbados.]

†This island is about thirty miles long and ten broad. Though not mountainous, it is rocky, and abounds with strong passes; so that a few of its inhabitants, who are indeed expert in the use of fire-arms, repulsed, with great slaughter, a considerable detachment of French, who made a descent thereon in the *war preceding the last*. Cotton and cattle are its chief commodities. Many of the inhabitants are rich; the captain-general of the Leeward-Islands nominates the governor and council. They have no assembly. ["The war preceding the last": the War of the Austrian Succession, 1740–1748, which preceded the Seven Years War, 1756–1763.]

There let philosophy conduct thy steps,
"For naught is useless made:"[111] With candid search,
Examine all the properties of things;
Immense discoveries soon will crown your toil,
Your time will soon repay. Ah, when will cares,   640
The cares of Fortune, less my minutes claim?
Then, with what joy, what energy of soul,
Will I not clime yon mountain's airiest brow!
The dawn, the burning noon, the setting sun,
The midnight-hour, shall hear my constant vows   645
To Nature; see me prostrate at her shrine!
And, O, if haply I may aught invent
Of use to mortal man, life to prolong,
To soften, or adorn; what genuine joy,
What exultation of supreme delight,   650
Will swell my raptured bosom. Then, when death
Shall call me hence, I'll unrepining go;
Nor envy conquerors their storied tombs,
Tho' not a stone point out my humble grave.

The End of Book III.

BOOK IV.
ARGUMENT

Invocation to the Genius of Africa.[112] *Address. Negroes when bought should be young, and strong. The Congo-negroes*[113] *are fitter for the house and trades, than for the field. The Gold-Coast,*[114] *but especially the Papaw-negroes, make the best field-negroes: but even these, if advanced in years, should not be purchased. The marks of a sound negroe at a negroe sale. Where the men do nothing but hunt, fish or fight, and all field drudgery is left to the women; these are to be preferred to their husbands. The Minnahs*[115] *make good tradesmen, but addicted to suicide. The Mundingos,*[116] *in particular, subject to worms; and the Congas, to dropsical disorders. How salt-water, or new negroes should be seasoned. Some negroes eat dirt. Negroes should be habituated by gentle degrees to field labour. This labour, when compared to that in lead-mines, or of those who work in the gold and silver mines of South America, is not only less toilsome, but far more healthy. Negroes should always be treated with humanity. Praise of freedom. Of the dracunculus, or dragon-worm. Of chigres. Of the yaws. Might not this disease be imparted by inoculation? Of worms, and their multiform appearance. Praise of commerce. Of the imaginary disorders of negroes, especially those caused by their conjurers or Obia-men.*[117] *The composition and supposed virtues of a magic-phiol. Field-negroes should not begin to work before six in the morning, and should leave off between eleven and twelve; and beginning again at two, should finish before sun-set. Of the weekly al-*

lowance of negroes. The young, the old, the sickly, and even the lazy, must have their victuals prepared for them. Of negroe-ground, and its various productions. To be fenced in, and watched. Of an American garden. Of the situation of the negroe-huts. How best defended from fire. The great negroe-dance described. Drumming, and intoxicating spirits not to be allowed. Negroes should be made to marry in their masters plantation. Inconveniences arising from the contrary practice. Negroes to be cloathed once a year, and before Christmas. Praise of Lewis XIV.[118] for the Code Noir. A body of laws of this kind recommended to the English sugar colonies. Praise of the river Thames. A moon-light landscape and vision.

BOOK IV.

Genius of Africk! whether thou bestrid'st
The castled elephants or at the source,
(While howls the desart fearfully around,)
Of thine own Niger,[119] sadly thou reclin'st
Thy temples shaded by the tremulous palm,   5
Or quick papaw,[120] whose top is necklac'd round
With numerous rows of party-colour'd fruit:
Or hear'st thou rather from the rocky banks
Of Rio Grandê,[121] or black Sanaga?[122]
Where dauntless thou the headlong torrent brav'st   10
In search of gold, to brede thy wooly locks,
Or with bright ringlets ornament thine ears,
Thine arms, and ankles: O attend my song.
A muse that pities thy distressful state;
Who sees, with grief, thy sons in fetters bound;   15
Who wished freedom to the race of man;
Thy nod assenting craves: dread Genius, come!

    Yet vain thy presence, vain thy favouring nod;
Unless once more the muses; that erewhile
Upheld me fainting in my past career,   20
Through Caribbe's cane-isles; kind condescend
To guide my footsteps, through parch'd Libya's wilds;
And bind my sun-burnt brow with other bays,
Than ever deck'd the Sylvan bard before.

    Say, will my Melvil,[123] from the public care,   25
Withdraw one moment, to the muses shrine?
Who smit with thy fair fame, industrious cull
An Indian wreath to mingle with thy bays,

And deck the hero, and the scholar's brow!
Wilt thou, whose mildness smooths the face of war,   30
Who round the victor-blade the myrtle twin'st,
And mak'st subjection loyal and sincere;
O wilt thou gracious hear the unartful strain,
Whose mild instructions teach, no trivial theme,
What care the jetty African requires?   35
Yes, thou wilt deign to hear; a man thou art
Who deem'st nought foreign that belongs to man.

    In mind, and aptitude for useful toil,
The negroes differ: muse that difference sing.

    Whether to wield the hoe, or guide the plane;[124]   40
Or for domestic uses thou intend'st
The sunny Libyan: from what clime they spring,
It not imports; if strength and youth be theirs.

    Yet those from Congo's wide-extended plains,
Through which the long Zaire winds with chrystal stream,   45
Where lavish Nature sends indulgent forth
Fruits of high favour, and spontaneous seeds
Of bland nutritious quality, ill bear
The toilsome field; but boast a docile mind,
And happiness of features. These, with care,   50
Be taught each nice mechanic art: or train'd
To houshold offices: their ductile souls
Will all thy care, and all thy gold repay.

    But, if the labours of the field demand
Thy chief attention; and the ambrosial cane   55
Thou long'st to see, with spiry frequence, shade
Many an acre: planter, chuse the slave,
Who sails from barren climes; where want alone,
Offspring of rude necessity, compells
The sturdy native, or to plant the soil,   60
Or stem vast rivers, for his daily food.

    Such are the children of the Golden Coast;
Such the Papaws, of negroes far the best:
And such the numerous tribes, that skirt the shore,
From rapid Volta to the distant Rey.[125]   65

But, planter, from what coast soe'er they sail,
Buy not the old: they ever sullen prove;
With heart-felt anguish, they lament their home;
They will not, cannot work; they never learn
Thy native language; they are prone to ails;   70
And oft by suicide their being end.—

Must thou from Africk reinforce thy gang?—
Let health and youth their every sinew firm;
Clear roll their ample eye; their tongue be red;
Broad swell their chest; their shoulders wide expand;   75
Not prominent their belly; clean and strong
Their thighs and legs, in just proportion rise.
Such soon will brave the fervours of the clime;
And free from ails, that kill thy negroe-train,
A useful servitude will long support.   80

Yet, if thine own, thy childrens life, be dear;
Buy not a Cormantee,[126] tho' healthy, young.
Of breed too generous for the servile field;
They, born to freedom in their native land,
Chuse death before dishonourable bonds: 85
Or, fir'd with vengeance, at the midnight hour,
Sudden they seize thine unsuspecting watch,
And thine own poinard[127] bury in thy breast.

At home, the men, in many a sylvan realm,
Their rank tobacco, charm of sauntering minds,   90
From clayey tubes inhale; or, vacant, beat
For prey the forest; or, in war's dread ranks,
Their country's foes affront: while, in the field,
Their wives plant rice, or yams, or lofty maize,
Fell hunger to repel. Be these thy choice: 95
They, hardy, with the labours of the Cane
Soon grow familiar; while unusual toil,
And new severities their husbands kill.

The slaves from Minnah are of stubborn breed:
But, when the bill, or hammer, they affect;   100
They soon perfection reach. But fly, with care,
The Moco-nation;[128] they themselves destroy.

Worms lurk in all: yet, pronest they to worms,
Who from Mundingo sail. When therefore such
Thou buy'st, for sturdy and laborious they,   105
Straight let some learned leach[129] strong medicines give,
Till food and climate both familiar grow.
Thus, tho' from rise to set, in Phoebus' eye,[130]
They toil, unceasing; yet, at night, they'll sleep,
Lap'd in Elysium;[131] and, each day, at dawn,   110
Spring from their couch, as blythsome as the sun.

One precept more, it much imports to know.—
The Blacks, who drink the Quanza's[132] lucid stream,
Fed by ten thousand springs, are prone to bloat,
Whether at home or in these ocean-isles;   115
And tho' nice art the water may subdue,
Yet many die; and few, for many a year,
Just strength attain to labour for their lord.

Would'st thou secure thine Ethiop[133] from those ails,
Which change of climate, change of waters breed,   120
And food unusual? let Machaon draw
From each some blood, as age and sex require;
And well with vervain,[134] well with sempre-vive,[135]
Unload their bowels.—These, in every hedge,
Spontaneous grow.—Nor will it not conduce   125
To give what chemists, in mysterious phrase,
Term the white eagle; deadly foe to worms.
But chief do thou, my friend, with hearty food,
Yet easy of digestion, likest that
Which they at home regal'd on; renovate   130
Their sea-worn appetites. Let gentle work,
Or rather playful exercise, amuse
The novel gang: and far be angry words;
Far ponderous chains; and far disheartening blows.—
From fruits restrain their eagerness; yet if   135
The acajou, haply, in thy garden bloom,
With cherries,* or of white or purple hue,

---

*The tree which produces this wholesome fruit is tall, shady, and of quick growth. Its Indian name is *Acajou;* hence corruptly called *Cashew* by the English. The fruit has no resem-

Thrice wholesome fruit in this relaxing clime!
Safely thou may'st their appetite indulge.
Their arid skins will plump, their features shine: 140
No rheums, no dysenteric ails torment:
The thirsty hydrops[136] flies.—'Tis even averr'd,
(Ah, did experience sanctify the fact;
How many Lybians[137] now would dig the soil,
Who pine in hourly agonies away!)   145
This pleasing fruit, if turtle join its aid,
Removes that worst of ails, disgrace of art,
The loathsome leprosy's infectious bane.

There are, the muse hath oft abhorrent seen,
Who swallow dirt; (so the chlorotic fair   150
Oft chalk prefer to the most poignant cates:)[138]
Such, dropsy bloats, and to sure death consigns;
Unless restrain'd from this unwholesome food,
By soothing words, by menaces, by blows:
Nor yet will threats, or blows, or soothing words,   155
Perfect their cure; unless thou, Paean,[139] design'st
By medicine's power their cravings to subdue.

To easy labour first inure thy slaves;
Extremes are dangerous. With industrious search,
Let them fit grassy provender[140] collect   160
For thy keen stomach'd herds.—But when the earth
Hath made her annual progress round the sun,
What time the conch* or bell resounds, they may
All to the Cane-ground, with thy gang, repair.

---

blance to a cherry, either in shape or size; and bears, at its lower extremity, a nut (which the Spaniards name *Anacardo*, and physicians *Anacardium*) that resembles a large kidney-bean. Its kernal is as grateful as an almond, and more easy of digestion. Between its rinds is contained a highly caustic oil; which, being held to a candle, emits bright salient sparkles, in which the American fortune-tellers pretended they saw spirits who gave answers to whatever questions were put to them by their ignorant followers. This oil is used as a cosmetic by the ladies, to remove freckles and sun-burning; but the pain they necessarily suffer makes its use not very frequent. This tree also produces a gum not inferior to Gum-Arabic; and its bark is an approved astringent. The juice of the cherry stains exceedingly. The long citron, or amber-coloured, is the best. The cashew-nuts, when unripe, are of a green colour; but, ripe, they assume that of a pale olive. This tree bears fruit but once a year.

*Plantations that have no bells, assemble their Negroes by sounding a conch-shell.

    Nor, Negroe, at thy destiny repine,   165
Tho' doom'd to toil from dawn to setting sun.
How far more pleasant is thy rural task,
Than theirs who sweat, sequester'd from the day,
In dark tartarean caves, sunk far beneath
The earth's dark surface, where sulphureous flames,   170
Oft from their vapoury prisons bursting wild,
To dire explosion give the cavern'd deep,
And in dread ruin all its inmates whelm?—
Nor fateful only is the bursting flame;
The exhalations of the deep-dug mine,   175
Tho' slow, shake from their wings as sure a death.
With what intense severity of pain
Hath the afflicted muse, in Scotia, seen
The miners rack'd, who toil for fatal lead?
What cramps, what palsies shake their feeble limbs,   180
Who, on the margin of the rocky Drave,*
Trace silver's fluent ore? Yet white men these!

    How far more happy ye, than those poor slaves,
Who, whilom,[141] under native, gracious chiefs,
Incas and emperors, long time enjoy'd   185
Mild government, with every sweet of life,
In blissful climates? See them dragg'd in chains,
By proud insulting tyrants, to the mines
Which once they call'd their own, and then despis'd!
See, in the mineral bosom of their land,   190
How hard they toil! how soon their youthful limbs
Feel the decrepitude of age! how soon
Their teeth desert their sockets! and how soon
Shaking paralysis unstrings their frame!
Yet scarce, even then, are they allow'd to view   195
The glorious God of day, of whom they beg,
With earnest hourly supplications, death;
Yet death slow comes, to torture them the more!

    With these compar'd, ye sons of Afric, say,
How far more happy is your lot? Bland health,   200
Of ardent eye, and limb robust, attends

*A river in Hungary, on whose banks are found mines of quicksilver [mercury].

Your custom'd labour; and, should sickness seize,
With what solicitude are ye not nurs'd!—
Ye Negroes, then, your pleasing task pursue;
And, by your toil, deserve your master's care.   205

      When first your Blacks are novel to the hoe;
Study their humours: Some, soft-soothing words;
Some, presents; and some, menaces subdue;
And some I've known, so stubborn is their kind,
Whom blows, alas! could win alone to toil.   210

      Yet, planter, let humanity prevail.—
Perhaps thy Negroe, in his native land,
Possest large fertile plains, and slaves, and herds:
Perhaps, whene'er he deign'd to walk abroad,
The richest silks, from where the Indus rolls,   215
His limbs invested in their gorgeous pleats:
Perhaps he wails his wife, his children, left
To struggle with adversity: Perhaps
Fortune, in battle for his country fought,
Gave him a captive to his deadliest foe: 220
Perhaps, incautious, in his native fields,
(On pleasurable scenes his mind intent)
All as he wandered; from the neighbouring grove,
Fell ambush dragg'd him to the hated main.—
Were they even sold for crimes; ye polish'd, say!   225
Ye, to whom Learning opes her amplest page!
Ye, whom the knowledge of a living God
Should lead to virtue! Are ye free from crimes?
Ah pity, then, these uninstructed swains;
And still let mercy soften the decrees   230
Of rigid justice, with her lenient hand.
Oh, did the tender muse possess the power;
Which monarchs have, and monarchs oft abuse:
'Twould be the fond ambition of her soul,
To quell tyrannic sway; knock off the chains   235
Of heart-debasing slavery; give to man,
Of every colour and of every clime,
Freedom, which stamps him image of his God.
Then laws, Oppression's scourge, fair Virtue's prop,

Offspring of Wisdom! should impartial reign,   240
To knit the whole in well-accorded strife:
Servants, not slaves; of choice, and not compell'd;
The Blacks should cultivate the Cane-land isles.

  Say, shall the muse the various ills recount,
Which Negroe-nations feel? Shall she describe   245
The worm that subtly winds into their flesh,
All as they bathe them in their native streams?
There, with fell increment, it soon attains
A direful length of harm. Yet, if due skill,
And proper circumspection are employed,   250
It may be won its volumes to wind round
A leaden cylinder: But, O, beware,
No rashness practise; else 'twill surely snap,
And suddenly, retreating, dire produce
An annual lameness to the tortured Moor.   255

  Nor only is the dragon worm to dread:
Fell, winged insects,* which the visual ray
Scarcely discerns, their sable feet and hands
Oft penetrate; and, in the fleshy nest,
Myriads of young produce; which soon destroy   260
The parts they breed in; if assiduous care,
With art, extract not the prolific foe.

  Or, shall she sing, and not debase her lay,
The pest peculiar to the Aethiop-kind,
The yaw's[142] infectious bane?—The infected far   265
In huts, to leeward, lodge; or near the main.
With heartening food, with turtle, and with conchs;

---

*These, by the English, are called *Chigoes* or *Chigres*. They chiefly perforate the toes, and sometimes the fingers; occasioning an itching, which some people think not unpleasing, and are at pains to get, by going to the copper-holes, or mill-round, where chigres most abound. They lay their nits in a bag, about the size of a small pea, and are partly contained therein themselves. This the Negroes extract without bursting, by means of a needle, and filling up the place with a little snuff; it soon heals, if the person has a good constitution. One species of them is supposed to be poisonous; but, I believe, unjustly. When they bury themselves near a tendon, especially if the person is in a bad habit of body, they occasion troublesome sores. The South-Americans call them *Miguas*.

The flowers of sulphur, and hard niccars* burnt,
The lurking evil from the blood expel,
And throw it on the surface: There in spots   270
Which cause no pain, and scanty ichor[143] yield,
It chiefly breaks about the arms and hips,
A virulent contagion!—When no more
Round knobby spots deform, but the disease
Seems at a pause: then let the learned leach   275
Give, in due dose, live-silver[144] from the mine;
Till copious spitting the whole taint exhaust.—
Nor thou repine, tho' half-way round the sun,
This globe, her annual progress shall absolve;
Ere, clear'd, thy slave from all infection shine.   280
Nor then be confident; successive crops
Of defoedations[145] oft will spot the skin:
These thou, with turpentine and guaiac pods,
Reduc'd by coction to a wholesome draught,
Total remove, and give the blood its balm.   285

　　　Say, as this malady but once infests
The sons of Guinea, might not skill ingraft
(Thus, the small-pox are happily convey'd;)
This ailment early to thy Negroe-train?

　　　Yet, of the ills which torture Libya's sons,   290
Worms tyrannize the worst. They, Proteus-like,[146]
Each symptom of each malady assume;
And, under every mask, the assassins kill.
Now, in the guise of horrid spasms, they writhe
The tortured body, and all sense o'er-power.   295
Sometimes, like Mania,[147] with her head downcast,
They cause the wretch in solitude to pine;
Or frantic, bursting from the strongest chains,
To frown with look terrific, not his own.
Sometimes like Ague,[148] with a shivering mien,   300
The teeth gnash fearful, and the blood runs chill:
Anon the ferment maddens in the veins,

---

*The botanical name of this medicinal shrub is Guilandina. The fruit resembles marbles,
though not so round. Their shell is hard and smooth, and contains a farinaceous nut, of admirable use in seminal weaknesses. They are also given to throw out the yaws.

And a false vigour animates the frame.
Again, the dropsy's bloated mask they steal;
Or, "melt with minings of the hectic fire."[149]   305

    Say, to such various mimic forms of death;
What remedies shall puzzled art oppose?—
Thanks to the Almighty, in each path-way hedge,
Rank cow-itch* grows, whose sharp unnumber'd stings,
Sheath'd in Melasses, from their dens expell,   310
Fell dens of death, the reptile lurking foe.—
A powerful vermifuge, in skilful hands,
The worm-grass proves; yet, even in hands of skill,
Sudden, I've known it dim the visual ray
For a whole day and night. There are who use   315
(And sage Experience justifies the use)
The mineral product of the Cornish mine;†
Which in old times, ere Britain laws enjoyed,
The polish'd Tyrians,[150] monarchs of the main,
In their swift ships convey'd to foreign realms: 320
The sun by day, by night the northern star,
Their course conducted.—Mighty commerce, hail!
By thee the sons of Attic's sterile land,
A scanty number, laws impos'd on Greece:
Nor aw'd they Greece alone; vast Asia's King,   325
Tho' girt by rich arm'd myriads, at their frown
Felt his heart whither on his farthest throne.

---

*This extraordinary vine should not be permitted to grow in a Cane-piece; for Negroes have been known to fire the Canes, to save themselves from the torture which attends working in grounds where it has abounded. Mixed with melasses [i.e., molasses], it is a safe and excellent vermifuge [anti-worm medicine]. Its seeds, which resemble blackish small beans, are purgative. Its flower is purple; and its pods, on which the stinging brown *Setae* are found, are as large as a full-grown English field-pea.

†Tin-filings are a better vermifuge than tin in powder. The western parts of Britain, and the neighbouring isles, have been famous for this useful metal from the remotest antiquity; for we find from Strabo, that the Phaenicians [i.e., Phoenicians] made frequent voyages to those parts (which they called *Cassiterides* [ancient name for the Scilly Isles off Cornwall, England] from stannum) in quest of that commodity, which turned out so beneficial to them, that a pilot of that nation stranded his vessel, rather than show a Roman ship, that watched him, the way to those mines. For this public spirited action he was amply rewarded, says that accurate writer, upon his return to his country. The Romans, however, soon made themselves masters of the secret, and shared with them in the profit of that merchandize.

Perennial source of population thou!
While scanty peasants plough the flowery plains
Of purple Enna; from the Belgian fens,   330
What swarms of useful citizens spring up,
Hatch'd by thy fostering wing. Ah where is flown
That dauntless free-born spirit, which of old,
Taught them to shake off the tyrannic yoke
Of Spains insulting King;[151] on whose wide realms,   335
The sun still shone with undiminished beam?
Parent of wealth! in vain, coy nature hoards
Her gold and diamonds; toil, thy firm compeer,
And industry of unremitting nerve,
Scale the cleft mountain, the loud torrent brave,   340
Plunge to the center, and thro' Nature's wiles,
(Led on by skill of penetrative soul)
Her following close, her secret treasures find,
To pour them plenteous on the laughing world.
On thee Sylvanus,[152] thee each rural god,   345
On thee chief Ceres,[153] with unfailing love
And fond distinction, emulously gaze.
In vain hath nature pour'd vast seas between
Far-distant kingdoms; endless storms in vain
With double night brood o'er them; thou dost throw,   350
O'er far-divided nature's realms, a chain
To bind in sweet society mankind.
By thee white Albion,[154] once a barbarous clime,
Grew fam'd for arms, for wisdom, and for laws;
By thee she holds the balance of the world,   355
Acknowledg'd now sole empress of the main.[155]
Coy though thou art, and mutable of love,
There may'st thou ever fix thy wandering steps;
While Eurus[156] rules the wide atlantic foam!
By thee, thy favorite, great Columbus found   360
That world, where now thy praises I rehearse
To the resounding main and palmy shore;
And Lusitania's chiefs those realms explor'd,
Whence negroes spring, the subject of my song.

Nor pine the Blacks, alone, with real ills,   365
That baffle oft the wisest rules of art:

They likewise feel imaginary woes;
Woes no less deadly. Luckless he who owns
The slave, who thinks himself bewitch'd; and whom,
In wrath, a conjuror's snake-mark'd* staff hath struck!   370
They mope, love silence, every friend avoid;
They inly pine; all aliment reject;
Or insufficient for nutrition take:
Their features droop; a sickly yellowish hue
Their skin deforms; their strength and beauty fly.   375
Then comes the feverish fiend, with firy eyes,
Whom drowth, convulsions, and whom death surround,
Fatal attendants! if some subtle slave
(Such, Obia-men are stil'd) do not engage,
To save the wretch by antidote or spell.   380

     In magic spells, in Obia, all the sons
Of sable Africk trust:—Ye, sacred nine!
(For ye each hidden preparation know)
Transpierce the gloom, which ignorance and fraud
Have render'd awful; tell the laughing world   385
Of what these wonder-working charms are made.

     Fern root cut small, and tied with many a knot;
Old teeth extracted from a white man's skull;
A lizard's skeleton; a serpent's head:
These mix'd with salt, and water from the spring,   390
Are in a phial pour'd; o'er these the leach
Mutters strange jargon, and wild circles forms.

     Of this possest, each negroe deems himself
Secure from poison; for to poison they
Are infamously prone: and arm'd with this,   395
Their sable country daemons they defy,
Who fearful haunt them at the midnight hour,

---

*The negroe-conjurors, or Obia-men, as they are called, carry about them a staff, which is marked with frogs, snakes, &c. The blacks imagine that its blow, if not mortal, will at least occasion long and troublesome disorders. A belief in magic is inseparable from human nature, but those nations are most addicted thereto, among whom learning, and of course, philosophy have least obtained. As in all other countries, so in Guinea, the conjurors, as they have more understanding, so are they almost always more wicked than the common herd of their deluded countrymen; and as the negroe-magicians can do mischief, so they can also do good on a plantation, provided they are kept by the white people in proper subordination.

To work them mischief. This, diseases fly;
Diseases follow: such its wonderous power!
This o'er the threshold of their cottage hung,   400
No thieves break in; or, if they dare to steal,
Their feet in blotches, which admit no cure,
Burst loathsome out: but should its owner filch,
As slaves were ever of the pilfering kind,
This from detection screens;—so conjurors swear.   405

    'Till morning dawn, and Lucifer withdraw
His beamy chariot; let not the loud bell
Call forth thy negroes from their rushy couch:
And ere the sun with mid-day fervour glow,
When every broom-bush* opes her yellow flower;   410
Let thy black labourers from their toil desist:
Nor till the broom her every petal lock,
Let the loud bell recall them to the hoe.
But when the jalap her bright tint displays,
When the solanum† fills her cup with dew,   415
And crickets, snakes, and lizards 'gin their coil;
Let them find shelter in their cane-thatch'd huts:
Or, if constrain'd unusual hours to toil,
(For even the best must sometimes urge their gang)
With double nutriment reward their pains.   420

    Howe'er insensate some may deem their slaves,
Nor 'bove the bestial rank; far other thoughts
The muse, soft daughter of humanity!
Will ever entertain.—The Ethiop knows,
The Ethiop feels, when treated like a man;   425
Nor grudges, should necessity compell,
By day, by night, to labour for his lord.

---

*This small plant, which grows in every pasture, may, with propriety, be termed an American clock; for it begins every forenoon at eleven to open its yellow flowers, which about one are fully expanded, and at two closed. The jalap, or marvel of Peru, unfolds its petals between five and six in the evening, which shut again as soon as night comes on, to open again in the cool of the morning. This plant is called four o'clock by the natives, and bears either a yellow or purple-coloured flower.

†So some authors name the fire-weed, which grows every where, and is the *datura* of Linnaeus; whose virtues Dr. Stork, at Vienna, has greatly extolled in a late publication. It bears a white monopetalous flower, which opens always about sun-set.

Not less inhuman, than unthrifty those;
Who, half the year's rotation round the sun,
Deny subsistence to their labouring slaves.   430
But would'st thou see thy negroe-train encrease,
Free from disorders; and thine acres clad
With groves of sugar: every week dispense
Or English beans, or Carolinian rice;
Iërne's[157] beef, or Pensilvanian flour;   435
Newfoundland cod, or herrings from the main
That howls tempestuous round the Scotian isles!

    Yet some there are so lazily inclin'd,
And so neglectful of their food, that thou,
Would'st thou preserve them from the jaws of death;   440
Daily, their wholesome viands must prepare:
With these let all the young, and childless old,
And all the morbid share;—so heaven will bless,
With manifold encrease, thy costly care.

    Suffice not this; to every slave assign   445
Some mountain-ground: or, if waste broken land
To thee belong, that broken land divide.
This let them cultivate, one day, each week;
And there raise yams, and there cassada's root:*
From a good daemon's staff cassada sprang,   450
Tradition says, and Caribbees[158] believe;
Which into three the white-rob'd genius broke,
And bade them plant, their hunger to repel.
There let angola's bloomy bush supply,†
For many a year, with wholesome pulse their board.   455

---

*To an antient Caribbean, bemoaning the savage uncomfortable life of his countrymen, a diety clad in white apparel appeared, and told him, he would have come sooner to have taught him the ways of civil life, had he been addressed before. He then showed him sharp-cutting stones to fell trees and build houses; and bade him cover them with the palm leaves. Then he broke his staff in three; which, being planted, soon after produced cassada. See Ogilvy's America. [John Ogilby, *America: being the Latest and Most Accurate Description of the New World* (London: Tho. Johnson, 1670).]

†This is called *Pidgeon-pea*, and grows on a sturdy shrub, that will last for years. It is justly reckoned among the most wholesome legumens. The juice of the leaves, dropt into the eye, will remove incipient films. The botanic name is *Cytisus*.

There let the bonavist,* his fringed pods
Throw liberal o'er the prop; while ochra† bears
Aloft his slimy pulp, and help disdains.
There let potatos‡ mantle o'er the ground;
Sweet as the cane-juice is the root they bear.   460
There too let eddas§ spring in order meet,
With Indian cale,‖ and foodful calaloo:#
While mint, thyme, balm, and Europe's coyer herbs,
Shoot gladsome forth, not reprobate the clime.

    This tract secure, with hedges or of limes,   465
Or bushy citrons, or the shapely tree**
That glows at once with aromatic blooms,
And golden fruit mature. To these be join'd,
In comely neighbourhood, the cotton shrub;

*This is the Spanish name of a plant, which produces an excellent bean. It is a parasitical plant. There are five sorts of bonavist, the green, the white, the moon-shine, the small or common; and, lastly, the black and red. The flowers of all are white and papilionaceous; except the last, whose blossoms are purple. They commonly bear in six weeks. Their pulse is wholesome, though somewhat flatulent; especially those from the black and red. The pods are flattish, two or three inches long; and contain from three to five seeds in partitional cells.

†Or *Ockro.* This shrub, which will last for years, produces a not less agreeable, than wholesome pod. It bears all the year round. Being of a slimy and balsamic nature, it becomes a truly medicinal aliment in dysenteric complaints. It is of the *Malva* species. It rises to about four or five feet high, bearing, on and near the summit, many yellow flowers; succeeded by green, conic, fleshy pods, channelled into several grooves. There are as many cells filled with small round seeds, as there are channels.

‡I cannot positively say, whether these vines are of Indian original or not; but as in their fructification, they differ from potatos at home, they probably are not European. They are sweet. There are four kinds, the red, the white, the long, and round. The juice of each may be made into a pleasant cool drink; and, being distilled, yield an excellent spirit.

§See notes on Book I; This wholesome root, in some of the islands, is called *Edda*: Its botanical name is *Arum maximum Aegytiacum.* There are three species of tanies, the blue, the scratching, and that which is commonly roasted. The blossoms of all three are very fragrant, in a morning or evening. The young leaves, as well as the spiral stalks which support the flower, are eaten by the Negroes as a salad. The root makes a good broth in dysenteric complaints. They are seldom so large as the yam, but most people think them preferable in point of taste. The French call this plant *Tayove.* It produces eatable roots every four months, for one year only.

‖This green, which is a native of the New World, equals any of the greens in the Old.

#Another species of Indian pot herb, no less wholesome that the preceding. These, with mezamby, and the Jamaica pickle-weed, yield to no esculent plants in Europe. This is an Indian name.

**The orange tree.

In this delicious clime the cotton bursts   470
On rocky soils.—The coffee also plant;
White as the skin of Albion's lovely fair,
Are the thick snowy fragrant blooms it boasts:
Nor wilt thou, cocô, thy rich pods refuse;
Tho' years, and heat, and moisture they require,   475
Ere the stone grind them to the food of health.
Of thee, perhaps, and of thy various sorts,
And that kind sheltering tree, thy mother nam'd,[159]
With crimson flowerets prodigally grac'd;
In future times, the enraptur'd muse may sing: 480
If public favour crown her present lay.

    But let some antient, faithful slave erect
His sheltered mansion near; and with his dog,
His loaded gun, and cutlass, guard the whole:
Else negroe-fugitives, who skulk 'mid rocks   485
And shrubby wilds, in bands will soon destroy
Thy labourer's honest wealth; their loss and yours.

    Perhaps, of Indian gardens I could sing,
Beyond what bloom'd on blest Phaeacia's isle,[160]
Or eastern climes admir'd in days of yore: 490
How Europe's foodful, culinary plants;
How gay Pomona's ruby-tinctured births;
And gawdy Flora's various-vested train;
Might be instructed to unlearn their clime,
And by due discipline adopt the sun.   495
The muse might tell what culture will entice
The ripened melon, to perfume each month;
And with the anana[161] load the fragrant board.
The muse might tell, what trees will best exclude
("Insuperable height of airiest shade")[162]   500
With their vast umbrage the noon's fervent ray.
Thee, verdant mammey,* first, her song should praise:

*This is a lofty, shady, and beautiful tree. Its fruit is as large as the largest melon, and of an exquisite smell, greatly superior to it in point of taste. Within the fruit are contained one or two large stones, which when distilled, give to spirits a ratafia-flavour [ratafia is a sweet liqueur], and therefore the French call them *Les apricots de St. Domingue:* accordingly, the *l'eau des noiaux*, one of the best West-Indian cordials, is made from them. The fruit, eaten raw, is of an aperient qual-

Thee, the first natives of these Ocean-isles,
Fell anthropophagi,[163] still sacred held;
And from thy large high-flavour'd fruit abstain'd,   505
With pious awe; for thine high-flavour'd fruit,
The airy phantoms of their friends deceas'd
Joy'd to regale on.—Such their simple creed.
The tamarind* likewise should adorn her theme,
With whose tart fruit the sweltering fever loves   510
To quench his thirst, whose breezy umbrage soon
Shades the pleas'd planter, shades his children long.
Nor, lofty cassia,† should she not recount
Thy woodland honours! See, what yellow flowers
Dance in the gale, and scent the ambient air;   515
While thy long pods, full-fraught with nectared sweets,
Relieve the bowels from their lagging load.
Nor chirimoia,[164] though these torrid isles
Boast not thy fruit, to which the anana yields
In taste and flavour, wilt thou coy refuse   520
Thy fragrant shade to beautify the scene.
But, chief of palms, and pride of Indian-groves,
Thee, fair palmeto,‡ should her song resound:

---

ity; and made into sweet-meats, &c. is truly exquisite. This tree, contrary to most others in the
New World, shoots up to a pyramidal figure: the leaves are uncommonly green; and it produces
fruit, but once a year. The name is Indian. The English commonly call it *Mammey-sapota.* There
are two species of it, the sweet, and the tart. The botanical name is *Achras.*

*See Book I. This large, shady, and beautiful tree grows fast even in the driest soils, and
lasts long; and yet its wood is hard, and very fit for mechanical uses. The leaves are smaller than
those of senna, and pennated: they taste sourish, as does the pulp, which is contained in pods
four or five inches long. They bear once a year. An excellent vinegar may be made from the fruit;
but the Creoles chiefly preserve it with sugar, as the Spaniards with salt. A pleasant syrup may
be made from it. The name is, in Arabic, *Tamara.* The Antients were not acquainted therewith;
for the Arabians first introduced tamarinds into physic; it is a native of the East as well as of the
West-Indies and South-America, where different provinces call it by different names. Its
cathartic qualities are well known. It is good in sea-sickness. The botanical name is *Tamarindus.*

†Both this tree and its mild purgative pulp are sufficiently known.

‡This being the most beautiful of palms, nay, perhaps, superior to any other known tree in
the world, has with propriety obtained the name of *Royal.* The botanical name is *Palma Maxima.* It will shoot up perpendicularly to an hundred feet or more. The stem is perfectly circular;
only towards the root, and immediately under the branches at top, it bulges out. The bark is
smooth, and of an ash-brown colour, except at the top where it is green. It grows very fast, and
the seed from whence it springs is not bigger than an acorn. In this, as in all the palm-genus,

What swelling columns, form'd by Jones or Wren,[165]
Or great Palladio,[166] may with thee compare?   525
Not nice-proportion'd, but of size immense,
Swells the wild fig-tree, and should claim her lay:
For, from its numerous bearded twigs proceed
A filial train, stupendous as their fire,
In quick succession; and, o'er many a rood,   530
Extend their uncouth limbs; which not the bolt
Of heaven can scathe; nor yet the all-wasting rage
Of Typhon, or of hurricane, destroy.
Nor should, tho' small, the anata* not be sung:
Thy purple dye, the silk and cotton fleece   535
Delighted drink; thy purple dye the tribes
Of Northern-Ind,[167] a fierce and wily race,
Carouse, assembled; and with it they paint
Their manly make in many a horrid form,
To add new terrors to the face of war.   540
The muse might teach to twine the verdant arch,
And the cool alcove's lofty room adorn,
With ponderous granadillas,† and the fruit

---

what the natives call Cabbage is found; but it resembles in taste an almond, and is in fact the pith of the upper, or greenish part of the stem. But it would be the most unpardonable luxury to cut down so lovely a tree, for so mean a gratification; especially as the wild, or mountain cabbage tree, sufficiently supplies the table with that esculent. I never ride past the charming vista of royal palms on the Cayon-estate of Daniel Mathew, Esq; in St. Christopher, without being put in mind of the pillars of the Temple of the Sun at Palmyra. This tree grows on the tops of hills, as well as in valleys; its hard cortical part makes very durable laths for houses. There is a smaller species not quite so beautiful.

*Or *Anotto*, or *Arnotta;* thence corruptly called Indian Otter, by the English. The tree is about the size of an ordinary apple-tree. The French call it *Rocou;* and send the farina home as a paint, &c. for which purpose the tree is cultivated by them in their islands. The flower is pen-tapetalous, of a bluish and spoon-like appearance. The yellow filaments are tipped with purplish apices. The style proves the rudiment of the succeeding pod, which is of a conic shape, an inch and a half long. This is divided into many cells, which contain a great number of small seeds, covered with a red farina. [Now known as *annatto.*]

†This is the Spanish name, and is a species of the *passiflora,* or passion-flower, called by Linnaeus *Musa.* The seeds and pulp, through which the seeds are dispersed, are cooling, and grateful to the palate. This, as well as the water-lemon, bell-apple, or honeysuckle, as it is named, being parasitical plants, are easily formed into cooling arbors, than which nothing can be more grateful in warm climates. Both fruits are wholesome. The granadilla is commonly eat with sugar, on account of its tartness, and yet the pulp is viscid. Plumier calls it *Granadilla, late-folia, fructu maliformi.* It grows best in shady places. The unripe fruit makes an excellent pickle.

Call'd water-lemon; grateful to the taste:
Nor should she not pursue the mountain-streams,   545
But pleas'd decoy them from their shady haunts,
In rills, to visit every tree and herb;
Or fall o'er fern-clad cliffs, with foaming rage;
Or in huge basons float, a fair expanse;
Or, bound in chains of artificial force,   550
Arise thro' sculptured stone, or breathing brass.—
But I'm in haste to furl my wind-worn sails,
And anchor my tir'd vessel on the shore.

    It much imports to build thy Negroe-huts,
Or on the sounding margin of the main,   555
Or on some dry hill's gently-sloping sides,
In streets, at distance due.—When near the beach,
Let frequent coco cast its wavy shade;
'Tis Neptune's tree; and, nourish'd by the spray,
Soon round the bending stem's aerial height,   560
Clusters of mighty nuts, with milk and fruit
Delicious fraught, hang clattering in the sky.
There let the bay-grape,* too, its crooked limbs
Project enormous; of impurpled hue
Its frequent clusters grow. And there, if thou   565
Woud'st make the sand yield salutary food,
Let Indian millet† rear its corny reed,
Like arm'd battalions in array of war.
But, round the upland huts, bananas plant;
A wholesome nutriment bananas yield,   570

---

*Or sea side grape, as it is more commonly called. This is a large, crooked, and shady tree, (the leaves being broad, thick, and almost circular;) and succeeds best in sandy places. It bears large clusters of grapes once a year; which, when ripe, are not disagreeable. The stones, seeds, or *acini,* contained in them, are large in proportion; and, being reduced to a powder, are an excellent astringent. The bark of the tree has the same property. The grapes, steept in water and fermented with sugar, make an agreeable wine.

†Or maise. This is commonly called Guinea-corn, to distinguish it from the great or Indian-corn, that grows in the southern parts of North-America. It soon shoots up to a great height, often twenty feet high, and will ratoon like the other; but its blades are not so nourishing to horses as those of the great corn, although its seeds are more so, and rather more agreeable to the taste. The Indians, Negroes, and poor white people, make many (not unsavoury) dishes with them. It is also called *Turkey wheat.* The turpentine tree will also grow in the sand, and is most useful upon a plantation.

And sun-burnt labour loves its breezy shade.
Their graceful screen let kindred plantanes join,
And with their broad vans shiver in the breeze;
So flames design'd, or by imprudence caught,
Shall spread no ruin to the neighbouring roof.   575

　　　Yet nor the sounding margin of the main,
Nor gently sloping side of breezy hill,
Nor streets, at distance due, imbower'd in trees;
Will half the health, or half the pleasure yield,
Unless some pitying naiad deign to lave,   580
With an unceasing stream, thy thirsty bounds.

　　　On festal days; or when their work is done;
Permit thy slaves to lead the choral dance,
To the wild banshaw's* melancholy sound.
Responsive to the sound, head feet and frame   585
Move aukwardly harmonious; hand in hand
Now lock'd, the gay troop circularly wheels,
And frisks and capers with intemperate joy.
Halts the vast circle, all clap hands and sing;
While those distinguish'd for their heels and air,   590
Bound in the center, and fantastic twine.
Meanwhile some stripling, from the choral ring,
Trips forth; and, not ungallantly, bestows
On her who nimblest hath the greensward beat,
And whose flush'd beauties have inthrall'd his soul,   595
A silver token of his fond applause.
Anon they form in ranks; nor inexpert
A thousand tuneful intricacies weave,
Shaking their sable limbs; and oft a kiss
Steal from their partners; who, with neck reclin'd,   600
And semblant scorn, resent the ravish'd bliss.
But let not thou the drum their mirth inspire;
Nor vinous spirits: else, to madness fir'd,
(What will not bacchanalian frenzy dare?)
Fell acts of blood, and vengeance they pursue.   605

---

*This is a sort of rude guitar, invented by the Negroes. It produces a wild pleasing melancholy sound. [The banjo.]

Compel by threats, or win by soothing arts,
Thy slaves to wed their fellow slaves at home;
So shall they not their vigorous prime destroy,
By distant journeys, at untimely hours,
When muffled midnight decks her raven-hair   610
With the white plumage of the prickly vine.*

Would'st thou from countless ails preserve thy gang;
To every Negroe, as the candle-weed†
Expands his blossoms to the cloudy sky,
And moist Aquarius melts in daily showers;   615
A woolly vestment give, (this Wiltshire weaves)
Warm to repel chill Night's unwholesome dews:
While strong coarse linen, from the Scotian loom,
Wards off the fervours of the burning day.

The truly great, tho' from a hostile clime,   620
The sacred Nine embalm; then, Muses, chant,
In grateful numbers, Gallic Lewis' praise:
For private murder quell'd; for laurel'd arts,
Invented, cherish'd in his native realm;
For rapine punish'd; for grim famine fed;   625
For sly chicane expell'd the wrangling bar;
And rightful Themis¹⁶⁸ seated on her throne:
But, chief, for those mild laws his wisdom fram'd,
To guard the Aethiop from tyrannic sway!

Did such, in these green isles which Albion claims,   630
Did such obtain; the muse, at midnight-hour,
This last brain-racking study had not ply'd:
But, sunk in slumbers of immortal bliss,
To bards had listned on a fancied Thames!

---

*This beautiful white rosaceous flower is as large as the crown of one's hat, and only blows at midnight. The plant, which is prickly and attaches itself firmly to the sides of houses, trees, &c. produces a fruit, which some call *Wythe Apple,* and others with more propriety, *Mountain strawberry.* But though it resembles the large Chili-strawberry in looks and size; yet being inelegant of taste, it is seldom eaten. The botanical name is *Cereus scandens minor.* The rind of the fruit is here and there studded with tufts of small sharp prickles.

†This shrub, which produces a yellow flower somewhat resembling a narcissus, makes a beautiful hedge, and blows about November. It grows wild every where. It is said to be diuretic, but this I do not know from experience.

All hail, old father Thames! tho' not from far   635
Thy springing waters roll; nor countless streams,
Of name conspicuous, swell thy watery store;
Tho' thou, no Plata,* to the sea devolve
Vast humid offerings; thou art king of streams:
Delighted Commerce broods upon thy wave;   640
And every quarter of this sea-girt globe
To thee due tribute pays; but chief the world
By great Columbus found, where now the muse
Beholds, transported, slow vast fleecy clouds,
Alps pil'd on Alps romantically high,   645
Which charm the sight with many a pleasing form.
The moon, in virgin-glory, gilds the pole,
And tips yon tamarinds, tips yon Cane-crown'd vale,
With fluent silver; while unnumbered stars
Gild the vast concave with their lively beams.   650
The main, a moving burnish'd mirror, shines;
No noise is heard, save when the distant surge
With drouzy murmurings breaks upon the shore!—

Ah me, what thunders roll! the sky's on fire!
Now sudden darkness muffles up the pole!   655
Heavens! what wild scenes, before the affrighted sense,
Imperfect swim!—See! in that flaming scroll,
Which Time unfolds, the future germs bud forth,
Of mighty empires! independent realms!—
And must Britannia, Neptune's favorite queen,   660
Protect'ress of true science, freedom, arts;
Must she, ah! must she, to her offspring crouch?
Ah, must my Thames, old Ocean's favourite son,
Resign his trident to barbaric streams;
His banks neglected, and his waves unsought,   665
No bards to sing them, and no fleets to grace?—
Again the fleecy clouds amuse the eye,
And sparkling stars the vast horizon gild—
She shall not crouch; if Wisdom guide the helm,
Wisdom that bade loud Fame, with justest praise,   670
Record her triumphs! bade the lacquaying winds

*One of the largest rivers of South America.

Transport, to every quarter of the globe,
Her winged navies! bade the scepter'd sons
Of earth acknowledge her pre-eminence!—
She shall not crouch; if these Cane ocean-isles,   675
Isles which on Britain for their all depend,
And must for ever; still indulgent share
Her fostering smile: and other isles be given,
From vanquish'd foes.—And, see, another race!
A golden aera dazzles my fond sight!   680
That other race, that long'd-for aera, hail!
The British George now reigns, the Patriot King!
Britain shall ever triumph o'er the main.

11

FROM

A General Description of the West-Indian Islands

JOHN SINGLETON

(fl. 1760s)

Singleton was the first poet to be influenced by the publication of James Grainger's *The Sugar Cane* in 1764. Turning from Grainger's georgic genre, Singleton wrote a blank verse topographical poem detailing his own travels through the Windward and Leeward Islands of the Eastern Caribbean. He acknowledges his debt to the "tuneful Grainger, nurs'd in Fancy's arms" in book II (line 20). Although not endued with Grainger's expert scientific knowledge, Singleton does provide intriguing details on matters of African and European customs in the West Indies, along with some well-phrased appreciation for the natural beauty of the islands.

Little is known of Singleton, except that he was a member of Lewis Hallam's professional acting company—the first such group of professionals in America. Hallam's troupe, founded in 1752, toured several of the North American colonies before traveling to Jamaica and the eastern Caribbean islands in the 1760s.

Singleton probably composed *A General Description of the West-Indian Islands* in Barbados, as it was first published there. A much abridged version was published in London in 1776 under the title *A Description of the West-Indies. A Poem, in Four Books.*

A General Description of the West-Indian Islands,
As far as relates to the British, Dutch, and Danish
Governments, from Barbados to Saint Croix.
Attempted in Blank Verse.
By John Singleton.
Barbados: Printed by George Esmand
and William Walker, for the Author.
M.DCC.LXVII.
[1767].

The FIRST BOOK.
The ARGUMENT.

The address. —Description of an island. —The hospitality of the inhabitants. —The cane plant and the West-Indian fruits particularly described. —The fable of Hippomenes and Atalanta[1] occasionally introduced. —Compliment to the inhabitants of all the islands, and some advice to the ladies. —The Indian barbecue. —The usual spot described. —This feast compared with, and preferred to, those of Ceres and Bacchus. — The several amusements in the morning. —The manner in which the barbecue is served up. —The customs of the turf, and the sports after dinner particularly described.

A General Description of the West-Indian Islands.
BOOK I.

On Daedalèan wing* the trembling muse
Attempts to soar, advent'rous, undismay'd,
If Pinfold,† gen'rous and humane, will stoop
To lend an ear, and patronise her song.
Then shall the bard, inspirited, resume   5
His sleeping lyre, and with exulting touch
Awake the joyful strings; happy if e'er

*Alluding to these lines of Horace:
Pindarum quisquis studet aemulari,
Iule, ceratis ope Daedalêa
Nititur pennis, vitreo daturus
Nomina ponto. —Hor. 1.iv.od.2.
["Whoever strives, Iulus, to rival Pindar, relies on wings fastened with wax by Daedalean craft, and is doomed to give his name to some crystal sea." Translation from *Odes and Epodes*, trans. C.E. Bennett (London: Heineman, 1915), 287.]
†Charles Pinfold, Esq. LLD. late Governor of Barbados. [Note from the second edition, 1776.]

A single note of his may aptly speak
His gratitude, his more than filial love,
To these indulgent isles, who, parent-like,   10
Within their hospitable shade, have oft
Refresh'd, and tun'd his drooping soul to joy.
    The pleasing subject, grateful muse, inspire,
Whether thou most delight'st to court the breeze,
That, sweeping o'er the spacious plain, salutes   15
Thy rosy cheek with a soft-temper'd kiss;
To wander pensive through the shady wood,
Or climb the summit of the topmost hill;
Alike each scene diversified attracts
The feasted eye.—Not fam'd Hesperian lands,[2]   20
Nor gardens of Alcinous,[3] could afford
Theme more delightful to the poet's pen.
Traverse with me the hills, the varied slopes,
The levell'd plains, crown'd with transcendent bloom;
Where ever-budding spring, and summer gay,   25
Dance hand in hand, and, with eternal joy,
Lead up the jocund harvest to the mill;
Whilst the rich planter, well rewarded, sees
Perpetual produce springing all the year,
And hospitable, at his plenteous board   30
Each welcome guest with various viands cheers:
Rich liquors oft in cups superb he quaffs,
(Thirst-sating draughts!) and each delicious juice
Unto the parched lip frequent applies;
Whilst mirth, with freedom, smiles at ev'ry meal.   35
Here Phoebus vertically darts his rays
From Capricornus to the Northern Crab,
Parching the thirsty ground with heat intense;
But milder Zephyrus,* with pity touch'd,
Calls up the sweet alleviating gale,   40
Whose balmy breath, with fragrant smells replete,
Skims o'er the golden vale and verdant mead,
Allaying sultry heat; whilst frequent show'rs,
Down from the mountain-cloud descending swift,

*_Zephyrus_ was the name given by the poets to the west wind; but it may be used in a poetical sense for any gentle breeze or trade-wind.

The burning bosom of the earth refresh.   45
Sometimes in gentle drops they kindly fall
Delightful o'er the plain; sometimes in puffs
The dang'rous flurries* break (with storm surcharg'd)
From forth the hollow of contiguous hills;
Then, with a rapid violence, they rush   50
O'er frighted Nature's face in whirlwinds dire,
And to the azure deep new horrors give.
With gentle breeze more oft the earth they fan,
Cooling the sultry air, with fragrance charg'd,
Caught from the scent of blooming fruits and flow'rs;   55
On Aura's[4] sportive wing they gently ride,
And sweeten all around, to man and beast
Delightful; whilst the sylvan choirs attune,
And all the warbling songsters† of the grove,
In vary'd harmonies, their Maker praise.   60
In high perfection here that plant‡ uprears
Its verdant blade, whose yellow ripen'd stem
Pours its rich juicy streams abundant forth,
And from its sweets bestows increasing pow'r,
Plenty, and ease, on its impatient lord.   65
Sweeten'd by this all-wond'rous plant,§ each fair
In India's sultry climes (abjuring wines)
The far-fam'd Chinese shrub‖ with pleasure tastes,
And satisfaction high, when oft they meet
Beguiling time; then Beauty's prattling lip   70

*These land-flurries are oftentimes very fatal to vessels, if the mariners are not exceedingly watchful to shorten sail on their first appearance; many having been overset and lost within musquet-shot of the shore, especially off Montserrat.

†Grainger says there are no singing birds.—I do not presume to compare them to the Canary bird, the linnet, or goldfinch; but there are thrushes in great abundance, and other birds of note, which inhabit the mountains, woods, and gullies, but they do not frequent the plain: I have often heard them, and many persons can attest the truth of my assertion.

‡The Sugar Cane. [Note from the second edition, 1776.]

§Very deservedly so stiled, for there is no Part of it useless: The body of the cane producing sugar and rum, the green tops feeding the cattle, and the mogoss (a term made use of in the leeward islands, signifying the same as mill-trash in Barbados: It is used to signify the reliques of the cane after it has gone through the mill) serving the furnaces with excellent fuel; the blades or trash serving for either manure or fuel, and making good litter for the stable, or thatching for poor houses.

‖Tea. [Note from the second edition, 1776.]

The vessel curious, wrought by Dresden art,[5]
From arm of alabaster hue receives.
No scandal then, or foul ill-manner'd speech,
Offends the ear; as when the midnight drums,
Sacred to fraud and ruin, cards and dice,   75
Destructive, hold their scandalous misrule.
Not so intemp'rate man its juice employs;
But its nutritious quality, for good
Design'd, to shameful purposes perverts:
He from the chymic[6] still extracts a fiend,*   80
When by excessive draughts he dims the light
Of reason, prime prerogative of man:
Th' intoxicated brain, by vapours fill'd,
Hurls wisdom headlong from her rightful throne,
And exil'd sense abjures the hated seat;   85
Folly usurps, and outrage oft employs
Her hellish train with mischievous intent;
Madness itself sometimes invades the man,
Fiery and wild, beast rather term'd than man:
For what is man of understanding void?   90
Who hath not read, how once the hoary sire[†]
Of postdiluvian race (when he the branch
Of olive saw, and, by divine command,
The ark on Ararat fast standing left)
With all his tribe descending to the plain,   95
Grosly abus'd the gifts all-bounteous Heav'n
Bestow'd? What time, deceiv'd by the rich grape's
Insinuating juice, th' unwary seer
All naked lay, expos'd to saucy mirth,
The impious mirth of his contemptuous son;   100
Who, lost to ev'ry sense of filial love,
Basely proclaim'd the weakness of his sire;
And dar'd, with bold derision, to survey
What nature's modest whisper bad him hide?

*Rum. [Note from the second edition, 1776.]
†Gen. ix. 22. ["And Ham, the father of Canaan, saw the nakedness of his father, and told his two brethren without." This was the act for which Ham was cursed by his father Noah. In the early modern period, some writers argued that Africans were the descendants of Ham, thus justifying their enslavement.]

So ever shall inebriated man,   105
By his own act of ev'ry sense bereft,
Fall a just victim to reproach and scorn,
And blush with shame, when cool reflection chides.

Nor does Pomona here with scanty hand
Heap on the damask'd board her ripen'd fruits   110
Delicious, and of flavour exquisite;
Fruits not unworthy Europèan soils.

Courting the taste, the luscious plantane* here
Within its yellow coat his tribute brings;
And sweet bananas (kindred fruit) their pulp   115
Luxuriant yield in rich abundant store,
By superstitious bigots sacred held.†

Here guavas, plums, and sapadillas bloom;
There juicy grape-fruits, burnish'd by the sun,
With rich forbiddens, grace the golden grove: 120
The bulky shaddock, and the citron green,
Which chearful dames in dainty pastries mix,
When, at the holy season, they regale,
And celebrate with joy a Saviour's birth.

Cool water-lemons to the fev'rish guest   125
Hold forth their grateful moisture, and invite
The gath'rer's hand; whilst, yielding to the touch,
The scented fruits enrich their bending vines.

The sweetly-poignant granadilla here
Spreads its broad leaf, advancing fast in growth,   130
Till with its weight th' umbrageous arbours groan.

There rip'ning melons strew unshelter'd beds,
And to perfection without art arrive.

Distent⁷ with nectar sweet pomegranates burst,
And in due season yield a grateful taste,   135
For use medicinal by artists priz'd.

*It has been objected, that the plantane ought not to be admitted into the catalogue of
fruits, because it is served to table as a kind of bread. It is granted, when half grown and roasted,
it makes very good food; but that ought rather to add to its value, nor can it any way lessen our
approbation of it as an excellent fruit when ripe.

†Some of these people fancy that the resemblance of a cross appears on every slice of the
banana, and therefore will not cut it.

Here Indian avocados plenteous hang,
Whose polish'd rinds, with various colours stain'd,
Replete with vegetable marrow swell.

The lofty tam'rind here (whose fruit, incas'd,   140
To thirst a slaking beverage affords)
Far over-arching, spreads its umbrage brown,
And to the weary traveller extends
An ample shade at Sol's meridian glow.
Oft times, beneath its cool inviting arms,   145
The bard to Celia's[8] eye-brow pens his lay;
Or, wrapt in grateful contemplation, hymns
The praise and glory of th' Almighty King,
His pious thoughts with rapt'rous zeal inspir'd:
Sometimes the epic strain delights his pen;   150
And oft the ditty by young Colin sung[9]
Am'rous, to sooth and charm the love-sick maid,
Which she delighted hears, and fans his flame.

The cocoa here, with rugged trunk* deform'd,
Winds in the air its long unwieldy bulk;   155
Or shoots, oblique, in many a wanton line,
And, scorning order, mocks the planter's care.
Forth from the nut cool flows nectareous juice,
Such as a god would scarce refuse to taste,
Though Ganymede[10] should not present the cup.   160
The nut itself might with the almond vie
For beauty, whiteness, and delicious food.

But let us turn to yonder fragrant grove,
Where hangs the orange, rich in burnish'd gold,
And by the fair seems eager to be pluck'd.   165
Not fairer fruit did swift HIPPOMENES,
The fav'rite of CYTHERA's queen,[11] receive
From her own hand, when ATALANTA's love

*On May the 4th, 1765, I saw at Mr. John Oxley's, in Barbados, one of these trees almost in the form of a cork-screw; the worm is amazingly regular, beginning at about two thirds from the trunk, and ending at the head. There is another one hundred feet long, whose branches are not more than twelve Feet from the ground; what is very remarkable is, that about a month before our last rains its trunk rested upon the stump of another old tree, but since then it has sprung eighteen Inches from its old support. The stump and the block of the cocoa, by long rubbing, are become as smooth as polished marble.

Urg'd on th' advent'rous youth to try the race.
He (subtle as he was) well knew the pow'r   170
Which the enchanted eye usurps o'er all
Of mortal frame, and artfully decoy'd
The eager fair, unable to resist
The sure temptation of the golden fruit.
Thus ART and NATURE ever will contest   175
In vain: She, steady goddess, perseveres
In her wise course, nor ever turns aside;
Whilst ART, still stooping to some luring bait,
Like ATALANTA,* labours still behind.

The clust'ring grape here spreads its branching vine,   180
And o'er each arbour throws delightful shade;
Inducing oft the am'rous youthful pairs
In moonlight hour to taste its fruit, and sip
The grateful juice.—And last,† though first in praise,
The luscious pine, of humble growth indeed,   185
But of majestic form, its mitred head
Uprears; ambrosial fruit its sculptur'd coat,
Diversify'd by Nature's hand, contains,
All fruits compriz'd in one; its flavours rich
By Heav'n upon itself alone bestow'd.   190
Not those which in Alcinous' garden bloom'd,
Nor those which grace our Europèan soil,

---

*Atalanta, who was exceeding fleet, contended with Hippomenes in the course, on condition that, if Hippomenes won, he should espouse her, or forfeit his life if he lost. The Match was very unequal, for Atalanta had conquered numbers to their destruction: Hippomenes therefore had recourse to stratagem; he procured three golden apples from Venus, and purposely carried them with him. They started; Atalanta outstripped him soon; then Hippomenes bowled one of his apples before her across the course, in order not only to make her stoop, but to draw her out of the Path. She, prompted by female curiosity, and the beauty of the golden fruit, starts from the course to take up the apple: Hippomenes in the mean time holds on his way, and steps before her; but she, by her natural swiftness, soon fetches up her lost ground, and leaves him again behind: Hippomenes however, by rightly timing the second and third throw, at length won the race; not by his swiftness, but by his cunning. *Vide Shaw's Bacon, vol. i. p. 563. this fable explained of the contest between Art and Nature* [*The Philosophical Works of Francis Bacon*, ed. Peter Shaw (London: For J. J. and P. Knapton, et al., 1733).]

†There are some other fruits, but they are not so generally esteemed as those I have particularised, viz. The soursop, the mammee, sugar, custard, and monkey apples, dunks, bully-berries, pimploe and prickly pears, &c.

And ripen, beauteous, on the sunny wall,
When Sol, with Virgo riding, autumn brings,
Could e'er the royal Indian pine excel.   195

Happy inhabitants of these bless'd climes,
Did they but know their own delights to prize!
Then peace would smile, and joy attend their steps;
Nor would they envy Europèan youths:
Then would they rarely quit their native soil,   200
To barter peace for equipage and state.
Our northern follies let them wisely shun,
Our foibles 'scape; the vicious joys they yield
(At midnight hour most sought) true joys destroy:
As when they croud to join the giddy herd   205
Of noble sharpers and polite buffoons,
Knaves, fools, and sycophants together mix'd,
By equal turns, the preyers and the prey:
Some trap the gold in honorable guise,
Whilst others strive to chase the hours away,   210
Affecting mirth with sorrow at their hearts,
Ingenious in dissembling what they feel.
O fools! deceiving and deceiv'd; for still
Ye lose, in seeking, what ye toil to find,
Content of mind, and precious ease of heart.   215
Joy dwells not there, no pleasures enter in;
True happiness from the detested group
Flies with expanded wing; and, in her stead,
Debauch, lewd riot, and disorder reign.
        Too soon, alas! such scenes from the lank cheek   220
Of sick'ning beauty chase the damask rose,
And the fair lily's gloss compel to fade,
Long e'er approaching age, with stealing pace,
Her erring steps o'ertakes; worse foes than Time;
For his attacks are gentle, mild, and slow,   225
And softly steal upon us unperceiv'd,
Almost unfelt; whilst riot's headstrong course
Scarcely permits our rip'ning into years.
But to you chiefly I address my song.
Ye fair ones.—O! avoid the fatal snare,   230
That spoils ye of your beauty and your health:

Ye sober matrons, and ye happy wives,
These orgies shun; fly swift, ruin unseen
Lies lurking deep, and the vast pit gapes wide,
To swallow down the vile abandon'd gang.   235
Leave that invet'rate rout to meet
Rashly to tread perdition's crouded path,
Where fraud and theft in rich embroid'ry stalk;
Where pride and sloth, parents of ev'ry sin,
Amidst the gay illuminations shine.   240
Then let us turn from such pernicious scenes,
And a more pleasing prospect set to view;
To tell what sportive harmless rites our youths
Throughout the far-fam'd western ind perform.

The BARBECUE*

Oft times beneath the wide extending shade,   245
Where wild figs shoot, and stately tam'rinds rise
Aloft in air, fanning the purling stream
Of some meand'ring brook, that creeping glides
O'er mossy beds, hard by the tufted lawn;
Or at a mountain's foot, amidst huge rocks,   250
Urges its latent course, our feasts we hold.
There the woo'd virgin, and the sprightly youth,
Am'rous and gay, the cool retreat enjoy;
Whilst pastimes innocent, and rural sports,
With high delight, the jocund hours beguile.   255
So once of old, in solemn grots and groves,
Or in the daisy'd lawn, or pasture green,
Where crystal streams in wand'ring mazes roll'd,
'Ere stately temples rear'd their incens'd heads,
The rustic pairs in am'rous parley met,   260
And felt the joys of conscious innocence,
Pure love, and transport, unallay'd with woe.
    A band select the chosen spot explore;

*The reader will be pleased to observe, that all the sports are not always used which I have
mentioned in the course of this barbecue; because the place chosen, wanting water sometimes,
will not admit of them. I have seen in Montserrat most of those herein described, and in very
high perfection; and I hope I shall not be censured for endeavouring to season my barbecue as
high and as richly as I possibly could.

Proud he who first his welcome friends receives;
Not with stiff Ceremony's formal brow,   265
But salutation free, and warm embrace,
With cordial love, and amity sincere.
The widow'd dame, and the stay'd sober pair,
Oft deign at these high revels to partake;
Nor does the matron grave, or sage deep read   270
In wisdom's solid page, avoid these rites
Of innocent festivity and mirth.
    Not those in honor of a goddess held,
Cerêalêan* call'd, which hinds of antient time
Grateful observ'd, when to her sacred turf   275
They brought, profusely grateful, their first fruits,
Which she, all-bounteous queen, profusely gave:
Nor those of Bacchus† on th'Ismarian mount,
Where noise and tumult held despotic sway,
And furious priestesses, with wine surcharg'd,   280
Intoxicated roam'd o'er Thracian land:
Not those, nor all which heathen story boasts,
Can with the Indian barbecue compare,
Whose harmless rural sports, and social joys,
In pleasure high the festival maintain.   285
A chearful glee in ev'ry face appears;
The sparkling eye speaks the delighted heart,
Free from hypocrisy, or smile constrain'd;
With freedom all elate, all what they seem,
Vie only with each other who can yield   290
Most satisfaction to the festive train.
The sable cooks, with utensils prepar'd,
Their sev'ral stations take, and crackling flames

---

*These feasts, sacred to Ceres, were celebrated with great order and decency, no wine being used at them, and the enjoyment of women entirely forbid. "Ceres was the first to turn the glebe with the hooked ploughshare; she first gave corn and kindly sustenance to the world; she first gave laws. All things are the gift of Ceres." Ovid, lib. v. fab. 6. lin. 341. [Latin in original; translation from Ovid, *Metamorphoses,* trans. Frank Justus Miller, vol. 1 (London: Heineman, 1984), 263.]

†These, on the contrary, were celebrated with all frantic demonstrations of joy, drunkenness, and riot; revellings and lewdness always prevailing even to excess, the mad multitude running about with cymbals and drums, making a hideous confused noise, and crying out, *Evoe Bacche, Evoe Bacche,* &c.

Enkindle; not with bellows, but with lungs,
Expert at blowing culinary blasts.   295
Whilst Cuffee, Lovelace, Talliho, and Sal,*
With viands stor'd, the loaded baskets bring:
This a variety of herbage holds,
And that the solid sav'ry meat contains,
The well cramm'd turkey and the rosy ham;   300
Nor is the mellow cheese forgot, of taste
High relishing, when silver-tipp'd black jack,[12]
Or tankard bright, fam'd Calvert's porter holds,
With flow'ry head high tow'ring o'er the brim.
The destin'd shoat[13] on Ethiop's shoulders swags,   305
Grunting, as to the rural shrine he's brought:
Here one beneath a load of liquors bends,
Cooling sherbets, and various dainty wines;
Another the capacious bowl conveys,
With sacharissian† loaf; the spirit fine,   310
From choicest cane‡ distill'd, mellow'd by age,
Within its glassy bounds alluring smiles;
Nor does the neighb'ring brook refuse its aid,
In mingling with the juice of yellow fruit,
Lemon or lime,§ which in contiguous groves   315
Upon the loaded branches fragrant hang.
      Now the bright sun to his meridian hastes,
And calls his children to the welcome shade;
Thither is brought the full salubrious bowl,
Heart-chearing sight! With lip impatient, all   320
Wait longing to salute it in its round:
Mean while the cooks their sev'ral tasks pursue;
The nimble butler now displays his part,
And on the turf the bleached damask spreads.
Some to the well-stor'd brook eager repair,   325

*Names of negroes who always attended at such entertainments.
†Sugar.
‡The Barbados spirit is made from cane-juice entirely.
§Limes arrive at great perfection in these climates, especially in Barbados, where there are some considerably larger than a man's head. The rind of these enormous limes is notwithstanding exceedingly thin, and they for the most part yield a great quantity of very grateful juice. What is more extraordinary, the seeds are as small as those of the common fruit.

Where in the deeps destructive nets they cast,
And num'rous fry emmesh; others with lime,
Or bark of wond'rous tree,* the waters taint,
And the swift natives of the fluid stream
In stupefaction† plunge; their sense benumb'd,   330
Intoxicated, oft they lifeless float,
And to the hand an easy prey become.
　　　Others from iron tubes the deadly ball
At the grey plover, or the harmless dove,
Or some superior songster of the wood,   335
With never-erring aim direct; down drop
The feather'd victims in their airy course,
No more, alas! to rise on tow'ring wing,
Or animate the grove with morning song.
　　　Others on tufted banks, in pairs drawn off,   340
With virtuous dalliance the sweet hours beguile;
Whilst harmony of thought, and mutual love,
Rise in each others souls reciprocal:
All unabash'd they toy, nor blush to meet
The chaste embrace, by chaste desire obtain'd;   345
Nor, cautious, from th' observing eye retire,
To steal, in secret, joys too dearly bought.
Love, urg'd in terms that speak the soul sincere,
The gen'rous fair with equal love returns:
Not like coy dames who over-rate their charms,   350
And oft their lovers with a frown reward
For many a vow sincere: Nor like proud jilt,
Or vain coquette, whose actions falsify
Their tongues, whilst in expression they pour forth
Soft protestations foreign to the heart.   355
　　　Some, on the sedgy bank, melodious notes
From the soft flute's enchanting tube command
Uninterrupted, save where echo sweet,
From distant hills and caves, returns the sound.
　　　But, hark! the gen'ral summon to the turf   360
Invites; all instant quit their sev'ral sports,

*Dog-wood, or manchioneil.
†This is called poisoning.

And each his fav'rite fair, smiling, conducts
Up to the sweet repast: The verdant earth
Spreads forth her matted carpet, sylvan seat:
The green sod first with circumspection swept,   365
Lest lurking thorn, or prickly pear, invade
The fair one's tender foot, they sit, they smile;
The smoaking BARBECUE in sight appears,
Escorted by a train of sable guards,
Wafting its favour tow'rds the jovial board,   370
All nicely brown'd and crisp. Transported they
View it approaching with an eager eye;
For the keen wholesome air, that gently breathes
Along the bubbling stream and fans the vale,
A never-failing appetite creates.   375
        Now all prepare; and one, with dextrous hand,
And knife of keenest edge, the shoat dissects.
The choicest bits each for his fair procures,
And all his care bestows to see her pleas'd.
Behaviour decent, and polite address,   380
These festive scenes adorn: Not like to those
In famous city oft, when lord-mayor's feast
Calls forth the well-fed alderman, prepar'd
The night before with an emetic,[14] sure
To whet the edge of sated appetite: 385
With sleeves turn'd up, and napkin to his chin,
He eyes the smoaking pasty, or the haunch
Four inches deep in fat; or takes his seat
Next the high-season'd turtle's calipee;[15]
Unhappy wretch! should other knife than his,   390
With scientific slice, monopolise
His fav'rite bit, or spring a mine of fat
Within the shaky shell, conceal'd, alas!
From his exploring eye:—Kind Heav'n forbid!
In other guise our chearful guests dispatch   395
The sweet delicious meal; pleasure reigns now,
And satisfaction beams from ev'ry eye.
Nature at length suffic'd, the cloth remov'd,
Each loyal health with flowing glass they crown,
And merry toasts the sprightly circle pledge   400

Alternate round the turf; high jests prevail,
With decent language grac'd; the artful pun,
The repartee unstudy'd, free from gall,
Diffuse sweet mirth and pleasantry around.
The rural banquet o'er, alert they rise,   405
And to the pastimes of the plain repair:
Some their brisk coursers mount, and to the goal
With rapid vi'lence rush, whilst the fleet steeds
Stretch o'er the ground, and fly through clouds of dust.
Others on foot with nimble ardour strive,   410
And struggle through the long laborious race.
In leaping some delight, whilst some the stone,
Of size unwieldy, cast to distance far,
And in athletic games their strength approve.
Judges of all, the beauteous tribe appear,   415
Seated to view the various manly sports,
And with soft praise the active youths elate.
Some foot it on the turf with nimble step,
And sprightly to the chearful measures trip:
Others, reclin'd, chant forth melodious lays: 420
All now is freedom, full content, and joy,
Without restriction, jarring feuds, or brawls.
        But see the sun, descending to the west,
Begins to hide his sinking head in clouds
Of purple tint, with golden boarders fring'd;   425
The glorious scene what painter can express!
When, at fair ev'ning's dusk, the setting God
O'erspreads the gilded vault with various forms,
And shapes grotesque, of unembody'd air;
Such as not fancy's richest pencil e'er   430
Knew how to picture out in Titian's school.[16]
Homeward he calls them from their sports away,
'Ere shrouded night brings on unwholesome dews,
And colds pernicious seize the tender frame.
Now from these rural, these enchanting scenes,   435
Uncloy'd they turn,—for innocent delights,
Such as I celebrate, can never cloy.
The willing steeds they mount, and ev'ry youth
Escorts his darling fair, whilst at her side

He chearful rides, till at their welcome homes   440
They safe arrive, and all to rest retire.
                The End of the First Book.

The SECOND BOOK.
The ARGUMENT.

The subject proposed.—Invocation.—Excursion to the Vale of Sulphur in Montser-
rat.—Description of the way, interspersed with occasional digressions.—Traffic for
negroes touched upon.—An African tale.—Prospects and descriptions of several isles
viewed from the top of the highest mountain in the author's way to the Sulphur, viz.
Saba, St. Eustatia, Nevis, St. Christopher, Deseada, Antigua, Guardaloupe and its de-
pendencies.—Journey to the Sulphur continued.—Obeah negroes.—A true story of
one.—The opening of the Vale of sulphur, and description of it.—Comparison of it
with the sulphurous lakes of the Dii Palici, the avengers of perjury, according to the hea-
then mythology.—The author's journey to the petrifying waters in Montserrat.—The
hospitality of his guide.—His farewel to that island, and his particular friends there.

BOOK II.

Deep in the briny bosom of the main,
Where aged Atlas reigns, fair Montserrat,
'Midst num'rous sisters of his antient race,
Exulting in its form, salutes the eye.
Awful appears its cloud-encircled brow,   5
Which the glad mariner delighted sees
Many leagues distant from the surf-lash'd shore;
Such a tremendous height the mount aspires,
Proud in superior grace: His wreathed head
Scowls o'er the vales below disdainful low'r,   10
As when a tyrant from his throne looks down,
And scornful sees (elate with eastern pride)
Beneath his feet submissive vassals crouch.
        Come, pow'rful genius of these fertile isles,
Though yet before thy shrine I have not bow'd;   15
Nor, conscious of my weakness, dare invoke,
Like bards superior, thy celestial aid;
Inspire me now, nor let my languid pen
Disgrace those climes, which late thy fav'rite son,
Thy tuneful Grainger,* nurs'd in Fancy's arms,   20

---

*The author of a poem called *The Sugar-Cane.*

So elegantly sung: Him (happy bard!)
Delighted thou hast led with list'ning ear;
Through each enliven'd scene his sprightly muse
Rejoic'd to traverse: O! disdain not now
To aid an humbler poet in his lays.   25
O'er yon stupendous mount* conduct my steps
Down to the bottom of the hideous gulph.
Teach me the fell Tartarean vale to sing,
And tell the horrors of the gloomy cave.

    A dreary pit there is, of deep descent,   30
Where Nature (ever studious to conceal
From mortal eye her dark mysterious ways,
Unfit for mortal eye to view) her stores
In secret hides; where sulph'rous atoms fume;
First found, through chance, by some delinquent slave   35
Flying the lash of his revengeful lord,
Or overseer more cruel. Once he dwelt
A native of rich Ebo's sunny coast,[17]
Or Gambia's golden shore; a prince perhaps;
By treach'rous scheme of some sea brute entrap'd,   40
When the steel-hearted sordid mariner
Shap'd out his wat'ry course for traffic vile,
Commuting wares for baneful dust of gold;
Or, what is worse, made spoil of human flesh.
Accursed method of procuring wealth!   45
By loading free-born limbs with servile chains,
And bart'ring for the image of his God.
Deal Christians thus, yet keep that sacred name?
Or does the diff'rence of complexion give
To man a property in man?—O! no: 50
Soft Nature shrinks at the detested thought,
A thought which savages alone can form.
    A wretch like this it was, who once betray'd
A sacred trust, which hospitality
And honor bound him to perform, and sold,   55

This mount [in Montserrat] is seen many leagues off in a clear day, and is esteemed as high land as any in the West-Indies: It abounds with wonderful curiosities, of which the author proposes to speak at large in the course of this book.

Like a base villain, for a little trash,
That pledge of friendship, which his royal host
(A king he was in Afric's sable realms)
Deliver'd to him with a parting sigh;—
His only son.—Him the fond father long,   60
Within his little empire, rear'd to arms
And virtue—virtue, such as Nature's sons
Are taught to practice, unallay'd with art.
Happy! thrice happy! had not Europe's fame
Induc'd the credulous old man to trust   65
With this false friend the darling of his age;
Hoping 'ere yet he reach'd th' approaching grave,
To see the youth return, with science stor'd,
And such accomplishments as Britain's sons
Had oft display'd before the Ebon king,   70
When fate had driven them to his sunny shore.
The specious friend accepted the rich charge,
And, with no scanty protestations, vow'd
To cherish as his own the fav'rite boy;
And, when instruction, with experience join'd,   75
Had form'd the stripling into perfect man,
Safe to return him to the longing arms
Of his fond parent; fond, alas! in vain
Of the dear boy, the pride of Afric's coast,
Whose precious sight no more shall bless his eyes.   80
For, O! the treach'rous friend, by love of gold
Allur'd, in some far distant isle exchang'd
His sacred charge for vile commercial gain,
Dead to the checks of conscience, and of shame.
Can such a wretch exist! nor feel the thorns   85
That goad and sting the perjur'd villain's heart,
Who dares, thus impiously, to violate
Earth's, Heav'n's, and Friendship's ever sacred laws?

. . . .

On boldly, curious traveller, nor dare
To view th' abyss beneath, o'er which thy steps
Ev'n now impend; whilst, on the widest part
If the tremendous verge's slipp'ry edge,
Thy treach'rous foot can scarce secure its hold.   330

There baleful weeds are said to grow; whose juice,
Th' experienc'd leech[18] among the sable tribe,
Extracting, turns to medicinal use.
For oft the crafty slave, affecting skill
In pow'rful herbs, calls magic to his aid;   335
And, when old age has silver'd o'er his chin,
Draws in the credulous, unthinking crowd,
To venerate his art, and fill his purse.
How gross soe'er the imposition seem,
Yet powerful fancy aids him in the cheat.   340
Sometimes, when his emollient hand's apply'd
To the complaining part, pins, crooked nails,
Flints, horse-shoes, broken glass, and leaden balls,
Have issued forth from arms, necks, legs, and sides,
Where none e'er enter'd in. Nay (strange to tell!)   345
These mock-physicians, by a single touch,
Will bring the patient, sinking to the grave,
To life again; and by emetic sure,
Eradicate a malady long fix'd,
(Past any pow'r of art but theirs to reach)   350
By easing the swell'd stomach of contents,
Such as no human stomach e'er contain'd.
    A true physician, who in vain prescrib'd
For a poor slave, by fancy once possess'd
So strongly, that no learned means cou'd cure,   355
Was led by curiosity to see
His patient treated with superior skill
By an old hag, who long had liv'd renown'd
For spells, drugs, charms, and knowledge physical.
With sapient face she handled ev'ry part;   360
Till, fixing on the seat of the disease,
She mumbled to herself some uncouth Words,
The myst'ry of her trade, and close apply'd
Her parch'd lips, by suction to extract
The cause of the complaint. Strange antick[19] tricks   365
She play'd; now sat, now rose; then on her knees,
And now erect again, she labour'd on
To charm, intice, or force, the cursed fiend,
That lurk'd within, to quit his wicked hold.

At length her pray'rs were heard; her art prevail'd;   370
And from th' affected part there issued forth
(Such is the pow'r of suction tow'rds some cures!)
Sometimes a pebble, then a horse's tooth,
With many a crooked pin, and rusty nail.
The doctor stood astounded all the while   375
To see the game the wrinkled sorc'ress play'd.
For these strange things, extracted with vast pain
Out of the writhing patient's tortur'd flesh,
Left not a wound behind to mark the place
From whence they issued: (Such is magic's force   380
When blended with true knowledge of disease!)
At last, impatient and incredulous,
Fast by the throat he seiz'd the ugly witch,
And out flew all her magazine of stores:
Teeth, pebbles, nails, and pins, her tools of trade.   385
O! bold deceit! to thee the universe
At times, becomes a prey. What being lives
Ungall'd by thee; who dost, by turns, delude
The ermin'd monarch, and the tatter'd slave?

.   .   .   .

The THIRD BOOK.
The ARGUMENT.

Voyage to Santa Croix. —View of the Narrows, Mount Misery, Brimstone Hill, St. Eustatia, St. Martins, Anguilla, St. Bartholomews, &c. &c. &c. —Description of the Virgin islands. —Wreckers and pirates in those seas. —The dangerous reef of rocks near Anegada. —Sea-view of Santa Croix at sun-set. —The same at sun-rise. — Description of the country. —Story of Aurelia and Philander. —A hurricane. —A negro burial.

BOOK III.

Now swift before the breathing gale we scud,
Cutting the curling seas with foaming speed,
Now in th' horizon sink the less'ning hills,
And from the poop Rodunda* seems to fly.
Thro' the smooth Narrows of the Nevian isle,[20]   5
By that huge bass which seamen call Nag's-head,

*A rocky islet. [Note from the second edition, 1776.]

We coast the shore of fam'd St. Christophers;
Where the black mount* its cloudy mantle wears,
Seldom conspicuous to the trav'ller's ken;
Or where brimstonic hill, a fortress vast,   10
Its ample strength conceals, impregnable,
Guarding the pleasant Villa,† and the point
Which terminate that island's western bounds.
Thence opens to the view the wealthy port
Of St. Eustace, mart of illicit trade,   15
Pleasant Anguilla, and St. Martins green;
And see what other charming scenes appear
O'er Sol's bright ev'ning mansions thickly strow'd.
The Virgin Gords,²¹ and Anegada rough,
Whose frightful reefs the pilot strives to shun,   20
Too oft in vain if adverse winds prevail,
Or currents draw him to the whirlpool's way.
Such sight the lawless wrecker's²² eye enjoys
When he beholds, high pleas'd, the gallant bark
Entangled fast within the stony net,   25
Beating amidst the surf from rock to rock,
Whilst raging billows foam on ev'ry side.
Then howls the conchs, resounding from the caves,
More dismal than the voice of bellowing storms,
Dire signal sure some shipwreck's on the coast.   30
Streight from the dark recesses of the wood,
Forth the remorseless sons‡ of plunder rush,
And furious mounting up her lofty sides,
The destin'd prize inexorable seize,
And cooly perpetrate the worst of deeds,   35
Too shocking for the poet's pen to draw
In softest lights, or human eye to view
Without a gen'rous sympathizing tear.
See where the rabble with their iron hands

---

*Mount Misery.
†St. Anns, and Sandy point.
‡These people sometimes live by fishing and cutting wood; and under such pretext screen themselves from the law, but when a shipwreck happens, I am informed that they are guilty of greater outrages than our *Cornish or Kentish men.* [Known for violent scavenging of shipwrecks and piracy.]

The stately bark disrobe.—Some fell the masts,   40
Which tumbling from the hull with ruinous crash,
Rend her firm timber'd sides; whilst others force
The full-stow'd hold, where all her treasures lye.
Some the rich furniture, and plate superb,
From the gay cabin, and the round-house rend,   45
To deck the cavern of their harden'd chief:
For e'en among these ravagers some laws
Obtain; and villainy transcendant gives
Superior rank, and high prerogative.
The leader of the ruffian band disdains   50
To claim an equal share. Before his throne
(Where, in mock-majesty, he holds his state)
The various spoils are pour'd, the richest find
A sure acceptance from the sov'reign's hand,
Which boastful he extends: Nor does his cheek,   55
Dead to remorse, turn pale, when he beholds
Ill purchas'd gold, wrung from the honest hands
Of industry, within his eager grasp.
      Thus, too, of old, St. Thomas and St. John,[23]
Lands of the Danish king, for pirates fam'd,   60
Within their fastnesses th' amphibious crew,
To all mankind detestable, receiv'd.
Ev'n yet old folks describe the hated spot
Where once their fortresses securely stood,
And shudder as they point to the deep vaults,   65
Whose mouths, they say, are now fill'd up by time,
Where treasures vast (for so the fable runs)
Still lye conceal'd. But still the hand of fear,
By childish superstition strengthen'd, checks
The poorest wretch from daring to explore   70
The real foundation of these fancied truths.
      But let us turn from these unpleasing tales,
And view the group of quays, extending wide,
Which in succession from th' horizon peep.
There thousands oft their barks and nets employ,   75
To take the hawksbil or the turtle green,
Whose flesh the epicure so oft delights,
When he with sauces rich, and high Cayenne,

Indulges luxury at health's expence.
  Tortola next her rugged clifts presents,   80
In uncouth order rising from the deep;
The last worth notice under British sway.
   And now at length, when ev'ning mild approach'd,
And dying gales stole o'er the peaceful deep,
In hillocks, rising from old ocean's edge,   85
Fair Santa Croix* her lovely isle presents.
The Phoebus shining sat, streaking with red,
Purple and gold the distant western sky;
And far into the glowing hemisphere
A thousand rays of various tincture shot;   90
With bright refulgent splendor he withdrew,
Nobly, majestic, cloudless, and serene.
Whilst the short ken of mortal eye pursu'd
Eager the glorious sight, in gazing lost;
To Thetis' briny lap he shining sinks,   95
And sets a period to the garish day.
Thus mighty Jove the gorgeous throne descends
Of star-pav'd Heav'n, in dazzling glory rob'd,
When he, paternal, lab'ring thro' the day,
To show'r down blessings on regardless man,   100
His council quits, and solemnly retires;
Whilst potentates, high pow'rs, and myriads crown'd,
Extolling round, the deity adore,
As he from care, with step majestic turns,
And seeks his consort in the realms of bliss.   105
   O'er the bright firmament a thousand forms,
Floating are lost in momentary change:
In marbled skies imagination shapes
Aerial palaces, temples superb;
The fiery dragon, or the griffin wing'd,   110
Beasts, birds and trees, mountains with flying caps,
And fleets of sailing ships, till by degrees
The vision melts, and night shuts up the scene.
Mean while the mariners on deck attend,
And chearful keep alternate hours of watch,   115

*Subject to Denmark. [Note from the second edition, 1776.]

Till to the eastern road of heav'n the day
Returns; bright Lucifer the gloom dispels,
And sweet Aurora, with her dewy hand,
Moistens the orient earth, or in mild show'rs
Descending slow, her morning pride displays: 120
The god, by fragrant aromatic gales
Attended, from the east the day renews,
With glories bright, and in the falling cloud,
By the refraction of his heav'nly rays,
In all its beauteous variegated tints,   125
Paints the gay-colour'd semicircled arch.
Not that more beauteous heav'n-born Iris bent
O'er the vast concave of the low'ring sky,
Where erst at Neptune's coral throne she bow'd
With awe, relating Juno's fell behests,   130
Impatient to destroy the Trojan race,
And reak her vengeance on Anchises' son.[24]
    The shore draws nigh, delightful landscapes rise,
A thousand beauties grace the varied scene;
Before us open all the level plains,   135
Rich canes wave their tall blades o'er ev'ry hill,
Whilst rising mountains, crown'd with tow'ring woods
Of stateliest trees, the prospect terminate.
The teaming soil sends forth abundant store,
And richly pays the lordly owner's cost: 140
Five times five seasons now have roll'd away
Since the young blade sprung up from parent earth,
And yet uncultur'd does the choice rattoon*
Far richer streams than annual plants produce.
Fat pastures here the lusty cattle brouze,   145
The sturdy woods with yellow mastic wave,
Gregory, and saunders, and the locust tall,
With lignumvitae, and the ebon hard,[25]
Which artists use to raise the sail-rigg'd mill.
There, where a stately forest once uprear'd   150

*Rattoons are canes that grow from the old stools. I have seen some growing at the estate
of Mr. Barnes Robinson, which I was informed had been planted twenty-five years; for the soil
is so rich and kind that they have very little occasion to grub up and plant, as is practiced in the
more windward islands, with great expence and labour.

Its awful head, like some vast theatre
Wherein old Rome receiv'd her conquer'd world,
Now swell the golden ear, or rip'ning cane.
Each spreading bush blooms with spontaneous fruit,
And berries wild in clust'ring bunches hang,   155
Of flavour exquisite, and luscious juice,
In beauty vying with the damsen plumb,
Or the rich cherry of the sable hue.
    Here gloomy manchioneils* thick branching spread
Their baneful foliage round, whose dealy shade,   160
Fair to the sight, extending far and wide,
O'er the salt beach, wash'd by returning floods,
The stranger oft with tempting guise allures,
To seek for shelter from inclement skies.
Loading the boughs, enchanting to the sight,   165
Variously streak'd, the pois'nous apples hang;
With scented fragrance all around they tempt,
And waft their odours through the gloomy grove:
Not unlike those the proud satanic host
Did annual taste (so sings the bard divine)[26]   170
When their great leader back to Hell return'd,
In guilty triumph o'er beguiled Eve.
Here to the plain the nimble steeds advance,
Train'd with high mettle for the ardent race;†
Whether from bord'ring Porto-Rico brought,   175
Or southern Curaçoa, full oft they strive,
And panting stretch o'er all the level course;
Nor unapplauded does the victor gain
The hard-contested palm. Thousands attend

*Much like a golden pippin in size and hue. These trees are common to all the islands, but I think the greatest numbers, and largest, are in St. Croix, there being extensive groves of them near the sea, almost all round the island. The tree on which this fruit grows is generally tall, and the limbs large: There is a milky juice distils from the leaf, that, should it fall on the face or hands, will immediately raise the most frightful blisters, and flay off the skin. The apples are counted deadly poison, although I have heard of women who, longing for them, greedily devoured five or six, without perceiving the least inconveniency.

†These races are very frequent in the leeward islands, and sometimes made for considerable sums; nay, horses are very often transported from one island to another for that purpose, and there is, in comparison, as much jockeying in the West-Indies, as at *New-Market* [Cambridgeshire site of horse races].

To cheer the straining coursers in their round.   180
Then oft th' indulgent youth leads to her seat
The blooming spouse, and by her beauteous side
Sits happy, time beguiling as they go,
With much endearing speech, and sweet content,
Which ease and affluence to the heart inspire: 185
For here the god of love oft revels high,
But Oh! too oft the avaricious sires,
For sake of gold, the tender lovers hearts
Asunder rend, and wound their childrens peace.
  The gay Philander, in the bloom of youth,   190
Whose soul (with lib'ral science richly stor'd)
Beam'd forth benevolent regard to all,
One tender she admir'd. Long he had dwelt
Beneath her father's roof, to bus'ness train'd,
In deep commercial schemes no mean adept;   195
For rich Avarus trusted to his care
The sole direction of his large concerns.
Tho' not to riches born, kind nature bless'd
The youth with all the choicest of her gifts;
A person elegant, a mind enlarg'd,   200
Susceptible of tenderness and love,
But with true greatness and with courage arm'd.
  The tender object of his gen'rous flame,
In shape and limb completely form'd, alas!
Few charms attractive in her looks could boast;   205
The fatal foe to beauty's cheek, long since,
In earliest youth had laid her beauty waste,[27]
Cropt the sweet rose, and, with an envious hand,
Rifled the blossoms of her lily skin:
But heav'n, indulgent, for the fatal loss   210
Full compensation made, and in its stead
Each grace the mind adorns, largely bestow'd;
In her bright soul seating angelic charms,
Such rare accomplishments as Britain's dames
In all their pride of youth and bloom display.   215
  Such was Aurelia, such the gentle youth,
When mutual passions warm'd their glowing breasts:
Ten years had pass'd, in which the lovers oft

Felt many a tender pang; in arts of love
Unskill'd they were, nor knew from whence the soft   220
Inchanting impulse sprung; still, as they grew,
The sweet affection rose by friendship's name,
Till friendship burst into a flame of love;
A flame which fear and prudence long conceal'd
From the stern father's penetrating eye,   225
For av'rice was the god of his desires.
      Such sordid parents prove their childrens bane;
And where the Hymenèal torch should blaze,
Discord and strife, vexation and despair,
Scatter, enrag'd, their fiery brands around.   230
      Philander, now, by industry possess'd
Of happy means to steer an easy course
Through the rough voyage of uncertain life
(For fortune dawn'd upon his first attempt)
With eager hope to gain his best belov'd,   235
Who, by endearments, sooth'd him to the task,
Flew to the presence of the rigid sire,
Told him the secret of their mutual love,
And, on his knees, implor'd th' unfeeling wretch,
To join two hands, whose hearts long since were join'd.   240
Enrag'd Avarus hears the fond request,
Reviles, upbraids, and spurns him from his feet.
Was it for this, he cries, I train'd thy youth,
And all the secrets of commercial gain
Implanted in thy breast? Or art thou lost   245
To gratitude so far, that thou'dst deprive
My feeble age of what I hold most dear?
Hence from my sight! these fost'ring mansions shun!
Avaunt, I say! nor trouble me in vain.
The youth, dejected, from the sire withdraws,   250
At his hard sentence shock'd; the pearly drops
Stole down his manly cheek; his noble heart,
With rage, with love, with indignation torn,
Broods o'er revenge, and meditates escape,
With his dear nymph, to some protecting pow'r,   255
Where British liberty should guard love's rights.
Mean while Avarus treats in cruel guise

His virt'ous daughter; prostrate on the earth,
To his detested threshold drags the maid,
Turns the harsh key, and leaves her drown'd in woe.   260
Philander, strait, the hagg'd duenna[28] seeks,
Who, for a well-tim'd fee, her trust betrays,
And to the hapless pair an interview
With art procures, shutting her Argus' eyes.
Quick at invention, love soon plann'd the scheme,   265
A bark's engag'd, the seas were lull'd to rest,
And gentle breezes aided the design;
When, at the hazard of his life and love,
Clasp'd in his arms Philander bears his prize
Swift to the beach, and hastily embarks.   270
His heart, elate, springs with extatic joy,
The gales arising swell the sleeping sails,
The watchful seaman chants his nightly lay,
And fond Philander tells his love-sick tale,
Till the slow morn appears, in roseate hue,   275
To grace the blest Aurelia's bridal day.
At length the wish'd-for gladsome hour arrives,
And in connubial bands the pair are join'd;
Philander in Aurelia's truly blest,
And she by him protected from the grasp   280
Of pow'r despotic, in a realm of peace,
Of justice, freedom, liberty, and love.
      But now the wand'ring muse, returning, points
Where the neat capital convenient lies,
Extending thro' the vales its ample bounds.   285
And, not content with circumscription, spreads
O'er two contiguous hills its mansions fair.
This beauteous spot a noble harbour boasts,
Where cautious mariners may safely moor
Their sea-beat barks,[29] and smile at threat'ning storms,   290
What time the Dog-star reigns,[30] and blazing fierce,
Autumnal Phoebus in th' equator shines;
Whilst the pale moon, full orb'd, encircled round
With hazy ring far distant from her sphere,
Starless, rides up th' orient path of Heav'n.   295
Then eastern winds no longer fan the sky,

But from th' unwholesome south hot breezes float
On wings contagious, and pollute th' air;
Or a dead calm ensues, or whiffling gales
O'er the smooth surface of the ocean creep,   300
Scarce wrinkling as they pass the glassy plain;
Then the light scuds from diff'rent quarters fly,
And low'ring clouds the darksome day obscure;
Fierce meteors blaze, and fiery vapours stream,
Thro' the thick concave of the gloomy night;   305
The livid lightnings flash, and balls of fire
Shoot o'er the singed surface of the earth;
Then heaving surges lash the sounding beach,
And south-west blasts, by currents strong oppos'd,
Drive the resisting waves with hollow noise   310
Upon the roaring strand, like thunder heard
Far off in distant clouds rumbling and hoarse:
Surge follows surge, the whit'ning breakers dash
Their hoary heads against the senseless rocks,
And in their rear, waves riding over waves,   315
Burst in a deluge on the trembling shore.
Then it behooves the skilful mariner
Careful to watch, and ride with tackle tough,
Lest he lament in vain his costly bark
Bulg'd on remorseless rocks, or useless plung'd   320
Fast in a bed of sand, a doleful sight!
When the loud tempest bellows thro' the deep,
And the dread hurricane affrights the ear
Of peaceful night, alarming nature's sons,
Yet some, incautious, oft their lab'ring barks   325
Neglect, forgetful of their freighted charge,
Whilst they to pleasure sacrifice the time,
Or, with the riotous debauch o'erwhelm'd,
In dangerous stews[31] intoxicated snore.
Others, more wise, prepare to ride the storm,   330
Or to th' approaching gale, with cautious hand,
Distrustfully extend the tim'rous sail,
And rather busk far off the raging deep,
Than trust their cordage to the restless winds,
Which now let loose, from out their caverns vast   335

Impetuous rush, and harrow up the deep.
From either pole the grumbling thunder rolls,
From ev'ry cloud the forked lightnings flash,
The dreadful storm from ev'ry quarter howls,
And the distracted deep runs mountains high;   340
Waves dash on waves, opposing foam to foam,
Th' insolent billows to the clouds ascend;
Wild rout and uproar thro' th' horizon reign,
The Heav'ns themselves, descending, seem to rush
From out their lofty spheres, and falling, mix   345
Celestial waters with the ocean brine.
Now, for a moment, all the weilkin[32] burns,
And one terrific blaze th' expanse inflames;
Ear-deaf'ning claps of thunder rend the air,
Kindling on high the elemental war,   350
Till with th' astounding crash all aether shakes:
Havock let loose, strews earth and seas around
With devastation wild; grim visag'd death
In various shapes appears, nor heeds the call
Of drowning wretches, who, with tearful eye,   355
And out-stretch'd arms, gasping their last, in vain
Implore a rescue from the wat'ry grave.
Here one awhile, undaunted, bold and strong,
Buffets the waves, and struggles with the storm;
Tho' well instructed in the swimmer's art,   360
In vain both hand and foot he stoutly plies,
Or, with the skilful stroke, plays on the wave,
Regardless of the furious dangers round;
Till weary grown, all spiritless and faint,
His languid limbs their wonted aid refuse: 365
Deep down beneath the wat'ry flood he sinks
O'erwhelm'd, soon he returns, aghast and pale,
Then eager strives, and on the surface toils;
Anon he cries aloud with mournful voice,
To earth, to seas, and man, with ceaseless tears,   370
But cries in vain, amidst the general wreck,
Nor earth, nor seas, nor man regard his pray'rs,
Here shatter'd barks lie tossing up and down,
Nor can their lacerated sides repel

The wasteful vengeance of the surly blasts;   375
For now the storm, increasing loud and high,
Renders the skilful pilot's art but vain;
Frantic confusion trammels up command,
From ev'ry quarter of the compass rage
The roaring winds, waging relentless war: 380
Heav'n, earth, and seas, the wild disorder aid,
Encreasing still the air-engender'd fray.
Here the stout prow the raging billows rides,
Once taught to humble to the rudder's beck,
But now, repugnant to command, she veers   385
With ev'ry blast, and drives before the storm.
Tremendous surges o'er the gilded poop
Impetuous sweep, and shatter all within:
The watchful mariner each danger views,
Trembling, aghast! nor can his skill direct   390
Aright what to command, or what forbid.
Th' inhospitable shore, with horror struck,
He dreads; and hears, or thinks he hears, appall'd,
The boist'rous surges bellowing on the rocks
With unavailing rage; too true, alas!   395
His boding fears inform! The billows break
With desp'rate force! the shore approaches nigh!
Whilst the huge-gathering surf impetuous rolls,
And the devoted bark high on the strand
Impels with ruinous shock, the dreary wreck   400
The rueful mariners forsake, quit the sad sight,
And wander thro' the storm-drench'd night forlorn.
Some vessels, with stout timber'd sides, awhile
The pityless storm's impetuous rage sustain,
But doom'd, alas! to still severer fate,   405
Scudding before two adverse winds they fly,
Or o'er the tops of heaving mountains dance;
Sometimes they seem the height of Heav'n to rise,
Dreading the hollow dismal vales below,
As Ach'ron deep, dark as infernal Styx:[33]   410
Sometimes, by wild outrageous blasts impell'd,
Deep down the wat'ry precipice they rush
With headlong speed, and from the gloomy pit,

The Heav'ns obscur'd behold, the blust'ring storm
Lab'ring they 'bide, and all at random roam,   415
Till, from two hollow seas rising, they meet,
And, with the surge, dash on each others bow
With force impetuous, and tremendous crash:
As when two bulls in furious combat meet,
And with ferocious ire their frontlets drive   420
Against each other in the bloody strife;
So these, in dang'rous fray encount'ring sore,
Engage, unwilling, and with dreadful force,
High o'er the waves uprear their fractur'd bows.
This plunges down, beneath the surface urg'd,   425
And found'ring sinks, with all her wretched crew.
That, too, had met the same distressful fate,
Had not cool prudence, in the pilot's breast
Unshaken, bore him thro' the dismal scene.
Now to the coast her shatter'd stem he plies,   430
Rather than perish in the raging deep;
Aghast the shore he seeks, and on the beach
Drives her devoted hull; then, with his crew,
Last quits the fatal scene, and from the sea
Turns his dejected eye, aiding the winds   435
With loud complaints and ceaseless piteous moan;
Whilst the new horrors of the land he views,
Sorely, with perils imminent beset,
For not less vex'd th' ruinous earth appears.
O'er nature's face the desolation spreads,   440
And thro' the gloom the tempest rushes wild;
The mountains from their firm foundations shake,
And rolling o'er their heads loud thunders crash;
The vallies tremble, whilst the frightful gust
With fatal blast destroys the hopeful field.   445
High over head, from sable clouds surcharg'd,
The streaming rains descend, and the huge floods
In wide extended sheets of waters rise,
O'er land dispreading vast extensive seas;
The furious whirl-winds gather in the vales,   450
And with destructive force uprend the earth;
Whilst torrents in collected bodies rush

With course impetuous from the mountain's height
Down the steep slopes, and deluge all the plain.
Rocks, stumps, and stones, and bulky trees they whirl   455
Adown their channels vast, with rumbling noise;
As once they say the furious gushing flood
Bore headlong with it from adjacent hills
The solid earth (sage men,* for truth renown'd,
This tale relate) then in main ocean fix'd   460
It firm foundation fast, and, for a while,
To antient Neptune a new island gave.
Mean while the blust'ring winds rage furious on;
High over head the spacious roof they bear
Of some gay lofty mansion; whirling it plays,   465
Like a light feather in a summer's breeze:
Dwellings entire, from strong foundations torn,
Are hurl'd from hill-tops to the neighb'ring plain;
The heads of huge enormous mills they send
To distance far, on hill or drenched vale;   470
Cattle, o'erborne, rush to the raging main,
And trees uptorn in rattling whirl-winds spin;
Earth to the deep her dreadful horrors sends,
And the mad deep worse horrors back returns;
Earth, air, and all the elements contend,   475
Till in the end, the howling tempest spent,
Ruin subsides, and all is hush'd around.
       Renewing filial and parental griefs,
Then frequent toll'd the doleful deep-mouth'd bell,
Foretelling the slow funeral's approach.   480
Distressful scene for melting hearts to view!
The wife, disconsolate, her widow'd bed
Bedew'd with tears forsakes; frantic she runs,
Lamenting, to her lord's new-open'd grave,
And, in a storm of passion, plunges in,   485
Eager to share his fate, and be interr'd
Alive with the dear object of her love.

*The honorable George Wyke, Esq; president of Montserrat when I was in that island, in-
formed me, that a huge piece of land was carried by the floods into the sea, at the mouth of Old
Road river; that it remained there some time, and that he himself had been on it, and fishing
round it.

Or else the lover, prostrate on the turf
Where all his joy's entomb'd, distracted raves;
Whilst the big tear bursts from his turgid eye,   490
And many an intervening sob breaks in,
Stopping th' impetuous torrent of his grief,
That vents its piteous moan, by turns, in vows,
In pray'rs, and passionate appeals to Heav'n.
        Ah me! how diff'rently th' untutor'd slave,   495
To no philosophy indebted, views
The obsequies of his departed friend,
And with his calm deportment puts to shame
The boasted reason of the polish'd world:
A moment dries his manly eye, untaught   500
To melt at death, the necessary end
Of all terrestrial things. His creed (the voice
Of nature) keeps him firm, nay, gives him joy,
When he considers (so the sages teach
Of Afric's sun-burnt realms) that the freed soul,   505
Soon as it leaves its mortal coil behind,
Transported to some distant world, is wrapt
In bliss eternal. There the man begins,
With organs more refin'd, to live again,
And taste such sweets as were deny'd him here,   510
The sweets of liberty. Oh glorious name!
Oh pow'rful soother of the suff'ring heart!
That with thy spark divine can'st animate
Unletter'd slaves to stretch their simple thoughts
In search of thee, beyond this gloomy vale   515
Of painful life, where all their piteous hours
Drag heavily along in constant toil,
In stripes,[34] in tears, in hunger, or in chains:
These are the ills which they rejoice to fly,
Unless, by partial chance, their lot is cast   520
Beneath some kind indulgent master's sway,
Whose hand, like their good genius, feeds their wants,
And with protection shields their helpless state.
        But see what strange procession hither winds,
With long continued stream, through yonder wood!   525
Like gentle waves hundreds of sable heads

Float onwards; still they move, and still they seem
With unexhausted flow to keep their course.
  In calm succession thus th' unruffled main
Rolls on its peaceful waters to the shore,   530
With easy swell, wave gliding over wave,
Till the spectator can no longer count
Their breaks incessant, but the numbers past
Are in succeeding numbers quickly lost.
Behold the white-rob'd train in form advance   535
To yonder new-made grave: Six ugly hags,
Their visage seam'd with honorary scars,
In wild contorsive postures lead the van;
High o'er their palsied heads, rattling, they wave
Their noisy instruments; whilst to the sound   540
In dance progressive their shrunk shanks keep time.
With more composure the succeeding ranks,
Chanting their fun'ral song in chorus full,
Precede the mournful bier, by friendly hands
Supported: Sudden stops the flowing line;   545
The puzzled bearers of the restive corps[35]
Stand for a while, fast rooted to the ground,
Depriv'd of motion, or, perhaps, impell'd
This-way, or that, unable to proceed
In course direct, until the troubled dead   550
Has to some friend imparted his request;
That gratify'd, again the fun'ral moves:
When at the grave arriv'd the solemn rites
Begin; the slave's cold reliques gently laid
Within their earthy bed, some veteran   555
Among the sable Archimages,* pours
Her mercenary panegyric forth,
In all the jargon of mysterious speech,
And, to compose the spirit of the dead,
Sprinkles his fav'rite liquor on the grave.   560
This done, the mourners form a spacious ring,
When sudden clangours, blended with shrill notes,

---

*i.e. chief magicians among the Obeah negroes.—*This word is often used by Spencer.* [E.g., see *Faerie Queene* 1.1.43.6.]

Pour'd forth from many a piercing pipe, surprize
The deafen'd ear. Nor Corybantian[36] brass,
Nor rattling sistrum, ever rung a peal   565
So frantic, when th' Idaean dactyli[37]
At their intoxicated feasts ran wild,
Dizzily weaving the fantastic dance,
And with extended throats proclaiming high
Their goddess Rhea,[39] thro' the giddy croud.   570
Thus do these sooty children of the sun,
"Unused to the melting mood,"[39] perform
Their fun'ral obsequies, and joyous chaunt,
In concert full, the requiem of the dead;
Wheeling in many a mazy round, they fill   575
The jocund dance, and take a last farewell
Of their departed friend, without a tear.

The end of the Third Book.

The FOURTH BOOK.
The ARGUMENT.

Address to the guardian angel of these climes.—A view of Barbados, sailing down the windward coast.—Grateful mention of a few select friends.—A description of the Mount and Gardens, and of the face of the country in general.—Scotland.—Mount Hellibe.—Run-away grounds, and astonishing gullies.—Cole's Cave and its wonders; occasional digression thereon.—The spout and animal flower philosophically described, and animadverted on.—The art of skinning the Face, &c. for a complexion, in what island used.—Advice most humbly offer'd to the consideration of the inhabitants in general.—Conclusion.

BOOK IV.

Thou guardian angel of this western ind,
Beneath the shadow of whose anxious wing
The blest inhabitants of these fair climes
Taste life's best comforts, unallay'd with pain,
And, strangers to those various ills that waste   5
Europa's sons, feel their soft hours glide on
Indulgently in elegance and ease,
Vouchsafe with me, thy much devoted bard,
To bend thy flight tow'rds yonder seeming cloud,
Which to th' approaching voyager unfolds,   10
By sweet degrees improving on the sight,

That view which most thou lov'st; that happy spot
Where thy Barbados feasts the ravish'd sense
With such a prospect as fair *Tempe*[40] once,
Or blest *Elysium* to the poet's eye   15
Presented, when in extasy he snatch'd
His harp, and boldly swept the speaking strings,
Bursting into a rhapsody of joy.
Oh! had I equal energy! my song,
Rising in just proportion to my theme,   20
Full of the love and gratitude I owe,
Should waft like incense o'er thy fav'rite isle,
The duteous tribute of thy poet's praise.
Blest isle, an abler pen thy praise demands!
Fairest, and first, of all thy sister train,   25
Spread num'rous thro' the vast Atlantic deep.
When first my ravish'd eye thy beauties caught,
To me another Paradise appear'd;
Gardens and palaces in mingled scenes
Rose to my view, and each a villa seem'd   30
Of some proud lord; as on Italia's shore
They stately rise, magnificent and grand:
Oh! how I once enjoy'd thee! blissful seat
Of love, of friendship, and of social joy!
Me thou receiv'd'st, with arms extended wide,   35
And thro' a series of indulgent years
Steep'd me in bliss complete; each day was crown'd
With happiness, each night with soft repose.
Whether with thee, exalted gen'rous S****,[41]
Mirthful, elated, all my mind at ease,   40
Warmly embrac'd by friendship's sacred arm,
Joyful I sat, and with the jovial group
Of friends select, laugh'd the short hours away;
Or, when by music's* soft attractive pow'r
Impell'd, we tun'd our instruments to joy,   45
High roll'd the tides of social pleasure then,
Whilst Pinder[42] with superior judgment sung,
And much-lov'd Horace† touch'd the trembling strings

*A concert was held by a set of gentlemen at their own houses, alternately.
†Mr. Horace Pine.

In manner exquisite, and taste refin'd.
How have I list'ning sat, elate to hear   50
Facetious worthy W***f**d chant his lay?
Or loyal Pierce to war and vict'ry tune,
Whilst the loud chorus round the table rung?
But ah! those happy days are now no more!
Yet mayst thou live in affluence and ease,   55
Belov'd and honor'd by that social band
Where peace and harmony conspicuous shine,
And soft-ey'd charity for ever smiles;
There mayst thou long with gentle sway preside,
And fill with dignity the mystic chair.*   60
  Hail, fairest Mount![†] thy antient mansions hail!
To thee old Ocean bows; and as he rolls,
Reflects thy beauties, whilst beneath thy feet,
Thy venerable feet, rich vallies rise,
And rip'ning harvests cover ev'ry slope.   65
All that the western ind can proudly boast,
Nice art and nature there combin'd bestow;
A garden fair and large, with all fruits stor'd,
Herbs of all scents, and flow'rs of ev'ry hue:
Delightful spot for ornament and use,   70
Richly with taste and elegance design'd.
Here all the gen'rous host demands to spread
His ample board, the cultur'd soil affords;
Thick stately woods, in walks diagonal,
Appear majestic, and to shade invite;   75
Long alleys green, and arbours wide and cool,
Present their calm retreats; where oft I sat,
And wrapt in pleasing solitude and thought,
At Contemplation's stream I drank and sipt,
The charms of sweet retirement and of peace.   80
  Thee, Oh my Florio,[‡] grateful I address;
How shall I sing thy worth? What words can paint
Thy undissembled truth and gen'rous love,
To me extended with a lib'ral hand?

*John Stone, Esq; was then Provincial Grand Master of Masons.
†The Estate of the honorable Jonathan Blenman, Esquire.
‡Hen. B - - - -s, Esq. [Note from the second edition, 1776.]

Stand forth, undaunted, in a virtuous cause,   85
And plead bold truths, deck'd with becoming speech;
For, bless'd by Nature with her choicest gifts,
A person elegant, a modest mein,
A mind instructed in each mystic page
Of artful law; a soul compassionate,   90
A heart to feel for objects of distress;
A happy genius to redress the poor,
And sweetest elocution to support
The injur'd client, and restore his right;
She now consigns your service to the bar.   95
Arm'd, then, against injustice and disguise,
With Ciceronean eloquence defend
The infant *ward* from the fell guardian's gripe;
The suff'ring widow from oppression snatch,
Arise for justice, and convince mankind   100
That truth and reason constitute the law.
      Should I, to celebrate thy worth presume,
My dearest Wh****n, I should sing all day;
But I forbear to raise the gen'rous blush
In learned modesty's ingenuous cheek.   105
Thy merits, worthy of a better muse,
Shall shine conspicuous to th' admiring world,
When, with his humble page, thy poet lies
In deep oblivion bury'd; yet pursue
Thy noble task, my friend, and thro' the paths   110
Of erudition lead the docile youth;
The rising genius form; teach the young mind,
Imbu'd with science, to enlarge its views,
And follow virtue, the sure road to peace.
Born, as thou art, with ease to exercise   115
Thy sacred function, speak the will divine,
Its laws explain; whilst bright example's weight
Gives strength and credit to the truths you preach.
But let me not attempt too great a task,
The praise of all that in Barbadian land   120
Are worthy praise to celebrate; alas!
My infant muse would sink beneath the load.
      Yet let me visit thy delightful plains,

Thou lovely Eden of the western isles,
Where Nature scatters, with a lavish hand,   125
Like a fond parent, all her choicest stores,
Marking, with partial eye, her darling spot.
The wide-extended prospect all around
Delightful scenes presents; each pleasant vale
Boasts its particular charms, and ev'ry hill,   130
Rising with easy slopes to gradual height,
Gives to the landscape sweet variety.
Thickly, around, the spacious mansions view,
With palms o'ershaded, or the tam'rind broad;
See! the nut-bearing coco's ample branch   135
Extends its leafy fans, and on the slave
Refreshing shade bestows, when on the ground
Humbly he sits to taste his noon-tide meal.
See yon majestic avenue* extend
In long array its rows of stately palms,   140
Which, like august Corinthian columns rise,
Waving aloft their flowing capitals,
Worthy to mark the temple of a god.
     Next, Fontabelle,† thy beauties let me sing!
Where oft in groves umbrageous I have trod,   145
Poring the melancholy tragic page:
Thy secret paths, thy rude embow'ring woods
To lonely solitude invite; by Nature form'd
To please the pensive mind, indulging woe.
Or in these shades the happy youthful pairs   150
Might wander with delight, and tell sweet tales
Of love, beguiling night, whilst the bright moon
Darts thro' the shading trees her silver beams,
And in the stream to ev'ry eye presents
Fair images of ev'ry object round.   155
     Now view the north of rich Barbadian land,
Where gloomy Hellebe his head erects,
And Caledonian hills in ridges spread
Enormous ranges to the roaring sea;

*At the estate in St. Thomas's called Farmers, now in the possession of Jonas Maynard, Esq.
     †The property of Mr. Martin.

Beneath whose feet the cheerful vallies smile,   160
And boast fertility that's not their own;
Whilst weeping hills their barrenness bewail,
Robb'd* of their native soil, which slides in flakes
With rapid force down their smooth slimy sides.
What time rough Boreas, with tempestuous blasts,   165
Rends up the solid earth, and torrents broad
Of thick descending rains rush from the heads
Of sloping hills, and sweep their sides away,
From the steep clift swift move the loosen'd canes,
And Devastation with her iron hand   170
Smites the afflicted earth; his sanguine hopes
Then oft the hapless planter sees destroy'd,
And where the canes their verdant blades uprear'd,
Gracing their gen'rous parent's teeming breast,
The face of Nature's chang'd, and nought but stones,   175
Or solid rocks, or barren sands appear.
More wonders yet! still more tremendous sights!
Thy curious search shall lead thee to explore:
And the dark melancholy gullies view,
Where dismal gloom and silence stilly reigns;   180
Save when the torrents with impetuous rush
Roll down the steeps and tear their entrails up,
Forcing a dreary pass thro' all they meet,
To mix their waters with parental seas.
      The curious nat'ralist, in this fair isle,   185
May find full scope for contemplation deep;
But pain and peril must attend his search,
Who would explore the subterraneous works
Of Providence, where Nature, as in sport,
Seems to have form'd a wild delusive scene,   190
To try the wisdom of vain shallow man;
Who, oft dismay'd by horrors such as these,
Has fondly thought, of old, in Pagan lands,
Some deity must needs inhabit there.
The mouths of these tremendous caves who dar'd   195

*In great floods the land on the sides of hills on the Clift and in *Scotland* [area in the north side of Barbados], slides away and settles in the low lands, thereby vastly impoverishing the one, and enriching the other.

Of mortal frame to pass? Thence groans and sounds
Of voices more than human issued forth,
And clanking chains were sometimes heard to fall,
Within the bowels of the awful den.
By cypress groves, and melancholy yew,   200
(Too sacred to be touch'd by ax profane)
Deep shrouded in a dim religious shade,
Which mortal fears had to each fancy show'd
More horrid still than to th' unbias'd eye
(Which ne'er thro' superstition's medium look'd)   205
The place in truth appear'd. With me descend,
If your heart fail not, into that steep cave
Which takes its name from Cole. Whether he first
Adventur'd down its frightful jaws, and gave
Its story to the gaping crowd, concerns   210
Not our inquiry: 'Tis enough to know
Its dreadful entrance in the hideous depth
Of a steep gully lies; where mould'ring clifts
Threaten to topple on th' advent'rer's head;
And uncouth rocks, of height enormous, peep   215
Between the gloomy tufts of branching trees.
Nor too secure, nor yet with fear, approach
The grim descent. Security, sometimes
Destroys the flush'd assailant, whilst chill'd fear
Deprives each corporal agent of its pow'rs,   220
And turns the coward to a lifeless clod.
Whilst down the craggy precipice you slide,
With vigilant eye, and cautious grasp, lay hold
Of all assistance in your slippery way:
Branch, twig, sharp-pointed stone, or root of tree,   225
Nor quit your hold with one, till t' other hand
Within its well-fix'd gripe has fast secur'd
Some help that's equal to sustain your weight;
For if you fall, you fall to rise no more.
When on the dewy bottom first you fix   230
Your aching feet, and all the danger's past,
You find yourself immur'd betwixt two rocks
Of monst'rous height, whose summits here and there
Let in, thro' mould'ring crevices, a light,

Glimmering like that which once (as Maro[43] sings)   235
Scar'd the thin subjects of grim Pluto's realms,
And made them scud to find a thicker gloom.
Various apartments here diversify
This subterraneous grotto: fit recess
For fam'd Aegeria,[44] or that prophetess   240
Sybilla[45] call'd, who, wrapt in times to come,
The fate of Rome in precious volumes told.
On either hand, and o'er the vaulted roof,
Thick incrustations, and clear icicles,
Distilling many a chrystal drop, appear.   245
Here you may see a limpid bason shine,
Reflecting ev'ry light that blazes round
This damp abode, and shews its hidden stores;
Whilst at a distance murm'ring waters break
The melancholy silence of the cave,   250
And with sweet draughts refresh the traveller,
Exhausted by fatigue and want of air;
There, when you've labour'd thro' a ruggid cleft,
(Tho' few dare go so far) ten thousand birds
Of night,[46] awaken'd by th' unwelcome torch,   255
Flapping their leathern wings, fly round the flame.
        But let us seek again the upper world,
And in the sunshine bask our chilly limbs:
There, from our fears releas'd, the mind at ease
May freely ruminate on those wise ends   260
Which these deformities in Nature's vast
Delightful landscape serve. Nor rock, nor cave,
Grotto, nor dread volcano's store-house, fill'd
With fire and vapours to alarm the sons
Of sinful man (just scourges of their crimes)   265
Have, in our worldly system, but to some
Great use been plac'd, by that almighty hand
Which governs all below. Our earthly globe,
Without these seeming foils, to its rare form
Might, probably, by dire succussions[47] torn,   270
For ever labour with convulsive throes,
Such as, pent up, wou'd dreadful havock make,
And shock the peace of man; whilst that great Pow'r

Whom all created beings must adore,
Would, by his trembling children, be more fear'd   275
Than worshipp'd, and his mercy, wonderful,
Ineffable to man, seem less divine.
      Next let us view what stores the waters yield;
To philosophic minds each element
Presents alike themes inexhaustible   280
Of silent wonder; whilst th' admirer, wrapt
In contemplation, hears still Nature's voice,
Thro' all her works, speak her Creator's praise.
      Near that fam'd spot where Ocean's angry waves,*
Within a rock's impending cavern pent,   285
With indignation force their rapid way,
And dart their foaming columns to the skies,
Inventive Nature (whose minutest works
Frequent display perfection most complete)
Within her secret habitations, long   290
Had treasur'd up, from vulgar eye conceal'd,
A prize which yet the sage philosopher
Never found class'd among his wonder's rare.
A flow'r it seems to less discerning eyes,[48]
But with true judgment view'd, the choice deceit   295
Gives signs of life and motion visible:
Not like the plant so celebrated once
By botanists, which sensitive is call'd;
That, like a sluggard, first must feel the stroke
Of th' assaulting hand, e'er it contracts   300
Its shrinking leaves, and shews a seeming sense:
But this, impatient of th' approaching touch,
Surprizes the spectator, who attempts,
Unthinkingly, to crop it for a flow'r.
No sooner is the hand stretch'd out in act,   305
To seize its little curious blooming prey,
Then th' eager fingers the delusion find,
And, losing the bright substance, press the air.
      Now let us visit the secure recess
Which Nature's hand enriches with these rare   310

*The Spout in St. Lucy's parish.

Marine productions.—Follow me, your guide,
To yonder point, and then, with steady eye,
The perils of the rocky clift survey,
Which looks, with rugged aspect, tow'rds the sea.
A steep descent your sliding feet must pass   315
'Ere you arrive within the spacious cave
That leads you to the object of your wish:
Whilst down the rock's rough sides you cautious try
To fix your painful steps, be not dismay'd
If the contending waves below should break   320
Incessant o'er your head, and from the top
Of this dread clift fall down in rattling sheets,
And drench your trembling limbs; firmly support
The brisk attack, till down the slipp'ry rock
(More slipp'ry made by this impetuous fall   325
Of waters) safe descended, you can gain
A resting place, and view the dangers past.
A wide extended cave first meets your eye,
Spacious enough for Neptune and his court
To revel in, whene'er the god should deign   330
With his wav'd trident to becalm the sea,
And view the surface of his wat'ry realms.
        The roof, imboss'd with incrustations hard,
Thro' slender tubes its limpid dews distils.
        Near this, a cave of smaller size attracts   335
Your eye; its bottom forms a standing pool
Of clearest water, briny as the wave
That from old Ocean's neighb'ring plain supplies
This standing bason with its frequent surge.
        Fast in the midst there stands a rock, that hides   340
Beneath the water's top its humble head.
Around its well-lav'd sides, at various depths,
These flow'rs, of wond'rous kind, perennial rise,
Resembling much the pale and love-sick hue
Of the jonquil, when delicate it wafts   345
From some fair bosom its soft languid sweets.
A tinge of green its variegated form
Most pleasingly irradiates: But to pluck
These tempting beauties from their rocky bed,

Wou'd seem a work for Tantalus himself.   350
Elusive to the touch, 'ere that arrives
To discompose its nice formation, back
With imperceptible retreat it flies
Into its hollow habitation; coy
As th' young virgin 'ere she feels the lip   355
Of her lov'd swain, whose soft enchanting kiss
Conveys a thrilling transport to her soul.
    Anon, some minutes counted, see the flow'r
Again advancing gradually in sight,
And opening cautiously its seeming leaves;   360
Till it appears in all its former bloom.
But shou'd th' admirer's restless hand again,
Darted with quickest motion, strive to seize
Th' alluring object, instantly again
It will recoil, reluctant to the touch.   365
    Wond'rous appearance this, that seems to speak
A being far superior to the class
Of vegetable things, which, justly rang'd,
In Nature's lowest order hold their rank;
Nor does it only *seem* to claim a place   370
Superior to the flow'ring class; convinc'd
By close inspection and attentive view,
Whoever sees with philosophic eyes,
Must soon perceive this seeming flow'r endu'd
With life no less than *animal.* What seem'd   375
Before like chives which from the center rose,
Now, like the spinner's slender legs, with quick
Spontaneous motion play around its sides.
    With these (if probable conjecture may
Be offer'd where experiment's untry'd)   380
'Twou'd seem that Providence, whose mercy reigns
O'er all his works, most wisely furnishes
This little creature, for the useful end
Of feeling out its food which, when (allur'd
By the bright colours of the shining rim)   385
The floating animalcules chance to reach,
With ease, these *feelers,* plying all around
Like forceps, seize their destin'd provender.

These are the island's treasures: Now its plagues
Demand a thought—a thought which the fond muse,   390
Trembling, suggests; unwilling to offend,
Yet studious to reform by soft advice
Where'er she finds a flaw. Know then, ye fair,
Among your plagues I count the negro race,
Savage by nature. Art essays in vain   395
To mend their tempers, or to tune their souls
In unison with ours: No doctrines touch
Their callous senses; no instruction wakes
Their drowsy faculties, nor bends their will,
Perverse and obstinate, to reason's lure.   400
Cruel and fierce, no admonitions tame
The brutal disposition of their souls;
Nor can "philosophy's sweet milk"[49] e'er quench
The flame that ever and anon springs up
To curse their beings, and to torture ours.   405
Then take, ye fair, the counsels of the muse,
Since for your peace, your happiness she sings.
If in the hymeneal state ye live,
And to your loves a happy offspring rise,
Should Nature to the mother's tender breast   410
The flowing streams of nutriment refuse,
Or sickness lessen her maternal care,
O! rather use all art the babes to rear,
Than e'er condemn them to the sable pap's
Infectious juice! for, with the milky draught,   415
The num'rous vices of the fost'ring slave
Deep they imbibe, and, with their life's support,
Draw in the latent principles of ill;
Which, brooking no controul, in riper years,
Grow with their growth, and strengthen with their strength.   420
Nor, when the babes to prattling years arrive,
Let fondling parents, or relations dear,
Teach the apt tongue an horrid oath to lisp,
Or phrase obscene; nor frame the ductile lips
Of innocence to utterance vile and base.   425
Taint not the minds with cruelty and rage,
Nor wantonly indulge a savage joy

To practice torments on the hapless slave;
Such dispositions ill become your sex,
Which but disgrace the rougher character   430
Of boist'rous man, the lord of all below,
Of man, whom your soft charms in bondage hold.
Exert your empire then, when rage hath rais'd
A storm which only beauty can allay;
Oh! then let meek compassion strongly plead   435
In the moist eye, then drop the melting tear,
And let a look, soft as the new-born babe's,
Disarm th' impending hand, and save the wretch,
Crouching beneath the vengeance of his lord.
    But most, oh! most beware of passion's gust;   440
That hellish phrenzy, cherish'd in the mind,
Reason dethrones, and sets a daemon there.
Soon shall the wrinkle those arch'd brows deform,
On which stern Anger oft triumphant sits.
    Whene'er the wretch, stretch'd on his parent, Earth, 445
Or to the stake fast bound, his pain endures
Of flaggelation dire, be far away,
And, if you can't prevent, urge not his fate.
    As Heav'n has form'd ye beautiful and fair,
Be wise, be good, be tender, and be kind,   450
And rather seek by gentle arts to win,
Your truant lord back to his joyless bed,
Too oft allur'd by Ethiopic charms,
And sinful made by an impetuous wife;
Be chaste, obedient, mild, sedate, and true,   455
With tender blandishments, and words of love
Reclaim your weaned spouse, meet him with smiles,
Let him find certain happiness at home,
And he'll not fly to looser joys abroad.
But above all, one impious act avoid,   460
If you wou'd beauteous live belov'd of man,
Ne'er steal in secret to remote abodes,
The desp'rate experiment to try
Of adding roses to the sallow cheek;*

---

*This desperate act of skinning the hands and face is thus performed; they bury the

Rather the freckled skin submissive bear,   465
Or face imbrown'd by Sol's irradiant beam,
Than practice such unwarrantable arts,
By fiends devis'd, by wrinkled hags perform'd,
With hellish spells, and damn'd ingredients stor'd.
And ye, experienc'd dames, for shame, desist,   470
Nor urge, by bold audacious speech profane,
The faultless fair to mend the work of God.
Fond nymph, what beauty does thy suff'rings add,
What charm increase, t' attract the lover's eye?
Know ye the mighty hazard which ye run   475
To gain the slight complexion of a day?
If chance the trickling tears shou'd plenteous start,
Impell'd by horrid pains, till then unfelt;
Or if the foul infernal mask shou'd turn,
Thy native beauty is for ever lost,   480
And in its stead distorted features rise,
With loss of sight perhaps; just judgment shewn,
As once it was on that presumptuous she
Who skinn'd at length her precious eyes away.
You great Creator dare not thus offend;   485
Did he not form ye lovely, soft, and fair,
And ev'ry feature to advantage place?
He gave you beauty to attract mankind,
Sufficient beauty; yet ye covet more.
Haughty of heart, and insolently proud,   490
Ye practice arts that beauty to increase;
His pow'r insult, his work complete destroy:
But know that momentary face ye own,
Got with the loss of many days ill spent,
Shall be the admiration of an hour;   495

---

cashew-nuts for nine days, then extract a poisonous juice, which, with a feather, they lay lightly
on the skin; this raises one continued blister, the head is swelled to an enormous size, the patient
must lie in one posture, and before the skin or mask of the face comes off, it turns black, and the
person so suffering becomes an horrid spectacle, being unable to smile, or even speak, or taste
any sustenance but through a quill.—Far be it from me to charge the ladies in general residing
in the West-Indies with this abominable practice. I must with justice acknowledge that until I
arrived at Montserrat, I never once heard of such an action, and I am not inclined to believe it a
general fault even in that or any other of the islands. If any should be offended at this relation, I
beg leave to say with the poet, *Quae, capit, illa facit.*

Shall no duration claim, but fade away
Like flow'rs that droop when the warm sun disdains
His cheering beams to lend; from pale to wan,
From wan to sallow hue, each face shall turn;
Such false deceitful charms the air shall blast,   500
And ev'ry wind the tender visage meets
Shall steal some beauty thence; till in the end,
All wrinkled, wither'd, hagg'd, ye sink with shame,
'Ere little more than half your days are spent,
To worse deformity than age sustains.   505
Then preserve beauty at a cheaper rate
And learn this truth, brighter your charms appear
In native hue, adorn'd with comely dress,
Than shall the vain coquette when she with paints,
And with a thousand washes artful daubs.   510
If you are fair, and would continue so,
These rules observe—Breathe the fresh morning air
'Ere Sol's fierce blaze obtains; with gentle pace
Walk forth, or on the ambling steed repair
To visit neighb'ring fields and wholesome springs,   515
And of their min'ral waters freely sip;
Or bid the milky udder yield its streams,
To furnish beauty with a healthful draught:
In the young cheek the rose and lily bloom,
When the veins thus with crimson tides are fed.   520
        Attend, ye sons of Caribbean lands,
For now to you the muse presuming speaks,
Intent on Reformation's arduous task.
From the destructive slumber rouze at once,
Nor in your odious lethargy dream on!   525
Awake at Nature's, Virtue's call, awake!
Shun the false lure of Ethiopic charms.
Wherein consists their beauty or their grace?
Perhaps the dark complexion of the slave
The eye enjoys, and in an aspect foul   530
Wanton delights, enraptur'd to behold
Deformity of features, shape and soul;
Detested composition! made more vile
By th' unsightly fashion of their garbs:

Or does the sable miss then please you most,   535
When from her tender delicate embrace
A frouzy fragrance all around she fumes?
Can such intice? For shame! the vice reform.
But above all, your marriage contracts keep,
Nor from the nuptial bed, at midnight hour,   540
With hasty steps depart, and leave forlorn
The pining fair, thro' the long night to sigh,
Torn with heart-rending jealousy and love!
O! strange infatuation of the soul!
Can youth and beauty claim no pow'r to please,   545
Nor virtuous love assert it's empire here?
Or, can the frightful negro visage charm,
Thro' vague variety, or wanton lust,
Whilst the blind fool an angel's bosom quits,
To pillow in a fiend's unnat'ral arms,   550
Where the fond master oft succeeds his slave?
Nor is the blame less just, as some may think,
Tho' the lewd spark the tawny shou'd prefer
To shining jet: Alas! that tawny draws
Its copper hue from such an odious source,   555
As Heav'n ne'er pointed out to nobler souls,
Form'd to be blest with elegant desires,
And to communicate the virtuous joy
To objects truly worthy of their love.
        Whene'er the slave a venial crime commits,   560
Th' hard'ning lash of public justice spare:
With gentle hand a mild correction deal,
For cruel treatment steels the stubborn mind,
And frequent stripes a callous skin create.
Think not I mean to banish from the land   565
Correction's useful stroke; or that the wretch
For heinous crimes unpunish'd shou'd remain:
Yet to the fault the punishment adapt.
Neither too lenitive, not too severe;
But, above all, no needful food with-hold,   570
And, parsimonious, stint the toiling slave,
Whilst you in pride and superfluity
Wallow content, nor heed thy servant's wants.

Too oft, alas! such practice, vile, prevails:
Oft have I seen th' unthrifty master shine   575
In gay magnificence, and pompous shew,
Whilst the poor slave, who labours to support
The wild profusion of his costly joys,
Fatigu'd by toil, and with sharp hunger torn,
For the bare life-sustaining morsel pines.   580
Such inhumane and sordid schemes reject,
And treat with justice those by whom ye live:
So shall the toilsome task of labour run
Far less tormenting thro' the torrid day,
And cheerful eyes survey th' arduous work;   585
So shall the slave with grateful heart repay
His gen'rous master's care, and bounteous love.
    Tho' by hard fortune he is doom'd to toil,
And never taste the sweets of liberty;
Yet know, thou lordly owner of his flesh,   590
His sable body cloaths a human soul,
To passion's impulse feelingly alive
As well as thine.—Not many years have pass'd
Since young Castalio,[50] in the prime of life,
Us'd with his sable Chloe to resort   595
Where a thick shade of tufted trees o'erspread
His aged parent's venerated grave.
There, aw'd by the religion of the place,
They lavish'd forth their vows and sighs sincere,
Till love at length united the fond pair.   600
But oh! that union prov'd the worst of ills
To both. Some moons had wasted, when the maid
In pregnancy advancing, caught the eye
Of her stern mistress; who, wrapt up in hopes
Of sordid gain, saw nature's gentle course   605
Monthly approaching to that destin'd point
When the poor slave no longer wou'd endure
Her usual toil, but sink beneath the task,
And, useless, bear no burthen but her own.
Strait were the cruel orders issued forth   610
Of separation, chastisement, and stripes:
Imprisonment, chains, tortures, death itself,

Was the hard doom, if e'er the lovers dar'd
Again to steal an am'rous interview,
Or to indulge soft Nature's dictates more.   615
Oft had Castalio, 'ere he gain'd his love,
Despairing, wander'd thro' the lonely night,
And to the forked light'ning bar'd his breast
Undaunted; nor, till now, had ever felt
A shock like that, which th' afflicting news   620
Of separation gave his drooping soul.
Alas! he knew the doom was fix'd, the word
Was past, irrevocably past; never again
Must he enjoy his Chloe's fond embrace.
Confin'd within a noisome dungeon's bounds   625
She lay, while all access was cruelly
Deny'd to her Castalio. Love, despair,
Rage, ev'ry wild emotion of the soul,
Seiz'd the unhappy lover's frantic brain.
Vacant his look, his eye-balls rolling, forth   630
He rush'd, and, with involuntary speed,
Raving he flew to the once happy spot
Where many a sigh and plighted vow has pass'd;
There, on the green sod, flooded with his tears,
He dash'd him down, and with a groan expir'd.   635
        Hence learn, ye fair, what Nature prompts the muse
(However partial to her fav'rite isles)
With gentlest lesson to inculcate: Learn,
That wheresoever Heav'n hath set its seal,
"To give the world assurance of a man,"[51]   640
Whether that being is to slav'ry doom'd,
Or shares an happier fate, yet, man is man,
And claims a milder treatment than the beast,
Who to his elemental dust returns,
And perishing, without the joyful hope   645
Of an *hereafter,* into nothing falls!
Learn, too, that mercy and benevolence
Ne'er shine with half that lustre, half that grace,
As when they're blended with a beauteous form.
Then only are the female charms complete,   650
When beauty, by its soft example, sets

The world a pattern of humanity.
    But now, my muse, whose timid pinion strove,
Not without pain, thus far to hold its course,
Here rests her wing; presumptuous deem her not,   655
Nor arrogantly rude, if from her tongue
Rash speech hath dropt, rash errors to reclaim.
Pardon her freedom, for she's British born,
And boasts no merit but an honest heart!
Submit to kiss the rod, by justice held,   660
Nor, falsely reas'ning, check the rising blush
Which Nature, passing sentence on herself
(Like an impartial judge in her own cause)
With sweet humility repentant wears.
So shall your virtues ripen day by day;   665
Such virtues as indear the marriage tie,
Such virtues as inspire the patriot's soul;
Or such as fill the artist's fertile mind,
When, thro' a length of useful study form'd,
The rich conception rises into life,   670
And proves a gen'ral blessing to mankind.
                  FINIS

"Carmen, or, An Ode," FROM *A History of Jamaica*

FRANCIS WILLIAMS
(b. 1697–1712, d. 1762–74)

Most of what is known about Francis Williams comes from volume 2, book II of Edward Long's three-volume *History of Jamaica* (1774). Long was an apologist for the slave system and what we would now call a virulent racist; he translated and published the following Latin ode by Williams in an attempt to discredit the literary ability of Jamaica's most educated free black as part of a program to buttress slavery by "proving" the inferiority of people of African ancestry. Long's attempt backfired, however: not only did he help preserve for posterity Williams's skill as a poet and Latinist, but he also provided an adept translation of the poem. Long even provides footnotes detailing which classical and Biblical texts Williams draws on in his ode, thereby inadvertently demonstrating the breadth of Williams's learning.

Williams's life story, detailed below by Long, was well known in his lifetime and may have been the inspiration for Robert Robertson's invention of John Talbot Campo-bell, whose 1736 *Speech* is included in this anthology.

The subject of Williams's welcome ode, George Haldane, arrived in Jamaica in April 1759. A native of Perthshire, Scotland, Haldane spent a career in the army before securing the Duke of Newcastle's appointment as brigadier general and governor of Jamaica. En route to his new post, Haldane commanded troops under General Peregrine Hopson in the expedition against the French West Indies, helping to conquer Guadeloupe in the spring of 1759. As a Scot, his appointment was not well received by the English planters in Jamaica, so Williams's welcome ode ought to be understood as being against the popular sentiment among powerful whites in the colony. Haldane died of a "putrid fever" in early August 1759, less than four months after taking office.

FROM

THE HISTORY OF *JAMAICA.* OR, GENERAL SURVEY OF THE ANTIENT AND MODERN STATE OF THAT ISLAND: WITH

Reflections on its Situation, Settlements, Inhabitants, Climate, Products, Commerce, Laws, and Government.

IN THREE VOLUMES. ILLUSTRATED WITH COPPER PLATES. . . .

LONDON: PRINTED FOR T. LOWNDES IN FLEET-STREET. MDCCLXXIV
[1774].

Chapter IV. FRANCIS WILLIAMS.

I have forborne till now to introduce upon the stage a personage, who made a conspicuous figure in this island, and even attracted the notice of many in England. With the impartiality that becomes me, I shall endeavour to do him all possible justice; and shall leave it to the reader's opinion, whether what they shall discover of his genius and intellect will be sufficient to overthrow the arguments, I have before alledged, to prove an inferiority of the Negroes to the race of white men. It will by this time be discovered, that I allude to *Francis Williams,* a native of this island, and son to John and Dorothy Williams, free Negroes. Francis was the youngest of three sons, and, being a boy of unusual lively parts, was pitched upon to be the subject of an experiment, which, it is said, the Duke of Montagu[1] was curious to make, in order to discover, whether, by proper cultivation, and a regular course of tuition at school and the university, a Negroe might not be found as capable of literature as a white person. In short, he was sent to England, where he underwent a regular discipline of classic instruction at a grammar school, after which he was fixed at the university of Cambridge, where he studied under the ablest preceptors, and made some progress in the mathematics. During his abode in England, after finishing his education, it is said (I know not with what truth) that he composed the well-known ballad of "Welcome, welcome, brother debtor, &c." But I have likewise heard the same attributed to a different author. Upon his return to Jamaica, the duke would fain have tried his genius likewise in politics, and intended obtaining for him a privy seal, or appointment to be one of the governor's council; but this scheme was dropped, upon the objections offered by Mr. Trelawny, the governor at that time. Williams therefore set up a school in Spanish Town, which he continued for several years, where he taught reading, writing, Latin, and the elements of the mathematics; whilst he acted in this profession, he selected a Negroe pupil, whom he trained up with particular care, intending to make him his successor in the school; but of this youth it may be said, to use the expression of Festus to Paul, that "much learning made him mad." The abstruse problems of mathematical institution turned his brain; and he still remains, I believe, an unfortunate example, to shew that every African head is not adapted by nature to such profound contemplations. The chief pride of this disciple consists in imitating the garb and deportment of his tutor. A tye perriwig, a sword, and ruffled shirt, seem in his opinion to comprehend the very marrow and quintessence of all erudition, and philosophic dignity. Probably he imagines it a more easy way of acquiring, among the Negroes, the reputation of a great scholar, by these superficial marks, which catch their eye, than by talking of Euclid, whom they know nothing about.

Considering the difference which climate may occasion, and which Montesquieu[2] has learnedly examined, the noble duke would have made the experiment more fairly on a native African; perhaps too the Northern air imparted a tone and vigour to his organs, of which they never could have been susceptible in a hot climate; the author I have mentioned will not allow, that in hot climates there is any force or vigor of mind necessary for human action, "there is (says he) no curiosity, no noble enterprize, no generous sentiment."

The climate of Jamaica is temperate, and even cool, compared with many parts of Guiney; and the Creole Blacks have undeniably more acuteness and better understandings than the natives of Guiney. Mr. Hume,[3] who had heard of Williams, says of him, "In Jamaica indeed they talk of one Negroe as a man of parts and learning; but 'tis likely he is admired for very slender accomplishments, like a parrot who speaks a few words plainly." And Mr. Estwick,[4] pursuing the same idea, observes, "Although a Negroe is found in Jamaica, or elsewhere, ever so sensible and acute; yet, if he is incapable of moral sensations, or perceives them only as beasts do simple ideas, without the power of combination, in order to use; it is a mark that distinguishes him from the man who feels, and is capable of these moral sensations, who knows their application, and the purposes of them, as sufficiently, as he himself is distinguished from the highest species of brutes."* I do not know, if the spec-

*The distinction is well marked by Bishop Warburton, in these words: "1st, The Moral Sense: (is that) whereby we conceive and feel a pleasure in *right*, and a distaste and aversion to *wrong*, prior to all reflexion on their natures, or their consequences. This is the first inlet to the *adequate idea of morality*; and plainly the most extensive of all. When instinct had gone thus far, 2d, The Reasoning Faculty improved upon its dictates; for reflecting men, naturally led to examine the foundation of this *moral sense*, soon discovered that there were real, essential differ-

imen I shall exhibit of his abilities will, or will not, be thought to militate against these positions. In regard to the general character of the man, he was haughty, opinionated, looked down with sovereign contempt on his fellow Blacks, entertained the highest opinion of his own knowledge, treated his parents with much disdain, and behaved towards his children and his slaves with a severity bordering on cruelty; he was fond of having great deference paid to him, and exacted it in the utmost degree from the Negroes about him; he affected a singularity of dress, and particularly grave cast of countenance, to impress an idea of his wisdom and learning; and, to second this view, he wore in common a huge wig, which made a very venerable figure. The moral part of his character may be collected from these touches, as well as the measure of his wisdom, on which, as well as some other attributes to which he laid claim, he had not the modesty to be silent, whenever he met with occasion to expiate upon them. Of this piece of vanity, there is a very strong example in the following poem, which he presented to Mr. Haldane, upon his assuming the government of the island; he was fond of this species of composition in Latin, and usually addressed one to every new governor. He defined himself "a *white* man acting under a *black* skin." He endeavoured to prove logically, that a Negroe was superior in quality to a Mulatto, or other cast. His proposition was, that "a simple white or a simple black complexion was respectively perfect: but a Mulatto, being an heterogeneous medley of both, was imperfect, *ergo* inferior."

---

ences in the qualities of human actions, established by nature; and, consequently, that the love and hatred, excited by the *moral sense,* were not capricious in their operations; for that the essential properties of their objects had a specific difference." Hence arose a sense of moral obligation in society, &c. Divine Legation, vol. I. p. 37.

It is this instinct which discriminates mankind from other animals who have it not, whereas in other instinctive impulses *all agree.* But the question is, whether all the species of the human kind have this instinctive sense in equal degree? If the brutal instincts impel the African to satisfy his appetites, to run from danger, and the like; why does he not exhibit equally the tokens of this *moral instinct,* if he really possesses it? would it not insensibly have gained admittance into their habits of living, as well as the other instincts, and have regulated and directed their general manners? But we have no other evidence of their possessing it, than what arises from the vague conjectural positions, "that all men are equal, and that the disparity between one man and another, or one race of men and another, happens from accidental means, such as artificial refinements, education, and so forth." Certain however it is, that these refinements must necessarily take place, where the moral sense and reasoning faculty are most abundant, and extensively cultivated; but cannot happen, where they either do not exist at all, or, are not distributed in such due portion, as to work the proper ascendancy over the more brutal species of instinct. ["Warburton": William Warburton, bishop of Gloucester, author of *The Divine Legation of Moses demonstrated on the Principles of a Religious Deist* (London: For Fletcher Gyles, 1738).]

His opinion of Negroes may be inferred from a proverbial saying, that was frequently in his mouth; "Shew me *a Negroe,* and I will shew you *a thief.*" He died, not long since, at the age of seventy, or thereabouts.

I have ventured to subjoin some annotations to his poem, and particularly to distinguish several passages in the classic authors, to which he seems to have been indebted, or to have had allusion; there may be other passages which have escaped my notice; I have added an English translation in verse, wherein I have endeavoured to retain the sense, without wilfully doing injustice to the original.

Integerrimo et Fortissimo

Viro

GEORGIO HALDANO, Armigero,

Insulae *Jamaicensis* Gubernatori;

Cui, omnes morum, virtutumque dotes bellicarum,

In cumulum accesserunt,

CARMEN.

DENIQUE venturum fatis volventibus annum[*]
Cuncta per extensum laeta videnda diem,
Excussis adsunt curis, sub imagine clarâ[†]
Felices populi, terraque lege virens.
Te duce,[‡] quae[§] fuerant malesuadâ mente peracta
Irrita, conspectu non reditura tuo.
Ergo omnis populus, nec non plebecula cernet
Haesurum collo te *relegasse*[||] jugum,
Et mala, quae diris quondam cruciatibus, insons
Insula passa fuit; condoluisset onus
Ni victrix tua Marte manus prius inclyta, nostris
Sponte ruinosis[#] rebus adesse velit.

[*]*Aspice venturo laetentur ut omnia* Saeclo. *Virg[il] E[clogues]* iv. 52.

[†]*Clara* seems to be rather an improper epithet joined to *Imago.*

[‡]*Te duce,* si qua manent sceleris vestigia nostri.
Irrita [*sic* for *Inrita*], perpetua solvent formidine terras. *Virg[il] E[clogues]* iv. 13.

[§]Alluding perhaps to the contest about removing the seat of government and public offices from *Spanish Town* to *Kingston,* during the administration of governor Kn----s. [Rear Admiral Charles Knowles, governor of Jamaica (1752–56).]

[||]Pro *relevasse.*

[#]Quem vocet divûm populus *ruentis.*
Imperî *rebus. Hor[ace] Lib.* I. *Od.* ii. [stanza 7.]

Optimus es servus *Regi* servire *Britanno,*
Dum gaudet genio *Scotica** terra tuo:
Optimus herôum populi fulcire ruinam;†
Insula dum superest ipse superstes eris.‡
Victorem agnoscet te *Guadaloupa,* suorum
Despiciet meritò diruta castra ducum.§
Aurea vexillis flebit jactantibus *Iris,*‖
Cumque suis populis, oppida victa gemet.
Crede, meum# non est, vir Marti chare! *Minerva***
Denegat *Aethiopi* bella sonare ducum.
Concilio, careret te *Buchananus* et armis,
Carmine *Peleidae* scriberet ille parem.
Ille poeta, decus patriae, tua facta referre
Dignior, altisono vixque *Marone* minor.††
Flammiferos‡‡ agitante suos sub sole *jugales*§§
Vivimus; eloquium deficit omne focis.
Hoc demum accipias, multâ fuligine fusum
Ore sonaturo; non cute, corde valet.
Pollenti stabilita manu, (Deus almus, eandem
Omnigenis animam, nil prohibente dedit)‖‖‖

*Mr. Haldane was a native of North Britain. [The eighteenth—century term for Scotland.]

†Tu Ptolomaee potes magni *fulcire ruinam.* Lucan. *Lib.* viii. 528.

‡This was a promise of somewhat more than antediluvian longevity. But the poet proved a false prophet, for Mr. Haldane did not survive the delivery of this address many months.

§Egerit *justo domitos* triumpho. Hor. *Lib.* I. *Od.* xii. [stanza 14.]

‖Botanic name of the fleur-de-luce [i.e., fleur-de-lis], alluding to the arms of France.

#*Phoebus,* volentem praelia me loqui

    Victas et urbes, increpuit lyrâ

  Ne. *Hor.* [Untraced.]

**Invitâ Minervâ. *Hor[ace] de Art. Poet.* [Line 385: "tu nihil invita dices faciesve Minerva" Ed.]

††*Maronis altisoni* carmina. *Juv[enal] Sat[ires]* xi. *ver.* 178. [*Sic* for lines 180–81: "conditor Iliados cantabitur atque Maronis / altisoni dubiam facientia carmina palmam."]

‡‡*Flammiferas* rotas toto caelo *agitat.* [Untraced.]

§§I apprehend Mr. Williams mistook this for *jubara,* sun-beams.

‖‖‖This is a *petitio principii,* or begging the question, unless with Mr. [Alexander] Pope,

    "All are but parts of one stupendous whole,

    Whose body nature is, and God the soul."

    But,

    "Far as creation's ample range extends,

    The *scale* of sensual *mental* powers ascends." [*An Essay on Man,* Epistle 1, lines 267–68 and 207–8.]

Ipsa coloris egens virtus, prudentia; honesto
Nullus inest animo, nullus in arte color.
Cur timeas, quamvis, dubitesve, nigerrima celsam
Caesaris occidui, scandere *Musa** domum?
Vade salutatum,[†] nec sit tibi causa pudoris,
Candida quod nigrâ corpora pelle geris![‡]
Integritas morum *Maurum*[§] magis ornat, et ardor
Ingenii, et *docto dulcis in ore decor;*[||]
Hunc, magè *cor sapiens, patriae* virtutis amorque,
Eximit è sociis, conspicuumque facit.[#]
Insula me genuit,[**] celebres aluere *Britanni,*
Insula, te salvo non dolitura patre![††]
Hoc precor; o nullo videant te fine, regentem
Florciites populos, terra, Deique locus![‡‡]

FRANCISCUS WILLIAMS.

The same, translated.

To

That most upright and valiant Man,

GEORGE HALDANE, Esq;

Governor of the Island of *Jamaica;*

Upon whom

All military and moral Endowments are accumulated.

An ODE.

At length revolving fates th'expected year
Advance, and joy the live-long day shall cheer,

*Mr. Williams has added a *black Muse* to the Pierian choir; and, as he has not thought proper to bestow a name upon her, we may venture to announce her by the title of madam *Aethiopissa.*

[†]*Vade salutatum* subitò perarata parentem [*sic* for "Perillam"] Litera. *Ovid.* [*Tristia* 3.7.2 "*To Perilla.*"]

[‡]See his apophthegms before-mentioned.

[§]*Maurus* is not in classic strictness proper Latin for a *Negroe.*

[||]Mollis in ore *decor. Incert.*

[#]Me *doctarum* ederae praemia frontium
. . . .
Secernunt populo. Hor. Lib. I. *Od.* 1. [Lines 29 and 32.]

[**]Mantua me genuit, Calabri rapuêre. *Virg.* [Untraced.]

[††]Hic ames dici *pater* atque princeps. *Hor.* [Untraced.]

[‡‡]Serus in coelum redeas, *diuque*
Laetus intersis populo. Hor. [Untraced.]

Beneath the fost'ring law's auspicious dawn
New harvests rise to glad th' enliven'd lawn.*
With the bright prospect blest, the swains repair
In social bands, and give a loose to care.
Rash councils now, with each malignant plan,
Each faction, that in evil hour began,
At your approach are in confusion fled,
Nor, while you rule, shall rear their dastard head.
Alike the master and the slave shall see
Their neck reliev'd, the yoke unbound by thee.
Ere now our guiltless isle, her wretched fate
Had wept, and groan'd beneath th' oppressive weight
Of cruel woes; save thy victorious hand,
Long fam'd in war, from *Gallia*'s[5] hostile land;
And wreaths of fresh renown, with generous zeal,
Had freely turn'd, to prop our sinking *weal*.[6]
Form'd as thou art, to serve *Britannia*'s[7] crown,
While *Scotia*[8] claims thee for her darling son;
Oh! blest of heroes, ablest to sustain
A falling people, and relax their chain.
Long as this isle shall grace the Western deep,
From age to age, thy fame shall never sleep.
Thee, her dread victor *Guadaloupe*[9] shall own,
Crusht by thy arm, her slaughter'd chiefs bemoan;
View their proud tents all level'd in the dust,
And, while she grieves, confess the cause was just.
The golden *Iris*[10] the sad scene will share,
Will mourn her banners scatter'd in the air;
Lament her vanquisht troops with many a sigh,
Nor less to see her towns in ruin lie.
Fav'rite of *Mars!*[11] believe, th' attempt were vain,
It is not mine to try the arduous strain.
What! shall an *Aethiop*[12] touch the martial string,
Of battles, leaders, great atchievements sing?
Ah no! *Minerva*,[13] with th' indignant *Nine*,[14]
Restrain him, and forbid the bold design.

*Lawn is used here in the sense given it by Johnson, viz. "an open space between woods;" which has a peculiar propriety applied to the cane-fields in Jamaica.

To a *Buchanan*[15] does the theme belong;
A theme, that well deserves *Buchanan*'s song.
'Tis he, should swell the din of war's alarms,
Record thee great in council, as in arms;
Recite each conquest by thy valour won,
And equal thee to great *Peleides*' son.[16]
That bard, his country's ornament and pride,
Who e'en with *Maro*[17] might the bays divide:
Far worthier he, thy glories to rehearse,
And paint thy deeds in his immortal verse.
We live, alas! where the bright god of day,
Full from the zenith whirls his torrid ray:
Beneath the rage of his consuming fires,
All fancy melts, all eloquence expires.
Yet may you deign accept this humble song,
Tho' wrapt in gloom, and from a falt'ring tongue;
Tho' dark the stream on which the tribute flows,
Not from the *skin*, but from the *heart* it rose.
To all of human kind, benignant heaven
(Since nought forbids) one common soul has given.
This rule was 'stablish'd by th' Eternal Mind;
Nor virtue's self, nor prudence are confin'd
To *colour*; none imbues the honest heart;
To science none belongs, and none to art.
Oh! *Muse,* of blackest tint, why shrinks thy breast,
Why fears t' approach the *Caesar* of the *West!*
Dispel thy doubts, with confidence ascend
The regal dome, and hail him for thy friend:
Nor blush, altho' in garb funereal drest,
Thy body's white, tho' clad in sable vest.
Manners unsullied, and the radiant glow
Of genius, burning with desire to *know;*
And learned speech, with modest accent worn,
Shall best the sooty *African* adorn.
An heart with wisdom fraught, a patriot flame,
A love of virtue; these shall lift his name
Conspicuous, far beyond his kindred race,
Distinguish'd from them by the foremost place.
In this prolific isle I drew my birth,

And *Britain* nurs'd, illustrious through the earth;
This, my lov'd isle, which never more shall grieve,
Whilst you our common friend, our father live.
Then this my pray'r—"May earth and heaven survey
A people ever blest, beneath your sway!"
                    FRANCIS WILLIAMS.

There is, in this performance, a strain of superlative panegyric, which is scarcely allowable even to a poet. *Buchanan* is compared with *Virgil*, and Mr. *Haldane* made equal to *Achilles;* nay, exalted still higher, for he is hailed the *Caesar* or emperor of *America.* The author has taken care, whilst he is dealing about his adulation, not to forget himself. His speech is represented erudite and modest; his heart is filled with wisdom; his morals are immaculate; and he abounds with patriotism and virtue.

To consider the merits of this specimen impartially, we must endeavour to forget, in the first place, that the writer was a *Negroe;* for if we regard it as an extraordinary production, merely because it came from a *Negroe,* we admit at once that *inequality* of genius which has been before supposed, and admire it only as a rare phaenomenon.

What woeful stuff this madrigal would be
In some starv'd, hackney sonneteer, or me!
But let a *Negroe* own the happy lines,
How the wit brightens! how the style refines!
Before his sacred name flies ev'ry fault,
And each exalted stanza teems with thought!

We are to estimate it as having flowed from the polished pen of one, who received an academic education, under every advantage that able preceptors, and munificent patrons, could furnish; we must likewise believe it to be, what it actually was, a piece highly laboured; designed, modeled, and perfected, to the utmost stretch of his invention, imagination, and skill.

Should we, or should we not, have looked for something better from one, upon whom (to borrow his own phrase) *omnes* artium, scientiarumque *dotes* Atticarum in *cumulum accesserunt?* or, is it at all superior, in classic purity of style and numbers, in sentiment and propriety, in poetic images and harmony, to any composition we might expect from a middling scholar at the seminaries of Westminster or Eaton? It is true, *poeta nascitur, non-sit:*[18] but the principal forte and excellence of this man lay in versification; however, as I mean not to prejudge the cause, I shall leave it to the fair verdict of a jury of critics.

The Spaniards have a proverbial saying, "*Aunque Négros somos génte;*" "though we are Blacks, we are men." The truth of which no one will dispute; but if we allow the system of created beings to be perfect and consistent, and that this perfection arises from an exact scale of gradation, from the lowest to the highest, combining and connecting every part into a regular and beautiful harmony, reasoning them from the visible plan and operation of infinite wisdom in respect to the human race, as well as every other series in the scale, we must, I think, conclude, that,

> The general *order,* since the whole began,
> Is kept in *nature,* and is kept in *man.*[19]
> *Order* is heaven's first law; and, this confest,
> *Some are,* and *must be, greater* than the rest.[20]

FROM

Jamaica, a Poem, In Three Parts

ANONYMOUS

(fl. 1 7 7 7)

Jamaica, a Poem, In Three Parts (1777) is an abolitionist text from the first stage of the abolitionist movement that peaked in 1788 before plummeting in the conservative reaction following the French Reign of Terror (1793–94). Despite the fact that only four copies of this work are recorded to survive, some of the poem's sentiments received a level of immortality by the quotation of 66 lines from the poem and the appended poetical epistle in John Gabriel Stedman's highly successful *Narrative* (1796) of the Surinam slave revolt in the 1770s, which itself became a major influence on subsequent abolitionist writers.

    Jamaica remains an anonymous work; the only biographical information is provided in the preface in which the author describes this poem as his "poetical maidenhead" written at "the age of eighteen." Judging from clues in the main poem and in the appended poetical epistle, the author had spent some years in Jamaica first as a manager of a plantation and then as a merchant.

    The poet appears to have been inspired to write, in part, in reaction to James Grainger's *The Sugar Cane* (1764). In his Argument to part 1, the poet writes "The Muse thinks it disgraceful in a Briton to sing of the Sugarcane, since to it is owing the Slavery of the Negroes." Much had changed in the thirteen years between the publication of these two poems: the North American colonies had declared their independence and were at war with Britain, the legal case of James Somersett (1772) had established a precedent that slavery was unlawful on English soil, and anti-slavery sentiment had spread far beyond its limited, mostly Quaker, constituency. *Jamaica* is an early and influential example of what would become a flood of anti-slavery prose and poetry in the decades to come.

JAMAICA, A POEM, In THREE PARTS. Written in that Island, in the
Year MDCCLXXVI. TO WHICH IS ANNEXED, A POETICAL
EPISTLE From the Author in that Island
to a Friend in England.

*Cum canerem Reges & prælia Cynthius aurem Vellit & admonuit; pastorem
Tityre (pingues oportet) pascere oves Et ne deductum dicere carmen.* —VIRG.EC.*

LONDON; Printed for WILLIAM NICOLL, at No. 51,
in St. Paul's Church Yard. MDCCLXXVII
[1777].

PREFACE.

A POEM, without a *name* to protect it, is like a *bantling* without a father to
own it: and the throwing of the one upon the Town without a *preface,* is like
the casting of the other upon the *parish* without a *shirt.* My name being insufficient to secure my works from criticism, I forbear to mention it; but, in
compliance to custom, beg leave to preface my *Poetical Maidenhead* with a few
words concerning its design.

Having gone to our principal settlement in the West Indies, at a very early
period, I was no less captivated with the beauty of the Island, the verdure of
the country, and the deliciousness of the fruits, than I was disgusted with the
severity of the inhabitants, the cruelty of the planters, and the miseries of the
slaves: the first I here endeavour to celebrate; the last to condemn.

To do justice to the fair Ladies of the Sugar Islands, to remove the vulgar
prejudices of narrow minds, to inspire the inhabitants with more generous
feelings towards the sooty race, and to advise the Planters, (for their own and
the interests of humanity) to adopt a mediocrity of punishment worthy the
citizens of a free and independent empire, and the partakers of mild and eq-
uitable laws:—These are the motives that induced me to attempt this subject.
Thus much for the design: as to the execution, with all the fears of a young author, it is laid before the tribunal of a candid and impartial public; knowing
that if it possesses any merit, it will acquire their approbation—If none, the
age of eighteen, at which it was written, will hardly be any alleviation of this
presumption.

*Virgil, *Eclogue VI,* lines 3–5. ["When I was singing kings and battles, Cynthius pulled /
My ear admonition: 'A shepherd, Tityrus, / Should feed his flock fat, but recite a thin-spun
song.'" Translation from *Virgil: The Eclogues,* trans. A. G. Lee (Harmondsworth, England:
Penguin Books, 1980), 71.]

ARGUMENT to PART I.
Of the COUNTRY, FRUITS, &c.

THE Subject proposed—*Address to the Rural Muse of Thomson*—*Picture of a Voyage along the Islands of* Deseada, Monserat, Antego, &c. *to* Jamaica[1]—*Its Beauties*—*The Fruits indigenous to it, and the other* West India *Islands, as*—*The Anana*[2]—*The Pear Melons*—*Cocoa-Nuts, &c.*—*Description of* Liguania—*The Rivers* Hope *and* Cobre—Drax-hall, &c.—*The Muse thinks it disgraceful in a Briton to sing of the Sugar-cane, since to it is owing the Slavery of the Negroes.*

JAMAICA; A POEM.
Part I.

Let some, enraptur'd with poetic strains,
Sicilian Muses* court, on British plains
Invoke the Naiads from some fav'rite stream,
Or in sweet numbers sing some darling theme;
In fields paternal woo their native loves,   5
And Mantuan garlands† weave in Albion's groves.
When midst her happy lawns I fondly stray'd,
And rov'd enraptur'd thro' the sylvan shade,
Ev'n I aspir'd to move the tuneful throng,
Live in soft numbers, and rebloom in song!   10
But now, far distant from my native soil,
I wake the lyre 'midst gay Jamaica's Isle;
Whose fertile vales ne'er with the Muses rung,
Whose fruits no bard, whose dames no poet sung,
Savannahs ope, hills rise, floods glide along,   15
And rills meand'ring, never liv'd in song.
Be these my theme: to tune the long-lov'd lyre,
When the *Cane Isles* and sun-nurs'd nymphs inspire;
To make the new to the old world be known,
And sing the torrid to the temp'rate zone;   20
Nor be thou envious, *Britain*, of the theme,
The tropic harvest, or the torrid dame:
Biennial springs, that double blossoms shoot,
And double Autumns crown'd with double fruit:
Since Ceres'[3] gifts your fruitful valleys shade,   25

---

*Sicilian Muses. Sicilidas Musae paulo majora canemus, &c. Virg. [Virgil, *Eclogue* 4.1. In English: "O Sicilian Muses! grant that I may sing a little grander!" (my translation).]
    †Mantuan garlands.—Virgil was born in Mantua.

And future navies rank the fertile mead:
While o'er the dale your siren daughters stray,
And shed new lustre on the smiling day!

    Since her own groves cannot her sons inspire,
Nor all the western world the poet fire;   30
Who shall direct the Muse's soaring wings,
Or what kind genius aid her while she sings;
What sun who o'er the eastern* world hath shone,
Light her to laurels in the torrid zone?

    O! thou, whom all the tuneful train inspir'd,   35
Fair fancy favour'd, and Apollo fir'd:
Immortal Thomson![4] wheresoe'er you stray,
In some kind sphere, blest with eternal day,
Preside propitious o'er thy sylvan strain,
Nor let a youthful bard invoke in vain!   40

. . . .

    But how can I forget the sugar cane?
The soil's warm sun, and planter's sweat-bought gain?
How, by the mill comprest, the liquor flows?
Boil'd by the jetty race, how sugar glows?   175
Or how the juice fermented and elate,
By the still's pow'r acquires a sprightly heat?
How Europe's sons with this debauch the day,[9]
With that her maids, in India's torpid tea?

    Here could I sing what soils and seasons suit,   180
Inform the tap'ring arrow how to shoot;
Under what signs to plant the mother cane,
What rums and sugars bring the planter gain;
Teach stubborn oxen in the wain to toil,
And all the culture of a sugar soil: 185
Th'ingrateful task a British Muse disdains,
Lo! tortures, racks, whips, famine, gibbets, chains,
Rise on my mind, appall my tear-stain'd eye,
Attract my rage, and draw a soul-felt sigh;
I blush, I shudder at the bloody theme,   190
And scorn on woe to build a baseless fame.
                 End of Part I.

*By this Europe is meant, being East in respect to America.

ARGUMENT to PART II.
Of the INHABITANTS.

THE Proposition—Invocation to the genius of Ovid, so happily attuned to soft descriptions—Encomium on the Creole Ladies (or natives of the West Indian islands)—The mixtures; as Samboes, Mullattoes, &c.—Their lasciviousness—The negroes; their music, dances, and employments—The independent spirit of the Indians—The cruelty of the first Spaniards to the natives of this and other islands—The Muse wishes, that while she displays their crimes, she could hide our own barbarities to the Africans.

JAMAICA; A POEM.
PART II.

NOW would my harp to fair creation strung,
Attempt a loftier theme, till now unsung;
In loftier verse the tropic Dames display,
And lay the torrid *beauties* ope to day!

O! thou, who sung the sympathizing groves,   5
The fruitful rivers, and the rural loves;
Naso,[6] descend! lo, suppliant at thy shrine,
I hail thy Muse, and bid her shine on mine,
That she, inspir'd, may sing so great a theme,
And graft immortal cyons[7] on thy fame!   10

Then first, O Muse! attempt the motly fair,
From lank and long, to short and woolly hair;
From white to black, thro' ev'ry mixture run,
And sing the smiling daughters of the sun!

'Tis true, few nymphs with British bloom we boast,   15
No rosy red adorns the tropic toast;
But* here the lilly sheds her purest white,
And well-turn'd limbs the panting youth invite!
While sportive Cupids circle round the waist,
Laugh on the cheek, or wanton in the breast!   20
Our sultry sun (tho' fierce in vertic rage)
Ripes the young blood, and nourishes old age;
O'er every limb spreads more than mortal grace,
And gives the body what he robs the face.

---

*By these are meant the Whites, or Creole Ladies.

Next comes a warmer race, from sable sprung,   25
To love each thought, to lust each nerve is strung;
The Samboe* dark, and the Mullattoe† brown,

The Mestize‡ fair, the well-limb'd Quaderoon,§
And jetty Afric, from no spurious fire,
Warm as her soil, and as her sun—on fire.   30
These sooty dames, well vers'd in Venus' school,
Make love an art, and boast they kiss by rule.
'Midst murm'ring brooks they stem the liquid wave,
And jetty limbs in coral currents lave.
In Field or household pass the toilsome day,   35
But spend the night in mirth-enlivening play:
With pipe and tabor woo their sable loves,
In sad remembrance of their native groves;
Or, deck'd in white, attend the vocal halls,
And Afric postures teach in Indian balls.   40
Not always thus the males carouse and play,
But toil and sweat the long laborious day;
With earliest dawn the ardent task begun,
Their labour ends not with the setting sun:
For when the moon displays her borrow'd beams,   45
They pick the canes, and tend the loaded teams,
Or in alternate watch, with ceaseless toil,
The rums distil, or smoaky sugars boil.
Ev'n while they ply this sad and sickly trade,
Which numbers thousands with the countless dead,   50
Refus'd the very liquors which they make,
They quench their burning temples in the lake;
Or issuing from the thick unwholesome steam,
Drink future sorrow in the cooling stream.

Why need I sing the Indian's copper hue,   55
Broad face, short size, lank hair, and scowling brow,

---

*The Samboe arises from the cohabitation of a Mullattoe man and a black woman, and *vice versa*.

†Mullattoe, from white and black.

‡Mestize, from white and Quaderoon.

§Quaderoon, from white and Mullattoe.

Unfit for toil? a mild, tho' gallant race,
Inur'd to war, and panting for a chace;
Born free, they scorn to brook a lawless sway,
Spurn the dire wretch who'd stripes for toils repay: 60
They pine! they sicken! hope their native sky,
Their friends, their loves—they languish and they die.

　　Here the fond Muse the Caribb* race would sing,
The painted people, and the plumag'd king:
Their feats in arms; in peace domestic toils;   65
The happiest people of the fairest isles!
Where thee, *Columbus!*† great as injur'd name,
Found a new world, and gain'd an empty fame.
Their sylvan sports along the sea-green shore,
What swarms *Domingo,*‡ what *Jamaica* bore.   70
But O! how vain the task! the theme how vain,
Their flitting shades still curse the faithless main,
Bare their gor'd breasts, and point at cruel Spain!

　　O that the Muse, who makes her cruelties known,
Could spurn her crimes, and not detest her own: 75
But lo! the Afric genius clanks his chains,
And damns the race that robs his native plains!
　　　　　　　End of Part II.

ARGUMENT to PART III.

THE vision of Liberty, addressed to Lord Camden[8]—*The proposition and invocation—Vision of the goddess Liberty—Her speech—The Muse advises the Planters to encourage their slaves—Picture of the punishments inflicted on the Negroes after a rebellion—Advises a mitigation, as most consonant to the spirit of a free people—Prayer to Liberty—Eulogium on Britain.—Conclusion.*

---

*The Aborigines of the West India islands, who were all extirpated by the Spaniards. [Another echo of the Black Legend of Spanish cruelty. For a brief overview of the controversy surrounding the received legends of the origins and fate of the native inhabitants of the West Indies, see Peter Hulme's chapter "Caribs and Arawaks" in *Colonial Encounters: Europe and the Native Caribbean, 1492–1797* (London: Methuen, 1986); for an archaeologist's account, see Irving Rouse, *The Tainos: Rise and Decline of the People who Greeted Columbus* (New Haven: Yale University Press, 1992).]

†C. Columbus was sent home in chains from that very world which he subdued and after the death of his patroness Isabella, treated very harshly by the court of Spain.

‡Hispaniola.

JAMAICA; A POEM.
PART III.

THUS far the Muse, when mad'ning at the scene
Of christian guile, and man enslaving man:
Around my head aërial phantoms rise,
And soothing slumbers seal my tear-stain'd eyes.

O! pride and glory of a sinking state!   5
Great in thy power, and in retirement great;
Tho' Lawyer, honest;—Courtier, sincere;
Patriot, unstain'd;—uncorrupt tho' a Peer:
Camden! a Bard unknown, would claim thine ear,
And mix the Muse's with the Patriot's tear.   10

The drowsy god had calm'd my troubled breast,
Charm'd every care and ev'ry limb to rest;
When lo! out-issuing from surrounding night,
The goddess *Liberty* arrests my sight:
A cypress garland round each temple twines,   15
And at her feet the British lion pines.
The sugar-isles with furious frown she eyes,
And I attend while thus the goddess cries:
"Lo! Afric from your furthest shores complains,
"Bares her foul wounds, and clanks your cruel chains;   20
"Polluted Gambia* mourns his country spoil'd,
"And wild Zaara's† fields become more wild:
"The peaceful Fauns forsake dishonour'd groves,
"And gentle Naiads leave their watry loves!
"Your cruelties reach beyond th'Atlantic main,   25
"A people sigh, but all their sighs are vain!
"These eyes have seen what this tongue can't reveal,
"These ears have heard what I would blush to tell;
"Whate'er the Briton, or the man could stain,
"Or give the Christian, or the Heathen pain!   30
"Thus Rome of old the barb'rous nations brav'd,
"Ev'n Indus saw his tawny sons enslav'd;
"Far to the North she spread her proud domain,

---

*A river on the coast of Guinea, much frequented by our trading vessels.
†A desart tract in Africa.

"And bound ev'n Britain in a gilded chain.
"But she who aw'd the world by arms and fame,   35
"Now smoaks by slaves, now stands an empty name!
"Fear then, like her, to meet an awful doom,
"And let your sea-girt shores still think on Rome;
"For your green isles, surcharg'd with bosom'd foes,
"May yield to slaves,—you feel the captive's woes."   40
This said,—the goddess sheds ambrosial tears,
Spreads her fleet wings, and instant disappears!

O Planter! be it yours to nurse the slave,
From Afric's coasts waft o'er th'Atlantic wave:
With tender accents smooth the brow of care,   45
And from his bosom banish dark despair:
So may rich sugars fill your roomy stores,
And rums in plenty reach your native shores:
So may no dire disease your stock invade,
But feed contented in the cooling shade!   50

Oft have I blush'd to see a Christian give
To some black wretch, worn out, and just alive,
A *manumission* full, and leave him free,
To brave pale want, disease, and misery!
A poor reward for all his watchful cares,   55
Industrious days, and toil-revolving years!

And can the Muse reflect her tear-stain'd eye,
When blood† attests ev'n slaves for freedom die?
On cruel gibbets high disclos'd they rest,
And scarce one groan escapes one bloated breast.   60
Here sable Caesars‡ feel the christian rod;
There Afric Platos, tortur'd, hope a God:
While jetty Brutus⁹ for his country sighs,
And sooty Cato¹⁰ with his freedom dies!

Britons, forbear! be Mercy still your aim,   65
And as your faith, unspotted be your fame;

*An instrument in writing used by masters in giving freedom to their slaves.

†During what the Planters term rebellion, but what a philosopher would call a brave struggle of an injured people for their lost liberties: During these, the Negroes will die amidst the most cruel torments, with the most obstinate intrepidity.

‡Names given by the Planters to their slaves. [See Aphra Behn's *Oroonoko, or the History of the Royal Slave* (1688), in which the hero's name is changed to Caesar once he is enslaved.]

Tremendous pains tremendous deeds inspire,
And, hydra-like, new martyrs rise from fire.

O hapless Afric! still the sport of fate,
Prey of each clime, and haunt of ev'ry state;   70
Lo! borne thro' sultry skies by fav'ring gales,
With ceaseless wishes and extended sails,
The restless merchant seeks thy hapless shore,
Sped by inhuman gain, and golden ore!

Inhuman ye! who ply the human* trade,   75
And to the West† a captive people lead;
Who brother, sister, father, mother, friend,
In one unnat'ral hapless ruin blend.
Barbarians! steel'd to ev'ry sense of woe,
Shame of the happy source from whence ye flow: 80
The time may come, when, scorning savage sway,
Afric may triumph, and ev'n you obey!

The Muse, fond wish, would hope some day may give
The world in peace and liberty to live!
Freedom descend! invigorate the whole,   85
And stretch your free domain from pole to pole;
Till the Cane-isles accept your easy reign,
And Gambia murmur freedom to the main!
Till Europe peace to Africa restore,
Till slav'ry cease, and bondage be no more!   90

O'er the warm South‡ extend your nursing wings,
Till future Incas rise, and future Kings;
Till captive tribes cease to be bought or sold,
And Chili's sons enjoy their native gold:
May Britain first her grateful tribute bring,   95
And all the world consenting Paeans sing!

Let the gorg'd *East* boast *China's* beauteous looms,
Golconda's gems,[11] *Sumatra's* rich perfumes;[12]
The sickly *South, Potosi's* pregnant ore,[13]
Peru's fam'd drugs, and *Chili's* golden shore: 100

---

*Guinea trade, execrable not only on account of its inhumanity, but also for the many villanies practised in it.
†America.
‡South America.

The frozen *North*, *Spitzbergen*'s mighty whale,[14]
Black *Hudson*'s ermine, *Zembla*'s spotted seal:
While the warm West her twice-impregn'd plain,
Twice vertic suns, and man enslaving cane:
Britannia! thine (the mighty boast below)   105
Is in what *freedom, commerce, health* bestow!

Hail, only isle![15] girt by the only shore,
Whose feeling* cliffs the captives rights restore!
Hail, happy shore! wash'd by the only wave
That bears to freedom the desponding slave;   110
Whose awful view unbinds his galling chain,
Whose sacred justice makes his bondage vain!
The joyous Muse could wanton in thy praise,
Proud from the theme to pluck unspotted bays;
Where freedom left her last best lumin'd ray,   115
And lighted Britain to a glorious day!

O that my theme could fire some greater breast,
Some loftier Poet in the Muses blest!
Laurel and bay their choicest boughs should spread,
And civic wreaths adorn his honour'd head;   120
While I, the humblest suppliant of the nine,
I, who in feeble verse attempt to shine,
An humble ivy, round the oak would twine!

But if my lays can chace one captive sigh,
Care from his breast, a tear wipe from his eye;   125
Dispel one gloomy woe-dejected brow,
Make one full heart with kind compassion flow;
Torture award from one desponding slave,
Or one poor wretch from fire or gibbet save:
This is my utmost wish—the envy'd prize;   130
Above wealth, fame, and honour, this my choice!

What tho' no laurel'd busto bear my name,
No flatt'ring marble raise an empty fame:

*Alluding to a famous decision of Lord Mansfield's, concerning the privileges of negroes in England. [William Murray (1705–93), first Baron Mansfield (1756) and first earl of Mansfield (1776), as Lord Chief Justice of the Court of King's Bench (1756–88) decided in the famous case of James Somersett (1772) that a slave could not be forcibly removed from England by his master. Despite the narrowness of the ruling, the Somersett case was hailed inaccurately as the abolition of slavery on English soil.]

Tho' Phoebus' self disclaim these youthful lays,
And dark oblivion with all my bays?   135
Tho' no proud wreaths around my temples ply,
And ere myself, these fancy'd honours die?
Some weeping friend may clasp my urn and say,   ⎤
"When freedom fir'd, he sung his virgin lay,   ⎬
"And scorn'd to flatter cruel savage sway!"   ⎦   140

A POETICAL EPISTLE, FROM THE ISLAND OF JAMAICA, TO A GENTLEMAN OF THE MIDDLE-TEMPLE.[16]

O POLLIO![17] can I here pretend to rhyme,
In such a warm, and such a sickly clime?
From Coke and Lyttleton,[18] from Law—attend,
And hear a Muse, by more than blood thy friend;
While midst th'Atlantic isle I fondly stray,   5
And in my mind the future bliss pourtray,
When fortune smiles, from these warm climes to roam,
And greet my friends, my country, and my home.

From where the sun burns with his fiercest ray,
To where, midst Britain, flows the temp'rate day: 10
Lo! England's beauties croud upon my soul,
And o'er my mind our former pleasures roll:
When gay with thee, Augusta,[19] I survey'd,
Or o'er thy *Kensington* enraptur'd stray'd!

These all are fled! ambition was my aim,   15
To raise a fortune, or erect a name:
Midst tropic heats, and sickly climes, to scan
The works of Nature, and the ways of man.

The Muse, when first she view'd the destin'd isle,*
(Where slav'ry frown'd, and fortune ceas'd to smile,)   20
Was forc'd by fate to pass her joyless days,
'Mong men unknown to sympathetic lays.
To see the captive drag the cruel chain,
Repaid with tortures, and solac'd with pain;
To give the Afric's fate the pitying tear,   25
And spurn the slavery that she could not bear.
But soon she scorn'd on human woe to rise,
Nor with a tort'ring hand would stain the bays.

*Alluding to the author's stay for a few months in the country, as a Planter, after his arrival.

If as the shoot shall spread the promis'd tree,
What can the smiling Muse expect from thee?   30
Shalt thou a *Thomson*, roll thro' fairy maze,
Or, with a *Pope*, dispute the equal bays?
Shalt thou a *Swift*, with satire's keenest dart,
Reform the manners, and correct the heart?
Or wilt thou still, more glorious as the theme,   35
Assert thy country's freedom, and her fame;
Teach Britain to resist tyrannic sway,
And drag her venal traitors to the day?

While, midst thy Britain surly Boreas reigns,
And rains congeal'd in crystal all her plains;   40
While snows descend in ev'ry fleecy show'r,
And nipping frosts deform the verdant bow'r:
With us, the fields enjoy one constant green,
No storms succeed, no tempests prowl the main;
No winter here—all is one constant spring,   45
And every month our feather'd chorus sing.

But here we pine beneath a sultry sun,
Scarce can th'expanded silks* his vigour shun;
He thins our aether with his potent rays;
Tho' mild our nights, yet listless are our days!   50
Our Creoles here no rapid Severn brave,
No Thames monarchial rolls his ample wave;
No flood-crown'd vill erects its lofty head,
No proud cascade reblooms the sun-scorch'd mead:
A Cobre only furious rolls along,   55
Alike unknown to commerce and to song!

Our tropic fruits, nurs'd 'neath a torrid sky,
With Britain's orchards, mild and fertile, vie.
Can England boast th'Anana's nectar'd taste?
The marrowy pear, a vegetable feast?   60
The flavour'd melon, or the juicy lime?
Or sugar-cane, the pride of India's clime?
Or milky apple, Venus to inspire?
Or cooling tamarind, that fans the fire?

*Umbrellas.

Can ye, midst winter, pluck the summer's pride,   65
When all your gardens glow one snowy void?
Or can ye sit by yonder fairy stream,
Where orang'd boughs preclude the scalding beam?

    But happy ye, who dwell midst Britain's isle,
Thrice happy men! if fortune deigns to smile.   70
No sighing slave there makes his heedless moan,
No injur'd Afric echoes forth his groan;
No tort'ring lord ransacks his fruitful mind,
Some unthought woe, some unknown rack to find.

    At each new crime this labours in my breast,   75
And this each night denies a quiet rest:
Some Afric chief will rise, who, scorning chains,
Racks, tortures, flames—excruciating pains,
Will lead his injur'd friends to bloody fight,
And in the flooded carnage take delight;   80
Then dear repay us in some vengeful war,
And give us blood for blood, and scar for scar.

Kingston, Jamaica,
20th May, 1776.
                FINIS

Notes

INTRODUCTION

1. Columbus to Doña Juana de Torres, October 1500, written by the imprisoned Columbus upon being returned to Spain (in *Columbus on Himself,* ed. and trans. Felipe Fernández-Armesto [London: Folio Society, 1992], 195).

2. E.g., Stephen Greenblatt, *Marvelous Possessions: The Wonder of the New World* (Chicago: University of Chicago Press, 1991); Peter Hulme, *Colonial Encounters: Europe and the Native Caribbean, 1492–1797* (London: Methuen, 1986); Philip Boucher, *Cannibal Encounters: Europeans and Island Caribs, 1492–1763* (Baltimore: Johns Hopkins University Press, 1992).

3. Prominent studies of the West Indies in this period include Richard S. Dunn, *Sugar and Slaves: The Rise of the Planter Class in the English West Indies, 1624–1713* (Chapel Hill: University of North Carolina Press, 1972); Jack P. Greene, *Imperatives, Behaviors, and Identities: Essays in Early American Cultural History* (Charlottesville: University Press of Virginia, 1992); William C. Spengemann, *A New World of Words: Redefining Early American Literature* (New Haven: Yale University Press, 1994); and Bernard Bailyn and Philip D. Morgan, eds., *Strangers within the Realm: Cultural Margins of the First British Empire* (Chapel Hill: University of North Carolina Press, 1991).

4. Quoted in David S. Shields, *Oracles of Empire: Poetry, Politics, and Commerce in British America, 1690–1750* (Chicago: University of Chicago Press, 1990), 240 n. 34.

5. *Robinson Crusoe: An Authoritative Text, Backgrounds and Sources, Criticism,* ed. Michael Shinagel (Norton Critical Edition; New York: W. W. Norton, 1975), 188.

6. Quoted in Hulme, *Colonial Encounters,* 216.

7. Although disease had depleted the populations of Native Americans in New England just prior to the arrival of the *Mayflower,* the continuing presence of native inhabitants along the frontiers of settlement ensured a persistent sense of cultural contact and conflict largely unknown in the small island colonies in the Caribbean.

8. Of the approximately ten million Africans transported through the Middle Passage, nearly five million landed in the West Indies (750,000 in Jamaica alone), four million in Brazil, and 250,000 in the British North American colonies.

9. T. H. Breen employs the term "charter societies" to describe the persistently powerful cultures of the founding groups in a given colony; see "Creative Adaptations: Peoples and Cultures," in *Colonial British America: Essays in the New History of the Early Modern Era,* ed. Jack P. Greene and J. R. Pole (Baltimore: Johns Hopkins University Press, 1984), 195–232.

10. For reasons not unlike the West Indian colonists', settlers in the coastal regions of the southern colonies on the continent frequently remigrated to England.

11. Hickeringill's verse is like Samuel Butler's *Hudibras* (which began appearing in December 1662) in its low humor, although with the exception of the "Epicurean Lullabie," it is decasyllabic, not octosyllabic.

12. See also Boucher, *Cannibal Encounters,* a study of European contacts with the Caribbean natives.

13. Other prominent studies of imperialism tend to take a postcolonial viewpoint, which, nevertheless, can also be useful in reading early modern examples of colonial discourse. A sampling of influential postcolonial studies would include: Patrick Brantlinger, *Rule of Darkness: British Literature and Imperialism, 1830–1914* (1988), Frantz Fanon, *The Wretched of the Earth* (1961) and *Black Skin, White Masks* (1952), C. L. R. James, *The Black Jacobins* (1938), Roberto Fernández Retamar, *Caliban and Other Essays* (1989), and Edward Said, *Culture and Imperialism* (1993). Although these authors address issues of universal applicability and choose examples from nineteenth- and twentieth-century texts, their consideration of the West Indies as central and seminal sites for the development of colonial discourse makes them useful for a nuanced understanding of the discursive products of the early modern Caribbean.

14. Among the many studies of race and gender useful to an investigation of British West Indian culture, some of the more prominent include: Winthrop D. Jordan, *White Over Black: American Attitudes Toward the Negro, 1550–1812* (1968); Henry Louis Gates Jr., ed., *Race, Writing, and Difference* (1985); Deborah E. McDowell and Arnold Rampersad, eds., *Slavery and the Literary Imagination* (1989); Paul Gilroy, *The Black Atlantic: Modernity and Double Consciousness* (1993); Frank Shuffelton, ed., *A Mixed Race: Ethnicity in Early America* (1993); Carl Plasa and Betty J. Ring, eds., *The Discourse of Slavery: Aphra Behn to Toni Morrison* (1994); Margo Hendricks and Patricia Parker, eds., *Women, "Race," and Writing in the Early Modern Period* (1994); Ivan Hannaford, *Race: The History of an Idea in the West* (1996). All of these works offer a variety of ways of reading the growth and change in concepts of race and gender, including discussions of such West Indies–related texts as Shakespeare's *The Tempest,* Behn's *Oroonoko,* and Charlotte Brontë's *Jane Eyre.* Another useful study of the intersection of gender with race and slavery is Barbara Bush, *Slave Women in Caribbean Society, 1650–1838* (1990).

15. Among the more prominent studies of the West Indies in these disciplines are George E. Marcus and Michael M. J. Fischer, *Anthropology as Cultural Critique: An Experimental Moment in the Human Sciences* (1986); James Clifford and George E. Marcus, eds., *Writing Culture: The Poetics and Politics of Ethnography* (1986); Arnold Krupat, *Ethnocriticism: Ethnography, History, Literature* (1992); and Nicholas Thomas, *Colonialism's Culture: Anthropology, Travel, and Government* (1994).

16. Available in an edition by William H. McBurney, *Four Before Richardson: Selected English Novels* (Lincoln: University of Nebraska Press, 1963).

17. A sampling of recent studies of piracy includes: Clinton V. Black, *Pirates of the West Indies* (Cambridge, 1989); David Buisseret and Michael Pawson, *Port Royal, Jamaica* (Oxford, 1975); Neville Williams, *The Sea Dogs: Privateers, Plunder, and Piracy in the Elizabethan Age* (London, 1975); Robert E. Lee, *Blackbeard the Pirate: A Reappraisal of his Life and Times* (Winston-Salem, N.C., 1974); Peter Earle, *The Sack of Panama* (London, 1981); Clive Senior, *A Nation of Pirates: English Piracy in its Heyday* (London: Newton Abbott, 1976); David Mitchell, *Pirates* (London, 1976); Edward Lucie-Smith, *Outcasts of the Sea* (London, 1978); Douglas Botting, *The Pirates* (Amsterdam, 1978); Frank Sherry, *Raiders and Rebels: The Golden Age of Piracy* (New

York: Hearst Marine, 1986); David Cordingly, *Under the Black Flag: The Romance and the Reality of Life Among the Pirates* (New York, 1995); and Margaret S. Creighton and Lisa Norling, eds., *Iron Men, Wooden Women: Gender and Seafaring in the Atlantic World, 1700–1920* (Baltimore, 1996).

18. See the editions of *Interesting Narrative* edited by Vincent Carretta (1995) and Paul Edwards (1990); Henry Louis Gates Jr., ed., *The Classic Slave Narratives* (1987); Adam Potkay and Sandra Burr, eds., *Black Atlantic Writers of the Eighteenth Century* (1995); and Vincent Carretta, ed., *Unchained Voices: An Anthology of Black Authors in the English-Speaking World of the Eighteenth Century* (1996). Other collections of narratives and sketches include Charles T. Davis and Henry Louis Gates Jr., eds., *The Slave's Narrative* (Oxford, 1985) and Paul Edwards and David Dabydeen, eds., *Black Writers in Britain, 1760–1890* (Edinburgh, 1991). Of related interest are Gretchen Gerzina, *Black London: Life before Emancipation* (1995); W. Jeffrey Bolster, *Black Jacks: African American Seamen in the Age of Sail* (1997); and Hugh Thomas, *The Slave Trade: The Story of the Atlantic Slave Trade, 1440–1870* (1997).

19. The ethnohistorical and ethnocritical studies by James Axtell (*After Columbus: Essays in the Ethnohistory of North America* [New York: Oxford, 1989]) and Arnold Krupat, among others, provide strategies for gleaning obscured information about subaltern cultures from the archive of European colonialism.

20. Scholars continue to privilege Samuel Sewall's *The Selling of Joseph* (1700) and John Saffin's reply to Sewall (1701) as the earliest "American" discussions of the issue, despite the fact that George Keith published seven years earlier (in New York) *An Exhortation and Caution to Friends concerning buying or keeping of Negroes* (New York, 1693). The West Indian contribution to early slavery writing is even older, with Richard Baxter, *Chapters from a Christian Directory* (1673); Morgan Godwyn, *The Negro's and Indians Advocate, Suing for their Admission into the Church: or, a Persuasive to the Instructing and Baptizing of the Negro's and Indians in Our Plantations* (London, 1680); and Thomas Tryon, *Friendly Advice to the Gentlemen-Planters of the East and West Indies* (London, 1684).

21. Richard Blome, *A Description of the Island of Jamaica; with the Other Isles and Terretories in America, to which the English are related, viz. Barbados, St. Christophers, Nievis* (London: T. Milbourn, 1672).

22. Sir Hans Sloane, *A Voyage to the Islands of Madera, Barbados, Nieves, S. Christophers and Jamaica, with the Natural History of the Herbs and Trees, Four-footed Beasts, Fishes, Birds, Insects, Reptiles, &c. Of the last of those Islands*, 2 vols. (London: B.M., 1707, 1725).

23. Mark Catesby, *The natural history of Carolina, Florida, and the Bahama Islands*, 2 vols. (London, 1731–48).

1. A TRUE AND EXACT HISTORY OF BARBADOS

1. Engine or machine.

2. Loblolly: thick gruel; bonavist: soup made from bonavist, or hyacinth, beans.

3. Plantains.

4. Maize, or Indian corn.

5. Peeling.

6. Referring to indentured servants, who were Europeans either transported to the colonies as punishment for crimes or who had contracted with a ship captain to trade passage to the colonies in exchange for a period of free labor, usually five to seven years.

7. Withes: twigs or slender branches.

8. A liquor distilled from sweet potatoes, or a punch made from this liquor.

9. Hammocks (a word of Carib origin), an invention of the Taino Indians, natives of the Caribbean.

10. Wear.

11. Humphrey Walrond (c. 1600–c. 1670), a noted Barbadian Royalist.

12. Reckless.

13. Guinny: Guinea, in West Africa; Binny: Benin, in West Africa; Cutchew: possibly Cuíto, a river and region of southwest Africa; Gambra: Gambia, a river and region of West Africa.

14. Chaste.

15. Precedents.

16. Posset: a drink of hot milk curdled with ale or wine; broath: broth; caudle: a warm drink of ale or wine with eggs, meal, and sugar; usually given to sick people.

17. Trade.

18. Sizes.

19. Fallen.

20. A large lute.

21. Small logs.

22. Pathways or roads leading to a church.

23. An instrument used in surveying.

24. Without dancing. With a satiric jab at Puritan objections to dancing on Sunday, Ligon here indicates that the Africans' dance involves more movement of the upper body than the feet.

25. A Jewish sect in ancient Palestine noted for their rejection of oral tradition, the afterlife, and the coming of the Messiah.

26. The coastal regions of North Africa.

27. Newly distilled rum.

28. Strong in the thighs.

29. Albrecht Dürer (1471–1528), influential painter, engraver, and printmaker of Nuremberg, Germany.

30. Kitten.

31. To count backwards.

32. A prominent Barbadian.

33. Stoccado: to stab with a pointed weapon; imbroccata: to thrust; pass: to lunge.

34. Exception.

35. Condign, suitable.

36. The mainland.

37. Cassava: a root, native to the Americas, used to make bread.

38. Triangular.

39. Elongated glass beads.

40. Purple.

41. I.e., a very good mind.

2. JAMAICA VIEWED

1. George Monck (1608–70), English general under Cromwell; created first duke of Albemarle for his aid in restoring Charles II.

2. Anthony Ashley Cooper (1621–83), Lord (later first earl of) Shaftesbury, politician noted for changing allegiances.

3. Thomas Woolston (1670–1733), a Church of England clergyman who published a series of deist tracts, for which he was indicted and imprisoned for blasphemy. He died in prison.

4. Henry St. John, first viscount Bolingbroke (1678–1751), leading Tory politician in the reign of Queen Anne; also a notorious libertine.

5. Thomas, seventh baron Windsor (c. 1627–87), was the first governor of Jamaica (1661–64) after the Restoration, replacing General D'Oyley. He was created earl of Plymouth in 1684. The stationer has confounded his earlier and later titles.

6. Edward D'Oyley (1617–75), the first governor-general of Jamaica (1655–62). In addition to defending the island from Spanish attacks, he helped make Port Royal the center of Caribbean piracy by inviting the privateers of Tortuga to relocate their base to Jamaica.

7. An error for 1661, which Bragg confirms earlier in his note.

8. Robert Venables (c. 1612–87) achieved prominence as a commander in Oliver Cromwell's conquest of Ireland, taking Belfast in October 1649. Cromwell's commanders were often rewarded with property in the West Indies and North America. Venables shared command of the Caribbean expedition with Admiral William Penn (father of the founder of Pennsylvania). As Hickeringill relates, Venables was distracted from military matters by the presence of his wife aboard the flagship to Jamaica.

9. Leaguer: a military camp; hence, a camp-following woman or prostitute.

10. Distasteful repetition.

11. "God gives little comfort to the pitiless."

12. "Of course Queen Money bestows trustworthiness and friendliness, both [in] kind and form, to a wife with a dowry, and persuasiveness and loveliness well adorn the rich."

13. Hunger for sacred gold.

14. Lust.

15. Nothing higher or better.

16. Bulimy: a morbid hunger, called a "canine hunger"; bulimia nervosa. Poludipsie: probably "polydipsey," which would suggest "many thirsts."

17. Adjectival form of "pica," a hungering for promiscuous or unnatural food.

18. "Scorching Phaëton does not terrify greedy hope." Hickeringill adds a spurious negative ("nec") to lines from Horace's *Odes and Epodes* (4.11.25–26), thus making the passage suit his imperial purposes.

19. Mulatto: the offspring of a European and an African.

20. The mobilization of a military force; the mustering of a militia.

21. "Whatever is under the earth, will come to the light in time."

22. After the Restoration, the harbor at Point Cagway was renamed Port Royal. Now known as Kingston Harbor, it is the seventh largest in the world. The Spanish name for Port Royal was Cagua.

23. Fort Charles, which was repaired after the 1692 earthquake and still stands.

24. Canoes. OED cites this passage.

25. Now known as Spanish Town.

26. In March 1643, Captain William Jackson (commissioned by Robert Rich, second earl of Warwick) led a series of buccaneering adventures against the Spanish colonies in America, including Jamaica.

27. Plural of "beef"; cattle.

28. Edward D'Oyley. See above, note 6.

29. Maroons, especially marooned sailors or pirates. OED cites this passage.

30. Modern Tortuga, a small island off the north coast of Hispaniola; after Port Royal, Jamaica, the most famous pirates' lair in the West Indies in the seventeenth century.

31. I.e., hunters in the forest. In classical mythology, Actaeon was hunting with his pack of hounds when he glimpsed Artemis in her bath. As punishment, the goddess turned him into a stag, and he was attacked and killed by his own hounds.

32. Apparently "Punic blood," in reference to the traditional belief that the Roman province of Hispania was settled by Punic refugees from destroyed Carthage; hence, Spaniards.

33. "Gaule" indicates the French.

34. Autume: to affirm, assert. OED cites this passage.

35. Quintus Fabius Maximus Cunctator (d. 203 B.C.); Roman general noted for his delaying tactics in fighting Hannibal during the Second Punic War (218–201 B.C.).

36. Marcus Claudius Marcellus (d. 45 B.C.); Roman statesman and general; passionate opponent of Julius Caesar in the civil war of 49 through 45 B.C.

37. George Kastrioti (1403–68), known as Skanderbeg, or Iskander Bey. Albanian hero of Serb descent who served as a general for the Ottoman sultan before changing sides, freeing Albania, and holding off the Turks for twenty years.

38. Apollo, as sun god.

39. Cassava. See chap. 1, n. 37.

40. A pyre. OED cites this passage.

41. Barbecue: to dry or cure (meat) over an open fire. OED cites this passage as the first example of its use.

42. Master.

43. A drunken monkey (Partridge).

44. Many of the first English settlers in Jamaica were recruited from the older English West Indian colonies, especially Saint Christopher and Barbados.

45. Classical god of healing and medicine.

46. The Parcae, or Fates: three sisters who spin out one's thread of life, measure it, and cut it short.

47. The thing that recommends the old man to others' company.

3. FRIENDLY ADVICE TO GENTLEMEN–PLANTERS

1. Silly talk.

2. Docile.

3. Wise man, sage.

4. Costly.

5. Biblical units of money.

6. Vapour: to bully or brag.

7. Shifty or fraudulent lawyers.

8. English silver coin equal to four pence; therefore, something of little value.

9. Common alternative spelling of "gaol" (jail).

10. Spread false rumors; perjure.

11. Untraced.

12. Lack.

13. Knock or beat.

14. Uniform.

15. Prov. 20:27.

16. Rabbis.

17. Galen (129 – c. 199 B.C.), Greek physician.

18. Philippus Aureolus Paracelsus (c. 1493 –1541) German-Swiss physician.

19. Square brackets in the original.

20. Have sexual intercourse with.

21. Precedents.

22. Eccles. 7:7.

23. 2 Sam. 22:27; Ps. 18:26.

24. Simile, in the obsolete sense of "similarity."

25. Latin for "root."

4. A TRIP TO JAMAICA

1. The third is the earliest extant edition.

2. For examples, see *A True Description of Jamaica* (1657); Edward D'Oyley, *A Narrative of the Great Success God hath been pleased to give His Highness forces in Jamaica* (London: H. Hills and J. Field, 1658); Hickeringill, *Jamaica Viewed* (chapter 2 of this anthology); John Ogilby, *America* (1671) and *Description and History of Jamaica* (1671); Richard Blome, *A Description of the Island of Jamaica* (1672); Thomas Trapham, *A Discourse of the State of Health in the Island of Jamaica* (1679); *The Present State of Jamaica* (1683); *The Truest . . . Account of the late Earthquake* (1693).

3. Gaol, or jail.

4. Untraced.

5. Square brackets in the original.

6. The stock exchange.

7. Lovers of money.

8. Most descriptions of the American colonies during the seventeenth century were designed to attract investment and immigration, and thus greatly exaggerated their appeal.

9. Partridge: "kidnapper; occ. kidknapper. A child-stealer, orig. one who sold the children he stole to the plantations in North America: 1678."

10. Partridge: "flip, n. 'Hot small Beer (chiefly) and Brandy, sweetened and spiced upon occasion' (B.E., ca. 1690): orig. nautical; but Standard English by 1800." "B.E." is "B. E.'s *Dictionary of the Canting Crew*, prob. dated 1698–9."

11. Amanuensis: a secretary.

12. "Creole" indicates a native of the Americas descended from Europeans or Africans. In the seventeenth and eighteenth centuries, climate was popularly thought to influence physical constitution profoundly and fundamentally. Europeans who spent many years in the tropics were thought to take on the coloring and stereotyped racial characteristics of tropical peoples.

13. Mulatto. See chap. 2, n. 19.

14. Moorfields was a market near the modern Moorgate underground station in London. According to Partridge: "sweetener. A decoy; a cheat or a swindler: c.: late C.17–early 19." "Luck in a Bag," apparently, is the sale of a bag of mixed goods bought sight unseen.

15. A farm laborer (scythe-man) from Monmouthshire, a historic county in east Wales, now divided among Gwent, Mid Glamorgan, and South Glamorgan.

16. Saracen: an Arab or a Muslim; signs depicting a Saracen's head adorned many public houses in England.

17. OED: "in forma pauperis, in the form or guise of a poor person (exempted from liability to pay the costs of an action . . .); hence, in a humble or abject manner."

18. Throwster: one who makes silk thread.

19. Fever.

20. Sailors. "Tar" is a common term for sailor. "Tar-jacket" does not appear in either OED or Partridge, but may refer to the oiled-canvas foul-weather clothes ("oilskins") worn by sailors.

21. A beggar.

22. An order returning a pauper to the parish of his birth for charitable maintenance.

23. Salé, a seaport in northwestern Morocco, now a suburb of Rabat. Salé was an independent republic in the seventeenth century and a base for Barbary pirates.

24. The Treaty of Ryswick (1697) marked the end of the war (1688–97) known variously as the War of the Grand Alliance, the War of the League of Augsburg, the Nine Years' War, and King William's War.

25. "The Ballad of Chevy Chase," one of the oldest English ballads, concerns the Battle of Otterburn (1388), at which the Scottish Earl Douglas defeated the English under Sir Henry Percy, who was killed in the battle.

26. The novella *The Jamaica Lady* (1720) borrows much from Ward's *Trip to Jamaica*, including the derogatory representation of dialect, adding Creole to the Irish.

27. Modern names: Désirade, a small island east of Guadeloupe; Montserrat; Antigua; Nevis; Saint Kitts, which became wholly British at the Treaty of Utrecht in 1713; and Redonda, a rocky island between Montserrat and Nevis belonging to Antigua; "Caribbee Islands" refers to the Lesser Antilles and the islands along the north coast of South America.

28. Phaëthon: son of Phoebus Apollo who drove his father's chariot of the sun too close to earth, scorching it.

29. Chlorosis, an iron-deficiency anemia in adolescent girls.

30. Iguanas.

31. OED: "A West Indian dish composed of meat (or fish, game, etc.) and vegetables stewed down with cassareep and red pepper or other hot spices." OED cites this passage.

32. Latin for "a rich man"; name of the rich man in the parable of the beggar Lazarus in Luke 16:19–31: Dives is condemned not for his wealth, but for his selfish pleasure in it.

33. OED: "Nightman. . . . A man employed during the night to empty cesspools, etc., and to convey away the night-soil."

34. Chimney sweeps.

35. These are heraldic terms. Escutcheon ("scutchion"): the shield upon which the arms are displayed; field: the background color; or: gold; charge: to apply designs to the field; proper: drawn true to life; sable: black; crest: a symbol or emblem that surmounts the helm; argent: silver.

36. The main port town of Port Royal, Jamaica, suffered a famous earthquake on 7 June 1692, destroying most of the town and ending Port Royal's fame as a center for piracy and debauchery. Among the many pamphlets describing the disaster are: *A sad . . . Relation of the . . . Earthquake . . . at Jamaco 7th July* [*sic*] *1692* (1692); and *The Truest . . . Account of the late Earthquake in Jamaica, June the 7th, 1692* (1693).

37. Street sweepers.

38. Mount Etna, active volcano in Sicily.

39. To move or clear the bowels.

40. Howard Troyer suggests that this line indicates that "most of them" were "ex-soldiers," apparently figuring that because of the Peace of Ryswick (1697), the island was filled with recently discharged soldiers. The fact that Ward lists only officers' titles suggests that this is not likely to be the case. Instead, Ward seems to be commenting on the colonial habit of using militia titles socially as a means of establishing a social hierarchy in a loose and promiscuous new settlement. Cf. Aphra Behn, *The Widow Ranter* (c. 1688).

41. An inexperienced pickpocket.

5. A SPEECH MADE BY A BLACK OF GUARDALOUPE

1. Son of Isaac and Rebecca, elder twin brother of Jacob, to whom he sold his birthright for some soup when he returned hungry from hunting (Gen. 25–33).

2. I.e., the law that makes slavery legal is, nevertheless, without foundation in justice.

3. Twenty pounds sterling.

4. Corpse.

6. THE SPEECH OF MOSES BON SÀAM

1. *Guinea's Captive Kings: British Anti-Slavery Literature of the Eighteenth Century* (Chapel Hill: University of North Carolina Press, 1942), 94.

2. *The Fortunate Slave: An Illustration of African Slavery in the Early Eighteenth Century* (London: Oxford University Press, 1968), viii.

3. I.e., Jamaica. The versions printed in the *Prompter* and the *Gentleman's Magazine* include the following epigraphs above the title (Robertson's appendix to *The Speech of Campo-bell* does not):

> *This is a* Black, *beware of him good Countrymen.*
> —Hor[ace].

> *Murm'ring, indignant, They the Mountains Shake!*
> *Yet, their* Commander *can their Fierceness Break!*
> *Nothing cou'd, Else, their whelmy Pow'r asswage;*
> *Nor* Earth, *nor* Sea, *nor* Heav'n, *restrain their Rage.*
> —Virgil—*of the* Winds.

7. THE SPEECH OF MR. JOHN TALBOT CAMPO-BELL

1. James Tobin, *Cursory Remarks upon . . . Mr. Ramsay's Essay* (London: G. and T. Wilkie, 1785), 131.

2. Throughout this document, square brackets in the text are Robertson's. Brackets in footnotes are mine, unless marked otherwise.

3. There are two epigraphs; first, in Greek, "[I]t is ridiculous for a man to reproach others for what he does or would do himself, or to encourage others to do what he does not or would not do himself" (*Aristotle: The "Art" of Rhetoric*, trans. John Henry Freese [Cambridge: Harvard University Press, 1926], 303); second, in English, "That which I see not, teach thou me: If I have done Iniquity, I will do no more" (Job 34:32).

4. The four Leeward Islands Robertson refers to are Saint Kitts, Nevis, Antigua, and Montserrat. Tortola and Spanish-Town (Virgin Gorda) are in the British Virgin Islands.

5. Oliver Cromwell sentenced hundreds of Royalist prisoners to transportation to the West Indies after defeating David Leslie at Dunbar (3 September 1650) and Charles II at

Worcester (3 September 1651). Those few Royalists who survived Cromwell's reign of terror in Ireland (1649–50) also added to the numbers of prisoners transported to the Caribbean.

6. Admiral Michael A. de Ruyter led the Dutch attack on English trading forts along the West African coast in May 1665, in retaliation for English attacks on Dutch West African forts in 1663 and on New Amsterdam in 1664. The Second Anglo-Dutch War (1665–67) was formally declared after news reached London of de Ruyter's attacks in Africa and against Barbados. The only significant change of territory resulting from the war was the trade of English Surinam for Dutch New Netherland (renamed New York in honor of the naval commander the duke of York, the future James II).

7. With the Treaty of Utrecht in 1713, which ended the War of the Spanish Succession, Great Britain won permission (the *Assiento*) to supply legally the Spanish American colonies with slaves from Africa.

8. Robertson's figures on the death rates are consistent with the findings in recent studies. The Middle Passage resulted in losses of 20 percent during the early period, improving to 5 percent at the end of the eighteenth century. A death rate of 40 percent during the first six to thirty-six months of so-called "seasoning" was common.

9. "To stand exposed for sale in the marketplace."

10. Thomas Woolston (1670–1733) was a Church of England clergyman who published a series of deist tracts, for which he was indicted and imprisoned for blasphemy. He died in prison.

11. Raw sugar.

12. Edmund Gibson (1669–1748), as Lord Bishop of London, published *Two Letters* (London: Joseph Downing, 1727). Robertson replies to this text in *A Letter to . . . the Lord Bishop of London* (London: J. Wilford, 1730).

8. THE STORY OF INKLE AND YARICO

1. Dark-skinned; not necessarily African.

2. "Barbadian" is probably intended.

9. POEMS FROM *CARIBBEANA*

1. Sea goddess; mother of Achilles.

2. Edmund Waller (1606–87), poet noted for his many love poems to "Sacharissa," Lady Dorothy Sidney.

3. I.e., 1734. Prior to 1752, when Britain adopted the Gregorian Calendar and made the secular date of January 1 "officially" the first day of the year, New Year's day was commonly observed in the spring, on March 25.

4. Wednesday, March 20, 1733 (i.e., 1734).

5. Corpse.

6. Richard Busby (1606–95), Anglican priest, headmaster of Westminster School (1638–95). Author of standard grammar texts, Busby became proverbial for a severe pedagogue. His students included John Dryden and John Locke.

7. John Dennis (1657–1734), poet, playwright, and literary critic, whose views and criticism were mocked by Alexander Pope in *The Dunciad* and elsewhere.

8. I.e., the letter concerning economic difficulties in the British colonies in the West Indies and North America.

9. Referring to Daphne, who changed into a laurel tree to escape Apollo.

10. Untraced.

11. See note 6 above.

12. Saturday, November 9, 1734.

13. Leander, a youth from Asia Minor, in love with Hero, who lived across the Hellespont in Greece. Leander would swim across nightly to visit Hero, guided by a lighthouse, until one night, when the light went out, he drowned.

10. THE SUGAR CANE

1. James Boswell, *Life of Johnson,* ed. R. W. Chapman (Oxford: Oxford University Press, 1980), 699 n. 1.

2. "And to be the first to stir with these new strains the nodding leaf-capped woods of Helicon, as I bring strange lore untold by any before me," Marcus Manilius (fl. first century A.D.), *Astronomica,* trans. G. P. Goold (London: Heinemann, 1977), 4.

3. Jean Baptiste Labat (1663–1738), author of *Nouveau voyage aux isle de l'Amerique* (Paris: Chez P. F. Giffart, 1722).

4. Samuel Martin, *Essay Upon Plantership, Humbly inscrib'd To all the Planters of the British Sugar-Colonies in America* (Antigua: T. Smith, 1750).

5. Greek epic poet (fl. eighth century B.C.), author of *Works and Days.*

6. Publius Vergilius Maro, or Virgil (70–19 B.C.), Roman poet, author of the *Aeneid,* the *Georgics,* the *Eclogues,* etc. Grainger refers to him elsewhere in this chapter as "Maro," and the "Mantuan Bard."

7. John Philips (1676-1709), author of *Cyder. A Poem. In Two Books* (1708).

8. John Dyer (1699–1757), Welsh poet, author of *The Fleece* (1757), a pastoral about the wool trade.

9. "I follow you, O pride of the Greeks / I eagerly press my feet in your / Footsteps, thus struggling with / Passion to imitate you."

10. Hesiod was a native of Ascra, near Mount Helicon.

11. Philips. Pomona is the Roman goddess of fruit, from which Philips's "cyder" is made.

12. Christopher Smart (1722-1771), classical scholar and poet, author of the blank verse georgic, *The Hop-Garden* (1752).

13. William Somerville (1675-1742), author of the four-book, blank-verse hunting poem *The Chace* (1735).

14. Marcus Aurelius (A.D. 121-180; reigned 161-180), Roman emperor and Stoic philosopher; author of *The Meditations.*

15. King George III (1738-1820; reigned 1760-1820).

16. Sirius, in Canis Major.

17. Region of central Sicily; said to be the place where Pluto seized Proserpina.

18. Well-watered.

19. Proserpina.

20. Untraced.

21. Ferdinand II (1452-1516), king of Aragon and, with his wife, Isabella I (1451-1504), joint sovereigns of Castile. Sponsor of Columbus's voyages of discovery.

22. Reward.

23. Soil.

24. Wagon.

25. Name of a plantation.

26. Dorsetshire, a county in southern England.

27. Legendary king of Ormenium, who refused Hercules his daughter.

28. From Edward Young (1683–1765), "Satire III: To the Right Honourable Mr. Dodington," line 10.

29. In classical mythology, wind spirits with birds' bodies and women's faces who are sent by the gods to punish wrongdoers.

30. Water nymphs.

31. Achilles.

32. A star in Canis Minor.

33. The Grampian Hills in central Scotland.

34. The peacock.

35. Eagle.

36. Roman architect and military engineer; author of *De architectura.*

37. Nymphs of the trees.

38. Name derives from Othello's predecessor as governor of Cyprus; Shakespeare, *The Tragedy of Othello, the Moor of Venice* (1604).

39. Tobacco, introduced into England by Sir Walter Ralegh.

40. Mother, by Jupiter, of Perseus.

41. First-century Roman medical encyclopedist.

42. Poet and landscape designer, famous for his pastoral poetry and for promoting the English natural landscape garden (1714–1763).

43. Roman god of fire and volcanoes.

44. Aurora borealis, or northern lights.

45. A gulf in Ecuador.

46. American vulture.

47. Of Mysia, an ancient region of northwest Asia Minor.

48. Dainties, provisions.

49. Major General James Wolfe (1727–1759), victor of the Battle of Quebec (1759), which secured Canada for Britain.

50. Refers to the immense stables of the mythical King Augeas of the Epeians. One of the labors of Hercules was to clean them out in one day; he did so by redirecting the Alpheus River through them.

51. The east wind.

52. The north wind.

53. Immaturity.

54. The south wind.

55. The sky.

56. Engines of war; artillery.

57. Adapted from Shakespeare, *Hamlet* 2.2.494: "The bold windes speechlesse, and the Orbe below / As hush as death."

58. Constantinople's Hagia Sophia.

59. Theodorus (fl. sixth century), lector at the Hagia Sophia, author of an influential church history.

60. Coruscation: a flash of light.

61. Scorched.

62. Sour.

63. Dazed, astonished.

64. Probably another stock pastoral name, but with echoes of Theano, a disciple of Pythagoras, who is thought to have written on philosophy.

65. English boys' boarding school, near Windsor.

66. Nickname for the Thames as it passes through Oxford.

67. To study (the nine Muses).

68. May refer to Monimia, the heroine of Thomas Otway's tragedy *The Orphan* (1680). The name Acasto may also derive from Acastus, one of the Argonauts.

69. Thomas Percy (1729–1811), antiquarian, publisher, and bishop, best known for *Reliques of Ancient English Poetry* (1765), which included a ballad by Grainger.

70. Poetic term for Italy.

71. River near Cognac, in southwestern France.

72. Robert Marsham (1712–1793), second baron Romney, husband of Priscilla Pym of Saint Christopher.

73. Untraced.

74. Divine name of Melicertes, who jumped off a cliff into the sea to escape his raging father, and then was made a god to whom sailors would devote prayers of thanksgiving following safe returns to port.

75. Meaning that the driver is a black, either slave or free, authorized to drive and punish slaves.

76. A ploughshare.

77. River and town, Dumfries, Scotland.

78. A painkilling drug put into Melelaus's wine by Helen, who had been given it by the Egyptian woman Polydamna (the physician Thone's wife).

79. From James Thomson (1700–1748), *Summer* (1730), line 104.

80. Lackey: to attend in a servile manner.

81. Mortised, secured with a mortise joint.

82. Purified.

83. Physician to the Greeks in the Trojan War, and son of the god of medicine, Aescalapius.

84. Farci: (in cooking) stuffed; tabid: wasted by disease.

85. Unending.

86. Cold.

87. Perflate: to blow through.

88. Ropy: viscous or glutinous; mucilage: gum or glue derived from plant matter.

89. Latin for "a bitter or sour substance."

90. Xanthippe, wife of Socrates, proverbially shrewish.

91. Barrels.

92. Untraced.

93. Poetic name for the River Severn in England.

94. Daughter of Acrisius, who kept her in a bronze tower to prevent any man from approaching her. Zeus descended on her in a shower of gold and she gave birth to Perseus.

95. Edmund Waller (1606–1687) addresses Bermuda in his poem "The Battle of the Summer Islands."

96. Name indicates a miser, from the Latin *avare* (miserly).

97. Probably after Vigone, village in the hills northwest Italy.

98. Drunkenness, from the Latin *ebrietas.*

99. Literary friends of Grainger's: the great critic Dr. Samuel Johnson (1709 – 1784); Bishop Thomas Percy (see note 69 above); and probably Gilbert White (1720 – 1793), curate of Selborne, Hampshire, author of *Natural History and Antiquities of Selborne* (1789).

100. Founder of Paeonia, a region in the Balkans; son of Endymion who lost a race with his brother designed to determine the succession to their father; exiled himself to Paeonia.

101. Western, from the Latin *hesperia.*

102. Roman goddess of war.

103. Ridiculously wild.

104. Greek poet and Spartan general who inspired troops to victory in the seige of Ithome (seventh century B.C.).

105. Dainties, delicacies.

106. Roman name for a proverbial glutton.

107. Mountains in Wales.

108. Portuguese. Lusitania was the ancient and poetic name for Portugal; Portuguese navigators explored the coast of Africa, opening trade (including the slave trade) between Europeans and Africans.

109. Probably Madeira or Canary wine.

110. Untraced.

111. From John Philips (1676 – 1709), *Cyder. A Poem. In Two Books* (1708), book I, line 98.

112. The spirit or personification of Africa.

113. People from the region around the Congo River.

114. The coast of the Gulf of Guinea, in modern Ghana, West Africa.

115. People from the region around Minna, a city in central Nigeria, north of the Niger river in West Africa.

116. The Mandingo, or Mande, people of West Africa, a predominately Muslim tribe, known for their widespread trading activities.

117. Obi, or obeah, is the traditional magic of West African polytheistic religion; related to vodun (voodoo) in Haiti.

118. King Louis XIV of France (1638 – 1715; reigned 1643 – 1715), called the Sun King, promulgated the *Code Noir* in 1685, which placed some restrictions upon the power of slaveowners over their slaves.

119. Major river in West Africa.

120. The fast-growing papaya tree.

121. Now called the Corubal River, in Guinea and Guinea-Bissau in West Africa.

122. River in Cameroon, West Africa.

123. Count de Melvil, a virtuous character in Tobias Smollett's novel *The Adventures of Ferdinand Count Fathom* (1753); he is the benefactor of the dissolute title character, who is, like Grainger, a physician.

124. Plough.

125. Rivers in modern Ghana, West Africa.

126. An African from the region around Cormantyne (or Kormantine), site of a Dutch slaving station in modern Ghana.

127. Poniard: dagger.

128. Apparently peoples originating in East Africa, who were associated with, or transported from, the Arab port of Mocha on the Red Sea.

129. A physician, so called because of the physician's former use of leeches to let blood as a cure.

130. The sun; Phoebus being the title of Apollo as god of the sun.

131. In classical mythology, the place in the Underworld where virtuous souls rest.

132. The River Cuanza or Kwanza, in Angola in southwestern Africa.

133. An inhabitant of Ethiopia, in East Africa, here representing Africans generally.

134. An herbaceous plant, native to Europe.

135. The houseleek, a succulent European plant with reddish flowers.

136. Former name for edema, the build-up of fluid in the cavities of the body, often due to kidney failure.

137. Inhabitants of Libya, in North Africa, here signifying Africans generally.

138. Dainty foods.

139. A surname or title for Apollo, the Greek god of medicine, music, archery, prophecy, and light.

140. Food for livestock.

141. Formerly.

142. Yaws, or frambesia: an infectious tropical disease of the skin.

143. Watery discharge from a wound or sore.

144. Quicksilver, or mercury.

145. Pollutions, defilements.

146. Classical sea diety, able to prophesy, known for assuming various shapes to avoid answering humans' questions about the future.

147. Personification of mania, or madness.

148. Personification of ague, or acute fever.

149. "Or the slow minings of the hectic fire," John Armstrong, *The Art of Preserving Health, A Poem* (1744), III.202.

150. The ancient Phoenicians, from Tyre in the Levant.

151. Referring to the long struggle by the Low Countries (modern Belgium and the Netherlands) to secure independence from the Spanish empire.

152. Roman god of the woods (*silva*).

153. Roman goddess of grain and harvests.

154. Poetic name for England, called white (*alba*) for the white cliffs of Dover.

155. Britain as ruler of the seas through naval and mercantile power.

156. Roman name for the east wind; here referring to the easterly trade winds.

157. Ireland's.

158. Carib Indians, native inhabitants of the Lesser Antilles of the Caribbean.

159. See Grainger's note to book 1, line 605.

160. The Phaeacians are the luxurious people of the island of Scheria in the Ionian Sea of Greece, whose king, Alcinous, harbors Odysseus in the *Odyssey*, and Jason in the *Argonautica*.

161. The pineapple (in French, *ananas*).

162. John Milton, *Paradise Lost* IV.138.

163. Cannibals, which the native Carib Indians were purported to be.

164. Cherimoya, a fruit-bearing tree of Central and South America.

165. Inigo Jones (1573–1652), architect of the Queen's House, Greenwich, and the Banqueting House, Whitehall, London. Sir Christopher Wren (1632–1723), architect of the plan of London and of Saint Paul's Cathedral following the Great Fire of 1666.

166. Andrea Palladio (1508–1580), influential Italian architect.

167. Indians of North America.

168. Greek goddess, mother of the Seasons, the Fates, and Prometheus; personification of Justice.

11. A GENERAL DESCRIPTION

1. See Singleton's note to book 1, line 179.

2. Hesperia, or western lands, may refer to Italy (west of Greece), Spain (west of Rome), or the islands of the Hesperides, daughters of Night and Darkness, who, with the dragon Ladon, guarded the tree that grew the golden apples.

3. See chap. 10, n. 160.

4. Short for Aurora, goddess of the dawn.

5. The German city of Dresden was famous for producing porcelain china.

6. Chemical.

7. Distended.

8. Perhaps suggested by Celia's character in Shakespeare, *As You Like It* (1599).

9. Referring to Edmund Spenser's allegorical pastoral, *Colin Clouts come home againe* (1595).

10. Greek prince favored by Jupiter because of his beauty and carried to heaven to be cupbearer to the gods.

11. Venus, who was born in the sea near the island of Cythera.

12. A leather covered drinking mug.

13. A young weaned pig.

14. Induced vomiting was thought to improve the appetite.

15. Yellow, gelatinous substance between a turtle's body and lower shell; considered a delicacy.

16. Titian (c. 1477–1576), celebrated Venetian painter.

17. The territory of the Ebo or Ibo, a large tribe in modern Nigeria.

18. Doctor or medicine man.

19. Using odd gesticulations.

20. The waters between Nevis and neighboring Saint Christopher.

21. Virgin Gorda, one of the British Virgin Islands.

22. The name they go by.

23. Islands of the Danish West Indies, now the U.S. Virgin Islands.

24. See Virgil, *Aeneid.*

25. Types of trees.

26. John Milton, *Paradise Lost.*

27. Referring to a pock-marked face resulting from smallpox.

28. Spanish term for an old woman or chaperone.

29. Ships just in from a sea voyage.

30. When the star Sirius, in Canis Major, is visible: summer.

31. Brothels.

32. Welkin: the sky.

33. Acheron, Styx: rivers in Hades.

34. Wounds made by whipping.

35. Corpse.

36. Frenzied (from the Corybantes, attendants of Cybele).

37. Mythological beings who inhabit Mount Ida.

38. Wife of Cronus, mother of Zeus; goddess of fruitfulness.

39. Untraced.

40. A proverbially pleasant valley in Thessaly in northeastern Greece.

41. Names are untraced unless noted.

42. Pindar (c. 522–c. 443 B.C.), Greek poet.

43. Virgil. See chap. 10, note 6.

44. In Roman legend, a water nymph who advised King Numa of Rome, and to whom women sacrificed to secure an easy childbirth.

45. Sibyl, a prophetess or witch (see Virgil, *Aeneid*).

46. Bats.

47. Shakings, convulsions.

48. A sea anemone.

49. Untraced.

50. Name refers to the spring of Castalia on Mount Parnassus, sacred to Apollo and the Muses.

51. Shakespeare, *Hamlet* II.ii.137.

12. CARMEN, OR, AN ODE

1. John Montagu (c. 1688–1749), second duke of Montagu.

2. Charles Louis de Secondat (1689–1755), baron de La Brède et de Montesquieu, French philosopher, author of, among many other things, *The Spirit of Laws* (1748).

3. Presumably the philosopher and historian David Hume (1711–76); quotation untraced.

4. Samuel Estwick, author of *Considerations on the Negroe Cause, commonly so called, addressed to the Right Honourable Lord Mansfield, Lord Chief Justice of the Court of King's Bench* (London: For J. Dodsley, 1772), an attack on Mansfield's 1772 ruling that the slave James Somersett was free by virtue of being in England, a ruling understood to emancipate slaves in England.

5. Poetic term for France.

6. Commonwealth, state.

7. Poetic term for Great Britain and the British empire.

8. Poetic term for Scotland.

9. French island in the eastern Caribbean. Occupied briefly by Britain several times in the seventeenth and eighteenth centuries.

10. The fleur-de-lys, symbolic of France, whose island of Guadeloupe was conquered by Britain in 1759.

11. Roman god of war.

12. Term used to describe black Africans and their descendants.

13. Roman goddess of war and wisdom.

14. The nine Muses, goddesses of the arts.

15. George Buchanan (1506–1582), Scottish poet, tutor of Montaigne and King James VI and I.

16. Achilles, Greek hero of the Trojan War, son of Peleus, king of Phthia, and the sea nymph Thetis.

17. Virgil. See chap. 10, note 6.

18. "The poet is born, not made."

19. Alexander Pope, *An Essay on Man* (1732 – 34), 1.171–72.

20. Untraced.

13. JAMAICA, A POEM

1. Modern names are Désirade (small island just east of Guadeloupe), Montserrat, and Antigua.

2. The pineapple; the term derives from the Peruvian name for the fruit, "Nanas" (OED).

3. Roman goddess of grain.

4. James Thomson (1700 –1748), Scottish poet, author of *The Seasons* (1726 – 30)

5. I.e., by drinking rum.

6. Ovid (Publius Ovidius Naso, 43 B.C.–A.D. 17)

7. Scions, descendants.

8. Charles Pratt (1714 – 94) was a close school friend of William Pitt the Elder and a jurist, who, as Chief Justice of the Court of Common Pleas (1761– 66) ruled the use of a general warrant to arrest John Wilkes for sedition illegal, which led to the elimination of general warrants entirely. As Lord Chancellor (1766 –70), he opposed the British government's policy of taxing the American colonies to pay for the expenses of the Seven Years' War without representation in Parliament, for which opposition he was dismissed as Lord Chancellor in 1770. When he was created first baron Camden of Camden Place in 1765, his maiden speech in the House of Lords condemned the Stamp Act. He was created viscount Bayham of Bayham Abbey and Earl Camden in 1786.

9. Lucius Junius Brutus (not his descendant, Marcus Junius Brutus, who was Julius Caesar's assassin) was the founder of the Roman Republic in 509 B.C.

10. Marcus Porcius Cato (234 –149 B.C.), important Roman statesman and writer.

11. City in Hyderabad, India, noted center of the diamond trade.

12. Island in the Indonesian archipelago; source of many tropical products.

13. Richest silver mine in the world; in modern Bolivia.

14. Island north of Norway; major whaling center.

15. Great Britain.

16. In *Capitalism and Antislavery* (New York: Oxford, 1986), Seymour Drescher links this epistle with a newspaper lampoon of William Beckford: "a West Indian grandee, [who] was called 'Alderman sugar-cane' and lampooned in political ballads."

17. Gaius Asinius Pollio (76 B.C.–A.D. 4), the addressee of Virgil's Fourth ("Messianic") Eclogue, was a poet, playwright, advocate, historian, Roman consul (40 B.C.), and champion of old republican liberty against the Augustan principate.

18. Sir Thomas Littleton (c. 1415 – 81), jurist, author of a treatise (c. 1481) on land tenures which formed the basis for early modern English property law. Sir Edward Coke (1552 –1634), jurist, whose *Institutes* (1628 –44, including *Coke upon Littleton,* a commentary on Littleton's *Tenures*) formed the basic textbook for law students for centuries.

19. Poetic term for London.